I0777864

PRINT EDITION

AGAINST ALL ODDS: 7 Stories of love in dangerous times © 2025 by Mirror World Publishing
Edited by: J.A. Dowsett and Robert Dowsett
Cover Design by: J.A. Dowsett

Published by Mirror World Publishing in May 2025.

Mirror World Publishing
Windsor, Ontario
www.mirrorworldpublishing.com
info@mirrorworldpublishing.com

ISBN: 978-1-998360-08-6

Against All Odds

7 stories of love in dangerous times

FOREWORD

Here we go. Since our last anthology a lot has changed AGAIN. We've survived a global pandemic, political turmoil, and as I write this, Canada is worried about a trade war and the collapse of relations with our southern neighbors.

Mirror World has always existed to provide an escape from all this, but more than that we want to hold up a mirror to the experiences of humanity as a means of providing a more hopeful vision of the future. That's where this anthology comes in. Because there's nothing more hopeful than love.

Last year we ran a contest. We asked authors to submit stories where love thrived despite the odds. Where romance and heartfelt dedication proved victorious in the face of strife. Well, these authors delivered.

I'm pleased to present to you seven stories that defy the odds and uniquely portray love in all its forms, whether that love is on another planet, between forbidden lovers, across cultures, for one's self, or one's friends. As always, we've incuded the bios and introductions from each of the winning authors so you can get to know the minds of the authors that dared to believe, even in these hard times that maybe, just maybe, love is worth the risk.

J.A. Dowsett

Publisher, Mirror World Publishing

ITINERARY

"Worldsteppers" by Jane Lupino

When Marik and his friend and colleague Vyla lead a group of tourists to the beautiful wildlife reserve world of Juriss, the last thing he expects to find is a love that challenges his very being. After just a few days on the tour, he and Vyla are ordered to bring the tourists back to Earth where they are shocked to find that Juriss is under attack from invaders from another world, who are using the StepZone technology owned by WorldSteppers to travel throughout the universe and wage war.

"Do It Yourself" by Titania Blesh

In a post-apocalyptic wasteland, Aurora wields an embarrassingly weak PowerTool against deadly energivores to rescue her father. Armed with little more than sheer determination and her quirky DYI tool, she discovers that survival takes more than power—it takes heart.

"The Pomegranate Question" by Mason Michalak

It's Abdon's first day in his position as handler for His God. What follows is a strange and dangerous affair like nothing he's ever experienced.

"The Value of a Sapphire" by Andrea Barton

Over the course of a century, sentient sapphire Nil Manel witnesses the lives and loves of its owners, but when it discovers devastating information about its history, it must ultimately learn the importance of self-love.

"Chasing Llyranite" by Shannon Nell

On Carthenwyl, love is a double-edged sword: admit to it, and you become mortal. As Calem and Eira brave the ocean depths during lightning storms to harvest the precious llyranite that powers their world, Eira must confront her fear of love and discover that embracing vulnerability may be the key to a life worth living.

"vAMP" by Taylor Calder

What if being a vampire was truly, truly awful? What if your life expectancy was shorter? What if you only developed preternatural abilities at the end stage of the disease, when you became a twisted shadow of who you once were? And what if, despite all of this, you fell in love?

"White Snake, Jade Terrapin" by Pat Woods

When Taiwanese high-schooler Xu meets Susan, an attractive Western girl, he has no idea where this encounter will lead him. Can their burgeoning romance survive the series of shocking revelations about Susan's true nature?

WORLDSTEPPERS

by Jane Lupino

'**W**HATEVER YOU WANT, WHEREVER YOU WANT, WE HAVE THE VACATION FOR YOU! WHETHER IT'S A FAMILY BREAK TO THE THEME PARK WORLD OF THORALTON; A ROMANTIC GETAWAY TO THE PARADISE LAKES OF LAVNOS; OR EVEN THE HEDONISTIC WORLD OF VIRDON, WHERE PLEASURES BEYOND YOUR WILDEST IMAGINATION AWAIT YOU. WHATEVER YOU WANT, WHEREVER YOU WANT, 'WORLDSTEPPERS' TOURS ARE OUT OF THIS WORLD'

More than a few pairs of eyes watched in appreciation as Marik entered the StepZone waiting area and sauntered towards the group of tourists. His body moved easily beneath the close-fitting, dark purple "WorldSteppers" uniform t-shirt.

Vyla moved away from the guests and greeted him. "They seem like a nice bunch." She glanced back at them. "The one with the blue backpack could become a bit of a handful, though."

Marik studied the small crowd of twenty, all strangers, all with one thing in common, the search for the holiday of their dreams. "I'm sure we'll be able to handle him," he said with a grin.

He strode across to them and Vyla suppressed the smile trying to force its way onto her lips. The view of Marik's delicious behind always did that to her. The way it looked inside his shorts, which stopped halfway down his thighs and showed off his well-muscled, tanned legs.

She followed and listened as he started the standard speech for all the vacations they led.

"It's great to see all of you looking so excited about this trip into the wild. The mountains and forests of Juriss are spectacular at any time of year, but right now is by far the best time to visit.

"Now, before we leave, I will just explain a little about the travel procedure." He looked around at them all. "Have any of you travelled with us before?"

A few tentative hands rose.

"Great! So, *you* know the drill. But, for those who've never done this before, firstly, where have you been? I'll tell you: you've been missing out on the best times of your lives!" He laughed and most of the people sitting listening laughed with him.

Marik waved his hands to bring them back to silence. "I'm kidding. It's great that you've joined us this time and hopefully the experience will be one that you'll remember for the rest of your life. Maybe it'll even tempt you into joining us again to try something different. Don't forget: if you book your next trip before the end of this one, you'll be entitled to a very substantial discount," he said, a true salesman to the end.

One or two people nodded and several others looked up with interest. Marik hoped that at least twenty-five percent of them would rebook so that he and Vyla would get a healthy bonus at the end of the season.

"Okay, so before we go, I'll just run through the routine. Vyla will go first so that she'll be there to meet you when you arrive. We'll go through one at a time. When I activate the StepZone, you'll feel a slight pull and may experience a moment of disorientation. This is perfectly normal and should pass within a few seconds. Very occasionally, someone may experience a mild episode of nausea, but again, this should pass quickly. The trip will take approximately 0.5 seconds and when you arrive, please step off the zone immediately so that your travel companions can come through. Are there any questions?"

The man with the blue backpack, who Vyla had pointed out earlier, put his hand in the air.

"Where, exactly, will we land?"

Marik smiled. "As was described in the travel pack you received, we arrive directly in the hotel lobby where we'll spend the first night before we set out on our safari."

"Thank you."

Marik held his arms out as if he would embrace them all. "Okay, departure will start in two minutes, so please gather your belongings and take your numbered position at the gate."

As he and Vyla watched them, a pretty blonde girl wearing a tight sleeveless blouse and very short denim shorts caught Marik's eye and smiled. He smiled back and held her gaze for just a moment longer than Vyla felt was absolutely necessary.

"Come on," she snapped. "We need to get going."

Marik winked at her, his deep brown eyes twinkling.

Vyla swallowed as the familiar jolt shot through her whenever he did that. She'd long ago given in to her feelings for him; his dark, curly hair and rugged good looks along with his amiable manner and gentle sense of humour had her hooked from their first trip together seven years ago. She'd also given up all hope of ever doing anything about it. For a start, he was too interested in the pretty young things who always seemed to find themselves on his tours. Plus, they had to work very closely together, and it would be far too awkward if things went bad. There was also the fact that he'd very early on given the impression that a quick fling on tour was about all the commitment he wanted to handle.

Marik stood by the departure gate, chatting with some of the guests, his easy laugh carrying across the waiting area. He nodded to Vyla as she approached and held the gate open for her.

"See you on the other side," he said, as he always did just before she went through.

She smiled and stepped onto a small square plate of blue light on the floor. It flashed green and she disappeared, the StepZone immediately returning to blue.

The last passenger to go through was the pretty blonde. Marik took her passport, brushing his finger across the back of her hand. "Okay…Ule, are you ready?"

Ule looked up into his eyes. "I'm always ready…for anything," she answered in a low, husky voice. She leaned in, giving him a good view of her cleavage.

Marik leaned forward, his mouth almost touching her ear. "I hope so," he murmured. "I'll see *you* on the other side for sure."

Ule pulled her passport out of his hand. "I'll be waiting," she purred. She stepped onto the plate and vanished.

Marik shook himself and grinned as he stepped onto the plate.

"So, I suppose you'll be hooking up with the blonde bimbo for the rest of the tour," Vyla sneered as she unpacked her night bag.

"And which blonde bimbo would that be?" asked Marik, not hiding his amusement.

Vyla straightened, and waggled her hands and arse. "Ule," she said in a silly girly voice.

Marik laughed. "Careful, I might think you're jealous."

"Huh! No chance!" Vyla turned her back and made a show of putting her nightclothes on her pillow. "But you're not bringing her back here!"

Marik smiled even as he felt a pang of guilt. He was fully aware of Vyla's feelings towards him, but he had tried to make it clear he wasn't interested without hurting her.

He watched as she busied herself filling the small water jug and setting it to heat for coffee. It wasn't that she was unattractive; she was very good-looking in a striking sort of way. Her short, dark hair framed her face, accentuating her high cheekbones and straight, narrow nose. She had a nice figure with a small waist and large, firm breasts, which looked good even in her uniform. But she was his closest work colleague and a good friend. He made it a rule never to mess with coworkers, especially one he spent so much time with.

"Don't make one for me," he said as Vyla got two cups out. "I'd better go down and intercept any issues before they arise. I'm sure someone will have too few pillows or the wrong room or something. You know what it's like, there's always one."

He heard the quiet sigh. "Alright," she said. "It'll be blue backpack man for sure."

Vyla's prediction proved accurate as Marik approached the front desk. Blue backpack man was indeed standing pointing at the receptionist, jabbing his finger at them.

"It's really not good enough," he was saying, very loudly.

The young person behind the desk was hastily typing something into their tablet, looking as if they were about to burst into tears.

"Everything all right, Collo?"

Collo, also known as blue backpack man, spun around. "No! Everything is not all right. In fact, everything is all wrong!"

Marik gave him a sympathetic frown. "Oh, what seems to be the issue?" He glanced from Collo to the receptionist and back.

"I asked for a mountain view and I can't get one! All I have is a savannah sunset and it won't change. I paid extra for changing views and I haven't got them! Also, I am certain my pillows are not hypoallergenic!"

The receptionist looked up in despair. "I can assure you they are of the highest spec allergy proof materials. All of our soft furnishings are! As for the view changer, I'll have someone come up directly and fix it for you, sir."

Marik put a hand on Collo's shoulder and addressed the receptionist. "That's okay, I'll go and have a look. I know these things can be a bit tricky for first-time users."

The receptionist looked relieved as Marik guided Collo away.

Outside, the real view showed the sun rising behind the tall buildings of the other seventy-three megahotels set within a three square mile area of the rainforest, which covered eighty percent of Juriss.

The rainforest sat within a vast circle of wide savannah spreading out for miles towards the ocean, which covered the rest of the planet. The gigantic island was the only landmass on this world. Many native tribes lived alongside the abundant unique flora and fauna, making it a perfect place to see a different culture and watch wild creatures in their natural habitats.

Vyla climbed out of bed and glanced at Marik's empty one. It was still made up, so he'd obviously spent the night elsewhere. No prizes for guessing where, but this was quick work, even for him. It was usually a few days before his quarry conceded, and Vyla thought it was probably the chase that excited him the most. Hopefully he'd soon get bored with this one, since she clearly hadn't provided him with much of a challenge. Vyla knew she should really report him; consorting with the guests was, strictly speaking, against the rules. But he'd been doing it for as long as she had worked with him, and probably longer, and management seemed to turn a blind eye.

She showered, dressed, and was combing her hair when the door opened and he came in.

He yawned heavily and glanced at her. "I need a shower," he announced.

Vyla wrinkled her nose. "Yes. You stink of sex. You look like you could do with some sleep too."

He backed into the bathroom, a lazy grin on his face and his arms spread wide. "What can I say? She's an animal!" He laughed and shut the door.

Vyla glared at her reflection. "Good," she muttered. "Maybe we can leave her here with the others then!"

She slammed the door as she went out, heading down to breakfast.

"Good morning, everyone," Vyla said when the group had assembled in the lobby after breakfast. "I hope you all had a comfortable night. We'll be roughing it from now on for the next two weeks, so I hope you made the most of it!"

Collo, standing at the front of the group in the centre, muttered something and looked unhappy, but he didn't say anything out loud so Vyla chose not to notice.

"Now," she continued, "we'll be travelling to the camp via StepZone again. Did anyone have any issues yesterday?" She scanned their faces, but most shook their heads and she was about to go on when Collo cleared his throat.

"Well, I must admit, I did feel a little queasy yesterday evening,"

Vyla smiled. "Oh, well that's probably not from the effects from the StepZone. If you had had any, they would've been immediate and passed very quickly. Perhaps you ate something that didn't agree with you. Anyway, as soon as Marik arrives, we can get going." She glanced at Ule and was surprised to see her blush.

Marik strode into the lobby looking his usual bright, confident self, eager to get going and clearly pleased to see them all. Straight away, the group gravitated to him, following him and chatting happily among themselves. Vyla shook her head; even after all these years, she still didn't know how he did it!

As always, Marik was the last to step off the StepZone. He had done this tour at least once every year for ten years and still this world, above all others, had the ability to render him speechless. The colours, smells, and sounds of this alien land held a beauty that he knew even Collo with his blue backpack would have to hold in awe.

Tall oomigong trees towered into the pale yellow sky, their tops disappearing into the blue clouds far above. Thick purple trunks held up multi-coloured translucent leaves ten feet long, which arched gracefully overhead to create a canopy of rainbow hues. The ground was thick with fallen flowers, leaves, and seeds, and everywhere, stark spiky anglan bushes grew, their dark yellow branches heavy with small pink leaves and bright blue berries, taking advantage of the many patches of white sunlight hitting the ground.

The Earth was now a major centre of technology, industry, and export, but had long since lost all signs of nature. The explosive growth of the human population had necessitated the need for every inch of land being used for housing, factories and all the infrastructure that went with it, until not so much as a single blade of grass grew naturally anywhere.Only a few native animals survived, in zoos and private collections. The loss of habitats and feeding grounds, mass safaris causing far too much disruption to wildlife, and a huge demand for illegal hunting had all succeeded in extincting most species by the end of the twenty-first century. Deforestation, intensive farming, and over-development caused the end of areas of natural life.

But here on Juriss, nature thrived. Strange bird calls echoed through the rainforest and the flutter of wings through leaves could be heard as the tourists stood, stunned by the abundance of beauty.

Some of the group were fanning themselves as they stared around with the maps they'd been given for the trip, and all of them were sweating in the humidity. Marik couldn't help noticing that it looked damn fine on Ule's supple, tanned skin.

He clapped his hands to get their attention and a flock of small, brightly coloured toki birds erupted from a nearby remped tree.

"Okay, we'll be heading off to the camp in a minute, but I just want to point out a few things. First of all, please don't eat any berries, fruit, or anything else without checking with Vyla or myself. Most of the plants here, while they are very beautiful, are also quite deadly. If we are lucky enough to come across any wildlife, please stay quiet. Take pictures if you wish; after all, that's why most of you are here, but please don't disturb any of the creatures." He nodded to Vyla, then turned and started to lead the way along a short, narrow path.

They came out a few moments later into a wide, circular clearing. Several large huts were placed around the edge and a large canvas-covered structure stood in the middle.

"Here we are," Marik announced. "You should all have been allocated your sleeping huts, but I'll just give you a quick tour of the rest of the campsite. The big tent here in the centre is the canteen. We'll all eat here together. Over there behind the end hut is the shower block and the toilets are behind them."

Collo snorted and muttered something under his breath as he tugged uncomfortably at the collar of his short-sleeved button-down shirt.

"I'm sorry, Collo, I didn't catch that," said Marik, smiling sweetly.

"Nothing. It's fine."

"No, no. Please, if you're unhappy about something, let us try to put your mind at rest."

Collo pulled a deep breath in through his nose. "I just wondered how hygienic these facilities are. Especially since they're communal."

Marik looked affronted. "I can assure you that all 'WorldStepper' facilities are maintained to the highest standards. After all, what better way to get to know your fellow travellers than sharing?

"Now, if you'd like to go and find your huts and get unpacked, we'll have lunch at around twelve-thirty. Then our forest guides will arrive, and we can go out for our first hike this afternoon."

"May I just ask what's the itinerary for this afternoon, please?" asked a middle-aged lady with short, black hair greying at the temples.

"Of course, Melda. Sorry, I should've told you. We'll have a six Juriss mile walk, which is equivalent to around two and a half earth miles, to get to the village. You'll meet the inhabitants and be able to buy some of their handicrafts if you wish. On the way we will hopefully see a few of the native wild creatures. The most common are the gyjahs, which are small, yellow humanoid creatures, about thirty centimetres high, with a long, prehensile tail. They're very brave and may approach, but be careful, they can bite and may try to steal anything they can get hold of. But don't worry, if they do take something, you will be able to barter for it back. They love Earth chocolate, but generally any food will do. We may even see one or two rangadang if we're lucky. They're large ground birds, about the size of an emu. They have orange and purple feathers, and bright yellow beaks. If we do see them, stay very quiet. They're very shy, but if they're startled they will spit. It's very unpleasant and burns if it gets on your skin or in your eyes.

"We'll stay at the village for our evening meal and then use the StepZone to get back here, since it's not entirely safe to walk through the jungle at night."

"Thank you," said Melda and some of the others murmured their own thanks.

Vyla came to stand beside Marik who was watching Ule's butt wiggle as she walked away and the rest of the group dispersed. "I notice you didn't mention in your little speech that they would be four to a hut. What's our friend Collo going to say about that?"

"Well, I thought it would be a nice surprise for him."

Vyla grinned and shook her head. "You're a wicked man, Marik!"

He laughed and put his arm around her shoulders. "Come on, we'd better get our hut sorted out. If it's bunks again, I'm on top."

Vyla raised an eyebrow. "I didn't realise you like to be on top. I imagined you preferring it the other way around!"

He grinned at her as they walked to their hut. "Oh, I don't mind either. I'll take it any way it comes."

"Yes, so I've heard!"

The beds were twins, so they picked one each and started to unpack.

"So you like to imagine me at it, then?" asked Marik.

Vyla turned away to sort out a pile of clothes, hoping he hadn't seen her blush. "It was a figure of speech. I can assure you, you do not feature anywhere in my fantasies!"

Marik chuckled and suddenly he was behind her. He slipped his arms around her and whispered in her ear. "Tell me about your fantasies."

Vyla shrugged him off and slapped his arm. "In your dreams," she said with a laugh.

"Oh, Vyla. You're always in my dreams!"

She pulled a boot out of her bag and threw it at him. He caught it easily and laughed as he tossed it back and skipped down the steps of the hut, heading off towards the canteen to check on the lunch.

Vyla closed her eyes. She hated it when he did things like that, building false hope and dashing it away with a joke. But if he ever stopped, she'd hate that even more.

The kitchen staff were clearing away after lunch and Marik was chatting to a few members of the group when Collo walked past with another tourist. He caught sight of Marik and stopped. Marik steeled himself, ready for the encounter.

"There are plenty of huts here, I don't see why we have to share," Collo snapped.

Marik stopped himself from scowling. This man was becoming a real pain in the arse. "Yes, there are plenty of huts. But there are also plenty of staff, as you can see. They need somewhere to stay. And it was stated in the brochure that accommodations would be shared."

"But I paid extra…"

"Which is why you have a larger hut with separate sleeping areas," Marik explained, cutting him off mid-sentence.

"But I assumed I would at least get a private room!"

"The accommodation dimensions are clearly shown in the brochure, even the luxury huts. This is a safari tour. We're here for two weeks of exploration, seeing the wildlife, and generally 'roughing it'. Believe me, this is real luxury compared to the tents we'll be using out on the savannah."

Marik took a deep breath to calm himself. "I'm sure you'll be very comfortable once you're settled in. All the beds have anti-insect and silence modes at the touch of a button. If you need help, just ask me or Vyla and we'll gladly be of service."

Collo huffed and frowned, but didn't say anything more.

As Marik watched him walk away, he was startled by a soft voice behind him.

"There is always one who will complain about being in such a glorious place."

Marik smiled and turned around. "Hello Xano. When did you get here?"

The woman was taller than Marik, slim and supple-looking. She had a sharp, thin face and her long white hair flowed around her shoulders in stark contrast to her royal blue skin.

She wore the traditional clothes of the Jurissan tribes, a brightly-coloured cloth sarong of orange and blue tied at the side of her waist and reaching to just above her knees. Her top was another piece of matching cloth tied around her chest and knotted at the front between her breasts. It was made of a lightweight material from one of Juriss' many fibrous plants.

"We have just arrived. Is he going to be trouble, do you think?"

Marik glanced in the direction Collo had gone. "Not really, he's just a moaner. We get at least one every trip." He looked over Xano's shoulder. "How many have we got this time?"

"I have only four of my people with me this year. I'm afraid the young ones these days are not as keen to stick to our traditions. They wish to explore other worlds and not their own."

"I guess that's the way it goes in all cultures."

"It would seem so. I only hope this world will not fall the way other worlds have, your own included."

Marik gazed around at the thick jungle surrounding the camp. "I can't see it happening. Hasn't the Director put a law in place that forbids any more construction or removal of the forests?"

"He has, yes. However, he will not always be the Director, and the next one may decide to change that law."

"I'm sure that won't happen. Your people receive a good income from 'WorldStepper' tours."

Xano inclined her head. "I hope it is always enough."

"Hi, Xano. Good to see you." Vyla stepped between the tall Jurissan woman and Marik.

"It is good to see you also," Xano replied with a wide smile.

Vyla turned to Marik. "They're ready to go. Even Collo seems quite excited, with his little blue backpack!"

Marik nodded. "Okay. Let's get going then, shall we?"

Vyla walked back towards the group while Xano called her team of forest guides over.

Everyone stared at the five tall, striking, blue-skinned figures. For some, it was their first time off-world, including, it seemed, Collo.

He stared open-mouthed. "They're aliens!" he said quite loudly.

Xano stepped in front of him and tilted her head to one side. "My friend, since this is *our* world, it is you who are the alien." She gave him a disarming smile. "I will introduce them now."

Collo shut his mouth and swallowed. He blinked up at Xano. "I-I'm very sorry, I, er, didn't mean to, er, offend you." He stuttered to a halt, still unable to take his eyes from her face.

She inclined her head and beckoned for the others to come forward. They were all dressed in the same clothing as Xano, although the males were bare-chested, and each wore different colours. The first guide was a tall male with the same blue skin, but his hair was a vivid yellow and hung in thick, shaggy locks around his head.

"This one is Zardir, he is my second."

Xano indicated the next two Jurissans, both a little smaller than Zardir. "These are Yindo and Yinda who are sisters."

Yindo had a shock of short, scarlet hair where Yinda's was an intense pink and hung in long, flowing waves around her face.

"This last one," Xano continued as a slim, muscular male with a shock of bright orange hair stepped forward, "is Zevyn."

As the guides turned away, the tourists saw that the hair of the two males continued down their backs to their waists in a tapering line. The female's backs were smooth without the manes.

Xano smiled at Collo. "Now we are friends," she said with a nod.

"You're beautiful!" Collo blurted.

Marik smiled. "Xano, leave the poor man alone. You know your Charm is too strong for most humans."

Xano looked at him. "I am not using it on him, I assure you. We do not need to, but anyway it has been forbidden to use the Charm on humans since your last visit here."

"Ah!" said Marik as he hastily stepped between the two. "Right, let's head out."

He led Xano away and left Collo looking on with wide, adoring eyes.

As they readied themselves, Marik glanced at the four other Jurissans. They were a handsome race, and possessed the 'Charm', an influence which could sometimes be used to compel others.

As he watched them, the younger male, Zevyn, turned and looked straight at him. Their eyes locked, and for a moment Marik couldn't move. The rest of the world disappeared, and he and this beautiful Jurissan were the only two beings left in the whole universe. Zevyn blinked slowly and the spell broke.

Marik gave a little gasp and felt a shock run through his body.

Vyla glanced at him. "Are you okay?"

Marik took a deep breath. "Yeah. Yes, I'm fine." He glared at the Jurissan and the tall male smiled shyly.

"Come on," Marik said to Vyla, his tone sharp. "Let's get going."

Xano and Marik led the way through the dense jungle. In some places they had to cut through the thick vegetation where it had overgrown the path.

"Take care not to touch the cut edges of these big red vines," Marik warned the group. "The sap is acidic and is strong enough to burn through your clothing."

They continued on with the Jurissan guides walking among the humans, chatting and pointing out plants and insects they passed.

Xano held up a hand and everyone stopped as she pointed to a small clearing where a herd of animals were grazing. They were the size of a large dog and their short, pink, velvety fur gleamed in the light through the trees, giving them a silky, glossy appearance. They had six legs, the front pair of which they used to separate blades of grass as they searched for insects and larvae. Their long, pointed snouts moved like an elephant's trunk, and were about twenty centimetres long. When they found food, a long, thin tongue like an anteater's shot out, poking into the ground.

Their large, blue eyes wrapped around the sides of their faces like a pair of sporty sunglasses, and they had long, straight ears, like those of a rabbit.

"They're beautiful," murmured a small, thin woman with short blonde hair. "What are they?"

"These are called onklong," Xano explained in a hushed voice.

One of the onklongs suddenly twitched its ears and looked up, turning its head towards the tourists. Its great ears were flicking back and forth, then it held its trunk up and sniffed the air. It opened its mouth and emitted a quiet but high-pitched peeping sound. Immediately the rest of the herd raised their heads and moved with a speed that shocked the humans. Within a fraction of a second, the clearing was empty.

"Well, that's just wonderful!" snapped Collo. "I've only just got my camera out. I didn't even get a chance to take a picture." He turned on the woman who had spoken. "Thank you very much indeed, Algam."

Algam blushed and muttered an apology. Melda, who was standing nearby, put her arm protectively around the smaller woman's shoulder. "Never mind, Al," she said soothingly. Then she glared at Collo. "Perhaps you should keep your camera on you, like the rest of us. That way you'll be ready as soon as you see something." She turned away and ignored Collo's blustering.

"They move so fast!" one of the men commented.

Beside him, Zardir smiled. "They do. They can reach speeds of ninety of your Earth miles per hour. And, as I believe the term 'nought to sixty' is popular among your kind, they would reach that in two Earth seconds."

The man laughed and shook his head. "Amazing! Look, I got some lovely pictures," he said, showing his camera to the guide and anyone else nearby.

Collo pursed his lips. "Well, lucky you!"

As they reached the outskirts of the village, they heard rustling in the nearby bushes. Suddenly, the party was surrounded by twenty or so of the small, yellow gyjahs Marik had mentioned. They looked like tiny naked humans with long tails swishing around like whips or curled around branches or twigs. One or two had small, blue half-eaten berries in their hands but all of them were watching the tourists and guides closely.

As the little creatures scurried around, some of them came closer, small smiles on their faces.

Ule grinned. "They're so cute! Look, that one's got a pair of sunglasses!"

Indeed, one of the gyjahs had the glasses, probably a prize from a previous encounter, perched at an angle over its eyes. The glasses were far too wide and lopsided, giving it a very amusing look.

Melda laughed. "How on Earth are those staying on? They're so big!"

Xano smiled. "These are very clever. She has probably tied them at the back with grass or vines."

As the gyjah turned away, they saw it was true. The arms of the glasses were tied together behind the creature's head with an untidy knot.

Melda nodded. "Did you say 'she'? It would have to be a female to be so ingenious." She laughed out loud, and to her surprise several of the gyjahs joined in with a shrill little cackle.

"Keep your belongings close to you," Marik warned.

A sudden cry went up from the back of the group and they all turned to see Collo wrestling with two gyjahs who had hold of his camera. "Let go! Leave me alone you little thieves!"

Vyla took a step towards them, but Xano put a hand on her arm. "Not yet," she whispered. "Let us enjoy this moment."

Vyla grinned at her. "You've met him, then?"

Xano smiled and narrowed her beautiful eyes. "I know his sort."

By this time, the gyjahs were tugging on the camera and had got round behind Collo. The strap was still around his neck and his face was red. He gasped as the creatures pulled on the camera, the strap choking him.

"Okay," said Vyla, still grinning. "I think I'd better step in."

She walked over, slower than she should've done, and took out a bar of chocolate. She unwrapped it and waved it around in the air near the gyjahs. They caught the scent and immediately lost interest in the camera. Vyla tossed the chocolate bar into the undergrowth and the gyjahs shot off after it. The sounds of bickering issued from the bushes and the tourists suddenly realised there were words amongst the squeals and growls.

"Mine!" "Mine!" "Mine!" "Give!" "Give!"

"Oh my god! I didn't know they could speak!" Algam peered through the shrubbery. "That's incredible!"

Xano looked almost proud. "As I have said, these are very clever. These can mimic other creatures, including both Jurissans and humans."

They walked into the village and Collo was making a big deal of coughing and massaging his throat, which was, to be fair to him, very red and sore-looking.

"I think you should've helped a little sooner than you did," Marik chided Vyla half-heartedly.

"I was going to," she explained, "but Xano was enjoying the entertainment."

Marik chuckled. "Good old Xano!"

He hung back a bit and waited for Collo. "Come with me," he said gently to the man. "I'll take you to the hospital. Best to get you checked out."

"They have a hospital here?" croaked Collo.

"Well, yes. All the villages do. This isn't the millennium age, you know!"

The hospital was a large, slab-built building, like all the houses and shops in the village. Marik led Collo inside and they stepped into a wide, airy lobby. Everywhere, blue-skinned Jurrisans walked or stood or sat. Some were clearly patients and others wore the long, blue coats of medical personnel.

A tall male with long lemon-yellow hair approached them. "Welcome," he said in a clear deep voice. "How may I aid you?"

Marik bowed his head to the doctor. "My friend here has had a run in with the gyjahs," he explained.

"It was more than a mere 'run in'! I was attacked!" Collo said, his voice squeaking from the damage to his throat. He coughed loudly and his face turned red, his eyes watering.

The doctor nodded and pointed to Collo's chest. "I see. You had this camera around your neck?"

Collo nodded, clutching his ravaged throat with one hand while the other held the camera close to his body.

"It is always best to keep the strap around across your shoulder instead, when you are in the territory of the gyjahs." He smiled benignly. "Come," he said and led Collo to a small examination room.

Marik left him and emerged into the bright, sunny square at the centre of the village. Humans and Jurissans were bustling around the many market stalls and tiny shops around the edges. Right in the centre of the square was the familiar gate where the StepZone they would use tonight was located. This was the only village on the planet to have one, making it the richest but still most traditional township here.

The Jurissan guides were busy explaining their culture and traditions to the tourists, and the ease with which both races interacted always surprised Marik. He wasn't a racist by any means, but most of the tourists who used 'WorldSteppers' had never seen other races before. It always seemed that after the initial introduction, most people simply accepted the differences and got on with having a fabulous vacation.

He was watching Ule bartering with a towering Jurissan female for a fine blanket made from the fibres of the goojang tree, a small, flowering tree that produced a soft, white, wooly fibre from its seeds that could be easily woven and dyed. As he watched, he felt the uncomfortable feeling of eyes on him and turned to see Zevyn staring at him.

He couldn't move. His body refused to respond, his feet rooted to the ground, and he realised that he wasn't breathing. When he let it out it came as a gasp but his eyes never left Zevyn's. His face was smooth and his blue skin shone in the sunlight. His short hair was a burnt orange colour and his eyes, large and almond-shaped, were a deep blue, almost black.

He stood tall and straight, his bare chest well-muscled, as were his arms and legs. He wasn't bulky, but slim and supple like all of his kind.

As he stared back at Marik, he smiled and gently bowed his head, his eyes never leaving Marik's.

Marik jumped suddenly when a hand landed gently on his arm.

"You okay?" asked Vyla, looking a little concerned. "I called you twice and you ignored me. Rude!"

Marik shook his head and looked at her. "Er, yeah. Sorry, I was…" He glanced across the clearing but Zevyn was gone. "Sorry," he said again. "What was it you wanted?"

Vyla raised her eyebrows. "Think you're losing it, old timer!" she said as she started to walk away. She turned back. "Are you coming or what?"

With one last glance back, Marik followed her. "Yeah. So what's the problem?"

Vyla led him to one of the stalls where a Jurissan elder, her green hair faded with age, was sitting behind a blanket laid out on the ground and covered with lots of brightly-coloured ceramic pots and bowls. The beautiful green and purple striped cloth she wore was longer, and it wrapped around the back of her neck where the two corners were tied neatly.

"No problem," said Vyla, pointing towards the stall. "But last time we were here you said you wanted a proper kalcho cup."

"Elder Qoza, are you well?" Marik asked, bowing politely as they approached the old female.

"I am well, friend Marik." Qoza held up a small beaker about the size of an eggcup. It was yellow with fine stripes of red and blue.

"You do not prefer to have the human size?" She indicated some smaller, thimble-sized beakers on display. "The kalcho is strong!"

Marik smiled. "I've developed quite a taste for it, as you well know, Qoza. The full-sized one in your hand will be just right."

Qoza chuckled as Marik handed her some coins and took the yellow cup. He held it up and inspected it. "Your craftwork is as fine as ever. The best in the land."

Qoza bowed her head in thanks.

"I shall use it tonight at the feast!" He grinned again and put the cup carefully in his pack.

"Rather you than me," Vyla quipped. "I can't stand the stuff!"

The feast was finished, the tourists full and content, and they were sitting around a large, round fire pit, with the Jurissan villagers among them, chatting and sipping kalcho.

Collo took a sip from his tiny cup and coughed sharply, spitting the drink into the flames. The fire roared for a second, white sparks flying up into the air.

"What is this stuff made from?" he croaked. The damage to his neck was gone, healed by the Jurissan doctor, but his voice was still a little strained.

Xano was sitting beside him and she slapped him gently on the back as he continued to cough. "It is fermented kalchaka weed. It is an acquired taste and very potent. This is why you have just a tiny cup." She sipped her drink from her own egg cup-sized beaker.

Marik inhaled the heady scent of spices and herbs issuing from the drink. He took a long, slow sip and swilled the liquid around his mouth, savouring the tingle as it slid across his tongue and finally down his throat. The liquid started off sweet from added manjar, essential for counteracting the bitter kalchaka, but slowly, heat from the alcohol spread quickly through his body and a lazy smile crept into his lips.

"Will you have more?" asked a young Jurissan girl as she moved around with a flask.

"No, I would love to, but I'm still working." He lifted his almost empty cup. "This is enough for me. Any more and I won't be able to stand!"

The girl laughed and left him. He looked up and caught sight of Zevyn. He watched as the Jurissan chatted and laughed with some of the tourists.

"He's really beautiful, isn't he?" Vyla commented.

Marik frowned and looked away from him quickly. "They're a beautiful race."

Vyla tilted her head as she watched the young male. "Yes, but there seems to be something about him. I don't know, I can't put my finger on it."

Marik grunted. "He's probably projecting the Charm."

Vyla glanced at her friend. "I don't think so. I've been subjected to that and you know it when it hits you! Anyway, Xano said they're not allowed to use it on humans anymore."

Marik checked his watch. "It's time to start getting them home," he said, changing the subject. He stood up too quickly and wavered slightly. He regained his balance and walked away, taking care not to look at Zevyn.

Vyla went through the StepZone first as usual, and Marik sent the tourists through.

The forest guides were there to see them off and Marik grabbed Zevyn's arm as he turned to go.

"Just stop it, do you hear?" he growled, not looking up. "Stop using the Charm on me. I'm not gay. I like females, not males, is that clear?"

The Jurissan took a step back. "I do not use the Charm, especially on humans, it is forbidden!"

Marik clenched his jaw. "So you say!"

"We do not lie. It has been told now that humans are too fragile. To use the Charm on you is unfair since you are too susceptible. Your emotions cannot withstand the power, and most cannot stop their feelings from taking over. There was an instance recently where a human took his own life rather than live without the one who put the Charm on him, even after it was removed."

Marik risked looking at him. He felt something stir inside and looked away. He moved out of the way. "Just leave me alone, Zevyn, okay?"

The Jurissan blinked. "I am sorry," he said as he turned away and disappeared into the darkness of the village.

Ule was waiting outside Marik's hut when he arrived back at the camp. She slid out of the shadows and gave him a sensuous smile.

"Aren't you a sight for sore eyes?" he murmured as he took in her tight blue shorts and another sleeveless blouse, this one pink, which was tied under her breasts to show off her ample bosom and narrow waist.

She pressed up against him and brushed her lips across his throat. He breathed in her scent and closed his eyes, his arousal becoming obvious to them both.

"Can we go somewhere?" she whispered.

"Who are you sharing with?"

"One of the old girls, that bloody annoying bloke with the backpack, and some other man."

Marik grinned. "Nice that you've got to know all their names."

Ule rolled her eyes. "They don't interest me. Why would I want to get to know them?"

"Well, that's kind of the idea of these tours, for people to meet like-minded people and hopefully make friends."

The girl shrugged and looked up at him. "I only came on this trip because a friend of mine went on one of your tours and gave me *all* the details! I decided to see for myself if they were true."

"Oh? Which friend was that?"

She stepped away and stared at him. "Oh my god! She was right, you really are man-whore, aren't you?"

Marik shrugged. "No, I wouldn't say so. I don't take payment for it. But if you mean I like to spend time with beautiful women who may be on my tours then, yes, I do. Do you have a problem with that?"

Ule looked him up and down. "Not especially." She smiled again. "You're worth it, I suppose."

He reached out and grabbed her hand. "Come with me, I need a shower."

When Marik walked back into their hut, Vyla was still up. She was sitting in her bed, propped up against the headboard, reading, and she looked up as he came in.

"You're back early!"

Marik undressed, not worried about being almost naked in front of her. "Yep."

Vyla put her book down. "Okay. What's up?"

He pulled on an old t-shirt that he used for sleep along with his boxers and flopped down on his bed. "Nothing!"

Vyla frowned. "Well, something is. You look well pissed off!"

He looked at her and ground his teeth. After a few moments of silence, he put his hands over his face. "No, I mean, *nothing* is up!"

Vyla shook her head. "What?"

He lifted his head and nodded at his groin.

Vyla looked confused for a moment then it dawned. Her eyes and mouth went wide. "Oh!"

She jumped out of bed and stood staring down at him. "No! Really?" She spun away and went to the other side of the room. When she came back she was grinning. "Really?" she squealed.

"It's not bloody funny!"

"No. Nope, you're right. It's not." She pressed her lips together. "Nope. Not funny. It's bloody unbelievable." She roared with laughter and fell onto her bed. "Oh my god! I never thought I'd see the day when the great Marik couldn't get it up!" She hugged herself, tears of mirth running down her cheeks.

Marik sat on the edge of his bed, elbows resting on his knees and head hanging down. "Yeah, that's it. Take the piss."

Vyla tried to pull herself together. "I'm sorry. It's just not something I ever thought would happen to you of all people!"

He glared across the room at her. "Yeah. Well it has."

Vyla bit her lip and watched him for a moment. He looked so forlorn she couldn't help but feel bad for him, despite the circumstances.

She went and sat beside him on his bed. She could feel the heat of his body through her pyjama shorts as her hip almost touched his. "I'm sure it's just a one-off, maybe you had too much kalcho?"

"I only had one cup!" He sighed. "I don't know what happened. I mean, I wanted to. She was there and she was…well, you've seen her, she's hot!" He paused and wiped a hand across his face. "I was, you know…*ready,* and then when it came to it…"

He closed his eyes and Vyla felt a bit uncomfortable; they'd never really spoken about anything this intimate before, but she was his friend and if he needed to talk she'd let him.

He stood up suddenly and paced across the room. "I've never felt so ashamed in all my life. I mean, this sort of thing just doesn't happen to someone like me!"

Vyla took a deep breath. "Well, I don't know much about it, but from what I do know, it happens to all men at some time or other. I wouldn't worry about it. The more you worry, the worse it'll get!"

Marik looked at her as if suddenly realising she was there. "Oh, well, that's all right then, isn't it?" he snapped. "That makes me feel so much better!"

She smiled sweetly. "Good. Glad I could help." She got up and climbed back into her own bed. "Can we get some sleep now, please?"

She heard him huff before she pressed a button on her headboard. A hazy cocoon enveloped the bed and all she heard then was silence. She switched off her light, turned on her side, and grinned to herself as she closed her eyes.

They breakfasted early the next morning. Vyla saw Ule watching Marik, but it appeared he had chosen to ignore the girl. Vyla felt quite smug about that and cleared away her breakfast things with a smile.

Marik picked up his tablet and scrolled through the day's itinerary.

"Don't forget to take your sunscreen with you, everyone, and make sure you have plenty of water pills. We'll be out on the savannah for most of the day and the sun can get quite fierce around midday.

"We should see quite a lot of wildlife. There are herds of onklong down there, and hopefully some dromlaks. You can't really miss them. They're bigger than the African elephants we used to have on Earth before they became extinct, and they have red skin with vivid green stripes. Unfortunately, I doubt we'll see any colveron, the only predatory mammal on this world. It's a kind of large cat about the size of a pig, and has a dark yellow coat with grey-brown stripes. They have three rows of very small, very sharp teeth and long, hooked claws. They are very efficient killers, but fortunately for us they choose not to attack people. They're very shy so we probably won't even get a glimpse. It's a shame, really, as they're stunning creatures."

Collo breathed out sharply. "Yes, they sound quite charming!"

Melda closed her eyes and huffed. "Why did you even bother coming on this trip, Collo? You've done nothing but complain! You don't even seem very interested in the wildlife or the native culture, which is what this tour is all about. I don't get you, why are you here?"

Collo blinked at her several times. "Well! If you must know, I won the trip in a competition at work. I thought it would be a nice break!"

Algam tilted her head towards Melda and Marik heard her mutter, "It would be for the rest of us if he'd just shut up!"

Marik suppressed his grin and turned as the forest guides arrived. They were all kitted out with a small pack slung over one shoulder, and three of them had small tranquiliser rifles as well.

"Guns?" blurted Collo, looking shocked.

Marik glanced at him. "They're just a precaution."

Collo continued to stare at the weapons. "I thought you said those big cat things don't attack people!"

"I said they *choose* not to. I didn't say they wouldn't if they decided to change their minds."

Collo paled. "Perhaps after yesterday's incident I should stay behind? My throat is still a bit sore and I don't mind not going today!"

Marik narrowed his eyes. "Well, you're welcome to stay behind…on your own…without any protection…with the gyjahs out there in the bush, waiting for a chance to come into the camp and see what they can steal." He smiled at Collo. "But just so you know, we won't be back for a few days."

As he turned away, he heard Collo muttering as he got up from the table and started to sort out his blue backpack. "Well, it would be a shame to miss out. I think I'd quite like to see the dromlaks. And as you say, it's unlikely we'll even see one of those beasts!"

As Marik walked away towards his hut, Vyla fell into step beside him. "You're going to hell, you know that, right?"

Once they were all through the StepZone, the tourists and guides boarded small, electric hover shuttles to take them out onto the savannah. Out from under the trees, the heat was intense but dryer than it had been inside the rainforest. The ground was a deep red, covered with tall and brittle pink, yellow, and green grasses. A few low, flat beedong trees dotted the landscape, their sparse mustard coloured leaves giving a little bit of shade here and there.

Inside the bullet-shaped shuttles, the air was cool and large panoramic windows gave perfect views from any seat.

The quiet hum of the engines was unobtrusive, and it wasn't long before they glided to a halt some distance from a large herd of onklong. The little pink animals looked up briefly as the shuttles stopped. The onklong were wary, but seemed unalarmed by the group's presence.

Xano nodded to Marik, then pressed a small button on the console at the front end of Shuttle One as she stood up. When she spoke, her voice could be heard in all three shuttles at once.

"You will find that some of the animals out here are used to seeing the shuttles but we do not get too close as we wish not to disturb them. They usually stay and allow us to watch. The only times they may not allow this are when they have very young calves, or when the males are ready and looking for mates. At this time they may become aggressive, and have been known to charge the vehicles!"

As they listened, the tourists watched the onklong grazing by using their front legs to search through the grasses, their long narrow noses poking around searching for prey.

Collo, along with most of the others, was taking photo after photo, making up for losing out yesterday when they came across these beautiful creatures.

Xano continued to tell them about the animals. "They live for around sixty of your human years, which is forty Jurissan years. They become sexually mature at twelve Jurissan years and usually only have one calf, although twins are not unusual. They eat grubs, rekig termites, most kinds of beetles, and their favourite food is zlirm, a long, thin slug which grows to a length of up to half a metre."

The onklong moved slowly as they fed, stepping carefully along as they searched the ground. All of a sudden, one of the creatures lifted its head and its ears rapidly flicked back and forth. It let out the high-pitched peep the tourists had heard before and the whole herd ran. Within seconds, the area was clear with no sign the onklong had ever been there.

Several of the tourists stood up and looked around, trying to find the source of the panic.

The Jurissan guides were scanning the grass and Yinda, her pink hair tied back today, pointed to a spot among a patch of yellow grass.

"There! A rapzeen!"

Collo, Melda and several other tourists stared out to see what she had seen.

Marik leaned towards the window and as he watched, a huge, long, red and green body slid through the tall stems. It came to the edge of the grass and hesitated. A large triangular head rose up from the ground and a long, blue tongue flickered out into the air. It moved slightly and another head appeared next to the first one. A moment later, yet another head appeared, slightly smaller, beneath the first two.

"Three of them?" asked Medla. "Do they hunt in packs? That's very unusual for snakes."

Xano smiled at her. "They hunt alone. The rapzeen are a species of triheads, three-headed reptiles similar to snakes."

The heads slid together as she spoke, the outside two pressing against the middle to make it perfectly streamlined. It slid further forward and carried on until it was completely clear of the grass. As its head passed the first shuttle, its tail was just level with the last.

"My god! It's huge!" exclaimed Collo needlessly.

"It is, but they have never been known to harm a Jurissan, or a human!" Yinda told him.

As the shuttles slipped across the plains they saw several more herds of onklong, and one or two small groups of danglinks, similar to Earth zebra but with one leg at the front and back and two in the middle, giving them a sort of diamond-shaped body. Their necks were short and their heads like an upside-down triangle with ears at the top two corners. They moved with an almost sideways gait that looked very cumbersome and slow. However, they took flight and ran away at considerable speed when the shuttles approached.

The tour stopped at midday in a small stand of the stunted beedong trees where WorldStepper staff had prepared a substantial lunch.

Vyla rushed over to Marik. "Did you see the size of that rapzeen? I've never seen one that big before! Wasn't it amazing?"

Even Collo got caught up in her enthusiasm and joined in. "It was huge, yes. I bet it could've taken three onklong in one go!"

Vyla frowned. "I know," she said quietly. "I mean, I know they've got to eat and all that, but the thought of it eating an onklong, well, they're just so cute!"

Marik burst out laughing. "Since when have you got so sentimental?"

Vyla shrugged. "I'm not. But you've got to admit, they are cute. With their little pink trunks and those funny long ears."

He put his arm around her shoulders, half dragging her along with him. "Come on, let's eat. I'm sure there won't be any onklong on the menu."

Night fell quickly on Juriss. Even out on the open plains of the savannah the sun disappeared quickly below the horizon. Stars pierced the sky in their millions, and with no moon they were the only source of natural light.

Marik was chatting quietly with a few of the tourists by a large open fire when he noticed Zevyn enter the circle of firelight. He felt his attention stray for a moment but forced himself to ignore the young guide and carry on with his conversation.

More than a few times, he caught himself looking across the flames at Zevyn. He pulled his gaze away, but it was harder to do each time. Finally he got up and walked over to where Vyla sat a few metres away from the campfire, sipping coffee and staring at the flames. She jumped in surprise as he sat down next to her.

"Sorry," he said. "I didn't mean to scare you. What're you doing over here?"

"Nothing. Just drinking my coffee."

He smiled at her. "You can come and sit by the fire, you know. It's quite safe."

She looked at him with troubled eyes. "I just can't do it! You know my worst fear is being burned alive." She heaved a great sigh. "It's strange, though. I'm terrified of fire, but if I get near enough it's like there's something strong pulling me towards it. I don't know why! It's like the fire is alive and it wants me. It's trying to drag me close enough so it can get me. Maybe I'm just weird!"

Marik chewed his lip, thinking. "I don't think it's that weird. It's like when you're up somewhere high and you stand near the edge. Sometimes it feels as if you're being pulled so hard you might go over. I guess it's the same sort of thing."

Vyla shook her head. "I don't know what it is. All I know is it scares me." She looked at him with serious eyes. "When I die, I need to be buried. Please don't let them cremate me. The thought of burning for eternity terrifies me."

He frowned at her.

"Please, Marik. Promise me."

He smiled. "I promise, but I doubt I'll still be around by then, so you'd better write a will and let people know!" He patted her leg. "Maybe you are just a bit weird, though."

She scowled and slapped his arm. "Anyway, what are you doing here? I thought you'd be off somewhere with your little blonde bit."

Marik glanced at Ule, who was chatting with Melda. She chose that moment to glare at him, her eyes hard as flint. "Ah, no. Not after last night. I can't even talk to her."

"Why not?"

"Er, it's a bit embarrassing, isn't it?"

"Why? Just because you couldn't get it up last night doesn't mean it's going to happen again. You haven't been drinking today!" Vyla said, her voice slightly shrill. She shrugged one shoulder, as if it was no concern to her, and took another sip of coffee.

Marik sighed heavily and closed his eyes. "No. I can't. It's not just because of the. It's worse, far worse."

"Oh? Tell me." She tipped the remains of her drink into the fire and turned to face him.

"I can't," he said very quietly.

"This sounds serious," she said with a grin.

"It's no joke, Vyla." He got up and walked away from the campfire.

He didn't go far since it wasn't safe to stray too far from the safety of the group, so he was more annoyed than surprised to hear footsteps behind him.

Vyla held her hands up in defence as he spun around, about to berate her. "I know you probably don't want to talk." She paused and lowered her arms, tilting her head to one side. "But I get the feeling you need to. What kind of friend would I be if I wasn't ready to listen?"

He folded his arms and stared into the distance. He really didn't need this.

"Look, wait here a minute. Please." She ran back to the fire and said something to Yinda. When she came back, she was carrying one of the tranquiliser rifles. "Come on, let's go for a walk."

Once they were far enough from the camp that she was sure their voices wouldn't carry, Vyla pointed to a large pile of rocks. They climbed up and sat on one of the higher ones.

Marik rested his elbows on his knees and looked out into the night. In the distance, he could see the pale outline of a small patch of water reflecting the starlight. He knew from previous tours that this was a lake, almost a mile wide in places, fed by a river that ran from the centre of the island. Together, they provided the only fresh water for miles around.

Vyla broke the silence. "Talk to me, Marik. I know something's on your mind, and not just from your performance, or lack of, last night. You've been a bit 'off' for a day or two. What's going on?"

He looked at her with a deep frown. But when he thought about it, he knew she was right. He had been distracted.

He sighed again and stared at the rock below his feet, which looked grey in the dim light. "I…I don't really know where to start, to be honest." He shook his head.

"How about you start with last night and why you think that happened?"

Marik growled out loud. "Ah, okay. But if you take the piss, we're finished. I won't work with you again. I mean it!"

Vyla leaned back. "Woah! Okay, I won't. I promise. It must be serious if you're making threats like that!"

"It is."

Vyla touched his arm gently. "So, tell me. Let me help."

He swiped his hand down his face, covering his mouth with his palm for a moment, then he looked away from her and started to talk.

"It was all fine at first. I mean, we were, you know, kissing and…things, and I suggested we go to the shower room for some privacy, because I needed a shower anyway. So, there we were, naked, wet…" He trailed off, closing his eyes. "I was ready, you know?"

He glanced at Vyla and was glad he couldn't quite see her expression.

"Go on," she said.

He heard the tight edge in her voice and knew she didn't really want the details. "I'm sorry," he said and squeezed her hand.

She shook her head. "It's fine. Go on."

"This is the worst bit. Because if I say this out loud, then…well, then it makes it real, you know what I mean?"

"Look. This is clearly something that's causing you a lot of trouble, so just say it quickly and get it out in the open."

"All right. I was about to do the deed, as it were, and suddenly there he was! In my head and I couldn't get him out!"

Vyla was silent. When he dared to look he saw her staring, her mouth a black 'O' in her otherwise dark grey face and her eyes wide enough to show the whites.

"Um," she finally managed. "Who, I mean, which 'he' are we talking about here?"

"Zevyn, of course! You must have seen the way he looks at me. He doesn't hide it."

Vyla coughed. "Zevyn?" she spluttered. "Jurissan Zevyn?"

"Yeah."

"Tall blue bloke, orange hair and a mane down his back? That Zevyn?"

He stood up quickly. "Yes. Tall, blue, Jurissan…beautiful Zevyn…"

When Vyla didn't respond, he turned and she was staring at him. He shook his head and sat down again beside her. "I don't know what's going on, Vy. I mean, he's a *he* for a start."

"Zevyn," Vyla said, her voice not much more than a whisper.

"Agh…I know. But I can't stop thinking about him. And the way I feel when he looks at me…" Marik threw his hands in the air. "I don't know what to do."

Vyla continued to watch him.

"I've never felt this way about *anyone,* let alone another bloke! At first, I thought he was using the Charm on me." He looked at Vyla, searching her face for any sign of what she was thinking. "We've both had the Charm put on us before, we know what it feels like, and this doesn't feel the same at all."

Vyla shifted her position. "He is very attractive, even by Jurissan standards. I mean, I would!" She shut her mouth and stared into the darkness for a moment. "Well, my friend, it sounds to me like you've fallen for him, big time!" she said finally.

"Oh, well that's a great help, thank you!"

She shook her head. "I'm sorry, I just don't know what to say to you! I mean, the news that you, Stud Machine Marik, had suffered a moment of impotence was one thing, but this, this blows it out of the water!"

Marik gaped at her. "*Stud Machine Marik?*"

Vyla smirked. "Ah. Yes. That's what they call you back at the office. Sorry, I wasn't meant to say that!" She cleared her throat. "If news about last night gets out…" She held her hand up. "Not from me, I swear! But I can't see Ule keeping her mouth shut about it, and from what I know of her, most of her friends have been on your tours and probably, well, you know. Then I guess if it gets back to the office, they'll have to change your name to Dud Machine Marik!" She grinned as he scowled at her.

"Mind you," she continued, "if *this* little nugget got out, they'd have to call you *Dude* Machine Marik!" She laughed out loud and he pushed her, almost knocking her off the rocks.

She took a deep breath and stifled her laughter. "I'm sorry. I don't mean to take the mickey, I just don't know what to tell you."

Marik sighed. "I know. I guess I'll just have to work it out for myself."

They sat in silence for several minutes.

"Why don't you just talk to him? Find out how he feels? Perhaps he's just being friendly and because the Charm is instilled in them he hasn't quite got control of it. Maybe it's, I don't know, leaking or something."

"Leaking?" Marik stared at her. "*Leaking?*" Then his face creased up and he laughed.

Vyla gave him a cautious look, then she started laughing with him.

Once they'd got themselves under control again, they headed back to the camp.

"Mind you," Vyla said as they made their way along a narrow game path through the tall grass, "I don't blame you, he is gorgeous! Those muscles and that hair! I could happily run my fingers through it for hours!"

Marik smiled. "I wonder how far down his mane goes."

"Marik!"

"What? You must have thought about it," he said in his own defence.

Vyla shrugged. "Well…maybe!"

They chuckled and walked on in silence for a few moments.

"So, do you think you're bi, then?" Vyla asked.

"I have no idea. I've never been attracted to a man before."

"Yeah, but, well, Zevyn's not technically a 'man', is he?"

"What do you mean? He's male."

"Yes," Vyla explained. "But he's not human, is he? So does that make a difference do you think?"

Marik paused. "I've never thought about it like that before! Huh! Maybe I'm not gay!"

"It's a well-known fact that the Jurissan's are all bisexual, or whatever, at least by Earth standards. They just pair up with whoever they're attracted to, whether male or female."

They got back to the camp to find most of the others had retired for the night. Only Yinda, Yindo, and Zevyn were left by the fire.

"It is good you have returned safely," said Yindo as he stood up. "We shall sleep now. Goodnight."

Yinda got up and followed her sister to their tent.

"Goodnight," Zevyn called after them. He looked up at Vyla. "May I take the rifle? I have the first watch tonight."

Vyla handed over the rifle and started to walk off towards her tent. "Now's your chance," she said to Marik as she passed him.

Zevyn glanced at Marik as he walked past him towards the perimeter of the campsite. He stopped at a tall, slim pole that was stuck into the ground and pressed a button on its top. A red light started blinking and he moved to the next pole several metres away. He switched it on and a green shield appeared, lit up between the posts.

Marik watched him, noticing the way his muscles fluidly moved under his skin then cleared his throat. "I'll give you a hand."

He moved around the remaining posts, going in the opposite direction.

Inevitably, they reached the same post at the same time. Marik reached out to switch it on just as Zevyn put his hand on the button.

Their fingers touched and Marik had a sudden intake of breath. The feel of Zevyn's smooth, supple skin under his hand was electric. He looked up into the taller male's eyes and held his gaze. In that moment it would have been so easy to reach up and press his lips against Zevyn's, but the moment was broken but a low growl from outside the perimeter and they both stared out into the darkness.

They parted and scanned the area.

"There!" Zevyn whispered and pointed at a patch of long grass.

They stayed motionless as the stalks parted and a long, low shape crept out into the open. As it moved closer, Marik could just make out the stripes. The colveron was perfectly suited to the terrain, its stripy coat blending into the grasses and making it all but invisible.

The shield light glinted off the rows of sharp teeth in the animal's open mouth as it padded along, panting and giving the occasional snarl.

"It's beautiful," Marik breathed.

"Stunning," Zevyn murmured his agreement. "But it is also too close to the camp."

"It can't pass the fence," Marik said.

"Are you sure?"

Marik smiled at him. "Yes. The fence is made to keep out even heavy dromlaks. Nothing can come through."

The colveron glared at them for a moment, then trotted past and disappeared into the night.

Marik started to walk back towards the camp, with Zevyn a step behind. He felt a thrill as Zevyn's hand rested on the small of his back.

Against every instinct in his body, he turned, and Zevyn's other arm encircled his waist. He reached up and their mouths met.

Marik was lost in the kiss that was both sensuous and sensual, arousing and reassuring at the same time. His hands were touching, searching Zevyn's skin and as his fingers found the long mane of hair down his back they sunk into the fur-like softness, stroking, grasping, never wanting to let go again.

Zevyn took control, one hand holding Marik in a close embrace, his other gripping Marik's head, pulling him deeper into the kiss.

With one hand in Zevyn's mane, Marik moved his other up the Jurissan's back, shooting the feel of the smooth skin and the hard muscles beneath. He wanted to feel this body, get to know every inch of it. He felt himself harden and knew that Zevyn could feel it too.

The Jurissan slid his hand down and pushed it up under Marik's shirt. The warm flesh of his palm was like soft leather. Long fingers pressed into him with an urgency, and he responded in kind, curling his own fingers into Zevyn's hair, trying to get closer still…

The sudden, urgent buzzing on his wrist took Marik's attention, and as he pulled away he saw Zevyn look at his own communicator.

"*Marik!*" Vyla's shout carried across the campsite, followed by the babble of voices from the tourists.

"Over here," Marik shouted back and started towards her voice. As he went, he checked the message that had clearly come through to everyone.

"*ALL WORLDSTEPPERS VACATIONS ARE HEREBY CANCELLED. ALL TOURISTS AND TOUR GUIDES ARE TO RETURN IMMEDIATELY TO EARTH VIA THEIR NEAREST STEPZONE. THIS IS NOT A DRILL. *REPEAT* THIS IS NOT A DRILL.*"

"What the hell is going on?" Vyla demanded as soon as Marik reached her.

"You've got as much idea as I have," he said as the others milled about, looking confused and frightened.

Ule was standing alone, her arms wrapped around herself, her face pale in the flickering firelight. Marik felt a faint pang of guilt as he passed her, leaving her to fend for herself.

Collo rushed out of his hut, his blue backpack in one hand. "We have to go. Now! That's what the message said. We have to go."

He stopped and looked at the others. "What are you all standing around for? The message says we have to go!"

Melda turned on him. "Oh will you just shut up, you stupid little arse! Just wait and see what's going on, will you? Like the rest of us."

She spotted Marik and Vyla and called out to them. "Do you know what's happening?" she asked as they stopped in front of everyone.

Marik held his hands up to quiet them. "I'm sorry, I'm afraid I don't have any more infor-"

At that moment, a bright orange flash lit up the sky some distance away, followed almost immediately by a loud boom.

Xano ran across the clearing. "It is war!" she shouted to Marik as she neared him. "The Chandarans. They have threatened war for decades, and now they attack!"

"Chandarans? Are you sure?" Marik asked quickly.

"But why? Why now?" Vyla asked in alarm.

Xano shook her head, her white hair flying around. "I do not know. But we must get your people home, right away."

Marik looked around quickly. He couldn't see Zevyn anywhere and his heart missed a beat as a split second of panic washed over him. He dismissed it and took a deep breath. He had to stay professional; the tourists were his main priority right now and he had to get them to safety. His watch buzzed again.

"ALL STEPZONES WILL BE CLOSED AT TWENTY-THREE THIRTY HOURS, EARTH TIME. ALL TOURISTS AND

WORLDSTEPPERS GUIDES MUST BE RETURNED BY THAT TIME."

"Shit!" Marik grabbed Vyla, pulling her away from the group. "Did you get this?" He showed her his wrist.

"Yes," she replied. "I'll get them all together, you prepare the shuttles."

Two more blasts hit, nearer this time, making the ground shake. Vyla was rushing around, pointing and giving instructions while the Jurissan's helped to get everyone's belongings together.

The ground rumbled again and loud honking sounds came from outside the perimeter fence. As everyone stopped to see what was happening, a huge shape lumbered at considerable speed from the darkness.

"Dinosaur!" someone yelled as people stopped and stared at the great beast running away from the blasts. Others followed quickly behind, and tiny yellow gyjahs darted all around their feet, trying to escape.

"They're dromlaks, and they're terrified! I've never seen them move at this speed before!" said Xano, as the huge clouds of dust mingled with the honks and bellows of the big animals. In their panic, a couple of them swerved towards the perimeter fence and collided with it, the impact hurling one of them into the other. They both roared in fright, the fallen one frantically scrabbling to get up. Others broke from the brush, running blindly. They didn't seem to notice their fallen sibling and it was soon lost beneath their great feet.

"Oh my god!" Melda stood with her hands over her mouth. "They're killing the poor thing. Can't we do something?"

Marik stared at the dying creature, left broken and bloody on the ground, as its pitiful cries became weaker. "We don't have time for this." He grabbed Melda's arm and herded the tourists towards the shuttles. "Quick as you can, please. Vyla, get them on board."

Vyla nodded and hoisted her bag onto her shoulder, pushing the tourists onto the shuttles waiting to take them to the nearest StepZone.

Zevyn appeared holding one of the tranquiliser guns. He switched off the perimeter shield and stepped towards the fatally injured dromlak. Without a second's hesitation he fired a dart at the creature, which instantly fell silent. His mouth was a tight line as he reloaded the gun and shot a second dart into the thick hide, and then a third.

Marik gave him a quizzical look.

"One dart will not be enough. Three will ensure it dies without pain." He slung the gun across his shoulder and Marik could see the pain in his eyes from what had just had to do.

"We must hurry now," Zevyn said. He pushed Marik towards the shuttles and followed him on board.

As soon as everyone was accounted for the shuttles raced off. They overtook many of the dromlaks but no one was looking at the beasts.

Ule sat alone with tears streaming down her face as the others comforted each other. Melda and Algam sat huddled, their heads close together and their hands clasped tightly. Marik watched as Collo moved over to sit beside Ule and patted her hand. "We'll be okay," he assured her. She smiled at him and wiped away a tear.

Collo glanced up and caught Marik's eye. Marik nodded to him and gave a tight smile.

They reached the StepZone back at the jungle camp and the tourists poured out of the shuttles.

"You first," Marik said, pushing Vyla towards the plate.

Another blast hit the ground just a few miles away. The ground shook again and the air was filled with the screeching of birds as they took flight in their hundreds.

"Quick. Get going," he said.

"What about you?"

He glanced at her. "I always go last, you know that. This is no different." He paused for a second. "See you on the other side."

Vyla disappeared and he turned away as the tourists all began to crowd around the entrance to the StepZone.

"One at a time, people. You know how this works!" Marik bellowed over the babble of panicked voices.

One man pushed his way through. "Get me out of here. Now!" He pushed at Marik's arm which was barring his way.

A hand reached through and grabbed the man. "The women should go first," said Collo, holding the man back. He glanced at Marik and gave a curt nod. Marik nodded back and started to usher the women forward.

Ule pushed her way to the front. She stared at Marik as if daring him to stop her.

He opened the StepZone and she stood on the plate.

"Get straight off at the other end so we can get the others through as quickly as possible."

Ule glared at him but said nothing.

He pressed the button and she disappeared. As soon as she'd gone, he ushered the next person on and sent them through.

To Marik's surprise, Collo made sure everyone was through before himself.

"Thank you," Marik said.

Collo shrugged. "I might like my comfort and not be the bravest, but I have every confidence in you. I knew you wouldn't let any of us get left behind, so there was no need for all that panic."

Another blast hit, much closer this time, and both men ducked.

"Go," Marik said.

Collo disappeared and the StepZone returned to blue.

Xano led her team over. "You need to go, Marik. I must reset the coordinates and get my own people back to their homes."

"You can't stay here. You'll all be killed."

Xano gave him a sad smile. "And what of our families and loved ones? What happens to them?"

"Xano…"

She leaned down and hugged him. "We will do our best to survive." She moved back and held him at arm's length. "We will meet each other again, my friend. Now you must go."

Zevyn came forward, his face full of anguish. "Goodbye," he said, his voice cracking.

Marik shook his head. "No. No…come with me, please!"

Zevyn kissed him, a long, passionate kiss full of longing and sadness. "I cannot."

They all cowered as another blast shook the ground. There was movement out in the darkness, lights flashed and voices shouting that Marik could not understand.

Xano spun around. "They are coming! We must hurry. Please, Marik. Go!"

He moved backwards onto the blue plate, not taking his eyes from Zevyn's, and pressed the button.

When he arrived at the main terminal on Earth, he hurried towards the group of tourists who were standing around looking shocked and lost. All around the waiting area, other StepZones were spilling vacationers from all over the universe.

Soldiers with large guns arrived and quickly spread out around each Zone.

Officials from 'WorldSteppers' moved around the groups, handing out advice and forms for the tourists to fill in; for what, Marik had no idea. This was not a normal situation, and he hadn't had any training for it!

There was a crackle and a voice came over the sound system.

"Would all tour guides please report to the main office immediately. All tour guides to the main office."

Vyla grabbed Marik's arm. "That's us, buddy. Come on."

He followed her away from the terminal and down a wide corridor. Dozens of other guides, all with the same WorldSteppers shirts were filing into a large room.

As they took a seat, Vyla glanced at Marik. "You okay?"

He nodded but found his voice stuck in his throat.

She put a hand on his arm. "I'm sure he'll be fine. I'm sure they all will."

Marik pulled his arm away. "You can't say that. You don't know. None of us does."

A short man in a shirt and tie strode into the room, and everyone fell silent.

"Thanks," he said abruptly, scanning the room with his gaze. "For those of us who have never met, I'm Kade. I'm your boss."

There were a few whispers but then silence prevailed once more.

"So, the situation is this: Chandar has declared war on all StepZone connected worlds. They are using the StepZones to infiltrate all areas of the universe and although they've made no demands, all we know is that that particular race are extremely unfriendly and it appears they're aiming to dominate as many worlds as possible."

Marik raised his hand. "They're already on Juriss. What are we doing to help the Jurissans?"

Kade flexed his jaw. Marik was well aware of the man's dislike of interruptions.

"*We,*" Kade answered, "are not doing anything. We don't have the manpower or weaponry to get involved on any level higher than protecting the StepZone terminals."

"But we can't just leave the other worlds to fend for themselves," Marik shouted. "Juriss and most of the others are peaceful planets. They won't stand a chance against the Chandarans."

Kade huffed and twisted away, his fist on his hip. When he turned back, he stared at Marik with open hostility, pointing a finger at him. "If you had let me finish, I was going to say that despite our inability to help, the Battarian militia are at this moment mobilising their forces. They're sending battalions to all StepZone worlds and their main force is heading to the planets that are under siege as we speak." He glanced at his wristwatch. "In fact, I would imagine they've already reached Juriss."

The door of the conference room opened, then a tall, thin man came in and whispered to Kade.

Kade nodded and the tall man left. "Right. I have to go to meet the battalion assigned to us."

He looked around the room. "For the time being, you're all to stand down until further notice. You receive full pay for the time being, and the situation will be reassessed at a later date depending on how long this damn war goes on for."

As Kade left the room, the chatter rose around Marik and Vyla. "Well, I guess we're getting an unscheduled paid holiday then," Vyla said. She watched Marik as he sat in silence, chewing the inside of his cheek. She recognised the rebellious look in his eyes and knew he was planning something.

"Whatever it is, please…don't!" she said.

Marik closed his eyes and sighed heavily. "I have to do something. I can't just leave them over there." He looked at her with a frown. "They're our friends, Vy. Surely you're as worried as I am."

She moved her head closer to his. "Of course I'm bloody worried. It must be terrifying there. But we've got friends on all the worlds we visit. We can't help them, any of them."

Marik stared over the heads of other guides who were still discussing the state of affairs. He shook his head. "I have to do something."

He stood up abruptly and walked to the door, weaving his way through the group.

Vyla hurried after him. As she neared the door, a young man grabbed her arm. "Hey, Vy. Some of us are going to grab a beer. You want to join us?"

Vyla removed her arm from his grip. "No. Thanks, Jomo. I'm a bit busy at the moment."

Jomo took a step closer to her. "He's never going to get with you, you know that, right?"

Vyla felt her face flush. "Of course I know," she snapped. "But he's my friend and he needs some help so I'm helping him, that's all."

"What kind of help?"

Vyla watched Marik disappear out of the door. "Look, I haven't got time at the moment, Jomo. I'll talk to you later, okay?" She squeezed his arm and dashed out after Marik.

Two Battarian soldiers were stationed at each of the StepZone gates in the main terminal along with the soldiers from Earth, their uniforms blending with their charcoal grey skin. Their bald heads shone in the harsh white lights shining down from the ceiling.

"Why are they here?" Vyla whispered. "The gates have been made inactive. Surely they don't need guarding."

Marik looked at each group of bored-looking guards. "They're probably making sure that people like me don't try to activate a gate and go through."

Vyla shook her head. "You're bloody mental. You'll never do it!"

"I have to, Vyla. I have to get back there."

Vyla huffed. "Then at least wait a bit. Let's talk about this and try to come up with some sort of plan or something. Just going off half-cocked like this is going to get you nowhere but thrown in prison or worse!"

He glared at the soldiers again. Finally, he nodded. "Okay. But you won't talk me out of it, so don't try."

She took a deep breath. "All right. Let's go get a beer or something and see what we can come up with."

Jomo and half a dozen of his friends were sitting at a table not far from Vyla and Marik. There were already several empty glasses on their table and more than a few full and half-full ones. The group were talking quietly, one or two of them looking up surreptitiously now and again.

Vyla had noticed Jomo glance across at her and Marik once or twice, and this time he held her gaze for a moment. He said something to his friends and got up, making his way to her and Marik's table.

He stood beside Vyla for a second and cleared his throat.

"Can we help you with something, Jomo?" asked Marik, his voice low and sounding bored.

Jomo took a deep breath. "No," he said quickly. "But we want to help you."

Marik pursed his lips. He looked up at the young man and frowned. "Help with what, exactly?"

Jomo looked from Marik to Vyla and back. "Whatever it is you're planning."

Marik shifted in his seat and leaned back casually, a small smile on his face. "And what makes you think we're planning anything?"

Jomo looked at them both again, then hurriedly pulled a chair from the next table and sat down. "Listen. Some of us are really not happy to just sit around and do nothing. We all have a lot of friends out there and we want to help them." He stared at Marik in earnest.

Marik picked up his beer and took a long, slow drink. He put the glass down carefully and looked back at Jomo in silence.

"You're our head guide, Marik. We all have a lot of respect for you, you know."

Marik barked a loud, sharp laugh. "Bloody idiots! I'm no one's head guide, where did that come from?"

Jomo shrugged self-consciously. "Well, you know, you've been around the longest. You've been to every other world out there. Believe it or not, a lot of us look up to you." He leaned in conspiratorially. "We know you must want to do something. You're not one to sit around and do nothing!"

Vyla glanced from one man to the other.

"Well, you clearly don't know me as well as you think. I'm not planning anything." Marik sat up and finished his beer in several great gulps, then he stood and glared at Jomo. "I suggest you go back to your friends, leave me to get myself another beer, and let me sit here and drink it in peace."

As Marik walked away, Jomo turned to Vyla. "Why is he lying?"

Vyla sighed. "He's not, you bloody idiot. He's trying to protect you!"

Marik was changing from his 'WorldSteppers' uniform into a red and orange camouflage jumpsuit. He was buckling on a heavy-duty utility belt when Vyla came in followed by Jomo and three of his friends.

"I told you no," Marik growled.

Vyla put her hands up in front of her. "Just hear them out, okay? They have a plan which I think will help us."

Marik straightened up. "There is no 'us'," he told her. "I'm doing this alone."

Vyla started to strip off her own uniform before taking out a similar jumpsuit to the one Marik now wore. "No, you're not. What kind of partner would I be if I let you go alone?"

"Vyla..."

"It doesn't matter what you say, Marik. I'm coming with you. We're partners. Where you go, I go."

He frowned at her.

She raised her eyebrows. "Deal with it," she snapped.

Marik huffed and glared at Jomo. "So what's this big plan of yours, then?"

Marik and Vyla waited at the edge of the terminal hall.

"Are you sure they'll be able to get this right?" Marik asked.

"They know what to do. Vadis is some kind of IT expert and should be able to get the relevant gates active without any problems." She checked her watch. "Should be any time now."

As soon as she'd spoken, the lights at one of the StepZone gates flickered into life. The Battarian soldiers jumped into action, their guns trained on the gate they were protecting.

From across the hall, a large group of people led by Jomo rushed into the terminal and headed for the gate.

The soldiers from several of the other gates, including the one for Juriss, hurried from their posts and ran to intercept the group.

The guides were trying to force their way through the gate to Thoralton, shouting and tussling with the soldiers.

The Jurissan gate flickered to life as soon as it was clear, then Marik and Vyla crouched low and crept from their hiding place, hurrying to the StepZone. As soon as they were through the gate, Marik stood on the departure plate and grabbed Vyla, holding her close to him. "I hope this works," he whispered. "I've never sent more than one person through at a time!"

"Great!" Vyla muttered.

Over her shoulder, Marik caught sight of Jomo as he was being led away by two of the soldiers. Jomo flicked his eyes in Marik's direction and nodded discreetly.

Marik nodded back and pressed the button.

The plate turned green and the pull they felt as they travelled through together was a little stronger than usual.

As soon as they landed, they almost fell off of the plate onto the soft, red Jurissan soil.

"Well, that wasn't as bad as I thought it would be!" Vyla announced. "Who knew we could send two at a time? Perhaps once this is over, we should let the company know. It could save them thousands!"

Marik made a face. "Huh, why should they benefit?"

He looked around, scanning the area where just a few hours before they had evacuated this campsite. The sun was beginning to creep over the horizon, turning the sky from black to deep purple. The place was eerily quiet; no birds called and even the sounds of the insects that usually buzzed, squealed, and whined all day and night were silent.

"Can you smell that?" Vyla asked.

"Burning? Yeah." Marik nodded towards the west. "Look over there."

Vyla followed his gaze and saw the unmistakable orange-yellow glow of fire. "Oh my god! Is that the village?"

"I think so, but we'd better not use the StepZone. We don't want to turn up in the middle of the square and get killed before we've even seen what's going on," Marik said.

"No," Vyla answered. "Much better to see first and then get killed!"

Marik flashed her a grin. "Pessimist!"

He took a small pistol from his belt and released the safety. Vyla copied him and they set off towards the burning village at a slow run.

They'd gone about three kilometres without incident before Vyla called a halt. "Sorry, I haven't run this far for a while. Can we stop for a minute?" she panted.

Marik glanced around. They were just at the outskirts of the main jungle where the trees were sparser and the undergrowth much thinner. "Can we get to the bushes over there? It's too open here for my liking."

Vyla grimaced but nodded and they jogged another half a kilometre until they were concealed within the brush. Marik took a couple of water pills from his belt and handed one to Vyla. She popped it into her mouth and sucked it.

"Thanks," she said. "How far is the village?"

Marik wiped his mouth. "Probably about another kilometre."

He stared into the thick undergrowth and watched the flickering light.

"That must be some blaze," Vyla said. "You can feel the heat from here!"

Marik took a deep breath. "Okay, let's get moving. I need to see how bad it is."

Vyla gave him a sympathetic smile and nodded.

They reached the edge of the village and waited in the shade of some low trees. The sun was warm in the early morning and the heat from the burning village was intense. The buildings were all but in ruins; some were smouldering, belching plumes of smoke, and some were still ablaze. The only one left standing was the hospital, which stood alone at the other end of the rubble-strewn town square. The bodies of dead Jurissan adults and children lay among the wreckage with clouds of insects buzzing around them.

Marik scanned them, checking the colours of their hair. When he was sure he didn't recognise any of them he signalled to Vyla, and they slipped into the shelter of a burnt-out house. The two rear walls were just about standing but the rest had tumbled down into huge piles of stone.

They hid behind a large chunk of rock and looked out at the hospital. As they watched, two red-skinned Chandarans moved towards the doors of the building dragging a young Jurissan female. Her dark green hair was matted, and red blood stained her face and clothes. The Chandarans were holding her under her arms and hauling her backwards. Her head was thrown back and she had a thick rope around her throat. Her hands also seemed to be tied behind her back.

"What the hell?" Vyla hissed.

Marik held his finger to his lips. "It looks like they're torturing the Jurissans," he whispered quietly.

"That's a female. I guess that figures."

"Why do you say that?"

Vyla glanced at him. "What do you know about these people?"

Marik shrugged. "Not much. We don't go there so I haven't really worried about finding out."

Vyla scowled at him. "You're so lazy!" she hissed. "Okay. Most of Chandar is populated by females. Most male babies are killed at birth, usually by the mother. The better specimens are kept for breeding and some are kept as slaves if they're low on captives."

They watched the Chandarans take their prisoner back inside the hospital.

"I suppose they torture females from other worlds because they think they're the stronger ones," Vyla mused.

The door opened again and more Chandarans came out. This time, the Jurissan with them was still walking.

Marik heard a sharp intake of breath from Vyla.

"Xano!" she whispered.

Xano's white hair was grey from the ash, and there were black and purple bruises on her arms, legs, and the parts of her body that were visible between her clothes, but her face was unmarked. The same thick rope was around her throat and her hands were tied high up behind her back. The ropes were connected so that if Xano relaxed her arms, she would throttle herself.

"We have to help her," Vyla said under her breath.

Marik shook his head then pointed to another derelict building to his left. Among the debris several dark grey shapes were moving, almost invisible in the shadows.

Marik heaved a sigh and started to back up. He stopped suddenly when he felt the unmistakable shape of a gun barrel in the small of his back.

"Why are you here, Earth Persons?" asked a quiet voice very close to his ear.

A hand reached forward and took his gun, while another figure stepped forward and relieved Vyla of her weapon.

"We're trying to save our friends," Marik hissed.

The rifle was lowered and the Battarian soldier holding it moved in front of Marik.

"You are foolish to be here. You will leave this to we who are trained in combat. We will save all." His voice was low and harsh. His hairless, charcoal skin and dark uniform seemed to blend with the shadows, making him seem nothing more than a slightly darker shape in the gloom.

Marik straightened to his full height and appeared to tower over the squat figure of the Battarian. "We can help. Please. I have to take them out of here."

The Battarian seemed unfazed by Marik's size. "You will not succeed. You will die," he whispered in a flat tone as if the whole thing bored him.

He looked from Marik to Vyla, sizing them up. "You may go, but you will die. We will not protect you. We are here to aid the Jurissans and do not have time for you."

Marik glanced at Vyla, and she gave him a quick nod.

"Fine," he said under his breath. He held out his hand and the soldier returned his gun.

The Battarian signalled for his men to move out. Before he followed them, he turned back to Marik. "You are alone, but I wish you luck. You will die but we will not be killing you."

Marik frowned. "Thanks for that!"

The soldiers crept out towards a demolished house on their right, so Marik and Vyla slid through the shadows of the ruined village to the left until they came around behind the hospital. The large windows facing the jungle had been shattered and the walls were dotted with shot blasts.

They could hear sounds of soft whimpers and someone quietly sobbing from inside the building. The smell of urine, sweat, and feces wafted up, and Vyla swallowed the bile rising in her throat.

Marik raised his head to see just above the sill of the ruined window. He saw a pile of blue and it wasn't until one of them moved that he realised they were the Jurissans, huddled together against a wall. One or two more bodies were lying not far from the prisoners. One of them was the green-haired female. She was untied but lay with one arm flung across her body and the other pinned beneath her. Her legs were bent at the knee and her eyes were closed.

There was a flash of red as a Chandaran guard walked past the doorway and the sound of commotion from the corridor as two more Chandarans burst in with Xano between them. Their bright red uniforms contrasted with Xano's blue skin and looked like thick, ridged leather covering their entire bodies. They wore rounded leather helmets, but their green faces and sharp, pointed ears were exposed.

Xano was covered with blood and Marik thought it seemed weird her blood was the same colour as his own.

She was thrown onto the pile of figures and one of them reached out for her, cradling her in his arms. Despite the dirt, grime, and dried blood, Marik felt a jolt as he realised it was Zevyn. He slid down the wall, leaning back against it with his eyes closed. He stifled the sob threatening to give them away, but all he could see was Zevyn's stricken face, bruised, swollen, and bloodied.

He felt Vyla's hand on his knee and looked up at her. "They're in there," he whispered beside her ear to keep his voice low. "There are about thirty of them and they don't look too good." He paused and ground his teeth. "They've just brought Xano back, she looks in a bad way. And Zevyn is there."

A shot rang out from the front of the building and suddenly voices were shouting in a language the humans couldn't understand. Then more blasts sounded and several of the Jurissans cried out in alarm from inside the ward.

Marik and Vyla glanced into the room. The Jurissans were pressed back against the wall, clinging to one another, but otherwise it was empty.

Marik climbed onto the sill and pulled Vyla up with him. They dropped down silently onto the flat, tiled floor and quickly moved towards the prisoners. The sound of fighting carried in from the front of the hospital.

Zevyn laid Xano down carefully and limped away from her. He reached for Marik and pulled him into a tight hug. "You should not be here," he said urgently. "It is too dangerous."

Marik shook his head. "I couldn't leave you here to die." He studied Zevyn's face, reaching out to trace his finger along a long, thin cut down the side of his head.

Zevyn winced and Marik pulled his hand away. "Your poor face."

Zevyn gave him a stoic look. "I am fine. Better than others." He glanced at the dead bodies across the room.

The sounds of fighting came nearer the ward and Zevyn rushed back to Xano, covering her body with his own.

Marik and Vyla aimed their pistols at the door as a red-skinned Chandaran ran in holding a blaster. Marik didn't hesitate. He pulled the trigger and a blast of white light shot from the muzzle, hitting the Chandaran full in the face. She went down and suddenly two more were standing in her place.

More shots rang out from Marik's and Vyla's pistols and the guards fell.

"We have to go," Marik called out. Xano heaved her broken body up from the floor and limped towards one of the fallen Chandarans. She stooped down and picked up the weapon, handing it to Zevyn.

"Many of us are injured. There are also old ones here," she said, indicating the Jurissan prisoners. Qoza sat huddled, her hair a mess and a large bruise across one cheek.

"If we stay here much longer, they'll be dead," Marik said as he looked at the wounded Jurissans. "Come on, those who can still walk must help the others. We'll help as much as we can. We'll have to try to get to the StepZone here."

Many of the younger Jurissans were still strong and able to walk, even though most had some injuries. They helped the old ones and those unable to help themselves to the broken windows.

As quickly as they could, they helped each other through and out into the shelter of the trees. Marik took Qoza in his arms and lifted her down. He was surprised how little she weighed but saw then how her blue skin seemed loose on her frame and realised she was not much more than skin and bone. As her feet reached the ground, she pulled herself upright and smiled at him. With a determined glare, she hobbled towards the trees where the others waited.

As they moved away, the hospital ward behind them was suddenly full of Chandarans, shouting, running, and trying to figure out where their captives had gone.

Blasts shot out through the window, shredding the leaves and scorching tree bark around the fleeing captives.

More shouts echoed and the gun blasts changed direction as the Battarians chased down their enemy.

Marik hurried the Jurissans, herding them through the dense brush towards the other side of the small town.

"What do we do about the StepZone? It's been shut down," Vyla said, her voice shaky.

Marik tapped his wristwatch. "We've still got a connection."

Vyla checked her own watch. "I'll get hold of Vadis. Hopefully he's still in the comms room."

"Marik!" Zevyn's voice was a harsh whisper as he called out.

Marik rushed over and saw Xano on the ground. He went to her, and she looked up with pain-filled eyes. "I am dead," she said.

Marik shook his head vigorously. "No. Not yet, you're not." He glanced up at Zevyn. "Help me."

Together, they hoisted Xano up and held her between them, while Vyla ushered the rest of the Jurissans on.

"Vadis is opening the gate. But it won't be for long, we need to get a move on. I'll keep an eye at the rear. Get her through first," she ordered.

They hurried forwards as fast as possible, stumbling through the undergrowth. Marik pulled up sharply as a figure leapt out in front of them. The dark face of a Battarian soldier stared for a moment, then he nodded towards the StepZone and hurried on into the bush.

A yell from behind stopped them for a second and they held their weapons ready. When no one appeared, they rushed on.

They reached the edge of a building and looked out into the village square. The StepZone was there and was live.

Marik scanned the area, but everywhere he looked Chandaran soldiers were running and searching. Shots rang out as Battarian soldiers burst into the square already firing and bodies from both sides fell.

Suddenly, the Battarian soldier from earlier was standing beside Marik. He hadn't heard the trooper arrive and spun around, pointing his pistol at the soldier's head.

The soldier looked at the gun and then at Marik, then shook his head. Marik lowered the gun. "Sorry," he muttered.

"You will get them out. We will aid you," said the Battarian quietly.

"You said we were on our own!"

"We are here to aid the Jurissans. That appears to be what you are doing. Therefore, we will aid you."

The square was still full of fighting soldiers and the StepZone was unreachable.

"How?" Marik asked.

The Battarian watched the action for a moment. "Wait," he commanded and disappeared into the trees.

Several minutes passed and Marik was beginning to think they would never get a chance to go when a sudden cry went up and fifty or so more Battarian soldiers appeared out of nowhere. The Chandarans immediately started to fire at the new troops and several fell within the first few seconds. The Battarians quickly spread out, returning fire with long, rapid bursts of light.

One of the Chandarans fled from the square, heading straight towards the escapees. A round of laser blast shot out, hitting the Chandaran in the middle of her back. The blast cut through the soldier's torso and Vyla put her hand over her mouth as the two body parts slid away from one another, landing on the hard soil with a wet 'flump' sound.

Within the space of an Earth minute the square was clear. Marik grabbed Vyla and dragged her forward. "Go," he hissed. He and Zevyn hurried the others after her, keeping Xano upright between them, and ran to the StepZone.

Vyla stood aside, her eyes darting all around as the sounds of fighting reached them through the derelict buildings. "You go first this time," she said to Marik. "Get Xano through."

Marik shook his head. "You always go first," he argued.

"Not this time. I'm a much better shot than you are. I'll make sure you get through and I'll see you on the other side!" She turned and grabbed the gun Zevyn was holding.

Marik swallowed, staring at his friend. Xano gave a small moan and sagged as her legs gave way.

"Get going you bloody fool. They could be back at any minute!" Vyla shoved them towards the plate.

Marik eased himself out from under Xano's arm. She managed to get her feet under her and stood limply, leaning heavily on Zevyn.

"I don't know if it can transport more than two at a time," he said. He reached out and stroked Zevyn's face. "Get her through and to the medical bay as quickly as you can. "I'll help get the rest through and come find you when I'm back." He stepped forward and gave Zevyn a quick kiss. "Go on."

Zevyn didn't say anything, but he held Marik's gaze for a long moment.

A blast rang out close by, starling them all. Zevyn helped Xano onto the StepZone plate and the pair disappeared.

Vyla hurried the others along, sending them through in pairs. As the last two disappeared, there was a movement in the shadows to one side of the square. Marik and Vyla pointed their weapons and waited. A moment later, three small blue faces appeared.

"Children!" Vyla gasped. "Where did they come from?"

"No idea," said Marik. He waved to the children to come over. The tallest one, a pink-haired female, looked wildly about and grabbed the two younger ones, hauling them in her wake as she dashed across the square.

The three faces were dirty but seemed unharmed. "Where have you been hiding?" Vyla asked.

The children stared at her but said nothing. "Do you understand our language?" asked Marik. They moved their gaze to him but didn't respond. The oldest looked like she wouldn't be much older than about six or seven. The other two, both with yellow hair, were much smaller and probably no more than two or three years old.

Marik looked at the female. "Only two can go at once," he said slowly, as if that might help her understand. She continued to stare blankly at him. He held up two fingers, pointed to the StepZone then at the two younger ones. "Two," he repeated. The female nodded then and said something in Jurissan. The two little ones huddled together and clung to her hand.

Marik was amazed as she calmly pulled her hand away and guided the little ones onto the plate. She kissed them both on the forehead, then turned and nodded to Marik. He pressed the button and the little ones went through.

A sudden shot blast hit the ground beside Vyla, so she turned and fired back as a Chandaran came rushing from the edge of a building towards them. Vyla's gun blasted again and the Chandaran fell just inches from her feet.

She turned around. "Get her out of here!" she yelled at Marik. "GO!"

More Chandarans raced out of the shadows. "We all go," Marik shouted. He pulled her and the Jurissan child onto the plate. Vyla fired at the oncoming soldiers, ducking the blasts aimed at them.

The pull from the StepZone was ferocious and Marik felt a wave of nausea hit him as he landed. The Jurissan girl vomited but managed to stay upright. She looked around and she ran to the two little ones as soon as she saw them, engulfing them in a fierce hug. One of the adults, a tall male with pale blue hair, gave a sudden howl and pushed his way through the throng towards the children. For a few moments they all stood and stared, then the male dropped to his knees as the children fell into his arms, sobbing and hugging each other.

People were milling around in the terminal hall, while the injured were being treated and taken to the medical bay. Zevyn had taken charge of his people and was working with the 'WorldSteppers' officials to tend to their needs.

As soon as Marik and Vyla had arrived, the StepZones went dark.

Marik gave a huge sigh of relief but found he was shaking as the adrenaline seeped from his body. "I can't believe we made it!"

He turned to Vyla and his face fell.

She was standing, just barely, her face white and her eyes unseeing. Slowing, she tipped forward and Marik caught her as she dropped.

As he held her, he saw a great hole the size of a dinner plate in her back. Her clothes and skin were gone, blackened around the edges, burned to nothing. Her spine was a mass of black, charred bones, crumbling as he watched and leaving her hanging like a puppet without its strings. Her internal organs were gone, all but the seared top halves of her lungs.

"No!" His voice was a harsh rasp and his breathing rapid gasps.

He felt his legs start to give way, but then strong arms were around him, engulfing both him and Vyla as they sank to the floor.

He turned her over and looked at her face. Her skin was white, and her beautiful brown eyes stared up at him but saw nothing.

"MEDIC!" he yelled but he knew it was too late.

Where is the blood? he thought. *There's no blood.*

The shot had left her cauterized, the blood flow stemmed, every vessel sealed by heat from the blaster. He couldn't help thinking that if she'd been shot with a good, old-fashioned bullet, there'd be blood everywhere. But she might not be dead…

A great sob forced its way from deep within him and he pulled her close, his head against hers, his tears soaking her hair.

And through it all, Zevyn stayed holding them both.

People arrived at their side. Someone reached down to take Vyla, but Marik held on. "No. Not yet."

"We need to get her to the crematorium," someone said.

"No!" Marik glared up at a small, pale man wearing the uniform of a low-grade medic. "I won't let her burn. I promised."

The medic shrugged and walked away.

They stood around the open grave at the base of a great oomigong tree. Zevyn held Marik's hand in support; Xano stood nearby, robotic aids on parts of her still-weakened body, keeping her pain free and able to stand and move. Many other Jurissans whose lives had been saved by Vyla's sacrifice were also there, most of them healed or healing. Jomo, Vadis, and many of the tour guides who had been her friends were among them, along with the tourists from her final tour.

Vyla lay wrapped in an exquisitely woven goojang blanket. Her pale face was peaceful, like she was sleeping, and Marik thought she looked happy to be laid here, saved from burning in the fire she'd so dreaded.

Qoza moved around the hole, speaking words in Jurissan and sprinkling coloured dust over Vyla's body.

Zevyn leaned his head close to Marik's. "She is saying that Vyla's body will stay here," he whispered, "becoming one with the earth, nourishing it with her vitality, but the herbs, spices, and seeds on her will release her spirit so it can soar in death as it did in life."

Marik suppressed a sob, letting his breath out slowly through pursed lips. Qoza held the bowl of seeds and spices to him, and he took a handful. He stepped to the edge and gazed down at his best friend.

"Goodbye, love," he said to her as he released the dust across her body.

A little later, as they toasted Vyla's life with Kalcho back at the jungle camp, Jomo approached Marik. Zevyn squeezed his hand and left them to talk.

"So, what now?" Jomo asked.

Marik shrugged. "Well, I know that the Chandarans have been driven back to their own world. The places they destroyed will start to rebuild and I imagine that the tours will start again sooner rather than later."

Jomo nodded. "We'll need to start preparing, then. Some places were hit worse than others, and one or two will probably be removed from our lists, at least for the time being."

Both men took a sip from their cups.

"What about you?" asked Jomo. "I suppose you'll be looking for a new partner now."

Marik took a deep breath. "No." He stared down at the cup in his hands. "I'm not coming back."

Jomo opened his mouth in shock. "What? But you have to! You're our leader!"

Marik gave a heavy sigh. "We've been through this, Jomo. I am not now, nor have I ever been your leader. I'm the oldest guide, yes and I've been doing it longer than any of you, but…" He paused and shook his head. When he looked up at Jomo, his eyes were full of sadness. "My heart just isn't in it anymore. I can't imagine working with anyone else now."

Jomo was watching him closely. "But you worked for years before Vyla, you had other partners before her."

Marik smiled. "But she meant more to me than any of the others."

Jomo chewed the inside of his cheek, his jaw flexing. "She loved you, you know."

"I know. And I loved her, very much."

"Then why didn't you tell her that?"

Marik closed his eyes for a second. "Because it wasn't the kind of love she wanted from me. I couldn't give her that."

Jomo glanced across to where Zevyn stood chatting with Xano. "But you can give it to him?"

Marik snorted a soft laugh. "I don't know. I think so. Maybe."

Jomo took another sip of Kalcho. "So, what will you do?"

"I'm staying here for a while…"

"With Zevyn?"

"…with Zevyn. We'll see how it goes. But I can't go back to Earth. I don't want to live on a dead planet anymore. I've seen too much death, Jomo. I need life around me." He looked up at the giant trees and the stunning yellow sky. "You hear the birds? I can't live without that anymore."

He stood up as Zevyn came back to join them. Jomo smiled. He looked hard at Marik for a moment then his face softened. "I get it," he nodded. "Good luck." He held out his hand and Marik shook it.

Zevyn led his team of forest guides into the WorldSteppers camp and looked around for the tour guides.

Jomo was standing with the group of tourists around him giving a rundown of that afternoon's itinerary.

"As soon as our forest guides arrive, we will prepare to go for our first hike of the vacation."

His words were not as slick as Marik's had been and he seemed a little nervous. Nevertheless, he was doing a good job and the tourists looked happy and engaged. All except one man who was sitting with a fluorescent green backpack clutched to his chest.

"I don't see why we can't just use the StepZone to get to this village. That's what they're for, isn't it?"

Jomo swallowed. "Erm, er…"

"Oh dear," said Zevyn under his breath.

Jomo puffed out his chest as he took a deep breath. "You see, if we take the StepZone, we'll miss out on seeing much of the jungle and its wildlife. The reason you're all on this tour is for the wildlife, so surely you'd want to see as much of it as possible"

Green backpack man huffed a little but nodded reluctantly.

The tourists dispersed and Jomo gave a great sigh.

"There is always one who will complain, even in this glorious place," Zevyn said in his ear.

Jomo jumped at the voice. "Oh my god! You scared the life out of me!" He laughed then and held out his hand. "Hello, Zevyn. It's very good to see you."

Zevyn smiled. "It is good to see you also. It has been a long time."

Jomo nodded as Vadis approached and greeted Zevyn.

"I can't believe it's been over a year," said Jomo.

"It has taken us this long to rebuild our villages. Yet I understand that our world is one of the first to reopen its tours."

"It is," Vadis told him. "Other worlds were hit even worse than here, but with the Chandarans under permanent house arrest on their own world, and thanks to massive interplanetary cooperation, it shouldn't be much longer before we're up and running at full capacity."

Zevyn smiled. "That is very good to hear."

"So," Jomo said, "how many guides have you got with you?"

"I have seven. And I think you know this one." He reached out towards a tall figure who came over, smiling.

"Marik!" Jomo shouted. He looked a little shocked as he regarded Marik's bare, tanned chest and the short green and orange patterned sarong he wore. "It's so good to see you! We wondered, well, hoped we would, didn't we, Vadis?"

Vadis was shaking Marik's hand vigorously. "We were just saying last night how great it would be if you were here!"

"We didn't know if you would be," Jomo continued. "I mean, well, we didn't know if things had worked out here for you or anything!"

Marik glanced at Zevyn and grinned. "Things are working out perfectly fine at the moment."

"We are still seeing how things go," Zevyn added with a wry smile. He winked at Marik then went off to greet the tourists.

Marik watched him go, his eyes full of love. "Although, we're hoping we'll see how things go forever!"

Jane Lupino lives in Chichester in the south of England with a mad goldendoodle called Stanley.

After being diagnosed with Fibromyalgia she had to make some serious life changes and found that writing, always a passion, became a great form of therapy.

She writes short stories which tend to become quite long and novels for young adults and children. She is currently working on four separate novels and one or two short stories. She has had three stories published so far.

"A smile can solve all problems." That's what Aurora's father always repeated, ad nauseam. A charming life philosophy, no doubt, but perhaps a bit out of place in a post-apocalyptic world where survival depends on makeshift DIY weapons known as PowerTools. And a smile definitely won't be enough to save her from the frightening energivores or a rival crew armed with electrotitanium drills and circular saws. But maybe—just maybe—the love for her best friend will.

Titania Blesh

DO IT YOURSELF

By Titania Blesh

To my Best Friend

Dad keeps telling me I need to think positive, even when everything is going to hell.

So here you go: the PowerTool about to pierce my jugular is an electro-titanium drill worth more than my life. And it's being wielded by *none other* than Loris Bae, my first crush when I was still a teenage girl stressed out by puberty hormones.

Yeah, Dad would be so proud of my positivity, if only he wasn't about to be devoured. And if only my plan to save him hadn't just gone to hell thanks to this jerk with the coolest drill on the construction site.

Outside my makeshift shelter of paint cloths and overturned bricks serving as chairs, the drizzle drums against the abandoned buildings of the city. Trying to appear as non-threatening as possible, I prop myself up with my elbows on the bags of mortar previously serving as my lookout just a moment ago. Yeah, lying on my stomach. Not the best position to be found in, in a world gone to hell so spectacularly.

"Only a noob gets caught with their back turned, you know, Aurora?" The tip of the drill caresses my trachea.

Noob. This moron still thinks he's in the middle of a LOL II match, but the only thing at stake this time are our lives. And the lives of the people I was trying to save, a moment before I was caught off guard like a chicken.

I can sense two people shifting behind me, the zooming of two energy Orbs powering their Tools right above their heads.

I have to play smart.

"I must admit it…you and your team have managed to equip yourselves surprisingly well." I only move my eyes and rest them on Dremel's circular saw, pointed too close to my kneecaps for my liking. I'm sure the rest of the gang is lurking nearby, the sadistic guy with the welder and that creepy woman with the pneumatic sandblaster.

"Do you think flattery will soften me up?" Loris leans over me and the piercings on his eyebrow glisten in the light of his floating Orb. "Where do you and the other noobs of your team keep your supplies?"

I try to crack a smile, even from my prone and undeniably disadvantaged position. Because '*a smile solves all problems*', Dad would say. Damn optimistic guru.

But hell, do I miss him.

"Listen, can we put our rivalries on hold?" I point to the crumbling square in front of us. Beyond a concrete mixer frozen in time, under a crane crumpled like an old dying man… there is the cistern.

A cylinder so rusty it weeps tears of blood with every drop of rain rolling down its surface.

Loris lets out a laugh that is somewhere between nervous and sardonic. "If you get close, you're dead. It's one of their lairs."

As if I didn't know that.

Positive vibes. Positive vibes.

"Listen, Loris." I stare at the dried paint on the sleeve of his overalls. "We can share the supplies. Let me put in a good word with Siria, and once we get our folks out of—"

"My folks are already dead, like most of them." He points to the cistern with his head and his jaw hardens. "They already spat them out, little more than bones."

A nasty chill grips my stomach, but I have to be optimistic. I have to. Dad would never forgive me otherwise. "I know, Loris, it sucks, and Siria has lived through this same tragedy, too. And that's why I believe that—"

"Your bitch of a leader would eat her own Orb rather than share a crumb with us."

I open my mouth to object, but he's fuming and his Orb crackles in response to his mood.

"And then, collaborate with your band of *losers*?" He turns to Dremel as if to seek support, but he remains silent and apathetic as always, dull-grey eyes under heavy eyelids. "Come on, what about that *noob* with the weed whacker?"

Hey, Hermes's weed whacker is a top-notch PowerTool. Even though there are no more lawns to weed. Even though he's probably waiting for me to attack the cistern as we planned, but instead I'm here with a high-end PowerTool tickling the back of my neck.

But there's no time for this kindergarten bickering.

They're coming back. The inarticulate cries echo among the buildings under construction, growls of voracity threatening to tear away the little composure I have left since they took all the adults. Uncles, grandparents, teachers. Everyone who had enough Orb energy to drain.

We should be fighting for our folks, for the ones who are left alive, but Loris seems stuck in perpetual primary school recess. Or in a state of loss too violent to really process. I wonder if it will happen to me too, if—or *when*—they devour Dad.

I stare back at the cistern. The urgency makes my hands tremble, and my Orb crackles with electricity. It hovers near my ear, a buzzing sphere discharging yellow-white bolts. Loris shoos it away with his elbow, but a moment later the Orb drifts back to my head.

"And anyway, what do you think you're gonna do against them, without a PowerTool?" He grabs me by the back of my overalls and lifts me up, placing the drill between my shoulder blades. I stumble over a pile of broken tiles, my ears burning with shame. Dremel takes a step back, points the miter saw down, and with a gesture of his chin he shoos away the Orb glowing brightly at the side of his cheek.

Loris gives me a shove. "Either your Tool sucks like your team's, or you're an idiot. Only an idiot would go places without the most important thing they own."

"And yet you go about without a brain, Loris Bae," a voice rings out from behind some rotten plywood panels, "but I don't hear anyone making a fuss about it."

My heart leaps in my chest with relief. My best friend, the leader of my gang, my savior—she is back. Siria leans nonchalantly against a barely recognizable Ikea Kallax shelf. The light of her Orb makes her shine with flashes of energy, as if surrounded by an aura. And indeed, to me she is divine. In one hand she clutches a worn pillowcase made into a sack. She found something to eat, finally. I swear if there's even one of those expired protein bars from 2024 that taste like acidic marble in there, I'm throwing the sack into the first batch of cement from one of the thousand construction sites in this dumpster.

"Ah, my food is here." Loris bares his teeth in a grimace and plants the drill against my neck again. I know he's not afraid to use it and reduce me to the only vegetable in this place. Siria knows that too.

The high-pitched whine of its engine fills the air.

I'm done.

Siria's Orb ignites with blue light. The sack of provisions falls to the ground. Various cans of beans, tuna, and lentils—a respectable haul that we would have really hated to hand to the bullies.

She raises her trigger arm and lifts the gigantic barrel of her leaf blower PowerTool as if it weighs nothing. A roar that is almost a howl explodes from the cheap plastic, and the Made in Italy cheap canvas sack—we can't afford quality Chinese stuff like the other teams—swells up suddenly.

The gust of wind hits us in a breathtaking jolt.

It throws me to the ground and I fall on one knee, scraping my fingertips and nails on the rough concrete to try to slow myself down. Behind me a crash thunders, an aluminum scaffold disassembles under Loris's weight and collapses with the rumble of an amplified xylophone.

Dremel's circular saw turns on with an ominous hum, judging by how his Orb dims to fill it with energy.

"Where's your Tool, Aurora?" Siria yells at me, spinning around to aim at the second enemy. Once again, she's caught me unarmed. Damn, now I'm more afraid of her reaction than of Loris's drill. But I mean, what can I do with the most embarrassing PowerTool in the—

A disjointed roar echoes among the buildings and the rusty cranes.

"Stop it!" I shout.

"What the hell was that?" Loris says. Dremel doesn't speak, but he's been silent since the energivores devoured his big sister, so no surprise there.

Siria powers off her Tool and her Orb returns to hover near her left ear, its size readjusting to that of an apple and its color returning from blue to its usual soft yellow-white. Loris gets up without a groan from under the collapsed scaffold, leans against an exposed plumbing pipe, and tiptoes over a slate slab.

A greasy drizzle drums on the puddles in the potholes on the road, filling the unfinished excavations.

Look through the rain to see the rainbow, Dad would say if he were here, and even if I miss him, I'm glad I don't have to listen to his bullshit for once.

"We have to hurry." My voice sounds so alien to me that I feel the instinct to turn around and see who spoke. No, it was definitely me. "Either we do it now while they're out hunting, or we may not have another chance."

Siria tightens her grip on her blower as if she's undecided whether to help me or hit me over the head with it. She's right. Without the rest of our team, there isn't much hope.

But the cistern is there, solitary in the rain. And we're here, fifty meters away. No more time for a plan. No more time for caution, because that stupid Loris screwed everything up and those things will be all over us any moment now.

We can't go on like this, alone, dog eat dog. Sooner or later, they'll come and get us too, when they're done devouring the last adults and their bigger, more charged Orbs. When they're still hungry, and there are only our tiny Orbs left.

And us.

Life isn't about waiting for the storm to pass, it's about learning to dance in the rain. I feel a little bit sick to my stomach to hear Dad's motivational phrases in my head again, but at the same time my chest tightens with guilt.

Because he needs me, this time.

Because he's in there, trapped in that cistern, and if I don't 'think positive' I'll be doing him an unforgivable wrong.

Siria hesitates. Loris grimaces.

Dremel remains silent and…a dark red spray erupts from his neck.

I scream at the top of my lungs.

Behind him, a shadow darker than black itself rises with a sinuous slowness, shapeless, the freshly spilled blood only outlining the profile of its zigzagging jaws, which close in one quick snap on Dremel's Orb.

It looks like someone turned off a light bulb.

Dremel flips backward onto the brick he had been resting his foot on and lands with a muffled 'oof'. Perhaps still in shock, he raises his circular saw, and the deafening hum fills the sky. His Orb's light filters through the energivore's jaws, and the screech of the blade grows louder.

The monster dives onto him, illuminated from within. It plants its black fangs in his ankle, but Dremel doesn't even scream. Then the light disappears, the Orb goes out, and the angle grinder stops buzzing and slows to a stop.

I fumble with both hands for my PowerTool, but, as always, I've left it somewhere out of reach.

"Move, Aurora!" To my right, Siria unsheathes the blower and raises it to shoulder level, bracing it against her collarbone to aim at the thing. Her Orb swells and the energy eater snaps around to face her.

Like a black stain, it lunges from the side and sends her rolling among the rubble and painting tarps of my little hideout.

I fumble with my tool belt for a few more seconds and tighten my fingers around the hammer. I turn to look for help, but Loris's back is already a blur in the rain. He's running away, the bastard. Abandoning his friend to die.

Siria flips over under the weight of the creatureand props it up with a knee to keep it at bay, but that monstrous body seems to be made of jelly. The jaws snap towards her Orb, trying to rip it away from her. First it feeds on the essential energy source, then on what's left in the emptied body. In the end, we're just electrical impulses—that's what we are.

With a shout, I tear the hammer from my belt and charge, taking a swing at the energivore. Its indistinct form crashes into the shelter of rags and tarps, and they collapse on top of Siria.

But it takes more than one hit to scare these things away. A normal tool is not enough, especially when the monsters are loaded with Orbic energy. The energivore lunges at Dremel again, extending a claw that seems to have come straight out of its ink-like body, and plunges it into his belly. It drags it down, opening a vertical slit from Dremel's diaphragm to his pubis.

Dremel presses his hands to his stomach to hold back the blood pouring out of the gash.

Not a word. Just red bubbles from his mouth.

I let out another strangled scream and take a step back.

"Aurora!" Siria rolls out from under the tent debris, with her Orb following in a crazy frenzy, and stops in a crouching position. She is holding a bulky tool with a backpack and a short barrel.

A PowerTool: the only effective weapon against energivores.

My PowerTool.

She throws it to me and tries to grab her leaf blower again, but the monster charges her. Damn, it's unstoppable.

I grab the backpack and sling it over my shoulder in one fluid motion. I clutch the lance and plunge the rear pump into the nearest puddle. Because my Tool has this cute little hindrance too—it needs water to function—as if the rest wasn't enough.

But I'm here, and I'm not backing down.

I pull the trigger on the spray gun. My Orb flashes, reverberates through every nerve fiber, as if it is sucking that same life force out of my muscles.

Because it is.

The pressure washer shoots out a cascading stream and…damn, even the humiliation manages to stifle my fear. Nothing more than a trickle of pee…this is my PowerTool. A tiny fountain. It could be a watering can, and no one would notice the difference. Good only for cleaning excess moss off driveways.

My dad would tell me to roll up my sleeves, stop whining like a brat and get to work, as "*if you want something done, do it yourself*".

Do it yourself.

But how can I exploit the true potential of my PowerTool when my Orb is smaller than a teenager's?

The energivore doesn't seem to care much about my paranoia. With a swipe of a claw, it sprays a shower of crimson droplets from Siria's shoulder and my best friend growls with anger.

Oh, no, you're not hurting her. I pull the trigger harder, and it actually seems to work. The jet comes out stronger, and it somehow grazes the monster. A small splash of black blood, nothing more than a scratch.

It's gratifying.

And a terrible, terrible mistake.

The thing is swollen with Orbic energy. Electricity runs through its undulating body in a series of violent discharges and the shock causes Siria to lose muscle control. She falls to the ground, shaking. Her Orb trembles in rhythm with her convulsions.

The monster's wide-open jaws close on the sphere of light, and the city seems to plunge into an abyssal darkness.

Siria screams, a moan that carries with it the most absolute anguish.

No. It's not possible.

All the times she saved me from bullies, energivores, and even my dad's sermons…and I'm just standing here watching her get devoured. First her Orb, and then her life will follow suit. She will have nothing left, her super blower off forever. Take a PowerTool away from a person and they can rebuild it, or get another one. Kill their Orb…and you've eaten their soul.

Please, don't take her away from me too… Another hysterical moan escapes my lips.

"*You just need to learn how to use it,*" Siria told me a few days ago. "*Listen, there was a guy who melted three energivores with a hair diffuser…*"

So it's not the type of Tool. It's the energy that rises from within. Your inner power. Your soul.

Your Orb.

I clench my jaw. *You won't take her away from me too!*

I raise the hose of my power washer and press the trigger. Electricity runs through my veins, *from* my veins, it shakes me, it strengthens me, and I growl in agony and ecstasy.

The energivore explodes like a balloon full of ink, splattering black squid ink in all directions.

Yeah! Take that, you disgusting sh—

A powerful hum rises from the scaffolding and beams.

My Orb swells, as big as my head, vibrating with barely contained power. It throws off blinding lights and flashes reflecting in Siria's wet eyes, who stares back at me in shock. Her work overalls hang on her so raggedly she looks like a scarecrow with sunken cheeks.

Damn, do I love her.

The wail of an energivore echoes among the half-constructed buildings. Then a second, a third, a cacophony. My Orb shines like a sun in the gloomy, gray air of what's left of this city.

I'm calling them, attracting them.

I'm causing one fuckup after another. At this rate—

I slap myself. A little lighter than Dad's smacks, but I'm not very good at disciplining myself yet. It's no use whining now, I must get my shit together. After all, *there's an island of opportunity within every difficulty, so stop whimpering.*

Siria is left without her Orb. The rest of our crew is far away. Dremel is gone. Loris has run off. And I've attracted the attention of every energivore in the neighborhood.

The uproar seems to shake the city like the rumble of an earthquake. On the second floor of a building without walls, I see the blue flashes of an oxyacetylene torch and hear the thunder of a pneumatic hammer.

"I'm done for." Siria clings to the water pump of my Tool; her lips are cyanotic, her hands trembling. She smells of something burnt, the tips of her hair curled and scorched.

"You're not done for." I squeeze her hand tightly. "I'm with you."

Because *this* is what real friendship is.

Love against all odds.

Even if anyone else would have abandoned her—now that she's dead weight.

She won't *ever* be dead weight to me. Sure, friendship can be a weight sometimes, but a weight I would carry forever. A weight that makes me stronger, like a gym plate. Or a bag of concrete.

And now I understand where my power comes from.

Holding Siria's hand, I sprint towards the cistern with all the breath in my lungs. And you have a lot of breath when you've spent the last few months running from bullets and killer monsters with a bulky contraption bouncing off your shoulder. I can't believe I chose this pressure washer, so many months ago, just for the satisfaction of spraying high-pressure water on a dirt stain.

And now I'm here, alone with my best friend, right in the nest of the creatures that are exterminating our society.

The roar of the energivores grows louder, more frantic. They're scrambling to reach us. I've never heard so many in my life, but I've never felt so much power inside of myself either. And I'm not sure this power only comes from my Orb, or my inner energy. There's something else.

What have I done? My mind keeps punching itself. On the one hand, guilt, on the other, Dad repeating to me with his unbearable conceit *'everything happens for a reason'*…but Siria's closeness is calming. Having your best friend's trust, and at the same time the task of protecting her, is the most encouraging thing there is.

That's where I get my energy from.

The cistern is half-sunk into a pool of murky, stagnant swamp where dozens of energivores are splashing around. Their slimy-coated forms move around rotting laminate and plywood waste, overturned paint buckets, and rusty nails.

I take a step in that direction and shapeless masses stir at the bottom of the swamp, as if I've activated an alarm. Zig-zag jaws open wide, a whining gurgle erupting from their bodies. There must be hundreds of them.

We're doomed.

Siria sets her jaw and squeezes my hand until it hurts.

From the center of the city, the mass of incoming energivores is like a swaying carpet rolling in our direction. A wall of darkness and serrated jaws. I don't think they've seen an Orb this big since they devoured the brightest of the adults', and I don't think I've ever seen so many of them together.

We're surrounded.

Siria slips a screwdriver and a cutter from her tool belt, but we both know they won't be of any use. I'm the only one who counts now.

I activate the pressure washer and its hum vibrates through my bones.

My Orb is huge now, a pulsating sun that scorches my ear, burning like my anger, my sense of revenge. I grab the pressure washer gun, adjust the fan nozzle, throw the pump into the swamp, and the internal combustion engine starts to hum in resonance with me. It vibrates so hard that my hands go numb.

They are coming.

I pull the trigger.

Eat this. Sixteen hundred bars of pressurized wet love.

The jet is so powerful that it throws me back, against Siria. She digs her heels in and grabs me by the chest, holding me up so I don't fall. The mud reaches our ankles, slippery and smelly.

The spray cuts through the first row of monsters like a blade, a laser beam. It mows them down, sending them flying in pieces everywhere.

I let out a cry of triumph. The energy of my Orb runs through my veins, reverberates through my nerves, contracts all my muscles, and straightens my hair above my head. Siria pushes against me and I pull the trigger until I can feel the pain in my index finger knuckle, but I want to destroy them all, turn them into ink broth until there's no trace of energivores left.

Live every day like it's your last. More of Dad's bullshit, but at least for these foul beasts it might as well be the last day.

Splosh. Splosh.

Ink balloons bursting everywhere.

Splosh. Splosh.

Ear-piercing screeches and black blood.

"Aurora!" Siria's voice is distant, muffled, and echoing in my ears. "Aurora, stop!"

My knees give way before my will.

I collapse to the ground and my friend's hands cling to my underarms in a desperate attempt to keep me upright.

I'm sobbing. My lungs hurt. It's as if even my tears have contributed to the power of my Tool. Every part of me has done it. Maybe even my soul, judging by how empty I feel.

"They're retreating." Siria hugs me tightly, her nose buried in the nape of my neck.

I raise my eyes and my vision is blurry. Black shadows take refuge in uncovered manholes, in pits in the walls, between the gratings of buildings. Like engine oil in a crack.

It was me. With my crappy pressure washer. I mowed them down. I drove them away. My Orb shrinks, dims until it looks like a nightlight. It's as drained now as I am.

An eerie silence hangs over the damp worksite.

"Aurora, look…" With a trembling finger, Siria points at the old cistern.

My pressure washer has left a horizontal cut on the rusty wall, and a thin sheet of metal has come off and is hanging all crooked.

The sheer power…

The last energivores splash away, plunge into the swamp, slip into the sewer pipes, and disappear.

And then, a pale hand clings to the sharp edge of the cistern.

"You did it…" Siria's voice is still a whisper.

A man I don't recognize stumbles out of the hole, sinking up to his ankles in the mud. He barely manages to stand up, glances around with a lost look on his face. His eyes are empty with terror, his cheeks sunken.

I can't move.

I struggle to focus my gaze. A buzzing sound lingers in my head like tinnitus. A part of me, deep down, always thought I would find only his bones. I didn't expect to see the flesh too, as little as it is.

A few coughs, and the man wobbles towards us. Dirty jeans and a frayed shirt hang on him like on a coat rack. Just a few months ago he had been plump and rosy-cheeked, with a joyful smile that never really extended to his eyes, especially when he scolded me.

Disciplined me.

Now he looks exhausted, but the smile remains.

The smile always remains.

And it widens as he sees me.

For half a breath, I tremble inside like when I was little, in dire expectation of something…not good. Then he rushes towards us. I can almost imagine him celebrating internally, as if all his forced positive thoughts *deserve* to be thought. As if they helped him *manifest* being rescued by me. As if karma had struck again, and all the usual bullshit.

But the truth is, this is just a slim victory. And not karma. Not positivity.

Just desperation.

The city is still overrun with energivores. Every adult without an Orb and a PowerTool is dead weight to carry around. But—being adults—with an added load of arrogance and paternalism.

Bitterness spreads in my mouth and I can't explain why.

I get up anyway.

All of a sudden, I feel like a baby. The little kid who always needed her parents, but had to put up an indestructible façade as the world kept collapsing. The kid who just wants to give up fighting and let the adults protect her with their infinite wisdom, their power, their strength. The kid who just needs a hug and some cuddles and some sweet, caring words whispered in her ears.

'All will be okay because I love you.'

I try to move toward him with outstretched arms, surrendering to that child in need of affection, but I collapse on my knees again and just burst into tears, trembling.

It's all wrong.

Something is blocking me, deep down, in my chest.

I can't speak anymore, so I hug my dad's knees, and his hands—once strong and hard and painful and now so weak—tighten on my shoulders.

He's alive. I saved him.

I'm the one who should tell him *'All will be okay'*.

Then why do I feel empty and desperate?

The future ahead of us is darker than ever, and this success feels *wrong*. Maybe my conscience is not so clean after all. Maybe I didn't want to get him out because he is *him*. My dad. Maybe I just wanted to save him for his gratitude. His admiration.

Am I so pathetic?

The guilt makes waves of nausea rise in my throat.

Siria at my side hasn't stopped squeezing my shoulder for the whole time, not a word escaping her mouth. Even now, even while I hug my father's knees, I can feel her there, not letting go of me. Never letting go of me.

I don't know how much time goes by, but my face is still buried in those gnarled knees I don't recognize. I struggle to think, a void filled by horror in my head.

"Aurora?"

I don't want to look up, it's all too difficult. Why did I save him?

I need a moment.

There's still an entire city to be liberated, and I feel alone and weak. And stupid. As if I've unleashed the worst of my liabilities. Worse than my ridiculous PowerTool. Worse than Loris's gang. Worse than the energivores.

"Aurora? What's wrong with you?" Dad asks, his tone flat.

Maybe I've gone mute like Dremel. Damn it, poor Dremel, what an atrocious end. I cling tighter to Dad's knees, sobbing.

I just don't want to look up. At that face. At that smile I've cringed away from for so long.

"Have we lost her?"

"Give her some time." Siria must have crouched down on the ground next to me. Her voice is soft, but it carries a trace of pain, of subdued anger. I know she doesn't look at my Dad's face either. She just can't. "For her—for all of us—it's been challenging to play the role of saviors…when we should have just had our parents' protection."

A hint of accusation. She just can't keep it in, even now.

Oh, my friend.

And she's so right. Maybe I never admitted it to myself, but the responsibility that fell on us crushed us, brutalized us. So little of our humanity is left that I cling desperately to that love.

Siria. And—

Dad jerks away from me. "Do you think I enjoyed being locked up by those creatures, in constant terror of being eaten alive?"

I slowly raise my chin and I see a twitch on the left side of his lip. *That* twitch.

Siria blinks with raised eyebrows. "Pardon?"

I try to focus my gaze on Dad's offended expression, on Siria's confused one, but I can't stop seeing that twitch. It's as if the smile wants to come back, the plastered, frozen smile he always wore when I needed to be taught a lesson.

"Do you think it makes me happy to come out now only after months of captivity, to find that the world is still hell on Earth?"

"You just asked me what's wrong with your daughter, Sir." Siria's tone is as sharp as Dremel's circular saw was, and she's not getting scared. She doesn't know what that twitch means. "And I'm just telling you that the last few months have been traumatic, to say the least, for Aurora, and me, and that for once you could at least—"

"Oh come on, what's with you teenagers and trauma?" Dad bursts into a shrill, terrifying laughter. "Your generation does nothing but complain!"

I wanted to go back to normal? Here it is, normality.

Those crazy eyes. The hidden threat. The smile hating on my rationality, the smile that always required a smile in return, or else…

The world is full of dangers.

And my father has always been one of them.

But now I know something: I'm capable of facing them. On my own. With a PowerTool and a best friend, not with a fake smile.

And I've found my safety. My *'All will be okay because I love you.'*

And it's not in the arms of this smiling man.

I stand up, my arms and shoulders heavy with the pressure washer that saved my life. That will save the *world*.

"You don't even know what real trauma is, girls. Now that I'm free, I'm gonna put a stop to this whining nonsense." He closes his fists by his sides, white and bony knuckles stark in the darkness. "Back in my day—"

This world is cruel, and it's time I begin to protect myself and the ones I love.

As my dad jerks toward Siria, I raise my PowerTool and pull the trigger.

Titania Blesh is a sci-fi and fantasy writer, best known for her historical fantasy trilogy A Colpi di Cannonau, Un Bagno di Sangria, and O Mirto O Morte!, published by Acheron Books in Italy. Her YA sci-fantasy Chelabron, won the Cassiopea Award for Best Italian Science Fiction Novel in 2022.

This story had a few working titles. I don't remember them all; I think at one point I'd saved the file as "The Servant."

The final title came before the idea of the pomegranate scene, and is thanks to my Grandma. One day, she brought home a large apple from the store. She showed it to me and told me, "I think this is a pomegranate." I told her it was an apple, and she insisted that the sign above it had been labeled "pomegranates." I had a laugh about this and sent a picture of the apple to my partner alongside the anecdote.

I meant to caption that photo, "the pomegranate in question," but due to a typo, it was captioned, "the pomegranate question." Right away, I thought that typo sounded like a good title for something.

I was working on this story at the time and after rolling it around a bit, I decided I could work with it. I'd already planned to write a hand-feeding scene, but the new title was what gave that scene its life. Pomegranates have significance in various religious histories—theorized by some as the fruit of the original sin—and, well...

The experience of eating a pomegranate is intimate. It's always messy and sticky; it stains your hands red and sour sweet. I wanted to bring that to my story. Working backwards from there, I had to come up with a reason why the story is called "The Pomegranate Question," and that's how the scene was eventually written.

Initially, my inspiration for this story was, well, religious kink! So much of kink is about exploring existing power dynamics and roles. I considered how interesting a reversed religious/worship dynamic between a god and their (Its?) worshipper would be.

This idea had been germinating for a bit before I came across the open call for Mirror World's anthology contest. Introducing the conflict of "love against the odds" is when I was able to transform it from just an idea into the story it is now. And the glaringly obvious, thematically appropriate option for the major conflict? Religious dogma.

The themes in "The Pomegranate Question" aren't new or unique; plenty of stories have been told about relationships and affairs that challenge peoples' ability (or perceived ability) to fulfill their roles and responsibilities within their communities. There must be a reason we tell these stories over and over.

All love ends in loss eventually. In some instances, it's even more clear just how much we stand to lose. I think we tell these stories again and again to try and say that love must be worth that inevitable loss.

And well...who among us wouldn't like to be close to divinity? So close that, at some point, you're not sure where God ends and your humanity begins? I imagine flying too close to the sun is far too easy after you get a taste for its warmth.

Mason Michalak

THE POMEGRANATE QUESTION

by Mason Michalak

*For all my wonderful kinky friends, and those throughout history
who have had to play in the shadows, for paving the road before me.
My life simply wouldn't be the same without your guidance.*

The slice of the ceremonial blade is a musical sound, the whine of a bloody instrument. My arms, covered in goose flesh—I'm looking down at you, but my eyes aren't focusing.
The sharp scent of iron and pure Faith in the air.
And you, leaking out of the divine vessel.
The Elder is saying something, but it's distant.
Far away, like we're underwater.
Yes, that's it.
We're underwater.
And I can't see you, even though I'm looking right at you.

All I can hear is the lone, violent chord he's strumming with that awful knife.

All I know is that I'm drowning.

And I think that maybe I never knew anything at all.

'The topic of the divine vessel is one that has been fraught for centuries, with no small matter of argument. While they may have at one point, both written and oral tradition fail to account for this in the present day. There are many theories—some say that it was created here, by and for our people; others say that it was found or simply turned up one day; and there are many who believe that it has always been here and always will be, far outlasting us. Due to the insular nature of our world, we have not had the ability to research or verify this.

'While highly contested, the divine vessel's origin is of less importance than the rituals of its maintenance. This text will detail the work required to maintain the divine vessel and its divine guest. For details about the process of exorcising and replacing the divine guest, see Chapter Ten.'

- Elder Alexandra, the introduction of *Book One: The Holy Texts of Divine Maintenance*

The sounds of my mother and sister arguing rouse me. The sun is just rising. I sit up and stretch with a groan, a couple of joints cracking. Then it's only a matter of minutes for me to brush my teeth and dress in my frocks.

I pass through the living room on my way to the kitchen, throwing an extra blanket on an asleep Grandpa Eli as I do—he always gets cold this early—and giving him a gentle kiss on the head.

As soon as I step into the kitchen, the arguing comes to an abrupt stop, and Mom and my sister, Mara, proceed to pointedly ignore each other.

"Good morning, Abdon," my sister greets me.

"Good morning. Tired of waking the dead?" I ask lightly before I begin setting the place mats out on the table.

Mara gives me a look that tells me we'll be talking later, which I simply return with a smile and a half shrug.

Mom snorts, the tension in her shoulders easing. "If we were loud enough to wake the dead, Pa wouldn't still be snoring in the other room."

"Mm, I think waking the dead would be easier than waking Pa." I step over to the cabinet to grab some plates.

I don't get a response to my quip. Instead, Mom looks over her shoulder at me, and at the plates in my hands as I turn around. "Don't bother setting a place for your father, he's already left."

This surprises me. "Must be some sort of emergency; everything this week was about how excited he was to see me off on my first day," I reply, putting a plate out at four mats, skipping the fifth.

"Dying sacrament for the Fisher boy, down the road," my mother says.

I pause. "Dying sacrament? What happened?"

Mara steps over to the sink and starts washing her hands. "Kid was out hunting last night and a tree fell on him," she explains over the noise of the faucet.

"Oh, Divine," I mutter, shaking my head.

"His dog ran for help and they were able to find him. Got the tree off him and brought him home, but there's not much they can do. He's in bad shape. Doesn't seem like he'll make it through the day—surprised he made it through the night, even." She dries her hands on a rag and turns to face me, leaning against the counter. "A damn shame."

"Well, you know that family never made him go to service," Mom injects, her tone condemning. "The Divine hasn't even seen him in what, ten years? And Its blessings only reach as far as It can see…"

I look towards Mara and her expression mirrors my own. Mother's rant continues even after the table is neatly set and her point is already well made, following us through breakfast.

After a hearty breakfast, I'm bombarded with well-wishes from my mother and grandfather, both of whom I give a hug and cheek kiss in farewell. Mara, meanwhile, insists on walking me to the temple, so she's right behind me as I step out the door into the cool morning. Our breath steams in our faces as we walk down the road, silent in each other's company. The morning is quiet and the sun shines brightly, lending us a subtle warmth.

"So, you and Mom were going at it this morning," I say after a few minutes, not turning to look at Mara. Her scarf is a splash of color in my periphery.

She huffs a sigh beside me. "It wasn't anything, really. Just that she's been rather terse with me as of late. Any excuse to chastise me. You know how she gets…"

I do, so I hum in agreement. "What is it, then? She's still upset about you apprenticing for the baker?"

"Probably. I think she's worried about losing the extra hand when I move out." She pauses. "…she doesn't seem thrilled about my entanglement with the baker's daughter either," she admits sheepishly.

My brows raise. "You made a decision on moving out, then?" I'm surprised that she's apparently gone with the choice that will distress our mother the most. "And you know she always hated my summer romances too."

She nods and pulls her jacket tighter around herself. "I won't be around enough to be much help anyway. Figured I might as well save myself the earache I'd get from her complaining."

"She never made so much fuss when I decided to apprentice as handler." I shake my head in sympathy.

"Well, you're the oldest, following in Daddy's footsteps in the clergy, who followed in his mother's footsteps before you. And you're a man." She pauses. "Though really just a boy still, Abby," she teases with a smile, poking at my stomach. "In your twenties but you've still got all that cute baby fat."

I smack her hand away and she cradles it dramatically. "Still more grown than you, Squeak. Body and mind."

"You know Mom hates when you call me that," Mara replies, sounding amused rather than admonishing. Squeak—my nickname for my sister for as long as I can remember, her little voice being the highest in our household by far. Not sure where she got it from, considering Mother's husky timbre and Father's baritone.

"Well Mom's not here," I shrug. "Unless she's hiding in the bushes." I jostle a nearby bush with my foot as we pass. "Nope—not here."

Mara snorts. "Goof." She bumps me with her shoulder.

I shoot her a smile before putting my arm around her. "You know she'll get over it eventually."

"Which part? The apprenticeship, the moving out, or the romance?"

"All three, I'm sure." I squint up at the bright sky. Little wisps of clouds are floating overhead. "She's never been able to hold a grudge for long. And you're her baby."

She sighs and leans her head against me. "I hope so, Abby."

Elder Cain is at the doors to the temple when Mara and I arrive. An ancient looking man who has been on the council since before I was born. He's fiddling with the message board outside the building and turns to face us as we approach.

"Good morning, Elder," I greet him as we come to a stop.

"Good morning, Abdon," he replies. Cain is not really a man who smiles with his mouth. Instead, he squints his eyes in what I've always assumed to be joy. He looks to my sister. "Do I have two students today?" he asks, a thread of amusement in his tone.

Mara returns his smile with a grin of her own and puts a hand on my shoulder. "No, Elder Cain. Just making sure this lamb didn't get lost on his way," she jokes.

"Well, you've done a fine job of it! He's here, and all in one piece, even. I daresay he almost looks presentable, too," he ribs me, eyeing my attire.

My cheeks flush and I huff. "Yes, thank the Divine she's here. I don't know how I'd manage otherwise," I joke with a shake of my head as I turn to face Mara. "Anyway, thank you for the escort. Get home safe." I start gently pushing her back the way we came.

"All right, all right. I'm going." She laughs. "Have fun today."

With that, I'm left alone with the Elder to start my first official day in my new role, and I walk through the temple doors in step with Elder Cain with the fresh eyes of a new handler.

'A divine guest is not human; it is not mortal. Through Its total essence, it is a being free of earthly desire. This is a key component in its ability to both absorb and distribute Faith among worshipers. To minimize the risk of corruption, we have established several holy laws. The guest is not to have skin-to-skin contact, is not to consume food or drink, and is not to be spoken to directly outside of prayer and instruction, lest it fall prey to temptation and desire.'

'Annotation: See accompanying historical texts for documented cases of Divine corruption.'

- Elder Alexandra, *Chapter One: Rules of Divine Engagement* in *Book One: The Holy Texts of Divine Maintenance*

After Elder Cain gives me a short tour—which is mostly a formality, considering I've already been shadowing my father all month for this role in a temple I've been coming to my entire life—I am led to your chambers. Through the cracked door, I can just make out the loveseat and the bookshelves filled with worn and dusty religious tomes. Before we even enter, though, I know what sight awaits me—an attached bathroom, a large canopy bed, a small desk and accompanying seat that have both seen better days. And of course, the ostentatious chair that can best be described as a throne. When we enter, Cain not bothering to knock, you're already seated in that throne, just as I imagined you would be. Though the sight of you is always sweeter, somehow, than I imagine it will be—still, posture rigid, and reminding me only slightly of the first time I saw you close up.

It's one of my first memories; I was so young. It was an unusually cold winter fraught with disease. Most who fell ill were only sick for a few days and recovered without issue. For those of us who were either very young or very old, it was dangerous. Widespread pain, fever, delirium, difficulty breathing, dehydration, and loss of appetite. In worse cases, weakness severe enough it caused an inability to stand. Worse than that, coma and death.

Being as isolated as we are, our town has limited options to treat the sick. We had even less at the time. I was one of the last to be afflicted, and my case was severe. After a week of failed treatments the local clinic advised my parents to start preparing funeral arrangements. My mother refused, bundling me up and taking me to the only other place she thought might help—the temple.

Fever-addled as I was, my memories of the day aren't clear. The desperation in my mother's tone as she begged for an audience with you despite the late hour sticks out in my mind. Your handler relented after seeing the state I was in. Sweating and shaking, my small body was laid before you, still covered head to toe with only my face showing. I was too weak to lift my head, but I'd seen you before when we attended service.

This was different. Your face was less than a foot from my own, and I remember seeing the universe in the expanse of your visage. Slow, swirling patterns of light moving against soft dark skin, reminiscent of a clear night sky. My flushed, gray and sickly form reflected back at me, more like a window than a mirror. My eyes wide at the little puffs of incandescent Faith billowing from your lips. Despite the background of Mother's desperate prayers, it felt like a private moment between the two of us.

You laid your hand ever so gently on the blankets layered over my chest. My memory of that moment is a feeling of weightlessness. According to my mother your hand lit with Faith, and that glow soon transferred into my small body. My eyes fluttered shut. The sound of my own rasping breaths faded away as I was filled with a gentler warmth than the fever that was killing me. It was like I was floating in this safe, inky space that I can only describe now as the feeling of *home*.

I was recovering by the next morning.

Thankfully this isn't the first time since that night that I've seen you close up, and while the memory is close in my mind, I'm not distracted by it. I've gotten used to being in the same room as you at this point, courtesy of shadowing my father in his role as interim handler. Elder Cain gives me a quick rundown of my duties for the day and then we're left alone.

Shortly after the Elder leaves, breakfast is delivered to me. After eating, I dust the bookshelves. The late morning through the afternoon are open hours for visitation. My job during that time is mainly supervisory, though it isn't unusual for those who visit to ask the handler for guidance. Occasionally it's even requested that the handler join them in prayer.

Today is a quiet day. Only a handful of people come to pray to you and whether it's because it's my first day or they truly don't require anything from me, I'm largely left to my own devices. I spend this time at the desk logging the visitors and their prayers, and reviewing logs from the past two weeks.

After I eat lunch I bring you on a walk of the grounds, making sure not to stray any farther than the temple garden. We sit on a bench for a while in silence. I sketch out some of the surrounding flora in my notebook, though my options are limited with the season. Once inside, we stop by the temple's archives so I can grab a few scrolls to study, which is how I spend the late afternoon and early evening.

Once I'm finished with dinner and I've set the dishes out in the hallway for pickup, I prepare for my last responsibility of the day. The door to your room closes with a creak. While washing my hands in your attached bathroom, I look down to notice I'm shaking. I take a deep breath and lean against the sink. This will be my first prayer to you as your new handler, alone, and while I've seen my father do it plenty of times by now, I'm nervous. For what, exactly, I'm not sure. This shouldn't be much different from any of my other duties. I splash some water on my face before exiting the bathroom.

You're still sitting on your throne where I left you when I return. I step forward, squaring my shoulders, then kneel before you, just like the earlier worshipers. I clear my throat.

"Holy Divine, I would like to thank you," I begin. Glowing tendrils of Faith begin to bridge the gap between us as I pray. "Myself and my family have always been very blessed, and I greatly appreciate the opportunity to serve as your handler." I bow my head. "Also," I say, quieter, "you may not remember, Divine, as I know all your responsibilities are so great, but many years ago I became ill. My mother brought me here, and you saw fit to save me." I'm glad my hands are clasped together because at this point, I feel like they would be visibly shaking again otherwise. "…and I wanted to say thank you for that.". Of course I don't expect a response; after all, you do not speak and it's taboo for you to communicate in any way outside the distribution of Faith, if that could be considered communication.

That's why my mind goes blank when I feel a warm weight on my head. It takes me a moment to realize you're touching me. You've reached your hand out and placed it on top of my head in what would be from anyone else a comforting gesture. And it's strange because I can *feel* that you mean it as one. But I'm more caught up in my own panicked thoughts and feelings. You *touched me*. No, you *are touching me*, right now. I wonder if you can feel my alarm in the same way I can feel your intent. Regardless, your hand remains.

I remember, Abdon, says a voice in my head. One that is not my own. It sounds like the humming of a bright star.

"D-Divine?" I whisper. "Is that you? You're not…not supposed to…" There's a thread of what feels like…***reassurance***, maybe, through the connection. I feel like I'll burst out of my own skin at any moment.

It is all right, Abdon. It is just you and I here.

I take a shaky breath. "Did you…do this…speak with your previous handler?" Your former handler, a quiet woman who retired about a year prior. Maybe the creeping dread I'm feeling is getting to you because your hand moves from the top of my head to my shoulder. I look up at you and your posture is more relaxed than it has been all day.

No, this is the first time.

I lick my chapped lips. My gaze searches your face. I don't know what I'm looking for. "Why?"

There's a long moment where we just stare at each other before you move your hand to gently graze the back of your fingers against my cheek. I flinch at the contact, startled by the feeling. It's like static, but through it I can feel your answer. It's like a pull in your chest—some sort of gravity tugging you closer to me.

I slowly nod. Then, in silence, I stand.

You're quiet, not even attempting to stop me as I walk out the door.

'Despite our best efforts, we are only human. Divine guests of the past have been tainted and given our flaws as mortal beings. It is likely that future guests will fall to corruption as well. When our holy laws are broken, and the divine guest is introduced to human touch, food or drink, companionship, or other worldly desires, It will stray from the path of Godhood and become closer to humanity. When this happens, a divine guest will act not in the interest of Its congregation, but will instead act in the interest of Its own impulses. Once this happens, it becomes necessary to exorcise the divine vessel and replace the guest via cleansing ritual.'

- Elder Alexandra, *Chapter Ten: Cleansing, Introduction* of *Book One: The Holy Texts of Divine Maintenance*

That night I go straight home. My father arrives home shortly after I do. He's tired, if the dark circles under his eyes are anything to go by. He must've been doing house calls all day then, after dealing with the Fisher boy. Still, he gives me a warm smile when he sees me.

"How was your first day?" he asks while hanging up his coat.

I think about the feeling of your hand on me. On my head, my shoulder, my face.

"It went well." I return my father's smile with a nervous one of my own. "Slow day, so it was easy."

He nods. "I told you you could handle it. Like I've said, the hardest part of that job is staying busy."

I nod slowly. "We spent some time in the garden today and I got some cleaning done. The door to the Divine's chambers needs some oil."

"That'll give you something to do tomorrow, at least. There should be something you can use for that in the supply closet. Cain should be able to show you if you can't find it."

"I remember," I assure him. "I think I'm going to turn in early tonight."

"Not a bad idea."

I head down the hallway to my room. With my hand on the door handle, he speaks a final time.

"I'm proud of you, Son."

I say nothing.

'The first recorded instance of divine corruption was the first recorded instance of a divine guest. Prior to the establishment of our holy laws, divine corruption was much more common. The first recorded guest to be given the title of Divine was corrupted within months. The concept of corruption as we understand it is new

to the last century, during which our laws have been developed and refined by the council, as advised by the scholars who have dedicated their time to this area of study. Previous guests were under no such restrictions as our present holy laws. As such, the first recorded Divine came to favor specific people and families in the distribution of Faith based on Its interactions with them, rather than more objective measures. Our town's first recorded instance of plague is now credited to this instance of corruption.'

- Elder Matthew, Introduction of *A Modern History of Divine Corruption*

Other than that first meeting, the first couple of weeks in my position as handler are shockingly mundane and I quickly settle into my new role.

I supervise and log worship, I study and copy various religious texts, I mop the floors and wipe the windows and mirrors, I attend weekly temple services and stand quietly at your side as you receive Faith from the prayer of the congregation.

It all becomes a steady rhythm that is comfortable, if a bit dull.

That first day starts to feel more and more like a fever dream, except I now feel that pull you introduced me to. When my mind wanders, I find myself thinking about touching you, speaking to you. Blasphemy.

In my third week, our routine changes. It's during my evening prayer on the second day of the week.

"Great Divine, I give to you, willingly, my Faith, so that I may receive your blessings. For I see the fruits of my worship. I see how you have blessed my studies, my family, m-" I have only just started my prayer when you interrupt me.

Abdon? you ask, in that ethereal not-voice.

The wisps of Faith curling out from my body peter out into the surrounding air and dissolve. You haven't said a word since that first day. A shiver runs through my body as I kneel before you. I'm not sure I'll ever get accustomed to you using my name like that, though it's rather presumptuous to think I'll have the opportunity.

I look up at your form, eyes widening when I see you've leaned closer. My initial instinct is to tilt forward, toward you. Even though I shouldn't. Instead, I am careful to remain still under your gaze.

"Yes, Divine?" I ask in return, feeling a little breathless under the weight of your attention, your proximity. And the fact that we're speaking to each other at all.

What does it feel like?

My brows furrow. An uncontrolled expression; I'm caught off guard. "What does what feel like?" I pause. "…*praying?*"

Yes.

"You could touch me to find out." My mouth is suddenly dry. I should feel ashamed to have even suggested it, and yet…

That charge in the air. The one that's been there since the first time you touched me. It's almost tangible now. You want this. And *I* want it, too.

Would you permit me to, Abdon? The way you ask is as soft as a whisper.

I wonder at that. You're asking permission, now? Are you nervous, after the first time? Puzzled that I didn't report you to the council? I am, too. A part of me is screaming at myself—I shouldn't be entertaining this. With each passing second, though, that voice gets fainter. Until at last, after a tense stretch of silence, it's mute. It isn't until then that I finally move.

Slow, but steady, I reach my hand toward you, until my nervous fingertips settle as a feather light touch upon your bare knee.

The connection feels no different from the first time we touched, though it's not a shock to me this time. I'm still on my knees in front of you, now staring up with the proper reverence at your glowing visage. Then, with my intention, there's a steady thrumming—*like the fluttering beats of my heart*—through our connection.

Devotion. *Service.* *<u>Surrender.</u>*
<u>Worship</u>.

You reach one of those smooth, glass-like hands of yours to caress my face, the gentleness of your touch mirroring my own. It's difficult to untangle the feelings I get back through our connection. I feel them as though they are my own, but that doesn't make them any easier to name.

> *Admiration?*

>> *Curiosity?*

>>> *Desire?*

After a few moments of silence, I begin my prayer once more.

"Great Divine," I start, my voice lower than before, "I give to you my Faith so that I may receive your blessings."

I pause to swallow, the intensity of your stare making me feel what I imagine a beetle might, having caught the attention of something hundreds—no, *thousands*—of times my size. "I see the fruits of my worship. I see how you have blessed my studies, my family, my..." I trail off, exactly where you interrupted me before, lost. Dizzy. I swallow again.

"I feel your blessings. Do you feel my Faith, oh Holy Divine?" I ask, now at a whisper myself.

Where our bodies touch, there are luminous threads of Faith, flowing from my skin and sinking into yours.

The pallor of your flesh reflects my own kneeling form back at me. Your thumb makes a soft pass over my cheek. I shudder and close my eyes, Faith thrumming through me in a way that gathers behind my eyes like tears.

Beautiful, Abdon. Thank you for sharing that with me.

Once more, things progress in a jarringly standard fashion for a few days. I launder the sheets, I supervise, I study.

Then one day I'm in your room after temple service, studying some passages about previous divines and corruption, when you decide to interrupt me again. As usual, you're sitting on your throne on the far side of the room while I work at the desk near the door.

I think I might like to try it, Abdon.

I'm left a little confused, unsure what you're referring to.

"What is it you think you'd like to try, Divine?" I turn in my seat to face you.

Warm colors ripple across the surface of the divine vessel, and I'm left wondering what that could mean when you say, *I would like to try praying.*

A beat of silence.

"What do you mean, Divine?" I think back to a few days prior. "Like what we did before?" I try to keep a neutral expression, but it's difficult not to let both my befuddlement and curiosity shine through.

You shake your head and the vessel flashes the same colors as before. You're quiet for what feels like a long time, and I wonder if gods need to gather their thoughts sometimes, too.

I would like to pray, you say, finally.

You seem to have a way of shocking me that often renders me speechless.

If you might permit it, as my handler, Abdon, you add after a moment, when I don't immediately reply.

"I…" I clear my throat. "Forgive me, Divine, but…how would that work? You want to…pray to *yourself?*"

Another pause.

Perhaps you could take my place.

…

"I would play as God, then?"

Only if you would like to indulge me.

My head is spinning as I imagine what you're asking for— what it would look like, what it might feel like. Brambles of desire bloom in my chest, catching me in their hooks. I take a breath to steady myself.

"All right." I get up from my chair and cross the room till I'm standing in front of you. Anticipation tingles across my skin. "Out of my seat, then. Down on your knees," I order.

You're quick to obey, standing and moving away from the throne and onto your knees in one fluid movement. I take your place in the chair, crossing one leg over the other. "Come and worship, then, if you're that desperate for it."

You crawl towards me on your hands and knees, and I realize I'm holding my breath.

And then you're there, in front of me, kneeling. I can see how flush my face is, reflected back to me in your refractory form; if that wasn't enough evidence of my interest, the steadily growing tent in the lower half of my uniform would be. "Oh, Divine…" I murmur, mostly to myself. "No; no, that's not right. What can I call you here, at my feet?"

I close my eyes for a moment. Then I open them before uncrossing my legs and leaning forward. My gaze catches the sight of my frocks in my reflection and I frown, looking down at the uniform loosely draping my frame, before an idea strikes me. I begin to unbutton my cassock.

"A worshiper should have the proper attire, don't you think?" I ask, not looking away from my task.

It doesn't take me long to fully disrobe, though I feel as though I should be more embarrassed than I am. Standing naked in front of my God, my arousal on clear display. But as I hold my frocks out to you, I only feel powerful. "Dress yourself."

You take the clothes from me without hesitation, then stand to ease the process of dressing.

I sit back down on your throne, enthralled as I watch you— the vessel shifts in size to accommodate the uniform perfectly, and you're surprisingly adept at dressing considering you've never done it before.

The final item is the collar, and your slim fingers make quick work of it before your gaze turns back to me.

Is this acceptable, Divine?

There's an innocence to the way you ask that sends a pleasant shudder down my spine. "More than acceptable," I reply. "To my feet again."

I pause.

"I still need a name for you."

You step back over to me, now looking the part of the worshiper, and kneel once more.

Forgive me if I'm speaking out of turn, Great One, but…you could always call me Abdon.

"Abdon, hm?" I think about it. I think about this role reversal we're doing and how you're on your knees for me, in servant's clothing asking to take a servant's name.

"A perfect name for a disciple." My head is spinning again. Maybe it never stopped. "Right, then, *Abdon*. Back to your worship, now."

You fold yourself into a bow, your head touching the ground.

Dear Divine, you start.

"No. Look at me when showing reverence."

Yes, Holy Divine, you reply, quickly sitting back up, your face turned to me once more.

Oh, Divine, you start again, *thank you for the opportunities you have given me. For every time you have touched me with your Faith, I have been nourished. Through your hands have you guided this poor acolyte through this world. You have led me to new and exciting pastures.*

By now my body is entirely flush. I can see the glazed lust in my own eyes reflected back at me and I wonder if you're feeling it, too. With more confidence than I feel I reach out to grasp your chin. And the feelings being sent through are a feedback loop. I see you, reverent on your knees in front of me and I'm sure you see it, too. I see myself from your eyes, towering over you, bare and powerful. A God and his worshiper. Mutual desire swirls through the link between us.

I live by your grace, and your grace alone.

"Oh, Abdon…" I mutter, the name its own prayer. My thumb swipes over your firm lips, and you open your mouth for me. I'm too enraptured by the sight to manage a smile, though I'm sure you can feel the happy buzz tingling across my skin as if it were your own. And perhaps some of it is. I dip my thumb past your lips, feeling my way into your soft mouth. It's not dissimilar to a human mouth—blunt, flat teeth, and smooth flesh that yields to my touch. The only difference is that it's a little drier. My thumb glides over the top of your tongue in a firm stroke and you just sit there, letting me.

"You're so beautiful like this."

It's another three days of silence from you while I complete my standard duties. It's not quite like before; I'm tempted now. To make the first move, to grasp your head between my hands just to know what you're thinking. Do you regret what we did? I don't think so. It didn't seem like it in the moment, or even after, when I redressed and rushed through my evening prayer before leaving.

But now three days of silence have passed and I'm not so sure.

On the fourth day, I gently close the door after your last visitor and nearly jump out of my skin when I turn around. You're standing right there, maybe a foot away. "Divine," I say, more a curse than an acknowledgment. "You startled me."

I apologize, Abdon.

I raise my brows. "You're finished with your silence, then?"

Your shoulders slump. I wonder if that's something natural, or something you've picked up from the people you've seen—trying to communicate with me in body language I have a better chance of understanding.

What we did…your indulgence of me. It was overwhelming.
"Yes, Divine. I'm aware."
I have been thinking.
"About what we did?"

In a way. I am not accustomed to emotion, and it is difficult to tell where your feelings end and my own begin. If I have any at all.

I sigh, moving past you to sit on the loveseat, and you turn to continue facing me, but stay where you are.

"Everything we're taught says you don't," I start, "but I don't know that I believe that anymore, if I ever did. You were the one who started this. What I get from you when we touch..." I trail off, trying to think of the right words, looking up at the ceiling. "Some of what I get feels like a reflection of my own thoughts and feelings. So much of it doesn't feel like my own, though. I don't know that it really matters, anyway." I look back at you. "What have you been thinking?"

You move to stand in front of me again, this time slowly kneeling so that you're looking up at me. It feels much more casual than the last time you knelt before me.

I have been thinking that...I may be sad. If we were to never do something like that again.

There's a long, still instant, though we're accustomed to sitting in silence with each other at this point. After a while, I look back down at you. "Okay. We need some ground rules if we're going to keep doing this," I say, finally.

What do you have in mind, Abdon?

"Well, obviously this needs to stay between us. You're lucky I haven't reported you to the council." I look away from you.

Will you?

"No." The *even though I should*, goes unsaid. "But I don't like the silence. I'm here with you every day. There are too many people around during the day, but in the evenings no one else is around. We can talk to each other then."

You can initiate, too, Abdon.

I grimace. You're not wrong, but...

"I have a lot less to lose than you do."

After a moment, you nod. Before me, you were never spoken to directly, but I'm certain you've sat in on enough sermons to know the consequences of getting caught.

"I'll initiate, though, if that's what you want. Just… know that we can stop at any time. If you decide you want to stop."

Or if you do.

It's a little jarring to me for you to give me that much consideration. Not that you haven't before, only that it's strange to think that a God cares about what I do or don't want.

I nod and tap my fingers on my thigh, a little lost in thought. "I think…" I look down at you. "I think I'd like to punish you."

'Before starting a ritual exorcism and cleansing, you will need the following:

— a white sheet soaked overnight in salted water, still damp;

— enough iron wire to adequately restrain the four limbs of the divine vessel;

— four grounded metal posts;

— four iron stakes;

— a ceremonial knife'

— Elder Alexandra, from *Chapter Ten: Cleansing* of *Book One: The Holy Texts of Divine Maintenance*

That's how we end up as we are now. It's after I've eaten dinner and you're bent over your bed before me. Once more you're donning my uniform, but now it's pulled up to expose the vessel's backside to me. The only thing I'm wearing is a pair of leather gloves, soft and broken in. I place my gloved hand on the curve of your ass. With the barrier of the leather, there is no connection here, which almost feels like playing with fire. You're used to being touched with gloves, but probably not here. And I'm sure you're not used to being struck.

"Before we begin, tell me you understand that you know you can and will stop this at any time, with only a word, if you desire to."

If I desire to stop, I will say something, Divine.

I stroke my hand along your skin. "Good boy. What we're going to do was common when my parents were young, but has fallen out of practice within the past few decades," I explain. "I want you to count each strike and thank me for them."

Yes, Divine.

"Good. Are you ready?"

Yes, Divine.

I say nothing else. I raise my hand back and bring it down harshly on the flesh of your ass. I'm not sure what I expected. The divine vessel isn't skin or flesh in the same way a mortal body is. There is no mark left. And even so, you gasp at the first strike.

One. Thank you, Divine.

I take that as my cue to continue. You're trembling at the fifth strike and part of me isn't sure how to take that. The other part of me thinks it's a beautiful sight, loves the power coursing through me, and is reassured that you never falter in your count and thanks.

After the twentieth strike, I pause and pick up the yard stick I'd borrowed from the archives before we set up.

Divine?

"Traditionally, this wasn't done with a bare hand, Abdon. Continue your count at twenty-one," I instruct before bringing the wooden yard stick down harshly on your ass.

It's louder than my gloved hand was and you jolt forward, as if shocked. There's a moment of silence. I wonder if you're thinking about asking to stop or simply gathering yourself.

Then, *Twenty-one. Thank you, Divine.*

I smile. "Good boy, Abdon."

I'm warm from exertion and arousal as we continue. At count fifty, I'm glistening with sweat, and I set the yardstick back down. I carefully remove the gloves from my hands before caressing your skin, warm from the abuse. The skin-to-skin contact is a reward for us both.   You're shuddering under me and now, with my bare hands, I can feel that it's pleasure you're shaking with. I lean my body against you and place a kiss at the back of your neck.

"You took your punishment so well," I murmur, pressing myself close.

I stay late that night, holding you close to me.

When I finally get home, only my mother is still awake. She's reading in the living room, and I enter the house as carefully and quietly as I can manage. She looks up at me when I enter the room and smiles.

"Late night?" she asks softly.

I nod. "I got caught up in copying some older texts." The lie feels sour on my tongue.

She puts her book down. "You know, your father was so worried when you started. You're the eldest, but he remembers how frail you were as a child. The job of a handler isn't hard, but it can be stressful," she explains. "It can be lonely."

I look away from her. "It does get lonely."

She stands and walks to me before putting a hand on my arm. "You're doing so well, though. Elder Cain is impressed, and so are many of our neighbors. Even if that weren't the case, though..." she trails off, like she's looking for the right words. "There's been a lightness to you lately," she says finally. "I'm glad you've found your place. We're all so proud of you."

I look back at her, my mouth dry, and say the only thing I can. "Thanks, Mom."

A few days later, I find myself tucked snugly into a corner of the loveseat in your room. I'm reading a loaned book on agriculture from the temple library this evening. You're sitting on the floor, leaning lazily against my legs, and I'm carding the fingers of my free hand through the dark locks on your head approximating hair.

We've been like this for maybe an hour when I find myself struggling to digest the words on the page in front of me. Perhaps noticing my focus shifting through our connection, you shift to look up at me. I swallow and pull my hand back from your head. Since I'm in my frocks at the moment and they're covering my legs, our connection is severed.

Abdon?

I sigh and put the book down next to me on the seat, face-down on the page where I'm stuck.

Something's been troubling me, but I've hesitated to bring it up or even put it into words. I should've known you'd be able to feel my tension through our connection at some point, though. I absentmindedly swipe my tongue over the inside of my teeth, tasting the ghost of my dinner as I consider how to word what I'm about to say.

After a moment that, at least to me, doesn't feel long enough, I finally speak. "I've been thinking about the standards imposed on the divine guests," I start. "About how living to those standards... it must be lonely. Maybe even more lonely than total isolation."

You tilt your head ever so slightly in a motion I take as encouragement to continue.

"You're with someone almost all the time, but you can't speak or be spoken to; you can't touch or be touched. Usually you're only ever addressed when someone wants something from you.

"We're taught early that because you're not human, you don't need things like that—things like touch or conversation." I pause and take a steadying breath before continuing. "I think... I think I've held on to that for as long as I have because a part of me knew if that idea is wrong, then we are the manufacturers of something truly terrible.

"And it's one thing to accept that I might be complicit in something like that. It's another to accept that my neighbors, my friends…even my family, are all perpetuating that cruelty—that we're all benefiting from it, even.

"I feel like I should apologize." My voice cracks against the weight of my effort to hold back tears. "But that seems trifling at this point."

We sit with the accompaniment of my shaky breathing for a few moments.

Abdon, forgive me, but…you are simply a man. You have been doing what is within your power to provide me with the things you have said I am deprived of.

I bark a harsh, self-deprecating laugh. "Sorry. Sorry, Divine. But you speak as though I'm doing any of this out of generosity, of selflessness. As if I'm not putting my own desires above your safety!" I shake my head with a grimace.

You shift further so your hands are resting on my legs before replying. *What more do you believe you could do for me? You did not write the Holy Texts and the rules that bind me—you have no more power than I to change them.*

I tap my fingers against the armrest of the loveseat. "I could petition the council—talk to my father or Elder Cain."

All you would succeed in is losing your position as my handler.

"Then I could speak to the congregation! Get them on my side, have a rallying force behind me."

Do you really think you could convince them, Abdon? Perhaps a few, but enough to make any difference? What would they stand to gain from believing you, from speaking against current doctrine and the council?

"Then we could run away together," I say, a tinge of desperation leaking into my tone now.

You would be hard pressed to succeed in getting yourself outside the walls of this town, let alone smuggle me out.

"That's not-" I let out a frustrated sigh. "None of that is the point!" I lay my head back against the seat and close my eyes. "The point is...I'm not willing to do any of that," I explain softly. "Whether because I'm a coward, or because I'm simply selfish."

*You are simply **human**, Abdon. Your reasons matter little when the outcomes would be the same. Please consider, dear one, that whatever time we have together, you are bringing me joy. That is the truth regardless of your motivations, which I believe are more complex than you give them credit for.*

"You are so much more than I deserve, Divine," I whisper.

I do not understand the concept of earning care, Abdon. The word "earning" sounds like a curse on your tongue. *There are only the delights and sorrows in which I may share with you.*

Tears leave silent tracks down the sides of my face that evening, though I don't let them fall until I'm alone in my own bed, where you can't see them.

"What was it like before you inhabited the divine vessel?" I ask you one evening, about a week later.

I'm currently working on copying texts regarding the philosophy of where divine guests come from. Back before the doctrine forbidding divine guests from worldly pleasures was established, there were several divine guests who explained, or attempted to, what they were and where they came from. It was never the same with any of the guests, and the question has been niggling me.

I put down my pen and turn to face where you're sitting on your throne.

It is...difficult to describe in language, you reply with a hesitancy that I'm not used to hearing from you. After a moment, you hold out your hand to me.

I stand from the desk chair and step quietly over to you, before taking your hand in my own and lowering myself to sit on the floor in front of you. Like I've done before, you stroke a thumb over my hand, the gesture familiar.

I was…the space between things, you explain, and alongside your explanation comes feelings through our connection.

The weight of the nothing in space between stars and planets.

The mass of the darkness that sits heavy in a cave.

The density of a deep hole in the ground.

Before I existed in this form, condensed by this vessel, I was not one thing, but many. I believe, also, that this form is simply part of what I once was, as emptiness continues to exist in my absence.

I think of that dark place where I felt your healing light.

There is…a feeling of loss, as I am now. Perhaps it was always there, as I am the embodiment of the empty. I am not sure I had the ability to feel in the same ways before I became bound to the vessel. It has been…disorienting, but had I not become your divine guest, there are many wonderful and otherwise interesting experiences I would have never had.

I feel my face flush as I think about some of the things we've done—a flush that creeps down my neck as I suspect you feel those thoughts through our connection. Then from you, through that connection, comes the feeling of a warm smile.

I am also content, knowing that I will eventually be returned to what I once was—the missing piece returning to the whole again.

My heart skips a beat. Though we've not been doing this— whatever *this* is—for very long, I have a difficult time imagining a future for myself without your presence.

You gently squeeze my hand, sending a current of reassurance through our connection.

I am in no particular hurry to do so, Abdon, you promise. *Perhaps you will even join me eventually—death is, of course, its own form of absence.*

It's probably much less comforting than you intend it to be, but it's hard to stop myself from smiling all the same.

Weeks pass.

It feels strange walking into your room today, but we've been talking more regularly since the spanking and there's a confidence I feel that wasn't there before. I trust now that you want this. More importantly, that you'll tell me if you don't. There's still a nervousness there—like we're teenagers sneaking around our parents. Well, this is worse than that; the stakes are much higher. At this point, though, it's become background noise. I consider whether that's a good thing or not as I set down the bag I brought. I can tell as soon as you spot it that you're curious—the only thing I ever bring with me is my journal. But you know our talks are reserved for the evenings, so you're good for me and say nothing.

We've had a lot of casual contact since I spanked you, but we haven't done anything nearly as intense. Most evenings are spent with you kneeling for me. Sometimes we talk; other times I'll read some texts aloud, usually with your head leaning against my legs like before, and a relaxed thrum echoing through our connection.

I wonder if anyone else can sense the nervous anticipation I see in you today. I watch your visitors closely, looking for any sign of suspicion, but the day goes by more or less as most of our days do. You're quick to talk, though, after I've set my dinnerware out in the hallway and shut your bedroom door.

What did you bring today?

I can't quite stop a smile from blooming on my face.

"It's a surprise. Get dressed and kneel for me at the foot of the throne," I order you, pointing to the spare set of frocks laid out by the desk—something I brought here a few weeks ago after our spanking session. "Leave the bag alone—no peeking. I'm going to go wash my hands."

In the bathroom, I strip myself of my own uniform and wash my hands, making sure to give you ample time to follow the orders I've laid out for you.

I'm pleased to see you've followed my instructions when I step back into the room. I grab the bag I've brought from the desk before walking over and sitting on the throne.

"You seemed distracted today."

My apologies, Divine.

"It's all right, Abdon. You're only human, after all." I pull out the first item from my bag—a black strip of cloth.

You watch me curiously.

"I did say I had a surprise for you." I lean forward to wrap the cloth around your eyes, tying it behind your head. "It wouldn't be much of a surprise if you could see it."

With that, I take out two other objects from my bag. A heavy, round fruit and a knife. I am slow with the process, cutting into the skin of the fruit and letting the scent float in the surrounding air. Once the skin is peeled back, I pluck out an aril.

"Open your mouth for me and stick out your tongue."

You're quick to obey.

I lean forward, the aril grasped between my thumb and forefinger, and hold it above your tongue before crushing it between my fingers. A single drop of juice drips down onto the vessel's tongue.

Your whole body shudders and I can hear you moan in my mind.

Divine? What—?

"Did you know that the corruption of the first recorded Divine is blamed on Its introduction to pomegranates?"

I stick my fingers in your mouth, feeding you the crushed aril. Then I hold those fingers in your mouth for a minute, feeling a deep sense of satisfaction when your tongue swipes over them to catch the residual juice.

"I figured you deserve a reward for taking your punishment so well before."

Over the course of the next twenty minutes I lecture you about the first recorded instance of corruption while gingerly feeding you more pomegranate arils.

Me, sitting on your throne, naked, with red stained hands and a pomegranate in my lap; you, blindfolded and supplicant at my feet, your mouth open to receive more little arils as blessings. This is the sight Elder Cain sees when he enters the room, not bothering to knock beforehand.

'The ritual begins by tightly binding the wrists and ankles of the vessel with iron wire, and securing each to the grounded metal posts. The Divine is unlikely to struggle, but there is often involuntary movement associated with the ritual. Next, the limbs of the vessel are to be secured to the ground with the metal stakes. Cover the vessel with the damp sheet. Underneath the sheet, use the ceremonial knife to make a deep incision across the neck of the vessel.'

- Elder Alexandra, from *Chapter Ten: Cleansing* of *Book One: The Holy Text of Divine Maintenance*

Everything that happens next happens in a blur. There's yelling, and then I'm being manhandled by the Elder. Before I know it, I'm dressed and sitting at the kitchen table of my house, the evidence of my deeds washed from my hands. Grandpa Eli is the only one missing from the room, having been put to bed already. My father and sister sit across from me and I stare down at the table as my mother paces nervously behind me.

"What did you do, Abdon?" my father asks.

I flinch at the question. "I..." I shake my head. "The Divine's really not that much different from us, is It?" My voice shakes.

My mother stops pacing and lets out a harsh bark of a laugh. "It should be! If It wasn't any different, any of us could do Its job!"

I shrink down in my seat. I don't know what to say. I don't want to say that you came to me with desire already in your heart, something that's true but feels like it would damn you even worse somehow.

My father takes a deep breath. "I think you and your sister should go to your rooms."

I don't argue.

On our way down the hallway, my sister grabs my arm.

"Abby..." Her eyes shine with concern.

I pull my arm back and we stand there, simply looking at each other for a moment.

"I'm sorry, Squeak." I'm not even sure what I'm even apologizing for.

I turn from her and enter my bedroom, shutting the door behind me, and then I try to sleep through the sound of my parents arguing.

"This divine guest has forsaken us;
for it has come to know worldly pleasures,
the seed of desire has been planted,
and it has germinated;
For the good of our people,
we pray one final time;
We demand that You,
our once honored guest,
vacate this vessel,
so that it may serve us once more,
as You have failed to,
and are no longer welcome."

- Elder Alexandra, from *Chapter Ten: Cleansing* of *Book One: The Holy Text of Divine Maintenance*

After that, my family seems to avoid me in my own house. I'm kept from you.

It's days, but it feels like so much longer, after being with you every day for months. No one tells me anything, and I'm too afraid to ask. As if knowing would make the consequences real. Part of me already does know, when my father tells me to put on my frocks and walks me to the town square.

It feels so silly that I finally get the courage to say something when approaching the gathering crowd.

"What are we doing here?" I ask my father, the same tremor in my voice as the night we were caught, as he leads us to the front of the crowd at the center of the square where four metal posts have been driven into the ground.

He won't even look at me, and the murmuring of the crowd is too indistinct for me to make anything out. The way heads turn our way and voices lower as we get closer makes me imagine what they might be saying. The pumping of my heart is the sound of blood rushing in my ears, echoing my thoughts: They all know. I keep my own eyes on the ground, not willing to face the disgust and judgment I'm sure is being directed my way.

We're not here for long before you arrive, escorted by several members of the council, including Elder Cain. It's then that I finally get the courage to turn my gaze from the dirt under my feet, looking up only to see you pointedly staring at the ground yourself, not meeting my eyes. You're led to the center of the square, and a hush falls over the crowd.

"Father, what are we doing here?" I ask again. My own voice sounds so far away.

"I would like to start by thanking the members of the congregation for coming to bear witness to today's events," Elder Cain's voice bellows through the square.

I feel rooted where I'm standing.

"There have been a lot of rumors the past few days, and I'm sad to report that many of them are true," the Elder continues. "Our Divine Guest has been corrupted by Its handler."

People in the crowd whisper to each other, many of them looking in my direction. I'm too focused on the heavy pit settling in my stomach to hear what they're saying.

"After investigation, it seems that this has been going on for months."

My mouth is dry. I wonder how much you've told them. Do they know how you've worshiped at my feet? How you've taken sacrament from my very hands? How we've turned my name into a blessing, and now a curse?

"As I'm sure you're all aware, the only way to cure Divine corruption is the exorcism and replacement of the guest."

My father puts his hand on my shoulder, but it feels less like comfort and more like a gesture to keep me from doing anything rash. I'm not sure I could in this moment, anyway.

It feels like everything after that happens behind a thick, glass pane.

You're instructed to lay in the dirt in the center of the metal posts, and you comply without complaint. I feel nauseous as your arms and legs are bound tightly with wire to the posts.

Elder Cain is handed a hammer and a metal stake. The sound it makes when the first stake is driven through your right wrist is indescribable. A loud crunch, echoing through the square. It makes me flinch hard, my own wrist aching and tingling in sympathy. The first time doesn't do anything to prepare me when that process is repeated with your left wrist and then both ankles. Your body jerks and shudders as you're brutally pinned to the ground, like an insect.

Next, a damp, white sheet is laid over you.

Sunlight glints off the blade of the dagger as it's handed to Elder Cain, kneeling next to the vessel. Kneeling next to you. He reaches under the sheet.

The slice of the ceremonial knife is a musical sound, the whine of a bloody instrument. My arms, covered in goose flesh—I'm looking down at you, but my eyes aren't focusing.

The sharp scent of iron and pure Faith in the air.

And you, leaking out of the divine vessel.

The Elder is saying something, but it's distant.

Far away, like we're underwater.

Yes, that's it.

We're underwater.

And I can't see you, even though I'm looking right at you.

All I can hear is the lone, violent chord he's strumming with that awful knife.

All I know is that I'm drowning.

And I think that maybe I never knew anything at all.

And yet...

I know your voice in prayer and gasping beneath me.

I know your hands and the curve of your ass.

I know your soft breath on my fingers, my face.

I imagine I know you better than anyone ever has or ever will.

Distantly, I feel tears dripping down my cheeks. A light that would be blinding if not for the damp sheet covering you emanates from where Elder Cain cuts you open. A soft, glowing mist spreads from your form and blankets the ground of the square.

Why aren't you doing anything to stop this? I think to myself. I wonder who exactly I'm asking.

There's a shift; a sad, tired tone rings through the clearing. Like a long, final exhale of breath, so thick that it's felt in the air.

It feels like you, wrapping me in your arms.

And it feels like that dark, inky space that I felt so long ago, when you healed me.

And more than anything it feels like *goodbye*.

Once it ends, I feel that the vessel, underneath its sheet, is empty.

My knees collapse under me as I choke on a sob. I shake my head, as if that will stop what's already happened. I reach out for you and I *pray*. I pray, mumbling to myself, and my father's grip on my shoulder tightens but he doesn't stop me. That luminous fog is clearing as Faith streams out of me and toward the vessel.

And it does nothing. My Faith moves past the vessel as if it's not even there.

I'm left there, on my knees, long after the crowd disperses, feeling like the Elder slit my throat and drained me out of my body, too.

'Throughout our history, many humans have aided in divine corruption. As we are flawed—and often misguided—beings, this is to be expected. It should be understood that those who aid in corruption of the divine guest are often doing what they think is just, and the loss of the divine guest they've corrupted is consequence

enough. That being said, anyone who has assisted in tainting a divine guest should be barred from any and all contact with the new Divine once a replacement guest is procured for the divine vessel.'

- Elder Alexandra, from the conclusion of *Book One: The Holy Text of Divine Maintenance*

Months pass.

Every day, nothing feels real. I can still feel your presence around me, like that fog, but you're not here in any way that matters. Of course I feel you heavily in this loss, this empty space you've left behind.

But I can't see you.

I can't hear you.

I can't touch you.

I spend so long wondering if it's worse than you being completely gone.

I go days without leaving my room, full weeks without uttering a word, simply going through the motions of life and doing the bare minimum to keep myself alive. Your absence feels tangible, and the fact that I'm still here is an agonizing reminder that, despite all our playing, I'm only human.

I can tell my family is worried about me. My mother dotes on me as much as she seems to think I'll tolerate. My father often just sighs and gives me piteous glances, as if he doesn't know what to say. Grandpa Eli is getting to a point where he doesn't much know what's going on anymore, so my interactions with him are limited. My sister moves back home, putting her apprenticeship on hold. Most days she comes to sit in my room with me, stroking my hair and speaking softly about small things, like the weather or the snails she encounters while tending the garden.

It's hard to care. It often feels like that thick glass pane is still there, between me and my own life. Sometimes that's better— better than facing the crushing agony of losing you, of being the thing that got you killed. Those nights, I lie in bed sobbing, clutching at a stomach that feels as if it's been stabbed over and over.

I rarely go out. When I do, I'm met with the judgment of my neighbors. No one says anything but I can always feel their eyes on me. Many of them look at me in disgust, but even more look at me with the same kind of pity I see in my father's eyes. It makes me want to vomit.

For a long time, nothing changes. Time moves forward, despite my wishes. Eventually I start having days where I feel a little better—almost normal, even. As normal as I think I can.

It's one of the better days that Mara brings me to the temple garden. It's summer by now, and we're sitting quietly under the shade of a large tree, listening to the calls of birds and the yells of children playing in the distance.

I'm staring up at the sun-dappled leaves that sway gently in the breeze, and I dig my hands into the dirt beneath me. I can feel that last, resigned sigh of yours, even in the dark soil, cool underneath my fingertips. Your presence remains in a way that tells me, *I'm sorry,* because we were not able to make it in this lifetime but for a moment. And I think to myself that you have nothing to apologize for. For *we*—your ever-devoted—were the ones who failed you.

Even if, in the end, you never blamed me.

Even if you don't now.

Even if you *never* would.

So I tightly grasp the earth in my palm, knowing—*and perhaps it's only wishful thinking*—that we will try again some day. Surely in another world, another time; surely one kinder than this, I will hold you again, more than simple loam in my hands.

And in this moment, I remember sadly, fondly, when you said that perhaps I would eventually join you in absence.

My good friend.

My Heart.

My Abdon.

I'm drawn to subversion; as a writer, as a person. That hasn't changed as I've aged—I'd say only that my taste for it has become more refined at 28. I write after my own heart and live with the hope that someone might follow.

Inspiration for 'The Value of a Sapphire' came when I inherited my grandmother's sapphire ring. She died when I was three, so I never really knew her, but I started wondering what this ring had seen of her life and wishing it could share her adventures with me.

My thoughts drifted to other experiences the ring might have witnessed. Gems can be bought, gifted, stolen, lost and found. Virtually indestructible, they land at the centre of myths and legends. Endless ideas formed.

Before I put any words on the page, I wasn't sure how to structure the story without jumping between the points of view of the people who'd owned it. I discussed the concept with my son, and he suggested telling the story from the sapphire's point of view. After that, the narrative fell into place.

I named my sentient sapphire Nil Manel and made it agender. While I allowed it to experience thoughts and feelings, it couldn't influence events. This meant I had to contravene story conventions in which the protagonist drives the action. Worried this passivity would frustrate readers, I discussed this concern with a writing coach, and she encouraged me to work with what Nil Manel could control: its feelings. I focussed on its emotional responses to each of its owners and its sense of impotence when it longed to intervene in critical situations but couldn't.

To give my character a backstory, I investigated how sapphires were formed and figured its mother was Mother Earth. In the first draft, I included a lot of information about how the sapphire was birthed, but this delayed getting to the heart of the story with Nil Manel's connections to its owners, so I removed most of that detail and filtered references to it throughout.

The first setting in the story is 1920s Ceylon, now called Sri Lanka. I chose Ceylon because my grandmother and mother were born there, and Sri Lanka is known for its gemstones. I visited with my family as a child and feel a strong connection to the country.

The rest of the story takes place over a century, and Nil Manel travels to England, Europe and Australia. Through travel and the passage of time, I aim to show how much the world changes, while Nil Manel remains physically unchanged. Its character development comes through its observations of others and its self-perception.

This personal growth had a natural fit with the theme of 'love against the odds'. Further, gems are often used as a symbol of love, whether in an engagement ring or in some other form. Nil Manel witnessed diverse love stories and experienced love for its owners, but it's not until its core identity is in question that it finds out whether it has the reserves of strength and courage to love itself.

Andrea Barton

The Value of a Sapphire

by Andrea Barton

For Grandma Ouida and her beautiful sapphire ring.

I arrived in the world in the early 1920s amid grunts, shovels, and flying mud in a small family mine in Ceylon. My first memories are of being tossed around, washed and scrubbed, cleaned, cut and polished, being transformed from a dull lump of rock to a shining gem.

When this torture was over, I lay naked under a bright light as a man appraised me. "Ah, it's a beauty."

A second man bent over a notepad, pen hovering. "Colour?"

"Blue as the deep sea."

The second man wrote something. "So, a sapphire?"

"It's a sapphire alright."

More scribbling. "Weight?"

"Twelve carats."

The second man whistled. "I might slip it into my pocket."

"Let's call it Big Blue."

"Nah. How about Neptune's Eye?"

"Huh?"

"You know, the sea god."

"Hmmm. Why don't we call it Nil Manel?"

"Perfect. A blue water lily." He noted Nil Manel on his notepad.

I glowed with pride. The funny thing about a name is it really does impact the bearer's self-worth. Shakespeare argues otherwise, but a rose would have a hard time holding up its head if it were called "thorny weed". In case you're wondering how I, Nil Manel, came to know about the literary greats, my most recent owner is an English teacher, but I'm jumping ahead of myself.

From the mine, I was sold to a jewelry store in Columbo run by Mr. Sanith Fernando, a fastidious man who always dressed in a three-piece pinstripe suit. Despite the tropical heat, he clung to British etiquette. Sanith sold me to my first private owner, a wealthy merchant named Roy Perkins.

A brute of a man with a head too small for his body, Roy came into the shop with a glint in his eye, energy in his stride, and a woman on his arm. He'd moved with the times and had ditched his waistcoat, opting instead for Oxford bags, a peculiar type of baggy trousers that fortunately went out of fashion as quickly as they came into it. The young woman looked ethereal in a flapper dress and a cloche hat.

He wasted no time on pleasantries. "I need an engagement ring. A magnificent ring. My Julia is a goddess who deserves a jewel to match her beauty." He beamed at his fiancée, a woman nearly half his height and half his age, who responded with a timid smile.

Sanith immediately recognized the sales potential—Burghers like Roy and Julia were known for their liberal spending—so he seated the couple at his consulting table and served them chilled water topped with slices of lime. "Sir, Madam, do you know what you want, or would you like to start by viewing our ready-made rings? We can custom make anything your heart desires."

Roy spread his hands wide. "Show us what you've got."

As Sanith unlocked a cabinet, Julia fidgeted and wiped a bead of sweat from her forehead. I sensed her perspiration was laced with nerves, although this was before the days of air-conditioning, so the only airflow came through the open door hung with strings of beads to keep out the flies.

Sanith presented a velvet tray showcasing his best rings: diamonds, rubies, emeralds, and a couple of sapphires. I was yet to be set, so I remained unveiled.

Roy waved the tray away. "Too small. What else have you got?"

Sanith gave a gracious smile. "Perhaps if you could tell me your preferred type of stone, I can show you our finest specimens."

Julia reached for a sapphire ring and Roy said, "Oh yes, blue to match your eyes, darling." He turned to Sanith. "Show us your biggest."

Within a week, I was set in a simple but elegant white gold ring and Roy slipped me on Julia's finger. I was immediately smitten with her. She treated everyone—from the gardener to Roy's parents—with respect and kindness, but that didn't mean she was happy. On the surface, it made no sense why someone blessed with beauty, intelligence, all the money in the world, and a doting, if overbearing, fiancé could be anything less than bursting with confidence and joy, but she approached every task with caution as if a calamity would follow. Before long, I saw that her father, an obnoxious man, vented his pent-up frustration on her whenever life's troubles grew too much. I was as relieved as Julia after the wedding took place and she moved out of her family home—only now, she worried her father would direct his anger at her mother.

Roy's house was beyond magnificent: a two-storey bungalow with big windows and doors that opened onto wide verandas. Julia spent hours in the manicured garden filled with palm trees, bougainvillea, and frangipani, delighting in the monkeys scampering around, the chickens kept for their eggs, and birdsong. She seemed lonely while Roy worked his long hours, but she came to life when he returned in the evenings full of anecdotes about his latest shipments and squabbles between the administration staff.

One morning after he left for the office, she fled to her opulent bedroom for privacy—a rare luxury, as they had many staff, overseen by Mary, the housekeeper. Lying on her four-poster bed as the fan turned its languid circles, Julia held up her hand and positioned me dead center on her finger.

"So beautiful," she whispered.

I shone more brightly to tell her she was as beautiful on the inside as the outside. Her face broke into a smile, so maybe she understood.

Despite Roy's puppy-dog obsession with Julia, I wasn't sure she was in love with him at first, but over time I believe she came to care for him deeply. Initially, I didn't think he was good enough for her. Sure, he was rich, but he was no match for her intellect, nor for her capacity to empathize with others, whether her mother's plight or Mary's occasional need to take time off. But in time, I recognized his strengths. What he lacked in pizazz, he made up for in loyalty and steadfastness. He showered Julia with gifts and learned to listen. When he spoke about becoming a father—which happened every time he passed a baby in a pram—he beamed like a child anticipating Christmas. The privilege of symbolizing such a charming union gave me an extra gleam.

About a year after we'd settled into our comfortable little trio, Roy arranged a lavish dinner for his father's birthday at the Galle Face Hotel. He told his household staff they could have the night off, doubtless planning to return afterward and take steps toward his goal of parenthood.

To his dismay, Julia woke up feeling sick the morning of the party. She tried to eat but couldn't keep anything down. I'd never known her to be ill before. Despite Julia's protests, Roy went out to find a doctor.

He returned with a fastidious young man, who poked and prodded Julia's stomach, asked about her toileting habits and the state of her breasts, and pronounced her pregnant. Julia cried happy tears, while Roy, to his credit, showed as much concern for his wife's health as jubilation over their news. That was the moment I knew he deserved her.

By the evening Julia felt better, but the doctor had prescribed rest, so Roy insisted she stay home.

After he left for the party, the enormous house became disturbingly noisy. Without the staff bustling around chatting and humming ragtime tunes, the creaking windowsills and complaining staircase filled the space. Wind moaned in the giant fig tree in the front garden and night creatures screeched. Bats? Owls? Julia shuddered, no doubt wishing she'd listened to Roy and asked Mary to stay with her.

She took *This Side of Paradise* to the living room and stretched out on the chaise lounge. Roy imported the latest books and gramophone records—they were among his best-sellers—and Julia had become an avid reader. Despite the rattling windows, she raced through the pages, transported across oceans to the United States of America.

A clatter near the entrance snapped her back to Ceylon. Her frown was soon followed by a gasp as the front door gave its distinctive creak. Soundlessly, she jumped up, leaving the book open, and hurried to the dark kitchen in bare feet. Her drop-waisted white dress flowed around her, making her appear wraithlike in the dim light.

Voices came from the living room. "The light's on and the lounge is still warm. Someone's home. I thought Mary said everyone would be out."

Julia stiffened, and I guessed she felt the same stab of hurt as I did. Our housekeeper had betrayed us. Fury made me shine at the thought of how loyal Roy and Julia had been to her. They'd trusted Mary and paid her nearly double the going rate to run the house. How could she set these criminals onto us?

"Dammit. Should we leave?"

"No chance. We're here now. I'm not walking away empty-handed. Let's find whoever it is and make sure they don't call the police."

Julia slunk into the pantry and hid in the shadows as footsteps headed toward us. The intruders' torch beam swept around the room. I glimpsed the pair of them, dressed in black with scarves tied around their faces to disguise their identities and cloth bags slung over their shoulders. They came our way. Julia held a lungful of air and clutched her hands to her chest. I could feel her heart pounding.

She flinched at the blinding light as the thieves reached the pantry entrance, towering over us.

"Hello, pretty lady." The man with the torch, the shorter of the two, gave Julia a once over. "We don't want to hurt you, but we can't have you running off to get help. Do as we say, and you'll be fine."

She cowered lower, speechless with fright.

Worried for her and the baby, I mentally urged Roy to arrive home early. If I could have, I'd have jumped right in, fists bared, and chased those men away, but my lot was to play the role of observer. I'd always been proud of my sapphire status, but for the first time, I resented my limitations.

The taller man pulled out a wooden chair from the kitchen table. "Sit here and we'll tie you up. When your husband gets home, he can set you free."

Trembling, Julia complied.

The taller man pulled a rope from his bag and wound it around her wrists. "Hey, get a load of this." He grabbed her hand and stared at me. "I've never seen anything like it. What is it? Seven carats? Eight?"

I bristled. What a Philistine! I was twelve glorious carats. But I had no time to fret over my bruised ego because the taller man twisted me off Julia's finger. I'd barely left her hand since the day Roy gave me to her—I spent more time with her than he did—and the thought of being separated from her made me wish magma upon the rotten thieves.

"No, please," Julia begged, "take anything else, but leave my ring. It's only money to you, but it's worth so much more to me."

The lowlife didn't listen. He shoved me into his pocket, then he and his accomplice searched the house, bundling valuables into their bags before racing out the door.

It happened so quickly I barely had time to realize I'd been stolen. I longed to race back to Julia, fearful that the shock of the home invasion might have harmed her pregnancy, but I remained impotent.

The next evening, the tall thief took me to a rowdy bar filled with a cross-section of the community: everyone from pen-pushers to railway workers to international travelers. The barman had just called for last drinks when the thief sidled up to a young British man in a loud purple shirt and pink cravat named Ned, a rep for a shipping company who was swaying on his feet. Most people shunned him, which made no sense to me but was convenient for the thief.

The pair held a hushed conversation in which the thief mentioned my suitability as an engagement ring, the depth of my colour, and a special price. Before he'd finished his beer, he'd pocketed an embarrassingly small amount of money and passed me over. I shouldn't have cared what the thief thought of me, but it was hard not to feel diminished by the exchange.

A week later, I found myself rolling and pitching on a boat back to London, and once there I remained locked in Ned's armoire for years, plenty of time to stew over what had happened to Julia:

Did they catch the thieves? Had Mary, the traitorous housekeeper, been punished? Had the baby survived the shock? Did Julia and Roy have any other children? Powerless to act and cursed never to know their fate, I lay passive, waiting for Ned to release me from my prison.

Apparently he had no use for an engagement ring, which isn't to say he had no relationships. Far from it, a steady stream of young men found their way into his bed. Every now and then, he'd take me out and stare at me wistfully. He never said much, so I wasn't sure whether he wanted to wear me himself but was afraid I was too obviously a woman's ring, or whether he was longing to find the right man with whom to share his life.

By the end of the 1930s, Ned had skidded into middle-age and found his true love. Emile, fifteen years Ned's junior, was a sergeant in the British Army with deep-set eyes that twinkled brighter than any jewel. The lovers couldn't acknowledge their relationship in public, but when they were alone their mutual attraction was evident. They shared a love of music, and Ned played the piano most evenings while they belted out popular tunes.

When war broke out they knew Emile would be called to the front, but Ned refused to talk about it, preferring a heavy dose of denial. He brought me out more frequently, holding me and muttering to himself as if rehearsing a solemn speech. I spent more time in a silk draw-string bag in his inside jacket pocket than locked away. Every ten minutes, his hand came to his chest as if to check I was safe.

One night, Emile's somber mood made it clear they could no longer avoid discussing his perilous future. They closed the damask curtains on the fast-darkening sky and stoked a fire in Ned's elegant living room. I'd grown used to the frigid London winters, but I still welcomed the fire, an elemental force that reminded me of my birth a mere million or two years ago. My mother, Earth, boiled magma for eons before it finally bubbled me toward the surface, spewing ash and lava.

Ned and Emile, side-by-side on the plush lounge, were about to face their own heat, an emotional volcano.

Ned drew a deep breath. "When?"

"Next week," Emile choked out the words then fell quiet. Normally he delighted in innuendo and quick-witted repartee, but this night he couldn't even muster a weak smile.

The fire crackled, sending shadows across the room. A spark shot across the hearth, and I caught a whiff of smoke. Ned jumped up to put it out, but rather than returning to his seat beside his love, he knelt on the Persian rug in front of Emile and took me out of his pocket.

He cleared his throat. "I want to propose marriage, but as we're not allowed, will you take this ring as a symbol of my love?" I'm not sure whether his or Emile's eyes welled fuller with tears.

Emile hesitated. "It's beautiful, but how can I wear this? How can I explain…?"

Ned gave a bashful smile and held up a silver chain. "Wear it under your shirt. That way, I'll always be close to your heart."

Emile's tears trickled down his cheeks. "Of course…and I…oh, I love you too."

They kissed, and for the second time in my life, I had the honor of symbolizing true love.

But we three didn't have time to enjoy our togetherness, because soon Emile was posted to the front. Strict protocol meant he couldn't even tell Ned his location.

On the battlefield, soldiers harnessed firepower and shot bullets across fields to kill the enemy. Death stole many souls, while the remaining soldiers wailed in anguish in their sleep. I feared for Emile, and even worried about my survival. We could be blown apart. Every day I hung around his neck as we went to face potential annihilation. Every night he wrote to Ned, then lay in bed, hands clasped around me. We drew comfort from one another.

One particularly cold morning, Emile prepared to attack, huddled in the trenches with his fellow soldiers and the smell of fear. Above their heads, frost had decorated the few surviving blades of grass and bejeweled a spiderweb. Emile's breath hung in the air—little clouds of hope and desperation. Instinct nagged me to make him turn and run home to Ned, but even had I been able, deserters were court-martialed and sentenced to execution, so he had no choice but to take his chances on the battlefield. I'd have done anything to put a stop to it, but once again my limits forced me to stand by and watch as someone I loved faced jeopardy.

Emile headed into no man's land, gun poised, a sitting duck for the enemy. His heart pounded against me like a horse's hooves at full gallop. Around us, men dropped, faces contorted by shock because even though the odds loomed taller than Everest against them, nobody ever wanted to believe their time had come.

I watched as guns blazed. A cacophony of war cries and agonized screams filled the air. Emile ran forward with courage that would have made Ned infinitely proud and impossibly sad. The bullet missed me by millimeters and pierced Emile's heart. I felt the impact as surely as if I'd been hit myself. He staggered forward, and for a blessed moment I thought he might survive, but then he fell to his knees. Blood surged from within him and enveloped me in wet heat. Slowly, he sank to the ground, into my mother's embrace.

As he took his last gasps, body coated in mud, he whispered, "I'm sorry, Ned."

I wanted to rant and rail, to call upon all that was sacred to keep him in this world. But of course, I could do none of that. I ached in silence. The only mercy was his quick passing.

I stayed with him as he turned cold, until medics recovered his body and took me away from him. An injured soldier carried me back to England and gave me to Emile's only surviving relative, his twenty-year-old sister, Carolyn. She looked just like a female version of Emile—a striking beauty with deep-set eyes. I assumed she would find out where I came from and return me to Ned. I belonged to him. But I only saw Ned once more.

The funeral, a solemn affair, took place in a cold echoey church with meagre stained-glass windows and a giant cross bearing Jesus in a crown of thorns that sent trickles of blood down the side of his face. I barely recognized Ned, slumped low in a pew. Puffy eyed and dressed for mourning, pain was etched in every feature. He barely spoke to anyone, until he approached Carolyn at the wake held in the church hall after the service.

He expressed his condolences, feet shuffling, eyes downcast. Then he asked, "Have his personal effects been returned? It's just...I gave him a ring to take away as a talisman." He grimaced. "It didn't work, clearly, but I hoped I could have it back, so I have something to remember him by."

Carolyn arched an eyebrow. "A ring?"

"Yes, with a blue stone, a sapphire. I bought it in Ceylon years ago."

I didn't understand her hesitation. I was right there in her pocket. She'd speculated with one of her friends that Emile must have bought the ring to propose to a woman back home, or perhaps a nurse he'd met while away. She'd brought me along to the funeral in case a grief-stricken girlfriend turned up. But she shook her head. "There's no ring, I'm afraid. Was it valuable? Maybe someone pilfered it."

Ned's shoulders stooped even lower, but Carolyn didn't relent. I was so close I could smell his fancy French cologne. If I could just reveal myself, he would grab me and take me back to the warmth of his fireside, caress me with his rough hands, and cherish me forever.

I glowered as Carolyn took me home, stuck me in a ring box and locked me in a safe. My fury against her festered; I should have been with Ned, sharing our grief, not locked away by a despicable liar.

She kept me there for three decades, until she inherited a house in Melbourne from her uncle. When she moved to Australia, she took me with her.

The plane trip was much faster than my ship ride from Ceylon, which had been renamed Sri Lanka, but I suffered terribly from being so high in the air. I was of the earth, not of the sky, and I'd never been so far from my mother's surface. Even at my age, I suffered the wrench. Relief flooded through me when we touched down in Melbourne.

I barely saw Carolyn until her deathbed in 2023, by which time I'd developed a profound dislike of her. On the rare occasions she brought me out to show her children, or later her grandchildren, I was introduced under the falsehood she'd created about Emile buying me for his fiancée. She developed a whole myth around her lies. Now in her late nineties, at home with full-time nursing staff, she had milky eyes and pure white hair. All the same, she reminded me of Emile. Given the chance, how would Ned's darling have aged?

When Carolyn knew her time drew near, she summoned her favorite grandchild, Amelia, and asked her to bring the contents of the safe. The live-in nurse raised the head of Carolyn's bed, propped her upright with pillows, then left to give the two women privacy. Sun streamed in the window and scent from the roses on the deep window-ledge made the air cloyingly sweet.

Amelia, an English teacher in her forties, pulled up a chair beside the bed and placed a plastic bag holding the safe's contents on Carolyn's lap. "Here it is."

Carolyn gestured for her granddaughter to pull her chair closer, then fumbled through the bag to find me. She opened the ring box and thrust me at Amelia. "I want you to have this."

Amelia had seen me before, but still, her eyes widened. "Wow, Grandma. Emile's ring. Thank you, I—"

Carolyn held up a hand. "Before you take it, I need to tell you something. I did a terrible thing."

"Grandma, you don't have to—"

"Hear me out. You're right, this was Emile's ring, but he didn't buy it for a fiancée. It was given to him by a man called Ned. At Emile's funeral, Ned told me about the sapphire and asked if he could have it back, but I told him it was never returned."

"Emile was gay?"

Carolyn's voice cracked. "Back then, things were different. Being…homosexual…was a shameful thing. I didn't want anyone to know."

"Do you want me to find Ned? To return it?" Amelia kept her tone almost neutral, but I caught the note of disapproval.

"It's too late now. Ned died years ago, and he had no children. No, keep it. I just wanted you to know the truth."

Amelia stared at Carolyn for a few seconds then held me up to the sun, watching the light stream through me. "What's it worth?"

"I don't know. I never had it valued. But a stone of this size?" Carolyn hesitated. "A substantial sum. You want to sell it?"

"Of course not. It's a family heirloom. I'm just curious."

So was I.

Carolyn's lips quivered. "Do you think I'm awful?"

"Grandma, it's not my place to judge. I love you just the same. I only wish you'd set things right before it was too late." Amelia tried me on, and I fitted perfectly on her right-hand middle finger. She admired me. "Beautiful. Just beautiful." For a precious moment, I caught an echo of Julia and ached to be with her.

A tear trickled down Carolyn's wrinkled cheek. Regret? I hoped so.

A few days later, Amelia took me to Tessa's, a trendy jeweler in one of Melbourne's cobbled laneways. Tessa, a tall thin woman with a pixie cut, tattoos, and a nose ring, served us. She listened carefully to Amelia's story about Ned and took me out the back, where she turned on a strong light and studied me under a loupe.

Rather than the oohs and ahhs I was expecting, she frowned and picked up a smaller loupe with stronger magnification. She shifted in her chair, clearly ill at ease.

After giving me a quick polish, she headed back to the shopfront, where Amelia looked up from a display case, tense with anticipation.

Tessa frowned. "I'm not quite sure how to tell you this, but it's not a sapphire."

Amelia's mouth dropped open. "Really? What is it then?"

"Volcanic glass, also known as blue obsidian."

What? Glass? Tessa was calling me glass? Surely, she was joking. Either she didn't know what she was doing, or she was trying to con Amelia. I searched the room for proof of her ignorance or dishonesty. Certificates on the walls testified to her knowledge, and Tessa wasn't old and doddery with failing eyesight; she was in her prime. Not ignorant then, she must be a charlatan.

Tessa passed me back to Amelia. "Naturally occurring blue obsidian is rare, but it's not valuable like sapphire, which has a different chemical composition. You might get a couple of hundred dollars for this, even a thousand, but a sapphire of this size and deep colour"—she whistled—"that would be worth tens of thousands. I hate to say it, but this is relatively worthless."

So, there it was: Tessa was conning Amelia; she wanted to buy me for a bargain price and sell me at a phenomenal markup.

"I'm sorry to be the bearer of bad news, but I'm afraid I wouldn't stock something like this." Tessa gave a sympathetic smile. "A smaller jeweler might buy it. As long as they declare what it is, it's perfectly legal for them to sell it."

Wait, what? Tessa didn't want me? She wasn't swindling Amelia, then. My mind spiraled. While I hated to admit it, volcanic glass had a frightening ring of truth—Mother always told me I was born of fire. Further, Tessa's reaction in the back room had shown sincere surprise, disappointment even.

I had to face it: I wasn't a sapphire. I was glass. Nothing but a massive fraud. My sparkle dimmed. I didn't know how to move forward with this shrunken status.

Amelia muttered a few words of thanks and left the store.

The whole way home, I mulled over how my new identity might change my life. What would Amelia do with me now she knew? I'd probably end up in the garbage like empty beer bottles and broken windows. I didn't want to leave her; she wore me openly, without a hint of shame over my provenance.

A few days later while I was still reeling from Tessa's brutal revelation, Amelia arrived at school to teach her English literature class. There were only ten students, so they were a tight-knit group. When Amelia had started wearing me, they'd asked where I came from, so she'd explained my background in World War II, which had seemed relevant as they were studying *All the Light We Cannot See*. They'd loved the fact that I'd been to the front with Amelia's great-uncle, so now I hoped Amelia wouldn't tell them about my reduced valuation, or I'd have to face their disappointment too.

Evidently, Amelia didn't pick up my concern and within minutes, she outed me to the class. They gasped in unison at my tainted pedigree. Her disloyalty stung. How could she leave me open to contempt like this?

"So, what do you think?" she asked. "Is it still valuable?"

The students, always keen for a rigorous debate, rushed to answer, jumping in on top of each other to demonstrate how clever they were.

"If you define value in dollars, of course, it's worthless."

"That's not the point. 'A rose by any other name'."

"You're talking about its appearance, but I think what really matters is its story. What it's been through."

"True, but its character is different now. It's not a sapphire."

"It was an engagement ring for a couple that couldn't marry. Nothing can lessen the poignancy of that beautiful tale."

"But it wouldn't have been used if they'd known it wasn't real."

"The mistaken identity makes the story more interesting."

Amelia leaned forward. "So, what should I do with it?"

In concert, they said, "Keep it."

"Why?"

I reeled. How could she ask such a thing? Of course she should keep me. I thought she was on my side.

The girl across from her said, "It's priceless. You can't buy a history like that."

Amelia's satisfied smile made me suspect she'd known all along how her class would respond. I relaxed. She'd never give me away. "You're right. And we only know what happened after Ned bought it. Who knows what adventures it had before?" Genuine joy lit up her face, and the fire within me made me sparkle brighter.

I still had no idea who I was or how to act now I knew that I was merely glass, but I was sure Amelia and I were going to get along just fine.

Andrea is the award-winning author of the Jade Riley Mysteries, The Godfather of Dance and A Killer Among Friends. Book 3, The Man in the Dam, is slated for release October, 2025. Besides writing, she runs the book editing company Brightside Story Studio, where she loves working with authors of fiction and memoir to make their stories sparkle.

From the tragic romance of *Romeo and Juliet* to tales of wars waged over lost love—and everything in between—the notion that love harbours the potential for danger is a theme as timeless as storytelling itself. When Mirror World's anthology theme for this year, *"love against the odds,"* was revealed, a compelling question emerged: What if the very act of admitting romantic love for someone made you susceptible to death? What if, until that moment, no lasting harm could come to you?

As I lay in bed one night, wrestling with this thought, images of a new world began to unfold, solidifying into what would become *Carthenwyl*. In this realm, those who have yet to experience romantic love—known as *Di-Os*—find physical pain to be a transient affair. They can brave the suffocating pressure of the deep ocean, survive deadly poisons, and withstand the fury of lightning, assured they will always heal and recover. However, the moment they confess their love, the essence of their being transforms at its core, and they become *Di-Byth*, where vulnerability becomes their new reality. Pain is no longer fleeting; it can be fatal. In *Carthenwyl*, love equates to death—and there's no escaping it.

To reflect this dichotomy, I aimed to create a fantastical realm where destruction and pain coexist with breathtaking beauty, mirroring the complexities of love itself.

As you embark on this journey through *Carthenwyl*, you'll discover that it's not just the characters who navigate their trials; it's a reflection of our own encounters with love's complexities, the risks we take, and the beauty we find amidst pain. I hope you find yourself swept away in this tale, contemplating the extraordinary nature of love against all odds and the splendour that emerges from the depths of its challenges.

Shannon Nell

CHASING LLYRANITE

by Shannon Nell

For Hayley and Katie–this exists because of you. Thank you.

Eira sank deep into the eastern *Môr làr* sea, eyes closed and unbreathing, savouring the silence beneath the waves as the storm churned the skies above. Icy tendrils crept along the edges of the otherwise clear mask suctioned to her face. She felt more than heard the faint cracking as the ice threatened to grow inward, only to find its progress blocked.

Like her full-body skin-tight suit, the front of her mask was coated in a thin layer of semi-translucent gel—*tanolithite*—emitting a faint amber glow. In these frigid seas, this gel was a necessary essence containing her body heat and preventing her eyelids from freezing shut. This gel—and its brother and sister versions—was the reason she and the three other amber-glowing figures were here.

To chase the elusive *llyranite*, capture its raw form, and thereby power the entire planet of *Carthenwyl.*

Her quad of Chasers lay in wait beneath the waves, poised for the storm of lightning to pierce through the waters and strike at the deep ocean minerals, sparking *llyranite* into existence. Then, their work would begin, a hectic but thrilling chase to catch the jagged, rapidly sinking shards of power before they vanished into the depths forever.

With the tempest of lightning yet to be broken, Eira was grateful for the shifting, multicoloured glow of the *lliwithite* embedded strips along her suit, at the edges of her mask, and in the flashlights she carried—its light pierced into the darkness where her amber *tanolithite* glow fell short.

Familiar pain clamped down on Eira—a relentless force squeezing her chest, popping her ears, and compressing her body until she thought she might implode. The instinctual desire to breathe despite access to oxygen sent waves of nausea surging through her, dizziness tugging her to unconsciousness with all its might. So she didn't try. Instead, she convinced her mind to accept that she was just holding her breath. For a while. And then another while. The life of a Chaser was primarily about learning to trick the mind, to silence the body's alarm bells and ignore the pain.

All was well. Eira had subjected herself to this for years, trained to endure it until the sensation became more than familiar; it was comforting. It was a place few dared to venture, even among the *Di-Os* like herself. *Di-Os.* Beings who could not die, all because they had never been in love—thanks to the magic of *Carthenwyl.* *Di-Os* and *Di-Byth.* The loveless and the lovers. The eternals and the mortals.

High above, the surface waters churned, and the gentle tug of subtly enlarging swells told Eira it was near time. Anticipation overpowered agony. *Di-Byth* often questioned her motives—why she willingly endured frigid waters, crushing depths, lack of oxygen, and lightning storms striking perilously close, threatening to encase her in its *llyranite* rock-like formations. Her responses varied with her mood.

"The pay is excellent."

"*Carthenwyl* needs *llyranite* to function."

"It makes me feel alive."

No one cared about her answers; they only sought to convince themselves of her madness while dismissing their own fears. Yet they knew they needed her skills if they wanted any semblance of comfort in their lives. While her answers always held some truth, the reality was far more personal, one that only Calem—Captain Calem, as of five short years ago—truly understood.

Eira shut her eyes and surrendered to the temptation of taking a breath. Instantly, her body spasmed, chest heaving violently as her lungs strained against the empty air. The shock was enough to banish thoughts of her old school—the *Ysgol Sâl*—from her mind.

You're holding your breath. That's all you're doing. You took a lovely deep breath moments ago, now hold it. Eira repeated the mantra until her body settled.

In control once more, she reopened her eyes and gazed upward through the dark, crystal-clear waters. Her home of the past seven years, *Islaw'r Tonau*, floated steadily at the surface. The old wooden ship glowed with the familiar, ever-shifting *lliwithite* covering its hull, casting a silhouette of multicoloured light against the encroaching darkness. A few clicks behind *Islaw*, a monolith of an iceberg plunged far deeper into the sea than it towered above, its shadowed peaks vanishing into the unknown. From her vantage point, *Islaw* looked like a small fish, unlike the twenty-five-foot-long hull it was in actuality.

The first of many muffled booming vibrations reverberated in the depths by Eira and her Chasers; the thunder had arrived. Eira sculled with her hands at her side to ensure she aligned with her quad: Lachlan and Alric to her left, Lyla to her right.

A rumbling from behind caused Eira to shift her body just in time. A creature swept past her in *Islaw'r Tonau's* direction, its bright lights unintentionally luring it in.

What are you doing here, tegwmor? Eira wondered as another boom echoed through the water. The creature remained undeterred, pressing forward toward its goal. *Strange.* She yearned to yell at the *tegwmor* to swim to safety, but all she could do was watch and study the creature few would ever see.

Its massive, bulky, muscular body was encased in thick, white fur that trapped heat and provided camouflage against the icy surroundings. Two large, intelligent eyes rested high on its rounded forehead, with a nose bulging outward and a mouth lined with sharp teeth. Fur rippled as its front fins and thick tail propelled it through the frigid depths, while its back legs with sharp claws—that could easily rip any *Di-Byth* apart in seconds—floated gently behind. It neared *Islaw* and rolled onto its back, tilting its head to study the strange object infiltrating its domain.

In an instant, a flash lit the sky above and penetrated through to the depths of the sea. The *tegwmor* fled, darting away with remarkable speed, a blur of white racing past Eira's quad.

Eira smiled; the storm had arrived.

In the blink of an eye, three more flashes lit the waters around the ship and continued down into the water, illuminating the underwater world far brighter than Eira's *lliwithite* did. The raw energy of lightning pierced deep into the *Môr làr* sea, straining to reach the minerals found beneath. Once found, the lightning erupted, twisting like cracks in glass. Each tendril spread faster than the eye could follow, expanding outward and solidifying into the sporadic designs of *llyranite*. A shockwave trailed just behind, warping the water with its momentum, sending vibrations of chaos past Eira.

As Eira embraced the pain building in her body, the first shockwave of a nearby lightning strike warped the water with its momentum. She remained calm. In pain—amid chaos—living without the fear of death, and *not* living in love, this was where she flourished.

Islaw'r Tonau rose and fell with the surging storm, perpetually illuminated by flashes of lightning. With hands that should be frozen, Eira forced her fingers to flex, relishing the sound of her cracking bones—a reminder of the frost that would cause a *Di-Byth* to lose their hands. But not her. She reached behind to the large, streamlined, power-infused pack on her back, ensuring her beacon was on. Her fingers found the rounded nob on the top of her left shoulder, where the pink-hued *pincdraenite* vibrated steadily. It acted as an invisible tether to the ship above, drawn to its sister mineral, the scarlet *cochdraenite.*

Confident her pack had passed the required checks before the chase, Eira manoeuvred to grab the thick chords from their holsters on either side. The small loop at the end of each chord slipped around her two middle fingers, the flat disk resting on her palms for easy access.

A heart-pounding beat passed, and the chase began.

The storm was unleashed. Eira spun and dodged as a barrage of lightning rained around her quad. Each bolt collided with ocean minerals, sending them expanding outward in rapid, chaotic succession from their cores, forming solid masses of prismatic tendrils reflecting everything around them. Eira dove after the nearest piece of newly formed *llyranite,* now sinking into the depths at breakneck speed.

A spike in water temperature near her was a warning coming too late. Vibrations shook her core, interrupting her pursuit of *llyranite*. A lightning bolt struck mere feet away from her face, too fast for her to dodge. It expanded into *llyranite*, spiking outward from its core and slamming across her stomach.

A strangled, noiseless grunt escaped her as her chest constricted—a reminder that air was needed to make a sound. She rolled through the water like a log tossed down a steep hill. Arms outstretched and body spread wide, she slowed and righted herself in seconds, relieved that the impact hadn't dislodged her mask. Her *llyranite* assailant was already long lost to the depths.

She glanced around, assessing the positions of her quad. Lachlan and Alric were close together, already hauling a piece of *llyranite* between them, tethered by their ropes. A swift scan upward reassured her that *Islaw* was still in sight, but her brows knit at the sight of a new figure plunging into the water. Even from afar, she recognized that form.

If Calem was in the water, something was wrong.

From high above, his head instinctively spun in her direction as another spike of heat and vibration reverberated through her. The strike posed no immediate threat, so she fixed her eyes on Calem, his urgency unmistakable. The light on his arm shook, frantically signalling to the depths behind her. Eira whipped her head around, her eyes landing on her fourth quad mate, Lyra, ensnared in *llyranite's* twisted tendrils and sinking into darkness.

The reason for Calem's uncharacteristic dive vanished from her mind as Lyra's descent pulled her heart down with it. Though *llyranite* at this stage was nearly weightless, its thick tendrils sank swiftly, trapping Lyra within. She struggled; her efforts to swim or access her pack were futile against its relentless hold.

Eira launched forward, short-finned feet allowing for increased propulsion and manoeuvrability as she kicked into high speed. Hands clasped tight into fists, they pressed into the disk in her palm, igniting the teal *teilwyrnite* energy in her pack. She shot forward with its blast of power. Calem may have spotted Lyra first, but he would never reach her in time. Eira didn't check if Alric or Lachlan had noticed; saving Lyra was her responsibility.

Arms tight to her sides, she forced as much power from her pack as it allowed, ignoring its strained hum under the pressure. Lyra was on the precipice where all light suctioned into nonexistence. She kicked feebly with her one free leg while her untrapped hand clawed desperately through the water, trying to grasp something solid that wasn't there. Even from this distance, Eira could make out the terror on Lyra's face—a fear Eira had never seen before. Fear of being dragged to the bottom of the ocean, where her body would be crushed yet undying, locked in an eternity of pain with no hope of rescue.

No.

Eira's kicks were small and rapid, her thighs burning, but the pain was trivial; her body could handle far worse. The moans from her pack grew louder—her *Di-Os* body could withstand this depth, but her pack power wasn't built for it. If she didn't pull up soon, the pack would implode, throwing her off course and sealing Lyra's fate. She slammed a fist against it, as if force alone would keep it going.

Come on! She gritted through clenched teeth, extending an arm to cut through the water at a speed sure to shatter a *Di-Byth's* bones.

Lyra's head turned, tendrils scraping her face as she looked up. Her free hand stretched toward Eira, her kicks weakening yet resolute. The pressure closed in, stiffening Eira's movements, but she would not relent. She reached out, muscles screaming against the force, and as her pack gave one final surge, her hand crashed into Lyra's, locking them together.

Eira ignored the superficial pop in her shoulder, tucking Lyra's arm securely against her body before flipping over and adjusting her trajectory upward. Her pack gave her five precious seconds before it sputtered and quit, the added weight of Lyra and the *llyranite* draining it completely. It didn't matter; those seconds were enough. With each passing second, they surged closer to the surface, and Eira kicked with more vigour as the pressure abated.

She didn't worry about controlling her speed as they could withstand the rapid ascent without damage. As they reached the turbulent lightning strike zone, Eira focused on instinct over thought, relying on a lifetime of anticipating lightning to guide her. She twisted and arched, maneuvering Lyra's *llyranite*-encased body in arching curves to dodge the strikes. Pain coalesced, flooding her senses—the ache of oxygen deprivation, the throb of her shoulder, the burning in her lungs. Her vision wavered, and her mind screamed that this should not be. Her body couldn't die, but it wasn't immune to suffering.

Suddenly, shadows flanked her. Alric and Lachlan materialized, illuminated by flashing lightning. They slipped in below her, each dragging smaller shards of *llyranite*, and took hold of the tendrils tangled around Lyra's feet, lending their strength to push them all upward.

As soon as they crossed the threshold of *llyranite*-forming depth, Calem arrived, wearing a larger pack than theirs. *Good. More power.* Eira's increasingly blurred vision barely made out what she knew were deep emerald-green eyes—though all she could see now were shadows, Calem's form, and a flash of concern before his strong arm wrapped around her waist. With his super-pack and Alric and Lachlan's support, Eira focused solely on clinging to Lyra as they rose to the surface at a steady rate.

She'd known this level of obscure pain a handful of times before. Her *Di-Os* body could endure endlessly, but her mind had a threshold—a cutoff point where it would shut down, leaving only the most basic functions intact until it could recover. Calem's arm anchored her, guiding them directly beneath *Islaw'r Tonau*, where the faint glow of *llyranite*-infused beams called to Eira with a welcome warmth as her vision cleared.

Before the ship's intricate carvings interlaced with flowing energy came into clear view, Calem angled them away from *Islaw'r Tonau*. Waves hammered against the hull, pushing against Calem's attempts to hold them steady. This was nothing they hadn't been through before, and as Eira's pain began to ebb, she strengthened her grip on Lyra. Calem's grasp remained firm around Eira's waist, steadying them against the chaos.

Above, the storm raged. Waves surged and collided in foamy chaos, driven by pelting rain and relentless winds. At least here they were somewhat shielded from the lightning.

Sturdy cables and tow lines from *Islaw* emerged within seconds of their heads bobbing above the water—a feat of skill under such conditions. The skill required to navigate the storm, winds, waves, and position of the tow lines was beyond Eira. On the ship's end of the line, at least two highly skilled crew members would be maneuvering the lines with precision, expertly adjusting levers to guide the cables. They manipulated the lines with practiced rhythm, using the same *pincdraenite*-powered technology as her beacon to maintain control in the storm's chaos.

When Calem relinquished his hold, Eira grabbed the floatation ring, wrapping an arm around it tightly. Lyra, still ensnared in *llyranite* tendrils, couldn't grip the ring, so Eira held her close, sacrificing Lyra's access to air to keep her secure. A hint of guilt touched Eira as Lyra's head remained below the waves, but the risk of loosening her grip was too great.

Eira's own head was another story. She leaned over the ring and yanked her mask off, savouring the first gulp of air just before a wave crashed, sending frigid water up her nose and into her mouth. It didn't matter. Air, blessed air, was hers.

Beside her, Alric and Lachlan approached a separate tow line. Keeping their *llyranite* haul tied between them, they latched onto their own ring, ready to be reeled in together. With Lyra's massive *llyranite* mass and Alric and Lachlan's smaller pieces, it was a successful haul—even with the near non-death experience.

Mask still on, Calem breathed heavily from exertion as he manoeuvred closer to Eira and Lyra's tow. Her mind clearer, Eira saw the simmering storm held within Calem's emerald depths as he assessed her. His gaze shifted to Eira's hand locked around Lyra's.

"Eira, are you alright?"

She nodded, "I won't let her go."

Calem's gaze lingered before he dipped beneath the waves to check on Lyra. Eira watched the water; even in the storm, she could follow his movements. The crystal clear water showed Lyra's blinking eyes behind the tendrils that covered her face. When Calem resurfaced, he gave her a brief nod, and those on *Islaw'r Tonau* reeled them in.

Islaw sailed upon calm waters, the chaos of the storm behind them, and a vast, cloudless sky overhead. The ocean's still surface reflected the dwindling icebergs, stretching them into larger creations than they truly were.

On deck, the essential crew kept to their stations, but all eyes tracked the progress of three knives as they sliced through the tangled mess of *llyranite* encasing Lyra.

Sweat and briny ocean water residue caked Calem's brow. He constantly brushed away strands of damp, wavy brown hair with a quick tilt of his shoulder, never faltering as he sliced one prolonged stroke at a time. His short-bladed, midnight black *llyranite* knife—-crafted through refinement in fire—only moved with the grain of the encasing tendrils.

Calem worked at Lyra's freed head, her face blank and unblinking as she stared at the sky, lips moving in wordless whispers. Eira cradled Lyra's head in her lap, gently wiping away the hair sticking to her forehead. She'd stayed like this for the last hour, trying to calm Lyra as the three knives sliced close to her body, though Lyra's unyielding fear unsettled Eira.

She's safe now, Eira thought, bewildered by Lyra's dark, dilated eyes. Even if a knife slipped—though it wouldn't—any wound they made would heal in a blink. But the fear remained; Lyra's jaw was locked tight, and her body trembled in small, uncontrolled waves. Eira's words had done nothing to calm her. Instead, she resorted to silent comfort, smoothing her hand across Lyra's forehead as Calem had shown her, watching and waiting as they cut.

Lachlan's knife bit into the *llyranite* with heavy, decisive strokes. At six-foot-one and built like a boulder, what he lacked in grace he more than made up for in sheer strength. His powerful cuts targeted the thickest tendrils around Lyra's torso—a near-solid, seven-inch bulbous barrier. As he worked, the gentle ocean breeze tousled his dirty-blonde hair, hints of ginger in his short, tidy beard catching the light as he kept his jaw set, eyes locked on his target.

By Lyra's feet, Alric followed Lachlan's cut in a single unbroken line, his taller, slimmer frame moving with careful, measured precision. His dark hair was buzzed short before each storm to avoid the very problem Calem was having, and he cut the *llyranite* in a continuous line to keep the mineral as unbroken and pure as possible.

Eira wanted to help, but Calem's cool glare and her exhaustion halted the arguments. However, she remained by Lyra's side, attempting to soothe her, even though she couldn't understand the reason behind Lyra's discomfort.

Finally, the *llyranite* split with a quiet pop, weakened by the combined efforts of Calem, Lachlan, and Alric. Lachlan gently pried his section off, mindful of any interlocked tendrils, while Alric manoeuvred the coiled strand from her leg. Silence fell across the deck as Lyra lay there, free from the restraints entrapping her the past few hours.

Freed, Eira expected her to leap up, test her muscles, and laugh off the ordeal as another wild adventure. Instead, tears sprang to life and sputtered sobs echoed for all to hear. There was no leaping. Lyra remained curled in place, arms wrapped around her knees as she rocked herself back and forth, muttering.

"I do. I need. I must. I do," Lyra whispered, her words muffled and half-lost against her sleeve.

Eira leaned closer, her voice soft but insistent, "What do you need?" She received only a shudder in response and a repeat of those words.

"Back to work," came the smooth timbre of Calem's voice, the Captain's calm authority cutting through the quiet. No crew member needed to be told twice; his command moved them without question. Though soft-spoken, Calem's quiet intensity resonated through the crew like a force.

To Eira, Calem's rise to Captaincy was inevitable. He had always carried that presence ever since she'd first seen him—a boy then, beaten and bloodied, surviving a barrage of sickness forced into his body, just as they had been into her. And his first words to her then had been a whispered "Thank you" cutting through all other noise.

Though his voice had deepened with age, his steady warmth, smooth timbre, commanding tone, and deliberate cadence that demanded attention had never changed.

Around her, the crew returned to their stations, some gathering the split *llyranite* to store it safely in the hull. Eira's quad of Chasers had completed their jobs, and by the Captain's orders, they were to rest for the remainder of the journey, whether they wanted to or not. Despite their *Di-Os* endurance, Calem firmly believed downtime was good practice—for both body and mind.

Eira hovered as Lyra rocked. The pallor of her fair skin was more pronounced than usual, and her damp, tangled locks appeared almost scarlet in the ship's light. Eira's attempts at comfort had failed miserably; seeing a *Di-Os* unravel this way was uncharted territory. Eira's solace lay in the knowledge that Lyra wasn't in love; otherwise, Lyra wouldn't be here, alive.

With a short nod to herself, Eira squared her shoulders. She took a step forward—still barefooted and in her wetsuit—only to be brought to a halt by a large, warm hand wrapping around her bicep. She recognized Calem's touch before he came into view.

"She needs to be alone right now." His clear, crisp words, though barely above a whisper, carried a weight that made her pause.

Eira scowled, glancing down at Calem's hand. He let go slowly. "Why? She's alive and unharmed. She should be celebrating her haul."

"I know for a fact that you know not all wounds are visible."

Straight to the gut, as always. Eira blew out a breath of air—a glorious breath of still frigid, albeit gradually warming oxygen— letting his reminder settle and pivoted toward the rail on the opposite side of the ship. Warmed by the amber *tanolithite*, the planks beneath her feet felt rough and reassuring.

"Where are we taking the *llyranite* this time?" Eira leaned against the simplistic wooden railing, containing none of the *llyranite* glow covering the rest of the ship.

Calem joined her quietly. "*Cofdeffro.*" He nodded towards the unobstructed horizon. "We've been a few times before." He turned his gaze back to Lyra as her head jerked upward.

As the sun set and stars sparked into existence, Eira scanned the horizon more intently. It wouldn't be long before the glow from clusters of coastal towns came into view, pulsing with shifting colours. The lights were thanks to various forms of *llyranite* powering the towns; as the raw form of lighting was an iridescent prismatic hue of shimmering, shifting colours, so was the energy drawn from it. The *llyranite*, when broken down, liquefied, placed in translucent copper pipes, and lit with a spark, created light of ever-shifting colours. The pipes were built into roadways, and there were more than a few homes with lanterns containing a few drops of liquid light to brighten the darkness. It was one of the most efficient energy forms harnessed from the *llyranite*, requiring minimal materials for a significant reward.

"Do you have a plan for the haul?" she asked, eyes still searching, wondering why they weren't headed for a closer port than *Cofdeffro.*

"We will distribute it where it is needed most, as usual. *Cofdeffro* is rich enough and large enough to utilize the most *llyranite*. The crew will likely have a full week off as a result. A little downtime will benefit everyone." He glanced at her, his expression unreadable. "I suspect we will also need to find another Chaser for your quad."

Frowning, Eira released her blonde hair from the crown braid she wore while swimming and massaged her scalp. She shivered as the breeze blew through her damp hair.

"You don't think Lyra–" Eira cut herself off as Calem handed her something, and she instinctively grabbed it.

"She has come to an important realization. She will not be coming back." The utmost corner of his lips dipped into an almost imperceptible frown, and he motioned to the object Eira held in her hands. It was one of his knee-length, fur-lined coats, and it was already warm. She blinked, surprised, meeting his steady gaze.

"How did you know I was cold?"

He regarded her, a faint smile in his eyes, as though the answer were obvious. "We are post-chase, and you are still in a wetsuit. And your hair, still damp, is loose. I know you, Eira—you never dress warmly enough on a good day."

"It's not like we *need* the layers," Eira countered, eyeing his thick fleece pants, puffy sweater, and coat. None of the crew minded the Captain's quirks, but his preference for layering was one they often teased him about.

Instead of rolling his eyes as Eira expected, he shut them a moment too long for it to be considered a blink. "We have had this debate countless times. Do I need to repeat it *yet again*?" Eira rolled her eyes as he continued without giving her time to answer. "We do not *need* them, true, but given how much pain we endure, it's a small comfort to take relief where we can. Why suffer when you do not have to?"

Relenting, Eira shrugged on his coat, immediately feeling its *tanolithite*-enhanced warmth seep into her skin. It carried the faint scent of sea air, a subtle blend of salt and memory that reminded her of their first meeting.

In the deepening night, with her hair free to dry in the wind, Eira snuggled deeper into the coat. Calem stayed beside her, one eye always on Lyra, content with the silence, listening to the sound of waves and the quiet creaks of the ship. Here, with no need to speak, they found solace. Some sought noise or laughter to fill the quiet, but Eira and Calem had always preferred the peace of silence—a silence that initially drew them to become Chasers. Under the water, beneath the waves, shielded by the ocean's immense weight, silence held a calm like nothing else.

Because if it was silent, that meant no one was screaming.

Eira awoke to the gentle sway of *Islaw* lulling her back to serenity. With her usual morning groan, Eira tossed her blanket aside bleary-eyed and stumbled out of her hammock in a fair imitation of a drunkard. By the time she trampled up the stairs to the main deck, the stars had since faded into the first colours of dawn, and they were almost upon *Cofdeffro*.

Crew bustled around her, preparing *Islaw* for her soon-to-be docking. Eira was sluggish despite at least nine hours of deep, dreamless sleep. At least no one tried to talk to her yet; she wasn't awake enough for that. But she *did* need to help. Her feet scraped and scuffed, dragging along the wooden planks as she eyed the other crew members, then made her way over to one of the still unsecured mooring lines.

As docking *Islaw* was something Eira could do with her eyes closed, this particular job suited her morning mood. The familiar routine, combined with the squawking gulls and increasing noise of workers at the waterfront, helped her get over grogginess; with practiced precision, in time with her crewmates, she secured her mooring line. Muscles flexed as she drew it taut, cinching the knot, and with the ship's next sway, Eira leaned back to test the tension of her line. Satisfied, she stepped back and turned her attention to the waterfront, and the glowing *llyranite* slowly winking out as the warm morning light of a new day crept over the docks.

The gangway thumped its connection to the dock, and before it was secured, a blur streaked past her. Calem was the only one on deck ready, almost expectant of it.

"Ensure the crew and *llyranite* remain secure until my return." First Mate Solem gave a sharp nod to his Captain, who was already chasing after the streak that had been Lyra. The crew exchanged startled looks, then resumed securing the ship once they grasped the Captain's intentions.

Standing an inch taller than Eira, with chiselled features, a pointed nose, and a stoic, unyielding jawline, Solem accepted his Captain's departure without a flicker of emotion.

All remaining sleepiness drained from her, and Eira didn't hesitate; she chased after Calem.

Impulsive fool, Eira rolled her eyes. *Ever the rescuer.* He too often ran to help others without thinking. As he so keenly mentioned the night before, just because he couldn't get hurt didn't mean she enjoyed watching him get into trouble. She never had. Not on the day she first saw him and not any day since. With Lyra acting the way she was, Eira had no doubt Calem was headed straight for it.

As she ran, the glowing world passed in a distant haze. She didn't care about the few early risers, the uneven cobblestone walkways underfoot, or the homes pressing closer together and diminishing *llyranite* the farther she went. The chill morning air was nothing compared to what she had experienced the day before in the *Mor lâr*, though the air tasted wrong on land. *Not enough salt.*

A far more skilled swimmer than runner, Eira barely kept up. Her legs burned as she forced herself not to lose sight of him.

Calem's foot rounded a corner, his shadow vanishing into a maze of stacked, interwoven homes. *Come on, Eira. Catch him before he turns again, or you'll never find him.* Then, she'd be unable to get him out of the trouble he was bound to find. *What a horrible way to spend your morning,* she thought, reaching the entrance. *Running. Ugh.*

She grabbed at the rough wall to arc her trajectory without slowing her speed, ripping her fingers in the process—and collided full force with Calem's firm back. He grunted as she toppled him over, her head slamming against the rocky ground of the alley. Pain exploded through her skull, blurring her vision before her body began to heal.

Ignoring the pain, Eira sprang to her feet.

"My bad," Eira's lips pulled back into an apologetic half-smile. A nigh-imperceptible frown, hard to distinguish in the dimly lit alley, was Calem's only response. The look didn't last long as Eira followed what caused Calem to stop.

Fifteen feet away, Lyra clung to another body.

She stepped forward to investigate when Calem's hand grabbed hers and tugged her back, warm but firm. He was only now getting up off the ground and gave a slight shake of his head, holding fast to her hand until she relented.

In the stillness and quiet of her racing heartbeat settling, Eira's ears twitched at the repeated whispered words reverberating off the walls of multiple brick homes squashed together, coming unmistakably from Lyra.

"I love you." Each word was a punch to the gut. "I love you." Eira's stomach churned at the proclamation. "I love you." Eira faltered back into Calem. He steadied her, letting go too soon, then folded his arms over his chest, face unreadable. Lyra's words reverberated in the alley, surrounding Eira, pressing down on her, trapping her in the echo chamber of love.

Lyra's grip tightened, and her determination not to let go was visible even through her still-unchanged wetsuit. Her partner reciprocated her enthusiasm and strength. It was hard to decipher who the person was in the dim light, but Eira didn't care. It was time to move on.

"Another one lost to love," Eira sighed, ensuring her voice was quiet enough not to carry in this echo chamber of an alley. *Lost to me. Lost to* Islaw. *Lost to death.* Just like her parents. Just like Calem's parents. Just like every person she'd ever known who had fallen in love. Her left hand gestured towards the couple; the pain in her fingers lingered as her body recovered from the rough turn that should have ripped them off her hand. Fingers always took the longest to heal.

"Almost succumbing to non-death does that to a person," Calem replied.

New lights sparked into life, throwing multicoloured luminescence on the couple and the overcrowded homes as people—Eira assumed they were relatives of whomever Lyra was declaring her love to—stepped outside the open door. Smiles of joy came crashing through as more joined the commotion. They kept coming, two, five, ten people from one of these tall, narrow, squashed homes. Their voices piled on top of each other; well-wishes poured out while Eira added her commentary to counter theirs.

"We knew it."

Ah yes, just like you knew the sun would rise, you knew *these two were simply* meant *to be together.*

"We're so glad for you."

Glad she can now die?

"Welcome to the family."

What, just because Lyra has declared her love, now *she can be part of the family? Not before?*

"I've never seen you two as happy as when you're together. It was inevitable."

Another person solely determines Lyra's happiness—as if she can't be, nor couldn't be, happy without them? Well, good luck to both of them since one will *inevitably be without the other. Where will that leave them? Love brings death.*

She'd seen it firsthand too often.

"I do not recall ever seeing *that* face before." Calem's crisp voice called her from descending into the depths of her past. The twisting inside eased, a flicker of relief amidst the turmoil as she turned away from the overt displays of love and faced Calem. His gaze swept over Lyra and the family, then fixated on Eira.

She frowned and brought a hand across her face, fingers pressing roughly against her skin to erase whatever expression he saw.

"Ya, well—" She couldn't find it in her to finish her thought; her eyebrows and shoulders lifted simultaneously with a shrug. She stayed this way for a beat, debating whether to unleash her thoughts, but their weight felt too heavy today.

Calem patiently waited for her to continue. He'd listen to whatever rant she wished to release—she'd done it plenty of times before—but this time she shook her head, spun away from Lyra, and marched back to the docks, Calem moving in step with her.

"You knew, didn't you? That's why we came here to *Cofdeffro*. Before she left the ship, you knew she'd fallen in love. And that her *person* was here. How?"

Calem tripped over the uneven laneway, delaying his response. Catching himself before falling again, he straightened, checked his boot for any tears or marks, and slowed them to stroll. "It was obvious."

Her eyes rolled of their own accord. "How? *How* was it obvious? How did you even know her lover, her *Di-Byth*, was in *Cofdeffro* when she didn't acknowledge she loved them until after her release from the *llyranite*? How do you constantly see these things that I don't?"

"Maybe you are not looking."

Eira blinked once, then widened her eyes, exaggerating them while they moved in all directions to prove him wrong.

Now in a more prominent part of town than Lyra's lover lived, the glow of *llyranite* lights fully illuminated the laneway beneath their feet. The cramped houses gradually opened up, spread apart, shrank in height, and widened in width as they walked closer to the docks and the number of buildings using *llyranite* increased. The sun was rising, but people in this area could afford to leave their lights on a while longer.

Even at this early hour, the keeper of an artisan shop was tinkering with the crystalline structures, which emitted a vibrant cerulean glow. The pieces were extravagant, artistic, bold, and sharp.

Useless. Horrifyingly expensive. Eira had to admit it took a lot of skill to manipulate the *llyranite* into this *llachadllyrite* form; however, the practical uses of spending that much money on decoration were nonexistent. There was no way Calem would sell their stock to this keeper.

As they walked side by side, their soft conversation blended with the distant sound of ocean waves. Eira's silhouette shimmered in the subdued light while the flickering of light and shadows concealed Calem's features.

"I am looking," Eira confirmed.

The corner of Calem's right lip tipped up—perceptible to her because she was, in fact, *looking*.

"When it comes to love, Eira, you are selectively perceptive."

"Selective in that I know it for the sham it is—you and I have *both* seen too many people die because of love."

They passed through a small square containing a striking fountain. Its rigid white *gwenithrynite* base was imposing and elegant, intertwined with delicate cerulean *llachadllyrite*. Together they formed a functional and beautiful structure of waves rising and falling in a never-ending cycle. Considering it provided a clean water source for the city, Eira didn't feel as uneasy at the wasted *llachadllyrite*. She could see the appeal of making one's city beautiful and functional on rare occasions, much like *Islaw* utilized both functional qualities of the *llyranite* and incorporated them into a strong, well-built, magnificent ship. The fountain's waters gleamed with soft hues of teal-white lights. They paused for a moment, watching the tumbling trickle of water.

"And how do you know it is a sham?" Calem's voice matched the falling water. Constant and calming, grounding her to her place of serenity beneath the waves.

"I've seen it."

"You have not lived it. Does it truly count if you have not been the one to experience it?"

"Just because I haven't experienced something doesn't mean I don't know what the result would be."

"Hmm." Calem turned them away from the fountain, and they continued their meandering. He was now scouting for the best candidate to sell their *llyranite* to.

"Don't 'hmm' me," she shot back, punctuating her words by punching him hard in the shoulder. He deserved it.

"Ow." Feigning exaggerated injury, Calem rubbed the spot, his mock grimace making Eira laugh despite her irritation.

The orange glow of dawn shifted to a bright yellow, marking the time for people to emerge from their nighttime slumber. Shop owners unlocked their doors and began to set out their wares for the day.

"I will overlook that you punched your superior officer—" Eira sputtered a cough of laughter. Despite Calem's recent tendency to remind her of his authority as Captain, their dynamic remained unchanged. She respected him as Captain, yet she relished the moments when their friendship returned to what it was at its core and she could tease him.

Calem glared with another corner smile that disappeared too soon. "Despite that, what I said remains true. You are selectively perceptive. And before you interrupt again, may I point out that while we have been walking, I have found two *llyranite* recipients." His eyebrows rose as he crossed his arms. They were back at their ship, and Calem took the opportunity to lean against a stack of crates nearby and gesture where they had come from. "Do you know who they are?"

Eira sucked in her cheek and chewed on the side while her lips pursed.

"Point for you, Calem."

The first buyer Calem scoped out could easily afford the high cost of raw *llyranite* and had a reputation for sharing its power generously—an unusual trait among the elite. By contrast, their current destination's recipient could not afford the resource but needed it desperately.

Eira walked a few feet behind Calem, in line with First Mate Solem. The chill morning air in *Cofdeffro* bit through her light coat, which lacked the white fur lining of the one Calem had given her back on *Islaw*. She wore a soft, billowy shirt tucked into tapered pants that bulged slightly where her black boots met her calves. Each exhale turned to a faint mist as she breathed in and out. The metal handle of the crate Eira held in tandem with Solem stung her ungloved hands with a cold sharpness, like holding onto a shard of ice.

Locked inside the crate were the remaining pieces of *llyranite*. Two days ago, Eira could have carried it alone, but once out of the ocean its weight transformed—growing exponentially heavier when removed from the water, as if absorbing the nearby air. Now, it took two of them to lift.

Solem, dressed in his usual stoic demeanour, wore his immaculate navy coat buttoned to the neck with no hair out of place. Unlike Eira's, his pants were so tightly secured in his boots that there was no hint of a bulge. His desire to uphold professionalism drove him to dress this way rather than his lack of love for the cold.

Calem, on the other hand, despised the cold, regardless of whether his body could handle it. Paired with his gloves, his musty maroon coat lined with fur stopped just above his knees. Eira noted the irony of the coat's lack of adornments with a frown—Calem resisted labels and attention, yet he was the type who drew notice without trying.

Captain Calem of *Islaw'r Tonau* and his crew were well known, particularly across port cities on the eastern stretch of the continent. Potential buyers, thieves, and swindlers knew they couldn't bribe, entice, or trick the Captain into selling them *llyranite*. He was not one for politics or the so-called rules of society. You'd only get *llyranite* from *Islaw'r Tonau* if the Captain deemed you worthy.

Their reputation preceded them, but Calem didn't take any chances. *Llyranite* was a power everyone wanted; the difficulty in Chasing and obtaining it steered people away. Stealing, however, was more manageable.

Calem quelled problems before they had a chance to start. Two quads surrounded their delivery the day before: a display of strength and a deterrent, a silent message that any attempts to reach their *llyranite* would be futile. The two quads, plus Solem, Eira, and Calem, were a force saying both, "*Llyranite* is here" and "You will not touch it."

Today, Calem didn't deem it necessary and instructed the rest of the crew to take the week off. They all now had twelve full days of freedom on land.

Eira readjusted her grip on the crate while Solem marched straight ahead, following his Captain.

As they marched, Calem and Solem each wore a mask of emotionless expression in entirely different ways. Eira found solace in Calem's calm presence—a steadying force against the unknown. By contrast, Solem held himself with tautness, his gaze intense, as if he was hiding something that no one else was meant to see. She couldn't decide if his secret was good or bad, and the uncertainty kept her wary, making her unable to fully trust him.

Calem maintained a steady and purposeful pace toward their destination. As he did, Eira felt a prickle at her neck—not from the shadow shifting by a vendor stall, whose owner was eying their crate with interest. Eira squinted her eyes, trying to find the source. Had it been a real threat, Calem and Solem would have already said something.

If you're so selectively perceptive as Calem says, how can you tell something is off while Solem and Calem seem unconcerned? Eira tried to pinpoint the source of her growing uncertainty. She didn't feel threatened—there was just something *wrong*.

Calem was his usual stoic self, especially with other people around, yet it was as if something integral to his innermost being was shifting. Eira shook her head, trying inconspicuously to study him as he walked ahead without alerting Solem to her oddity.

If they both aren't noticing anything, perhaps they both already know? But why wouldn't they tell me?

They followed a similar path to the one they'd taken in following Lyra, passing weathered wooden market stalls adorned with colourful fabrics and spices flourishing in the light of day. Calem halted at the corner of a moss-covered stone wall, lifting his hand to rest on it while his eyes scanned the area. Eyes narrowed, Eira took this momentary pause to study his posture.

By all appearances, he was the same. Same brown shaggy hair falling just above his eyebrows. Same muscular arms hidden beneath a thick coat. Same straight-backed stance exuding confidence.

But then, as Eira's gaze lingered, she pinpointed the subtle difference. He was leaning—a slight tilt to the side, hand resting on the wall as if burdened by an invisible weight. A minuscule lean, barely noticeable, but to Eira it spoke volumes. She was not able to ponder his position for long, as Calem pressed off and diverged from the route she expected.

They navigated through the laneways—dark despite the sun having risen well in the sky—with no *llyranite* to light the decrepit buildings rising on either side. Vines grew from the ground below, their tendrils creeping upward and clinging to the walls as if holding them up, snuffing any light or sound from entering—or exiting—the windows. The air around the building carried a musty scent, a blend of dampness and neglect. The salty ocean scent she loved—fresh and ancient, wild and natural—was tainted with the melancholic perfume of sickness and decay.

Calem slowed as they approached a lone woman sitting on the staircase ahead of them. Vines crawled up the side of the singular door, entwining and filling in the cracks in the wall as they made their way up and up. Sitting on a pile of broken vines—perhaps to cushion the uncomfortable staircase—the woman hunched over and pounded the side of a copper casing with a jagged-edged rock.

"How many are here?" Calem asked by way of introduction. Her head lifted a fraction when the crate was lowered.

"Why do you care?" Clang. Clang. Clang.

Less patient than Calem, Solem grunted and stepped forward. His movements were gentle yet purposeful and happened before the woman realized what he was doing. The copper casing clanging against her rock was now in Solem's hand, hovering near the crate. Annoyance barely had time to cross her face when the copper—now near the crate—vibrated. *Llyranite* sparked in flashes, easily visible through the cracks thanks to the alley's darkness. Solem's eyebrow rose, ensuring she took note, before handing the buzzing copper casing back to her. She frowned at it, still reverberating in her hand.

"How many?" Solem's voice rose a fraction.

Eira stepped in, crouching to the woman's level, making herself impossible to ignore.

"We just want to help."

"Who's to say we want your help?"

The glare didn't deter Eira. She shrugged and plastered on a smile despite the muffled screams behind the door.

"No one, I suppose. Doesn't mean it's not needed."

A thump brought everyone's attention to the boarded-up, vine-covered window above them.

"Listen, they're going through enough as it is; might as well give them a glimmer of comfort while it happens."

Though there was no smile as Calem leaned down, he managed a more genuine tone than Eira and Solem. "You remember what it was like, do you not? Pain is pain; ultimately, they are at your *Ysgol'Sâl* now so that they will survive later. But having a working toilet—or whatever you choose to use this for—isn't going to deter from that. There can be comfort in pain."

The woman pursed her lips, set the rock she'd been smashing on the step by her feet, and frowned at Calem.

"Why would you help?"

"Because we can."

"How much would it cost?"

Calem raised himself back up as Eira did, removing his gloves. He tucked them into his coat pocket before repeating his question, "How many are here?"

"Fifty-seven. Plus the workers."

"Fifty–!" Solem blurted before remembering himself. He coughed and skirted his eyes to take the building in properly.

This is what happens to those who can't afford the affluent sick schools. Eira's jaw clenched. Children stuffed like *macrell* in a tin, forced to ingest countless pills laced with every imaginable illness. All done in the futile hope that when they grew up and found love, they wouldn't succumb to something as mundane as sickness. *Not to mention, of course, the inevitable fighting.* It amazed Eira that even in constant sickness, children would fight—were indoctrinated to fight. To "build their immunity" to everything the world would throw at them. Eira shuddered, shaking off her memories. *How can a world so enraptured by love send children to such a place?*

The woman smirked as if wanting to prove nothing they could do would be of any benefit. She did not know Calem. He didn't hesitate. "A gift, then."

"I–what? *Maddeuant*?" In her flurry to stand up, the woman stood on the back hem of her skirt and fumbled backwards up the stairs. While Eira contemplated the necessity of helping this woman who didn't look to be in love, Calem leapt forward. Her hands clasped Calem's coat and right arm; his muscles flexed as he was pulled forward hard to the ground.

The woman remained unharmed; her head hovered just above the sharp edge of the top step thanks to Calem's stabilizing grip on her collar while his other hand landed with a sharp thud behind her.

Kneeling on the step, Calem held her steady as he tilted his head, "I take it you choose to accept our help?" He lowered her the remaining few inches as she nodded slowly. Calem moved his body back, flexing the fingers of the hand that hit hard, and remained kneeling on the ground.

"Perfect. Lead the way." At his word she stood, taking care not to rush, brushed herself off, and unlocked the door with a specialized *llyranite* key. The motion caused the door to glow in a cerulean-hued lightning pattern.

Eira fumbled to carry her end of the crate as Solem leapt into action and followed her in. She stopped at the top of the stairs at Calem's voice.

"Eira, I have a favour to ask." Her abrupt stop stirred a grumble from Solem, who determined he could drag the crate himself now that they were up the stairs and through the door. Calem was still kneeling, dusting himself off meticulously and moving the bucket and copper casings to the side so no one else would trip.

"Sure." Eira hesitated in the doorway, then pointed inside. "Can it not wait unt—"

"I need you and Solem to finish this. Make sure it goes well, and those kids are," he faltered, "as good as we can help them be, at least. See if there is anything else that would help ease their time. Be sure they know how to refine the *llyranite* and hire a crew to oversee they're using it properly—not just for themselves."

She squatted in front of him on the step, balancing on her toes, her brows furrowing. "Why are you being so—"

"I have to go." He cut her off again.

Eira's head tilted to the side. "Right now?"

"Yes."

She searched his eyes and face for any change to his expression. Any hint at what was going on. A clue to point her toward *what* exactly was odd about Calem other than his earlier *lean*.

"That's it? That's all you're going to give me?" Elbows came to rest on her knees and her head between her hands as her eyes narrowed. They held each other's gaze, matching intensity, until his lips slipped up a fraction. Still, he did not reveal any more. With an exaggerated eye roll and a huff, Eira dropped her arms and stood back up. "Fine. Be cryptic. I'll see you later, then?"

"Beneath the waves," Calem whispered. The familiar words were a promise forged in fevered dreams back when sickness blurred their lives, and all they'd clung to was the hope of a quiet place beyond the pain. Before Eira overthought his invocation at this moment, he continued, "I'll want a full report."

"Beneath the waves," Eira returned, shook her head, and entered the doorway. The screams were louder, and she sucked in a sharp breath.

"You are helping them. Remember that." Calem stood and turned away from her as he looked over his shoulder. His hand fisted at his side, peculiar, except she noticed her own were fisted as well. Calem's stare softened as he leaned forward with a slight eyebrow raise.

One deep breath later, Eira returned to the door and walked through.

The tour and ensuing *llyranite* transfer brought back haunted memories of her own time in the *Ysgol 'Sâl*. Inside, she'd been unable to shake the bone-chilling cold permeating her core, spreading outward and sucking the colour of everything around her. As Eira followed Solem outside, the few rays of sun fighting for space through the darkened alley's towering buildings were life-giving.

A weight heavier than the *llyranite* they had delivered released from her shoulders. They'd done as Calem asked and ensured the *llyranite* would be used appropriately at this *Ysgol 'Sâl*. Eira struggled to suppress her resentment towards the caretakers; it wasn't their fault the children were there. It wasn't their fault children were sick, crying, on the verge of death, yet unable to die. It had to be done. It was the way. This was the world. If kids weren't exposed when they were young, they would die from sickness when they were in love. Their bodies had to be prepared.

There has *to be another way*. Her personal vow to never love wouldn't solve the problem for these kids.

To their credit, the caretakers tried—at least minimally—with their funds. Most money went into purchasing pills concentrated with various diseases the kids had to swallow daily; the remainder went into supplies to keep them comfortable. Comfort was relative.

You're doing what you can, Calem's voice sounded in her mind. He was right, of course. *Yet, it never seems to be enough.*

When Eira went to her *Ysgol 'Sâl* the first time—when she was two or three, she never remembered—she shared her room with another. They had one caretaker to look after them both, all twenty-seven hours of the day, twelve days a week. In this place, there were two caretakers to look after fifty-seven.

At eight, she had her own room with a bed, a long skinny window where the ocean was visible in the distance, offering a glimpse of freedom, and copper piping in the floors to light it when it got dark. She was in a dorm with ten other girls, all between five and ten years old. They had functioning washrooms and soundproof walls, sparing them the agony of hearing anyone else's screams. Although, at times, it had been a comfort to know they were not alone. In this place, the kids were ten to a room with a latrine, which was not emptied nearly enough, and candled lights too sporadic to be of use.

At fourteen, Eira's last summer of schooling was horror sharpened to a point. By then the kids were "broken in," resigned to pain, their bodies and minds capable enough to endure the daily doses of illness. Every child had a bed—but piled so high they sagged like deflated lungs, so worn they seemed to breathe out dust and mildew. Wafer-thin sheets crumbled in their hands as they huddled for warmth.

Here was where Eira's and this *Ysgol'Sal's* similarities started. And where they ended.

Here, with their meagre funds, the kids were only given the cheapest diseases —not the *prestigious* drugs of rich schools.

However, here, children could move and roam if they chose. With only two caregivers to look after them, less fighting was encouraged; they didn't want to deal with the repercussions of inevitably repairing broken objects. There were arguments, but they did not *fight*.

Eira's *Ysgol'Sâl* consisted of endless moments of calculated suffering to produce resilience in their bodies. It was torture with a goal. Caregivers encouraged fights—spurred on by the knowledge that anything broken could be repaired. Their pills were endless, all-consuming, pure pain.

Eira shook away the memories. At least at her *Ysgol'Sâl* she'd found Calem.

The llyranite will help. Eira squeezed her eyes for a moment, phantom pain returned to her stomach, and her hand reached down to grip her puffy shirt into a fist.

The moment passed.

With her head down, when her eyes opened they were drawn to a dark spot on the staircase. Solem continued without notice or care, or perhaps with a desire to get out of there for his own traumatic reasons. He left her behind as Eira pulled towards the darkness. Frowning, she bent down and grazed her finger lightly over the top.

A deep, rusty-brown stain had dried and set into the wood of the stairs. The *llyranite* rock, which the caregiver, Nova, had used to try to ignite her copper casings, was missing. While it wasn't uncommon for such an item to go missing due to the residual energy it still held, Eira was certain its previous position matched the exact spot now stained with darkness. She cocked her head.

Had the stone *leaked* somehow? That didn't seem right. *Llyranite* didn't melt or leak unless put under extreme pressure and heat. She bent her head down to smell the substance. The metallic, musty scent clicked in her mind. She hadn't seen it in years, so it hadn't registered. It wasn't a stone leaking. It was a human leaking. Blood.

Whose blood? Thoughts spiralled. *Nova is Di-Os; it couldn't be her. Solem hadn't walked this path. And it didn't come from me.*

The phantom stomach pain clawed its way upward, and suddenly it was as if the vines creeping along the building's walls had invaded her chest, twisting tight around her insides. There was only one other person whose blood it could be—barring the even more absurd happenstance that a random *Di-Byth* came to this exact stairway and fell. *Calem.*

"Impossible," Eira muttered, her breath catching in disbelief. *Impossible.* Calem was the Captain of a *llyranite* Chaser Ship, for *blathryn's* sake! He was unshakable, the one constant she could always rely upon in a world of shifting tides of lovers. Eira's feet couldn't find the ground as she frantically tried to latch on to something real.

People blurred around her, moving in disjointed steps as if they'd all forgotten how to walk; their faces trailed after their bodies like echoed shadows. Eira stumbled, pushing through the haze, trying to focus on reaching Solem. He was real. Right?

The proposed reality her mind struggled to accept was illogical. Yet her gut had warned her of something amiss with Calem. Now Eira couldn't shake the question: how long had she been blind to these strange occurrences around him? Calem said she was selectively perceptive; had she only begun to notice his oddity because her subconscious had finally kicked in, or was it that she hadn't cared to see until it demanded her attention?

A distant voice nagged for her attention but slipped away from her focus until large, rough hands shook her shoulders.

"Hello? Eira?"

Blinking rapidly, she shook her head, eyes struggling to focus on the hands finally grounding her to reality. Solem stood before her, and their ship loomed tall and proud behind him.

We're back? Her journey from the *Ysgol'Sâl* to the docks had felt endless, her mind disoriented—but now that they were here, it seemed they'd arrived all too abruptly. She rubbed her eyes vigorously, trying to shake off the disorientation that still clung to her.

Waves. Focus on the waves. Beside her, water lapped gently against the hulls of anchored ships—a steady and calm lullaby from the sea. She let the lapping sounds envelop her, breaths slowing to the rhythm of waves as they rose and fell. Gradually, other sounds crept back in—screeching gulls, merchants calling out their finest wares, and the bustle of people going about their day—a lively scene, as busy as her thoughts, yet not as chaotic.

"Yes, Solem?" Her voice came out raspy, and she tried to clear it, arms folding, then unfolding. Then she slipped her hands into her pants pocket instead. *How do I normally stand?* Eira floundered.

Solem eyed her, his expression as unreadable as ever and repeated, "I said I'll be back in a few days."

Eira nodded slowly. *Yes, of course, he's leaving. He's earned his break. Nothing is wrong.*

He hesitated, hand raised once again as if to reach out to Eira, but dropped it. She didn't need comfort. She was fine. She was *Di-Os*.

"Go," Eira said as he continued to linger, somehow plastering a smile on her face. She pulled her hands from her pockets and gave him a gentle shooing motion. "I'm fine, just lost in my thoughts." She waved a hand near her head, mimicking said fluttering thoughts.

"He'll be back. You know that, right?"

She laughed, high and shrill. "Who? Calem? Of course he will." *Deflect, deflect, deflect.* Eira grabbed his arm and turned him around with more force than necessary. In her haste, the pack on Solem's back—*when had he grabbed that?*—smacked her in the face. Another chuckle came as she brushed her now frazzled hair out of her face. "Go, enjoy your time off. You've earned it."

He left, disappearing back into the crowd, free to spend his week however he wished. But why did she now wonder where he was going? What was he doing? Had he not seen the blood? *I couldn't possibly be more perceptive than him. Why did I not just ask? Wait—was he going to find Calem now?* Without *me? Why would he do that?*

She knew the answer. They weren't friends. Eira knew little about him—and anyone else aboard *Islaw,* for that matter. It was always better not to form attachments with anyone; there was no chance of falling in love if you didn't know them.

Yet Eira had known Calem for a long time. He was the exception to her rule. Why? Why did she stay with him when she knew the potential consequences?

More importantly, where is Calem now?

She discarded thoughts of consequences. Calem had always been the exception, constantly defying her self-imposed rule. It didn't matter right now. Right now, she needed to find him and uncover the truth herself. Letting her imagination run wild would serve no purpose. Locating him was the first step. Demanding answers would come soon after.

The few stragglers Eira questioned on shift to guard the ship were no help.

"We assumed he'd be with you," they all replied.

The fifth time someone said that Eira couldn't restrain herself. She looked pointedly at Elin, one of their *llyranite* Converters.

"Oh, right. How silly of me. Here he is right beside me. He simply turned invisible with the newly discovered form of *llyranite* and used it to prank me."

Elin ignored Eira's glare, unperturbed and returned to her notes. "Guess so."

"Thanks for the help," Eira muttered with a heavy sigh.

After that, she took it upon herself and searched the ship with frenzied urgency; her fingers grasped at ropes and crates as if they could hide a full-grown man while she navigated *Islaw's* deck. With each passing moment her anxiety mounted, driving her to search even more fervently. The creaking of wooden planks beneath her feet mingled with the distant sounds of the bustling port, creating a clamour of noise and fuelling her determination. Her eyes darted from one shadowy corner to the next, hoping to glimpse Calem's familiar figure, yet everywhere she looked turned into another dead end.

"Blathryn!" As she came to a stop, the stitch in her side flared before melting away. Her breathing was ragged from the exertion, but her already-healed body was ready to go. The problem was, go where?

Calem claimed they'd been to *Cofdeffro* multiple times, yet to Eira, it looked infuriatingly ordinary. No distinguishable feature set the city apart from any other port, and there was no indication of where Calem might have run off.

It was early evening on the twelfth day. Rumblings around the latest brewing storms in the *Môr làr* and *Môr Cryf* were at the height of discussion amongst the crew, wondering which storm the Captain would choose to chase.

With every second, Eira's panic elevated. This new pain was unlike anything she'd known before. It tore at her from within, relentless and unhealing, not something her body could recover from.

Where *was* he? The question ruminated in her mind; it was practically the only one she could think of anymore. That and the one she suppressed—the one that caused her insides to squeeze far tighter than any pressurized depth the ocean had ever been able to do.

What if he died?

Because if he died, that meant he was in love.

Eira paced the top deck, scanning the docks for any sign of Calem. She ignored the crew's furtive glances and how they mirrored her unease. Their usual jovial chatter, present after a week off, faded to muffled whispers as they shuffled about, preparing *Islaw* for the Captain's supposed arrival.

"Eira." The voice wasn't Calem's, so she didn't turn.

The voice came again, harsher, an order. "Eira, come."

Her hesitation brought forth a rare glare from Solem. He was First Mate, and on this ship there was no hesitation when a superior gave an order. As minute as it was, Eira grunted frustration at her own insubordination.

Her thoughts drifted in and out of focus, and the crew's noise dimmed as she trailed Solem below deck.

In the crew's quarters, dim lanterns of multicoloured *lliwithite* flickered, casting a soft glow on the weathered wooden beams and hammocks spread throughout. Carys, the quartermaster, a hard and determined woman Eira struggled to get along with on a good day, was already there—her presence commanded attention with ease.

Lachlan entered behind Eira, and she spotted a new flash of colour. His muscular frame was highlighted by a new outer tattoo on his upper arm, faintly glowing with a crystalline cerulean hue.

Di-Os couldn't receive real tattoos due to their impenetrable healing skin, so this piece was instead intricately woven and attached almost seamlessly to his skin. It pulsated with the energy of *llachadllyrite*, expanding and adapting as his muscles flexed beneath it.

It looked good on him and suited him well, but in Eira's state she was frustrated by Lachlan's frivolous spending on something that would not last.

Lachlan, Carys, Solem, and Eira faced each other, the four crew members who had been with Calem the longest.

As all but Eira settled onto the stools scattered about the hold, the faint scent of salt and sea mingled with the musty aroma of aged wood. The space was clean and organized, warm and inviting thanks to Carys—a stark contrast to Eira's agitated state.

"Eira, you need to calm down," Carys said evenly.

Eira looked up sharply, a retort ready when Solem spoke over her.

"The Captain will be returning tonight, Eira. Your needless worry has unsettled the crew and needs to stop."

"How do you know that?" Eira ignored his words and focused on his confidence. "Have you seen him? Have you spoken with him this week? Did you—"

"He said he would be back today," Solem reiterated, again cutting her off. "Today isn't over yet."

Eira huffed in disbelief, a weak laugh escaping her lips. "You do realize Calem has *never* left the ship this long. Never left—" She stopped. Everyone knew what she was going to say but chose to politely ignore her insinuation.

"You trust him, though, right?" Lachlan pushed back on the rear legs of his stool, balancing with ease as he gestured around. "We all do. We all know Calem, Eira. He said he'd be back—he'll be back."

"And it would help the crew if you'd calm yourself and remember that," Carys repeated while glaring at Lachlan to sit respectfully. He pushed himself into balancing on one leg instead. She continued, "We *should* talk to the crew, however. Put them at ease. Consider keeping Eira out of sight until Calem shows up, *if* he happens to be late."

Eira's hand shot out, her fingers splayed wide in disbelief at Carys' contradiction.

"You don't believe he'll return!"

"This is moot." Solem sighed, preemptively breaking up the argument between Carys and Eira. Eira was glad for the intervention, even as her anger simmered. She was too tired, confused, and worried to argue anymore.

Solem pulled a logbook off a hook by the door, glanced at it, and continued. "Calem will be back tonight. While we wait, Eira and Lachlan can start prepping the *llyranite* to convert into *porfforddwrithite*. Elin said we will need more to distribute across the ship to balance *Islaw'r Tonau* for the next storm. Carys and I will—"

Everyone froze. The feet of Lachlan's stool landed with a soft thud, and the dim light through the small windows shifted.

The ship was moving. There was only one reason for that—Calem was on board.

Eira barely registered Solem muttering, "Typical," as she flung the door open—uncaring as it slammed into the wall—and sprinted up the stairs to the deck. In her haste, her fingers jammed against a splintered piece of wood on the staircase railing. A shooting pain ricocheted down her index finger as the wood attempted to penetrate her skin. She gritted her teeth and continued her run, pulling the piece away and tossing it to the side.

A brisk, salty sea breeze caressed her face on deck as *Islaw* gracefully slipped away from the bustling harbour. The scent of open ocean on the horizon embraced her, calming her mind as her focus intensified, her eyes scanning for Calem.

He stood, as he always did, at the helm. His hands deftly manipulated *Islaw's* wheel, navigating them through the maze of other ships and smaller boats coming in and out of the harbour. The soft glow of *llyranite* around the wheel was just visible in the fading daylight, casting a subtle and shifting illumination on the contours of his face.

Eira stormed up the stairs to the helm, her own fury rolling like a tempest on the edge of exploding. His crisp voice cut through before she had a chance.

"Ah, there you are, Eira. New storm brewing, a big one."

She missed her next step, but with swift reflexes, Calem caught her with one hand. She shoved his hand away with more force than necessary, and it went back to the wheel.

"Here *I* am?"

"Right off the coast of *Cofaelog*. We need to hurry if we want to catch it in time. *Cofaelog* is a fair distance from here—two days if the winds favour us."

"Calem."

"Where is Solem? If we plan it right, this haul could keep us from chasing for *months*." He turned to avoid yelling in Eira's face, "Hoist the main!" The crew sprang into action, pulling on halyards to raise the mainsail, unfurling it as it ascended.

"CALEM."

"Can you imagine what we could do with months of *not* chasing storms? We could travel, explore on *our* time, try something new."

Enough.

With a surge of determination, Eira launched at Calem. His attention wavered, and that was all she needed. She hooked one foot at the wheel's base in a spontaneous, agile motion, using it as leverage. Simultaneously, she applied pressure to Calem's torso, unbalancing him. The unexpected manoeuvre caught him off guard, and before he could react, she completed the flip, sending him sprawling backward to the ground.

She guided their fall, landing them harmlessly on the deck as she straddled him. The ship's wheel held its position despite no longer being secured by his hands, unperturbed by the unexpected turn of events. The atmosphere between the two of them crackled with charged energy.

"Was that entirely necessary?" He looked resigned more than shocked to find himself in this position. Eira lost it.

Her voice shook, but her gaze held steady. "Yes, it *blathryn* well was necessary! Calem, you were gone for a *week*! No word. No sign. Gone. We didn't know what you were doing—if you'd return. I didn't know if you were—" She still wouldn't let herself fully form the words.

"So you do care." His words were soft, a near-silent secret he didn't want revealed. Her grip relaxed, and she shifted herself off his body. To their credit, the crew ignored them. He sat up and stretched his neck from side to side, placing a gentle hand on his left knee. Eira stared at that knee; now seen, it was impossible to tear her eyes away.

"Eira." His voice wasn't enough to pull her gaze. Words failed her, hitching in her throat, too afraid to ask the question that infiltrated everything she was for the past twelve days.

Solem's feet appeared in her periphery as he helped his Captain up.

"Everything alright, Captain?"

"Yes," he replied, not caring to explain anything of what had transpired. Eira remained on the ground, squeezing her eyes shut against the mix of anger and relief while Calem told Solem where they were heading. The planks creaked as Solem shifted and left Calem with her once again.

"Oh, we have a new chaser on board. Gwen." Solem's feet stopped at the edge of the stairs leading to the main deck. "She was a Messenger across the *Tir'pergl Plains* before she got into healing, so her skills transfer nicely. And before Carys asks, yes, we went through the proper authorities to get her on board. Be sure she is brought up to speed."

A strange curdling sprang to life inside Eira, twisting her thoughts. Was *that* where he'd been? With Gwen? And why did that gnaw at her so fiercely? Eira's gaze fixed on Calem's knee, tracking its every subtle shift.

"Eira." She blinked as gloved hands touched her face, lifting her chin and the rest of her body with it. "We will talk later." His hands dropped as soon as she stood, leaving a chill where warmth had been only moments before.

They stood close, closer than Calem usually liked to.

"Later? And what will we discuss later? The report you requested from Nova's *Ysgol 'Sâl*? Or perhaps instead, where the *blathryn* you've been and why you invoked 'beneath the waves' and *didn't come back*?"

"*Technically*, this *is* later," he replied, a hint of a smirk playing on his lips. "I did not lie. And I *did* come back."

"You—" He held a gentle finger up to her lips, eyes darting around as he shook his head. She frowned, noting the familiar strangeness lingering in his movements despite his week away.

"I'll tell you, Eira," he said, his tone softer, more secretive. "*Beneath the waves*. I promise. Right now, I need to Captain this ship."

Sighing, Eira noted the line of crew Solem was trying to pacify as they had their own questions for their Captain.

"At least this time, you can't just disappear." She gave him a look, then gestured for Calem to depart, lips curving slightly, almost daring him. He may hold the title of Captain, but he wouldn't dare leave Eira's side without her consent. Not again.

For every one of the next two days' fifty-four hours, Calem was otherwise occupied. Inspecting the ship, catching up on what he missed, briefing the crew on the storm ahead, reviewing *Islaw 'r Tonau*'s readiness and equipment, and going over contingency plans—Eira couldn't shake the thought that Calem was keeping them buried in tasks to avoid their overdue talk.

Eira kept her complaints to herself, if only to prove Carys wrong about her lack of restraint, though a few grumbles and mutterings still slipped out. She understood the need to prepare the ship and crew for the storms, but they had to do this for every storm, regardless of how big it would be. This was nothing new.

Busy, busy, busy. Everyone was busy. That was a fact of life. But *blathryn*, sometimes you had to *make* time.

Resigned, Eira was limited to hovering at the edges of his conversations, watching his every move, determined her sheer will would reveal his hidden truths.

In some ways it was a relief when she was ordered to another task. Busy work gave her mind a respite, and she moved through her tasks efficiently, ready in case Calem stopped by.

Her task for this hour was to sit in the dark hold—a windowless room sealed off from the rest of the ship—with the new chaser, Gwen. Their faces were covered with the same masks they wore when diving into the ocean—designed to limit air circulation, trapping the fine dust in airtight containers as they worked.

Hand-sized chunks of *llyranite* sat beside them in piles, which they positioned one at a time over a grinder to capture the violet dust—*porffoddwrithite*—in its bucket below.

Gwen was as good as Calem made her out to be, adapting naturally to any task. With her background as a Messenger on the *Tir'pergl* Plains, this was no surprise.

A Messenger's job was similar to being a Chaser, in a way. Instead of diving into the ocean to chase fallen lightning, they ran across a deadly desert wasteland amongst countless animals who wished to rip apart anything that crossed their path—all to deliver a message. Eira's brief consideration of joining the Messengers ended with the simple truth: powering the world was more important than delivering a letter, and running was about as appealing as becoming a *Di-Byth*.

Eira was surprised to see Gwen's nimble fingers moving with such practiced precision as she expertly handled the *llyranite* in the small, dim room; Messengers were known for swift feet, not deft hands—carrying messages demanded speed and powerful, well-defined legs, often at the expense of upper-body strength. Eira shrugged as she tried not to look too long at Gwen and continued with her task.

Without portholes, they relied on the faint glow of *llyranite* lights to illuminate their workspace, necessary to keep the integrity of the *porffoddwrithite* as pristine as possible. Lighter than air, the *porffoddwrithite*—strategically placed throughout the ship and on its sails—was a marvel. This powerful mineral made ships exceptionally buoyant, keeping them afloat even against waves that would otherwise overwhelm them in a storm.

Eira focused as well as she could, though curiosity drew her to Gwen. Gwen's presence was striking, her stature tall and commanding. With short, wavy, chestnut brown hair framing her sun-kissed face, the faint traces of freckles across her nose and cheeks were a testament to her time spent outdoors. With every movement, the muscles of her firm, defined frame flexed beneath her clothing. Sitting on a low stool, toes on the ground and heels on its legs, a cerulean hue of an outer tattoo like Lachlan's was exposed on her lower right ankle, rising up her calf.

Who are you? Curiosity churned into something darker, and she had to resist the urge to glare at this stranger who knew Calem.

This stranger who was doing precisely as told, applying the exact gentle pressure required to properly produce the fine powder without generating excessive heat and thereby altering the properties of *porffoddwrithite*. She was doing an excellent job of it; Eira had no right to feel this anger towards her.

The repetitive grinding was mind-numbing and required meticulous focus to ensure all the shavings were deposited correctly from the grinder into the buckets. If any escaped for a prolonged period, it would throw off the ship's balance.

The already confined air was thick with Eira's unspoken questions as they worked in silence, her mind buzzing with painful persistence. Where did Gwen come from? What sparked her desire to become a Chaser? How did she know Calem, and for how long had she known him? Had she been the one to hold him back from coming back to Eira? When did she undertake the test to prove herself as a *Di-Os* and earn a place on the ship?

Eira hadn't noticed the scowl etched into her face until her jaw protested. She released the pressure by massaging her cheek, an echo of pain lingering as her body healed. Gwen paid her little mind, and the frown returned unbidden.

"It is later, if you would like."

Eira jumped at the unexpected voice. Instead of the small *llyranite* piece gently pressing against the grinder, her hand slipped onto it. The pain was a thousand times worse than a spark abrasion, but Eira endured it for a second before her added pressure made the grinder topple, dislodging it from the bucket.

"*Lleugor*!" A cloud of violet dust erupted, sparking out in every direction.

"*Gwyrthol*, Eira! I did not mean to startle you." Calem shut the door swiftly and rushed to her side, cupping his gloved hands to catch the escaping sparks. Gwen sprang into action, precisely placing her bucket and grinder down before grabbing a *drith-net* to catch the dust.

Righting her bucket, Eira focused on not letting any more escape. With the *drish-sweep*, she swept and gathered the dust on the floor. Luckily, the violet dust was easier to find in the darkened room.

In less than twenty seconds, the dust was mostly contained. Eira exhaled in relief; the *porffoddwrithite* hadn't been out long enough to cause lasting damage. They merged all the pieces they found together, letting them flow down the funnel and back into the bucket before sealing it properly.

A few stray sparks of violet glittered where Eira had been working. She moved to pick them up, but Gwen stopped her.

"It's alright, Eira. I'll clean the rest up."

"But I—"

"The Captain wants to speak with you. I am the lower-ranking crew member. Go. There's barely anything left to clean up." She shooed Eira away with her hands and reached over to a shelf to put another set of goggles over her mask. They would help her scout out more of the missed *porffoddwrithite*.

Calem raised his eyebrow, a smirk playing on his lips. "She is not wrong."

Eira almost fumbled her bucket again. Calem full-on *smirked*—right in front of someone else. And it *lingered*.

"Come on," he said, taking her bucket and placing it firmly on the ground, out of her reach.

Eira narrowed her eyes but determined not to let her stubbornness ruin this chance to finally talk. She straightened, placed her mask on a hook at the entryway, and followed on Calem's heels as they made their way to the Captain's quarters.

Calem's quarters were small—nearly square, but he had the space to himself. A hammock stretched widthwise across the walls, held in place by scarlet *cochdraenite,* while a simple, unadorned wooden desk sat on the opposite side, its contents tucked securely within its drawers. A single porthole above the desk allowed in faint light, and a couch barely able to fit two people sat in the middle. The base of each piece of furniture glowed scarlet with sticky *cochdraenite,* meant to keep everything secure during rough seas.

Closing the door behind them, Calem headed straight for the couch, slumping into it with unrestrained relief. He leaned against its side, his elbow resting on the armrest and his hand soft on his left knee.

"Well," he started with a slow blink. *He's tired*, Eira noted, adding to her mental list of what was different about Calem. In the comfort of his room, his facade faded, his features softened, and his mask of withheld emotions lowered for her to see. *And Gwen, apparently*. Eira itched at her skin.

"Would you sit down?" He motioned to the space beside him, Eira's gaze following the gesture to his gloved hands, tracing the fabric that concealed whatever lay beneath.

"Why are you wearing gloves?"

Calem didn't flinch at the odd question, answering without hesitation.

"Because I like to keep warm."

"You don't need to keep warm." *You don't. Tell me you don't, Calem.* Her heart pounded in her chest, desperate for the truth.

He sighed and shut his eyes, further relinquishing his guard—revealing so much in that small motion. His typically straight posture was slouched, and the once-firm lines around his eyes softened with weariness. Fleeting vulnerability flashed across his expression, aspects of himself he was too fatigued to conceal.

"I *like* to keep warm, Eira."

"But we are inside."

"Is this really what you want to talk to me about? Gloves?" He opened his eyes, tilting his head to the side, resting it on the couch.

She swallowed, trying to calm the rush of emotions. "No."

"Then what would you *like* to talk to me about?"

Her feet shifted, unsure of where to go or how to begin, frustration bubbling up. Why wasn't he coming straight out and saying it? Was she foolish for wanting answers? Anger threatened as she chided herself for wanting to demand an explanation when she had no claim on him—no right to him.

Despite being with each other practically every day since leaving the *Ysgol 'Sâl* together, going a week without him was mind-boggling. Why did he leave? What had happened? Did he think she wouldn't search for him? Why the persistent knee holding? The silence gnawed at her—and yes, *blathryn,* Calem!—*why* the gloves?

She strode forward, ready to release the flood of questions swirling within her, and settled on the couch. Her legs folded beneath her, and as she met Calem's gaze the words that had been on the tip of her tongue evaporated.

Instead, she studied those deep emerald eyes, weariness lingering in their depths; a cloud of exhaustion dulled their usual brightness. But there was more—a longing, a need for her to ask the *right* question and a desire concealed for so long that he couldn't suppress it any longer. Whatever happened during his time away changed him. For good or bad, Eira was almost too scared to find out.

Silence—broken only by the sound of their breathing and waves slapping against the closed porthole. A sharp intake of breath and Calem's lips moved.

"Just ask, Eira," his voice soft but urgent. "I need you to ask, please."

The question she'd buried deep inside sprang out of the box she thought she'd locked and buried it in. Her lips pressed together, and her breath hitched as the question loomed. She couldn't ask him. Not that. Anything but that.

She was losing the battle. The words surged forward, refusing to be pushed aside, demanding release.

She shut her eyes, counting to five as her breath slowly steadied.

Calem's weary and subdued voice cut through the noise. There was a subtle yearning beneath it, a plea that latched onto to the question in her mind. "Please, Eira."

After one more breath, her eyes opened. Calem shifted closer. His left leg remained extended outward, while his right was now bent and brushed against hers. He leaned further forward, his eyes intense, as if proximity would urge her on.

The words tumbled out.

"Are you in love?" She flinched over the word, but Calem's unwavering gaze held her captive, locking her in place. This was it; she *needed* to know the answer.

The world shifted, and she felt as though she stood on the precipice of her first leap into the ocean of storms. In that moment it was only her and Calem, and the mounting pressure between them tightened, painfully close.

"Yes." His voice, now crisp and clear, bore no hint of exhaustion. The pressure in the air thickened as her heartbeat thudded in Eira's ears.

"Gwen?" Eira couldn't believe how small her voice sounded when she uttered the name. Calem blinked at her, and then, in a shift she hadn't witnessed in years, his entire expression transformed. It was a laugh she hadn't heard since he rose in rank to Captaincy. Perhaps even longer. He laughed—a slight chuckle, yet for him and Eira witnessing, it meant everything.

"No, not Gwen." The smile lingered on his face, and for a moment Eira forgot everything else. She never wanted him to stop smiling. That's what had drawn her to him in their *Ysgol'Sâl*, and it drew her in again now.

"Then who?" His answer alleviated some of the pressure but was swiftly replaced by her plummeting heart, no longer anchored where it should be.

"Not Lyra? This—this all started after Lyra declared her love. Did you know then it was her? That you loved her? But…how would that work? She loves someone else."

"Love doesn't depend on reciprocity," he said softly, as though the words carried years of meaning.

"So it *is* Ly—" she began, but Calem's hardened sailor hands gently caught her flailing ones, guiding them down to the couch. He shook his head, and the smile that adorned his face slipped.

"Selectively perceptive. You've always been that way—a defence mechanism you built long ago."

The hands still holding hers were uncovered, gloves removed at some point unnoticed by her. Eira's eyes flickered between his hands and his face, a deep frown furrowing her brow in confusion.

"Wait—" Her eyes darted back down, and she gasped, reaching out to grasp his hand. She pulled it gently up, studying his palm in disbelief. "You have scars?" She traced multiple semi-raised faint red lines and a few others—white ones—on his palm with a feather-light touch, afraid of making them worse or reopening the wounds. Each line held a frightening truth, a story she had likely been a part of but never fully known.

"Rocks are hard, and *Di-Byth* get injured when they fall." He tried to shrug it off, tugging his hands away as if to hide the truth, but Eira's grip tightened, unwilling to let him deflect.

"No—these are *scars*." Her finger trailed along a white line on the side of his index finger. It was small, smaller in length than the nail of her pinky finger, and white. Glowing against his dark, tanned skin.

"This is healed over, Calem." She didn't think her eyes could widen further. "*How long* have you had these scars?" She spoke more urgently now, her voice rising with each word. "*How* have you managed to get past screenings? And—wait. That is why you were gone, isn't it? I saw the blood on the stairs. You fell. You hurt yourself. Your knee."

Without thinking, she leaned forward, her legs straddling his as she reached for his pant leg, tugging it out of his boot to expose his injury.

"Eira, I think you're missing the point."

"The point?" He didn't try to hold her back or stop her. The pant leg tightened before she got to his knee, but there were scratches and other scars on his leg, leading to a white *gwenithrynite*–enforced bandage starting just below the knee. The *gwenithrynite* was soft to the touch. Breathable but secure. His knee would not be moving in this.

He sighed and pulled her upwards to face him again. Her legs were half over his, thanks to her scramble, but even the uncomfortable position couldn't make her move.

"Selectively per—" he whispered, cutting himself off with a roll of his eyes. "It seems I need to be more clear. It is about time I was."

Eyes fixed, Eira stared at his knee and thought about all the scars along his leg. She was brought out of her contemplation only when Calem's hands tenderly cupped her head.

"Eira. I am in love. I have been for *years*." He paused, steady and sure, unwavering with conviction. "With you."

The words tumbled over her, rising like a wave, then passing by, not landing; she could not comprehend.

"Eira, it's *you*. I *love* you."

"Um." She paused, her hands reaching toward the arms holding her face, but froze an inch away. "What?" The ship rocked. Or was it her that was spinning?

"Love, Eira." She faltered at his words, then sank back into the couch, sliding subtly off him. The weight of his confession hung in the air. His hands lowered, pulling their warmth until one settled against his chest.

"I, Calem," he reached out with the same hand toward her, "love you, Eira." His smile returned, but this time sadness lingered in its corners.

"That's not possible."

"I beg to differ." His hand dropped back in his lap while Eira's remained frozen mid-air.

"You don't fall in love. *We* don't fall in love. Not with each other." Her head shook, refusing to stop. Why was it more plausible to believe his love for Gwen or Lyra? But *her*? Eira? Impossible.

"To be fair," Calem lowered Eira's hands for her, "I did not fall. Falling implies an accident—an unintentional misstep. No, Eira. This was a choice. A purposeful step. Towards you. Always towards you."

"You *planned* to lo—" She faltered, the word 'love' lodged somewhere in her throat, unable to string together a sentence that would equate to Calem loving her.

"Well, no. Not exactly. But also, yes, exactly. Since the moment you tackled Owain to the ground as he was beating me, I have had feelings for you, Eira. I let them grow. I did not—could not, and would not want to—stop them. Was not hard to do, considering."

"Considering what?"

Calem's head tilted to the side. His brown, messy curls were shorter now after his week away, no longer falling into his eyes. He smiled again, but it was different this time. Not grand or full-toothed, but subtle—a glimmer of warmth lighting up his entire face.

"You."

Eira sprang up, unsteady and tripped over her own feet. She needed to leave, create space between her and Calem—but the tumble turned to pacing, unable to pull her eyes from his face. His eyes bore into hers, letting out everything they'd ever concealed. Love for her. Sadness at her incomprehension. Need for her to stay. He longed for her to listen, to ask whatever questions it took.

"You can't," she began. "I'm not—" Her head shook, her steps clumsy in the small room. "Ugh." She tossed her hands in the air, then ran one down her face, the weight of everything crashing in on her. Flashing moments with Calem flickered through her mind— hints of the truth she'd ignored.

Every time his eyes found her first when they entered the same space; the way he moved towards her instinctively—even in the depths of the ocean. Every time he insisted she keep warm, eat, or *not* be in pain—not because she couldn't handle it, but because he didn't want her to.

And every time she punched him—now she worried—had she bruised him? And if she had, he'd never said anything. Every injury she thought inconsequential to her and the crew was made real because Calem had taken them all too. Without complaint, and, more notably, without anyone noticing.

Eira halted in the middle of the room. Calem, still seated, massaged his knee, and she glared at him. "Why, Calem? Why me? Why submit yourself to torture for years?" She took a breath, words spilling out, "Why not leave? Take yourself away from the danger?"

He lifted his straightened leg with both hands, forcing his knee to bend, wincing without care if she noticed. Eira's feet nearly moved on their own, rushing her to his side. He was in pain, and it was absolutely entirely her fault.

"You really don't understand love, do you?" He murmured, knee finally bent as he set his other leg on the floor. He rose, favouring his right leg, and she winced at the slight wobble in his stance.

"You ask 'why you'? Because you are fierce. Because you went through *Teyrnoeth* as a kid, yet still found it in your heart to come to the aid of another. To stop bullies from beating me, even knowing the pain wouldn't last—knowing I wouldn't die. Even though you *refuse* to 'be in love', you show me every day what it means to care. Love is not just romantic entanglements. It is compassion, resilience, unwavering support."

"I've hardly—"

"No." He took a purposeful step towards her with his bad leg. "*Think* about it, Eira. When have *you* ever left me? When I rose through the ranks and you did not. When I became Captain and gave you orders. You were never bitter. You were excited. You supported me from day one and have never deigned to think of stopping since."

He took another step, his voice steady and intense. "Why torture myself? I ask you the same thing. You submit yourself to pain every day.

"Every time you enter those waters in the *middle of a raging blathryn lightning storm*, you literally *stop* yourself from *breathing*. But that's not why I do it. You're asking the wrong question. It is not torture. Yes, it is agonizing to watch, wondering if this will be the time you're dragged to non-death. But I get to see you every day. See you doing something you believe in—something that helps other people. You are willing to sacrifice yourself to endless pain, even non-death, to power other people's lives. You and our small crew are a testament to how few are willing to do that."

Another step.

"No. It is not torture. Even though my heart burns every time I watch you dive into a storm. Even though it tears me apart to see pain inflicted upon you. Even though I'm *terrified* of what you will do now that you know I love you. Even though it might be hopeless, Eira, you must see this truth. I'm not giving up. I will never give up. And I'll always be with you, return to you, no matter what.

"Because I love you. And if living this insane life of chasing storms is what it takes to be with you, I'll do it. Every *blathryn* day."

His face was inches from hers, and Eira felt her heart beat like thunder, echoing in her head. Yet it was a mere whisper compared to his declaration.

Voice hoarse, it came out as a whisper, "Why now, then? Why wait all this time to tell me?"

He reached up as if to tuck a piece of hair behind her ear, but his hand hovered momentarily. Thinking better of it, he dropped his hand and ran it through his shaggy hair instead.

"Lyra…seeing what happened to her made me realize. I cannot wait any longer for you to know how I feel. I cannot wait until I'm dead. And I do not want to waste any more time, even if you never love me back."

"Why didn't you come find me like you said you would? Why disappear?"

"I couldn't *walk*, Eira," he said, humour and pain interlaced. "I half dragged myself to Gwen's."

"Gwen?"

"She is a healer. I've sought her aid many times in *Cofdeffro* before. She's like a cousin to me; our families lived beside each other before we were sent to different *Ysgol 'Sâl*. I made it to her that day, and she refused to let me leave. She forbade anyone from seeing me until I got my head on straight. Once again, she tried to convince me to revoke my Captaincy and find a safer life—but I held firm. I had to. I knew you would not leave. Instead, somehow—impossibly—our negotiations resulted in her agreeing to come aboard *Islaw*. She'd had enough of me showing up broken time and again. If I was determined to remain Captain, she figured she might as well be here to put me back together as quickly as possible."

Another emotional punch to her stomach nearly toppled Eira over. *She'd had enough of him coming to her broken. Broken.* How often had he come to her or someone in another town to heal him? Broken because he couldn't bear to leave Eira?

Calem's hands came up to grip her shoulders, steadying them both in the ship's sway and her thoughts. She turned away, needing space, when the ground beneath her shifted.

Islaw'r Tonau tilted sideways, and the world around them spiralled into chaos.

A deafening roar filled the air as *Islaw* lurched violently, throwing them both off their feet. In a split second, Calem's arms wrapped around Eira, shielding her from the blow as his body slammed into the opposite wall.

Calem's silence and his lack of a groan sent a shockwave of panic through Eira. As *Islaw* switched directions again they were thrown to the ground, tumbling over the couch in a dizzying blur. Eira leapt out of Calem's arms, her heart racing as her eyes darted over him, terrified of what she might find. Dizziness clouded his vision, but Calem forced his body to obey, his bad knee buckling as he regained his balance.

Solem crashed through the door, his voice strained with urgency. "Captain, we've got a problem." His boots, glowing with scarlet *cochdraenite*—designed to keep him anchored through even the most violent shifts—flickered as he clung to the doorframe.

"There always is," Calem muttered, not masking his exhaustion.

Eira was prepared for *Islaw*'s sporadic tilts and shifts this time, and she grabbed hold of Calem to keep them both steady.

"We've found the storm, Calem. Or, the storm found us—as in, sprang up and swallowed us. It's a mite bit bigger than anticipated."

Calem looked to Eira, expression flickering with concern, illuminated by the jagged flashes of lighting that struck around *Islaw'r Tonau*. The storm's rage echoed violently through the hull.

"Can we do it? Is it worth it?" Calem's question hung heavy in the air.

Solem nodded, his gaze sharp. "If we're quick, it could be the biggest haul *anyone's* ever done." His eyes flicked toward Eira, lingering longer than necessary before returning to Calem. "You'd be set."

Eira's jaw dropped, her mind reeling from the implication in Solem's voice. *Did Solem* know *about Calem?*

"Then we better get what we came for and get out of here."

Solem dipped his chin in acknowledgement and raced away. Calem shook Eira's hands off him, and used *Islaw's* next sideways tilt to his advantage, launching forward and sliding on his knees to reach the trunk below his hammock.

"Calem, what are you doing?" Eira stumbled over to the doorway to grab hold of the frame as Solem had. He ignored her, steady hands working the lock before the lid swung open. He held the lid firm with one hand so it wouldn't slam shut as he dug through.

"You need to get out of here!" Eira's voice pitched as the roar intensified. "Calem! You can't stay in this storm! Not now! Not when you're—"

The trunk's lid slammed shut with a jarring crack and Calem latched it, his fingers tightening around whatever he'd found.

"I am exactly as I have been for the past five years, Eira." His voice was annoyingly calm and piercing as he ran and slid over to her. "Here." He revealed two thin strips of unused *cochdraenite*, ready to be stuck, and offered them to her. She refused to move.

"Calem, you could *die!*"

"And you could *not-die!*"

They froze, their breath sharp and ragged. Wind howled like a beast; waves crashed against *Islaw's* sides with brutal force. The ship tilted again, yet Eira and Calem stood as if they were the only solid things in a world on the verge of unravelling. Everything else spun and swirled, but they remained rooted in place, the centre of gravity amidst the storm.

Calem had yelled at her. His eyes blazed with fierce intensity, a volatile mix of worry, anger, and frustration. His jaw clenched tight, a muscle ticking under the strain, and every ounce of him vibrated with tension and concern for her.

Calem took Eira's shock as an opening, lifting her feet and slapping strips of *cochdraenite* on her boots with swift, practiced precision. His arms spread to either side of the doorway as he rose, towering over her.

He continued as if there had been no pause.

"Forcibly dragged to the bottom of the sea, crushed but not crushed. The pressure suffocating you, the darkness pressing in until you can no longer breathe, move, or think. *That* is what awaits you. *That*, Eira, is worse than death.

"And you face it every time we come out here. So don't you dare tell me how *I* might die when *you* could be lost to endless agony, forever. I love you, Eira. And I know you. You would never let me or anyone else stop you from doing your job. So don't try to force me to do otherwise."

Calem pried her hand off the frame and pushed past her.

"The sooner we get in, the sooner we get out. If you want us to leave, I suggest you get to your station."

Calem sprinted down the hall and up the stairs without a backward glance.

"Calem, wait!" He'd always been faster than she was on land, and she yelled louder as she trailed after him, "Where are *your cochdraenite* strip*s*?"

The deck was a storm of its own, organized chaos as the crew battled to maintain their position. Calem took two precious seconds to assess the situation, then his voice cut through the bedlam—a beacon of control amidst the rainless storm. His crew, attuned to his barely audible voice and hand signals above the increasing roar of wind and waves, responded without hesitation.

Eira arrived atop the staircase in a daze, her feet the only thing anchored to the ground. Her eyes followed as Calem approached the wheel and took control.

"Stick to the outskirts. Avoid the eye. There's plenty of lightning right here." A boom loud enough to hurt her eardrums resounded, followed by four more as if to prove Calem's point.

The outskirts. Finally, Eira focused on something other than Calem and faced the storm wall. At that moment, it felt as if her world had shifted into slow motion. Before her loomed a formidable wall of black—like the night sky itself had descended to meet the raging sea, brimming with malevolent energy. Inside its depths, streaks of lightning flashed and vanished, each bolt carving brief scars in the darkness. The air was thick with the metallic tang of charged particles, and the sea churned as if possessed by unrestrained fury.

Luckily—if that word could even apply here—this trip had not carried them into the iceberg-infested waters of *Môr lâr* to the east. Instead, they were further south, in the heart of *Môr Cryf.*

No icebergs to dodge. But what they had ahead was far worse.

They sailed through an ocean trapped between two masses of land, where the cold, unforgiving waters of the northeast collided violently with the warmer currents. This passage, unbroken by land, became a funnel for relentless winds, their speed and fury growing as they circled all of *Carthenwyl* and converged here, where the storm now awaited.

The ship pitched and rolled, the storm dragging it further into its grasp. Monstrous waves rose on either side, rising like wrathful giants bent on crushing the vessel.

Calem was undeterred; his stubbornness and determination outmatched even the storm. Eira couldn't shake the thought that the only thing keeping them afloat was the *porffoddwrithite* spread meticulously throughout the ship and *cochdraenite* holding *Islaw* together. She hoped Gwen had gathered the remaining pieces of *porffoddwrithite*, fearing her earlier blunder had affected the ship's balance.

There was no time to wish Calem would change his mind and take them away from the storm—not that she believed they could anymore, even if they wanted to. Even on the outskirts, towering waves crashed down relentlessly. Eira and the entire crew were drenched in a heartbeat.

It got worse. Colossal, unforgiving waves loomed overhead, crashing down with brutal force. *Islaw*, barely holding on, was tossed like a rag doll.

"Eira!" Calem's voice snapped her back to reality. Two waves crashed together behind him, hurling them into the sky like a towering monolith. Lighting struck in that instant, illuminating the waves' interior. As the bolt collided with the ocean minerals, it solidified into *llyranite*, then plummeted to the depths. A new fear struck her. They'd never had to fear lightning striking the ship since it was drawn only to the minerals in the sea. But with waves this high, those minerals were being lifted.

Llyranite could form and expand *onto Islaw*, threatening to sink them all.

"Do your job!" Calem yelled, one eye on her and the other on navigating the storm. He couldn't afford to lose focus now—if he were to survive this storm, Eira would have to go in.

Eira allowed one last look at Calem. His muscles were taut, jaw set as he gripped the wheel. Ripping her gaze from him, she stripped off her outer layers.

Alric and Lachlan helped Gwen suit up and were strapping her pack on when Eira reached them—a *Teyrnoeth of a storm to have your first chase in*. Deft fingers tightened the straps around her waist and shoulders. The bulky pack spanning the entirety of her short torso did not deter Gwen; she would not let the quad go in without her.

Alric watched Gwen closely, offering sharp instructions whenever she faltered. Eira tested her shoulder release, clicking and snapping it back to ensure it wouldn't hinder her if she needed to drop the pack in the water. Despite her delayed start, she finished her checks in sync with the others.

Prepared and tense with anticipation, Eira eyed her quad, performing her own mental checks on each. Years of working with

Lachlan and Alric had ingrained trust in these stormy seas. But Gwen was a different story.

As Eira watched Gwen take in the storm for the first time, she saw her fear. But beneath that fear, Eira saw something stronger—a desire, a willingness to sacrifice. Gwen was here to protect Calem. She had kept him safe for years—something Eira hadn't even known she should have tried to do. Eira didn't need to know Gwen the way she knew Alric or Lachlan. Gwen had sacrificed much in taking on the role of a Chaser solely to protect Calem. That alone was enough to earn Eira's trust.

They exchanged nods of confirmation; words weren't needed now and wouldn't be used below. They couldn't die, so what was there to fear? *Except Calem. Calem could die. And I could succumb to non-death.* Eira shook the thoughts away, forcing herself to focus. She had to put Calem out of her mind—hard as it was.

With the last deep breath she was bound to have for a while, she steeled herself against the tempest. An unspoken word moved them to the gap in the railing made for them, and as one unit, her quad leapt into the raging ocean.

Eira did not fall. Instead, a wave surged as she leapt, crashing against the ship and lifting her. For a fleeting moment, she glimpsed *Islaw's* deck through the frothing water, the crew scurrying like ants—then the wave pulled her under and she plunged downward.

Within the wave, her world morphed into a chaotic dark abyss, the ocean's muffled murmur replacing the storm's roar. Today, there was no solace in the silence.

The water's unyielding force enveloped her. Relentlessly tossed and tumbling, entwined in the relentless current, she lost all sense of direction in a whirl of darkness and froth. Her arms flailed, erratic and desperate, twisting in ways that would have shattered bones if she weren't *Di-Os*. Eyes squeezed shut against the disorienting darkness; she focussed all her energy on reclaiming the pack's handholds, torn from her grasp in the tumultuous torrent.

She gritted her teeth and, still spinning in the current, strained to manoeuvre her arm to her chest, down her body, and toward the attachment at her waist. Following the line to its end, her fingers closed around the lever. With a determined squeeze, she activated it, propelling herself—she hoped—downward, away from the relentless thrashing of the surface above.

A lightning bolt illuminated the abyss, offering a fleeting glimpse of her surroundings. Determined, she dove downward, using each flash to guide her to safety. Gradually, the tempest above grew distant, replaced by an uneasy calm as she reached the depths where the water was more tranquil and the currents less wild.

Now below the churning waters, Eira could focus again. The faint glow of her head and hand lamps was dim compared to the lightning flashes. She spotted Lachlan nearby, coming out of his daze. They locked eyes and swam toward each other, scanning for Alric and Gwen. Lachlan flashed his handlight at Eira and pointed in the opposite direction. Ahead, Alric was tugging Gwen downward, having miraculously attached one of his lines to her in the chaos.

The quad reunited. Eira noted Gwen, shaken but recovering fast, already orienting herself with a grim determination. They surveyed the water together, devoid of marine life—a small blessing, as it meant clear paths ahead. Their only real threat was the *llyranite*, now raining down with unrelenting fervour and expanding in never-ending flashes.

Islaw'r Tonau loomed above, silhouetted by a constant barrage of lightning. Eira realized surfacing for each piece of *llyranite* would not be an option today.

Attuned with her thoughts, telltale signs of *clymuwr*-ropes appeared, tossed over the ship's edge. Thin lines shimmered, then stretched, dragging deep into the water. At each rope's end, a *llyranite* light encased in protective housing—much like their headlights—glowed faintly, sinking nearly as deep as they were. The ropes were made for rough waters, though Eira feared they'd still be challenging to use.

But they had a mission, and it was time to work. With quick hand signals, Eira reminded them to stick close and always deliver *llyranite* in pairs. No matter its size, no one was to dive too deep or chase pieces too dangerous to obtain. The constant flashes striking around them promised plenty to collect.

Paired with Lachlan, Eira kept glancing at the ship, telling herself it was to ensure their beacons were working and they stayed on course. But the truth, pounding at the edges of her mind, was Calem.

She couldn't afford the distraction. Lightning flashed, solidifying into *llyranite* pieces plummeting at dangerous speeds. Dodging them alone demanded total concentration.

Hundreds of pieces littered the water around them. Eira soon realized resurfacing for each one wasn't feasible, so she began tying them to one of her lines as she went. Once her pack grew heavy enough to complain, she and Lachlan swam up to the *clymuwr*-ropes, cut their line, and secured the *llyranite* together.

Eira wasn't sure how long to keep at it. Their first collective haul surpassed the total they'd gathered from their last trip. But the *clymuwr*-ropes were cleared of their burden and tossed back overboard. Calem wanted more. *Why*?

As she squeezed her hands for an extra power boost to dodge an expanding piece of *llyranite*, the question remained: *Why does he want so much*? The answer hovered just beyond reach. She couldn't afford to dwell on it; every ounce of her focus was on staying clear of the currents and avoiding *llyranite* entanglements. Dodge the strike, chase after *llyranite*—that was her focus. Dodge, chase, and catch.

Lachlan and Eira's fourth swim to the *clymuwr*-ropes was complete; Gwen was doing well with Alric as her guide, coming up with their own smaller, third batch. This *had* to be enough. Eira signalled Lachlan with her handlight—a pattern telling him to stay below, where the lightning couldn't reach. She was going up to talk to Calem. Lachlan hesitated for a moment, then nodded and left to inform the others.

Eira powered her way to the surface, the ascent easier than their earlier descent; she could now see the currents and moved with them to carry her up. As she broke the surface, only her pack's power and the *pincdraenite* beacon's pull toward its counterpart on *Islaw'r Tonau* kept her from being ripped away. She rose and fell to massive heights with the waves, battered by wind and rain that had finally broken through the clouds.

Her gaze found Calem before she realized it, as though her eyes always knew where he was, even if she didn't. Relief flooded her at the sight of him still standing, still in control. The crushing weight of the ocean below was nothing compared to the growing pressure within.

Towering waves crashed over *Islaw* again and again, hammering the ship. Calem handed the helm to Solem and rushed to the railing, locking eyes with Eira just as she spotted him. She couldn't hear Calem, but she read it in his eyes. One more haul. One more, and they'd be set.

A colossal wave loomed, casting a shadow over the ship as it tipped sideways. Calem wrapped himself around the railing, clasping it tight. Lightning struck the rising water beside *Islaw* with a blinding flash, drawn by minerals closer to the surface than usual. *Llyranite* solidified, expanding outward as the wave crashed over the deck.

Towards Calem.

Claw-like tendrils wrapped around Calem, and in an instant he was ripped from *Islaw* and flung into the ocean.

Eira's heart dropped, and she lurched down after it, desperation and determination propelling her into the dark abyss as the sea swallowed them both. Calem's shadow plummeted, spiralling with lightning, *llyranite*, and debris. Her quad was somewhere below, but the chance they'd spot him in the chaos was slim. *Get to him. Just get to him. He will be okay.* She forced away thoughts of the crushing pressure, lack of oxygen, and the *llyranite* encasing his fragile *Di-Byth* body.

Everything else blurred as Eira dove deeper, faster than ever before—even faster than her pursuit of Lyra. They'd charged their packs fully for this trip, though they hadn't anticipated this many dives. Her heart hammered in sync with the relentless rhythm of the storm as every part of her strained against the drag.

For every two inches gained, one was lost to the relentless currents. Her only solace was that the water would affect Calem similarly. Her determination sharpened—she wouldn't let the *Môr Cryf* claim him.

These once-peaceful waters became her battleground. With every surge forward, the weight of the ocean pressed against her.

Lightning struck just ahead. Rather than dodging, she hurled herself into it, seizing the growing tendrils to spin and launch herself closer to Calem. The *llyranite's* weight and desire to plunge to the depths increased her speed. She kicked hard, adding a burst of power, thankful for her short-finned feet. The race against the ocean's pull intensified as Eira battled the forces trying to claim Calem.

Calem's face came into view; his eyes were closed, one arm floated limp as he was dragged down, the other trapped within the encasement of *llyranite*. In the near darkness, her headlight revealed shadows radiating from his body.

Her hand shot forward, gripping a jagged spike of *llyranite*. The piece, though smaller than Lyra's, wrapped tighter around Calem. Blood leaked from multiple wounds. Eira didn't let herself think. With her hand locked on, she flipped over and adjusted her trajectory, plunging a line from her pack into the *llyranite* while shooting them upwards again.

She felt nothing of the ocean's crushing weight any longer. Didn't register their speed or the toll this could take on Calem's frail *Di-Byth* body. Her only thought was getting Calem to the surface— and never letting go.

Islaw'r Tonau came into hazy focus. She didn't need her beacon to find it now. The call of safety for Calem drove her on, and she answered. Roaring through the depths, Eira aimed to crest a wave, to launch herself and Calem onto the ship. She halted—realizing that landing that way would hurt Calem even more. Instead, she guided them as close to the ship as she dared.

A rope dangled within reach; the moment her fingers found it, she wrapped it tightly around Calem and the *llyranite*. A second rope came down for her, which she looped around her arm. The crew heaved them up, but it was too slow. Eira shook her head, searching wildly for another way.

She spotted a ladder built into *Islaw's* side and moved instinctively. Using what slack she had, she lunged for it. She missed once and slammed in hard the second time. The crew's grip slipped and both ropes sagged, but the second she released hers, Calem bounded up. She winced every time his body struck the ship's rocking side.

She couldn't cling to the ladder for long; its narrow boards were meant for calm waters—used in tandem with ropes and pulleys to hold someone in place while inspecting *Islaw*.

The current tugged at her as a wave built up. She glanced up—Calem was nearly over the railing. She could wait, hoping her grip would hold, or take her chance.

There was no real choice: either the ocean would rip her away, or she'd let go on her terms. The wave tugged at her; she released, her fingers tearing free from the ladder as the current whipped her backward and flung her onto the ship. Pain meant nothing as she tumbled across the deck, her body crashing and scraping along the floor, rising just as Calem was lowered onto the deck.

"Get us out of here!" she yelled to anyone who would listen from the top deck where she'd landed. But they were already on it. *Islaw'r Tonau* jolted as it turned. A small part of her registered Lachlan and Alric climbing onto the lower deck by Calem, with Gwen stumbling behind. Relief, mixed with guilt for forgetting her quad, flickered through her.

Eira scrambled, falling down the stairs and slipping on her knees toward Calem as she tore off her mask and pack. Gwen arrived before her, hands hovering over Calem's body, assessing him. *Llyranite* encased him almost entirely, sparing only his chest and right shoulder. Gwen leaned in close, cheek by his face, then tilted his head back and pressed her lips to his. *Kissing* him.

"What are you doing?" Eira demanded, shoving Gwen aside and pulling a short-tipped knife from its sheath in her suit pocket.

Gwen, undeterred by Eira's shouting or the knife nearly grazing her cheek, leaned back over Calem. She placed her hands on the exposed part of his chest and pressed down repeatedly. With each compression, blood pooled thicker around Calem. Eira's eyes darted, her dread mounting as the volume of it all sank in.

"He's bleeding! You need to stop the bleeding!" Another wave crashed over the ship, but Eira barely noticed. She gripped her knife and began hacking at the *llyranite*.

"Stop!" Gwen broke from her rhythm to slap Eira's hand away. Furious, Eira snatched up her knife and shifted to the other side, out of Gwen's reach.

"I thought you were a healer!" Eira yelled, slicing a piece by Calem's shoulder and tossing it aside. "HEAL HIM!"

"I AM!" Gwen snapped back, matching her intensity. "But he needs air first. Oxygen. And if you keep cutting away what's likely holding him together, Eira, *you'll* be the one who kills him."

The knife clattered from her hand, "He's...I–".

"Get her out of here," Gwen ordered, and, surprisingly, the crew obeyed. Rough hands seized Eira's arms, pulling her back. She fought, insisting she had to stay with Calem, but she was drained and their grip was unbreakable.

Everything inside her shattered. She was exhausted; the pain of the last few hours was nothing. Even the storm fading as they sailed away was mute.

All she saw was Calem, his chest unmoving, his face pale, his eyes shut tight, wounds from the *llyranite* criss-crossing his body—and the spreading pool of red beneath.

Her week without Calem had been tormenting, but seeing him like this was infinitely worse. He was here, exactly where she wanted him, yet not here at all—and she could do nothing about it. Her helplessness was infuriating. What was one supposed to do when nothing could be done? When the very person who guided her every action now lay unmoving?

When that person might be dying because of something as senseless as *love*. *Why* did he have to love her? *Why* did he let himself fall into its snare?

Soaked to the bone, with seawater still clinging to her skin, tears Eira didn't bother to stop flowed freely.

A guard was placed outside her door, trapping her below deck while Calem fought for life above. All because of her. She wasn't even allowed by his side.

Perhaps that was best. She caused this. This was her fault.

All she could manage was to curl into herself, much like Lyra had what felt so long ago, and whisper Calem's name over and over.

Nothing else registered—not food, sleep, her own body's needs, nor the words of those around her. Everything felt muted; she was powerless, and so she became nothing. And nothing needs nothing to survive.

She didn't even notice when they docked in a new port town; not until Gwen's boots appeared in her downcast gaze, shadowed outlines against the floor. Gwen, who had worked the chase just as tirelessly as she had—for the first time—and then spent hours saving Calem. Gwen's voice was the only thing that pulled Eira's focus, faintly lifting her from the fog. But as she looked up, the first thing she felt was her stomach churning, the urge to hurl rising.

Calem's blood covered Gwen, seeping into her suit in dark stains against dark fabric. Eira couldn't bear the sight. Her stomach lurched uncontrollably, choking her as she doubled over, coughing up its contents.

Gwen manoeuvred around the sick and stacks of *cochdraenite*-stuck boxes to reach the corner where Eira had barricaded herself. She slumped beside Eira, her head knocking against the wall as her eyes closed.

"He's with the town's healers," she began. Eira wiped her mouth in silence, avoiding Gwen's gaze. "We got him breathing again." Silence followed. Eira sensed what was coming and knew she could do nothing to stop it. *Nothing does nothing.*

"The *llyranite* was wound so tightly around him; I couldn't tell if it was holding him together and keeping him alive." Eira waited for the inevitable "but." It was coming, and she had no idea what she'd do when it did.

"When the healers took over, I stayed with him. They found his trapped arm positioned—squashed—across his stomach." Gwen reached forward, taking Eira's chin and turning her face to meet her eyes. "The *llyranite* pierced his arm, not his stomach."

Her heartbeat was steady and slow, as if it remembered it was nothing—nothing had no heartbeat, so it should just stop or at least be quiet.

Eira didn't understand. "I think I'd like you to get to the point, Gwen." Her voice came out husky and raw, broken.

Gwen tilted her head, forcing herself into Eira's line of sight. The concern and fatigue plastered across Gwen's face meant nothing to her. Eira felt almost disgusted with herself. Almost.

Gwen's jaw tightened. "He is breathing. His arm protected his internal organs. The *llyranite* did not pierce his stomach—not in a debilitating way. Those are good things, Eira. But." *There it was.* "He was in the water too long. The pressure at those depths and the speed of his descent and ascent were too much for a *Di-Byth*."

My fault again. Eira clenched her teeth, forcing herself to hold her breath. It was better than the ragged gasps she couldn't control. She held the tears back this time, focusing instead on the pain of not breathing.

"And?"

"He remains unconscious. What happens next depends on him—his body, his mind, and how they handle the stress." Gwen rolled her shoulders, twice forward, once back, then stood, taking a shaky breath. "Solem will take you to him when you're ready."

Eira was off the ground before Gwen finished speaking. She wasn't sure if she was ready to see him—to watch him suffer—but she *had* to go. The pull toward him eclipsed every other thought and feeling. If she could just reach him, that was something. She didn't have to do nothing, wouldn't be nothing.

Solem waited outside the door, his face stern and lined with worry, his hands clenching and unclenching. Their eyes met briefly when he saw Eira emerge, and he turned to lead the way. Her steps faltered as the weight of Gwen's actions hit her, grounding her in a moment of sudden awareness.

Gwen wiped her face of tears. Her short chestnut waves, usually swept back, had turned to half-dried, wild ringlets—a frizzed chaos. Eira composed herself long enough to turn back and place a hand on Gwen's shoulder.

"Thank you, Gwen," she murmured, pouring all her remaining feelings into the words. Tears welled again in Gwen's eyes, and a small, sad smile emerged, accepting everything Eira couldn't say.

With a final glance at Gwen, Eira raced after Solem.

Eira stood in the doorway, a thin barrier between Calem and the world of the living. Everything around her was colourless, dull, and unnoticeable. She didn't remember the route Solem led her down, the building they entered, or whether she'd opened this door herself or if it had already stood open. It was all meaningless, fading into nothingness—except for Calem.

Calem's body was the only touch of colour in her world, yet even that was fading fast. The deep brown of his hair, once as warm and rich as mahogany, now muted; his curls flattened, the colour dull as weathered and untreated wood. His tanned skin was pale, his face drained of warmth, heat, and light.

He just lay there, still and silent. Breathing ragged, disrupted, agonizingly soft breaths, as if each one might be the last, his body almost entirely swathed in bandages. A bland beige blanket covered him, concealing the worst of his wounds—but Eira knew.

"Calem," she whispered, her eyes burning as they filled with tears. Eira's three calming breaths came out shallow. She almost preferred the familiar pain of holding them in, but Solem had told her to talk to him, to let him know she was there, which meant she needed air.

Her legs felt limp as soggy noodles, barely able to carry her as she stepped inside. The scent of medical antiseptics mingled with the unmistakable iron tang of Calem's blood—a smell she would never forget—lingered heavily in the air. She willed herself to his side, where his one uninjured arm lay over the blanket, his hand—that so often made an excuse to hold hers—now lined with scratches.

"Calem," she choked out again, dismissing the chair beside his low bed and sinking to her knees instead. She took his hand in hers, deliberately choosing, for the first time, to be the one reaching for him. Leaning in, with her upper body resting on the bed and knees pressing into the hard ground, she let her head settle against his arm, gingerly squeezing his hand.

Tears returned, and she cared little for any onlookers who might see. She cried, allowing herself to embrace vulnerability she had never shown before. Her face flushed as salty water— not from the ocean—streamed down, soaking Calem's arm. For the first time in her life, she wasn't afraid to reveal her tears and emotional scars. She could acknowledge that all her past pain paled in comparison to this current agony. And it was the first time she realized that every past hurt had been worth it as long as Calem had been by her side.

This was why she'd stood up to Owain and the other bullies all those years ago. She'd seen Calem, who, like everyone in the *Ysgol'Sâl*, had been sent by their wealthy parents to save their futures. To build their immunity so that when they inevitably fell in love, they'd survive whatever life threw at them.

No one cared that the schools were deteriorating, failing in more ways than one. It wasn't just sickness they faced; creatures—

likely taken from the *Tir'pergl Plains*—tormented them in the night, friends turned on each other for scraps of comfort, and bullies took out their frustration on anyone weaker.

On her first day at the intermixed *Ysgol'Sâl*, fourteen-year-old Eira saw a boy—Calem—mid-beating, and it ignited a fire within her. She couldn't restrain herself, rushing in to stop the injustice. She had no idea how they fought them all—she barely remembered the fight itself—only that her goal was getting to this boy and ensuring he was alright. And then, when she reached him, he smiled at her—after being beaten. It was the first genuine smile she'd seen at the *Ysgol'Sâl* in all her years of attending.

After that, people claimed Calem followed her around like a puppy. Now she saw they were wrong. It had always been her following him, needing him and his smiles that shone through any pain.

"Smile for me one more time, Calem. Please."

Over the years, something had diminished his smiles. With new insight from what he revealed before everything fell apart, Eira realized his smiles must have faded when he knew he loved her. He'd hidden his emotions, not wanting anyone to find out he was *Dy-Byth* and tear him from her. Eira cursed herself for being so blind.

Time slipped by until all that was left of Eira were red, puffy eyes, dried tear streaks on her cheeks, and hair—once secured in its braided crown—-now loose, a mass of tangled flyaways. Her grip on Calem's hand was loose, and she reached to pull the chair closer with her other hand. It was low, like the bed—a design choice in case patients rolled off. Settling down, she pulled her legs up, crossing them so they rested half on the bed and half on the chair.

"Why did you take us into that storm? Why risk it?"

"Surely you know by now?" Solem's voice startled Eira, making her knees bump against Calem's arm. She winced, fearing the motion might hurt him, but he remained unperturbed, unmoving. "He did it for you, Eira. Every bit of it was always for you."

Solem entered, carrying a small pitcher of water.

"But *why*? Why that storm? Why didn't we wait? There's *always* another one."

"The nurse says he needs water." Solem ignored her question. "Care to help?" He brought the pitcher to the other side of the bed as Eira nodded. Even without an answer, Eira resolved to do all she could to help Calem. She couldn't let him down again.

Eira moved onto the bed as if to lift Calem. Solem shook his head.

"He cannot drink—not how we'd like, at least." He pulled out a short stick with a green sponge on the end from behind the pitcher. Eira's hands hovered over Calem, half relieved they didn't have to move him, half terrified at what it meant if a *Di-Byth* couldn't even drink water. Solem dipped the sponge into the pitcher, squeezed off the excess, and handed it to her.

"Roll the sponge gently over his lips—keep them moist, keep them from drying. That's all we can do." He gestured for her to begin. Still on the bed, Eira delicately brought the sponge to his lips and rolled it across. There was no movement, no stirring as the cool water made contact. Trembling, Eira continued, watching a few drops slip between his parted lips.

"That's enough. The nurse says to do that whenever it looks like he needs it." Solem took the sponge from Eira's trembling hands and set it on the table beside the pitcher. Eira's eyes bore into him.

"Solem…*why*?"

He sighed. As Eira looked at him, she noticed his eyes were redder than usual—a small, unwanted spark of colour in her otherwise colourless world.

"He couldn't wait any longer to tell you how he felt. He knew the storm was coming, and he thought if he gathered enough *llyranite*, the earnings—along with his savings—would be enough. Enough to give the crew an extended break while he tried to convince you to take another path. Anything else would have been safer than being a Chaser. He wanted time with you, simply to *be*.

"And he hoped that, with time, you'd understand. That you'd no longer want to go back to *Islaw'r Tonau*—or any other ship—if he could find something you liked more, something more enticing. He dreamed that you might want him more than his ship one day.

"And if his hopes proved fruitful, he wanted the crew taken care of until we could find someone to replace you both." Solem gently touched Calem's head, smoothing his limp curls before he stood. "Eira, he just wanted to be with you and offer you a life free from pain. Calem would never force you into it—he just thought you might try, if he told you it was something he wanted. That storm was intended to be his last." His voice lowered, hitching as he murmured, "And I suppose, intended or not, it was."

Solem's large, dark hand, stark against Calem's pale face, lifted as he left the room. Denied the opportunity to ask more, Eira was left with the undeniable truth: he had known everything all along.

Cautiously, she resumed her place beside him, her hand gripping his and knees touching his arm as she leaned close to his face. Her other hand found his hair. She hadn't realized his tangled hair's softness, even with the few dried specks of blood missed during cleaning. Eira ran her hands through, over and over, untangling every last strand with each pass.

Of all the pain she'd known, this was the worst—and there was nothing she could do. This pain would not fade with time.

"You've tried for a long time, haven't you, Calem? Tried to get me to leave the crew and *Islaw'r Tonau*. I thought you were joking—as if you knew as well as I there could be no other life. The thrill of it. The joy of providing a lifesource for others.

"Except, you weren't joking. I misread you, Calem. I'm sorry. You wanted a different life—planned for it. And now, I can't imagine any life worth living if you're not there." Eira let out a dry, disbelieving laugh, wiping her eyes on her shoulder so she wouldn't have to stop holding him.

"I sound like those *Di-Byth* idiots I loathe. Except you're one of them—*Hirwel*, you're one of them. And you are *certainly* an idiot." Another maniacal laugh escaped. *But I don't care anymore.*

Her back ached from her hunched posture, but she straightened, bringing both hands to cover his.

"You've always been here, Calem. You say I rescued you that day? You're wrong—you rescued me. Without you, I would have grown sour and bitter against the world—well, *more* sour and bitter. You showed me…" Eira hesitated, voice catching before letting the word flow freely, "Love. You showed me love. What it could mean—not how I thought I saw it in the world.

"Love was never a weakness for you. It didn't change who you were. It didn't stop you from doing what needed to be done. Love never made you soft or weak. Calem, I think it made you the strongest person I've ever known.

"No one else could remain *Captain* of a *Chaser* ship, knowing full well they might *actually* die at any moment. No one." Her body trembled. "Who in their right mind would do that? Only you. Calem, you fool. You incredible, self-sacrificing, patient, ever-loving fool."

With her nose dripping, Eira sniffed, unable to stop the tears—or the smile that came with them this time. She laughed as she cried.

"I think I'm going crazy." She kept wiping her cheeks and nose, but the tears wouldn't stop. "Calem, you make me crazy."

Ignoring the pain flaring in her back, she leaned forward, eyes closed, and rested her forehead against Calem's.

"I think I understand now," she whispered, hoping he could feel her words through their connected foreheads. "What it means. It's not fleeting. It's not only there in the good times—when you're the 'happiest you've ever been'. It's stronger in shared pain. It grows. It's not a fall; it's a slow, simmering pot that boils over until you can't stop it. It's not bad. It doesn't make you weak. And it is okay to feel."

Her heartbeat increased, and her eyes opened enough to see his still, pale face. Of all the pressure building inside her, there was a minuscule pinprick of release; a small hole had been punctured, gradually releasing the air.

Her tears stopped. She wiped away the drops that had fallen onto Calem, still with a gentle smile on her face.

"I'm sorry, Calem. I'm sorry I waited for you to die to realize it. I'm not afraid anymore." She paused, "Well…no, I'm *terrified*. But I'm not afraid to say it." Her aching back solidified her resolve, and the words came as easily as her *Di-Os* body would once have healed. "Calem, I love you."

The pressure slowly easing exploded, releasing a rush of air that lifted the crushing weight from her chest.

"I love you, Calem. I need you. Live, please, Calem. Live so I can tell you and see the light in your eyes. I don't care about the scars. I don't even care if you can't walk. I just want you to live so I can tell you. Live so I can see your smile. It's been hidden for too long. Please."

Eira repeated the words, thinking that if she said them enough times—once for every day she'd known him, once for every time he'd wanted to say them to her but never did—he would hear her. He had to. If he would only let it, if he knew, he'd will himself to wake up.

He did not.

Solem came and went, accompanied by nurses who tended to Calem's needs—refilling his water, wiping his face, and setting out food for Eira. She did as they asked: adjusting Calem to prevent bedsores and checking his wounds, all while holding him. Every word, every action was centred on repeating those three words. Even in her sleep, she never let go, curled up on the bed beside him, and told him.

Days passed with no change. Whenever the nurses grew skeptical, Eira tossed money at them. As long as he was breathing, Calem would stay here, and they would try. Until he *knew*.

Every night, Eira slept beside him. On rare nights, her dreams were filled with her expressing love for him and hearing him say it back. More often, nightmares haunted her—visions of him never waking, of him dying over and over, and her inability to stop it.

A pressure she thought was long gone shocked her awake. Her eyes snapped open, locking onto Calem's closed lids. No movement. It was dark and quiet—like the deep ocean. Eira shifted, her hand tightening around his.

"Beneath the waves, Calem. Our calm place, returning to us even here. Just you and I, and silence. Remember? Remember, I love you." Her eyes fluttered shut again, and the pressure returned as she drifted. This time, it had come from her hand. When she looked down, her hand was heavy, drained of energy, resting beneath Calem's.

Beneath?

His hand tightened. Eira bolted upright. "Calem?"

There was no response. Her shoulders slumped, eyes fixed on their joined hands. "Calem, I love you." A weak squeeze returned. Hope surged through her. She repeated it. He squeezed again. Every time she said it, he squeezed back. He was there. He knew.

Hope ignited faster than lightning. She resolved never to stop telling him how much she loved him. Whatever came next, he knew. Eira fell asleep whispering her truth, squeezing back every time his hand squeezed hers.

Born in South Africa and now living in Canada, Shannon Nell is captivated by the magic of storytelling. As a lifelong fantasy fan, she finds inspiration in worlds of adventure, wonder, and epic magic systems. When not tucked away lost in a book, Shannon loves to travel and appreciate the beauty around her through photography.

A central theme of many vampire stories that being a vampire is a deeply hollow experience. Vampires are tortured creatures whose eternal life and unearthly beauty mask a lonely soul. For all its superficial appeal, to be a vampire is to suffer a gilded curse, and those afflicted yearn for the restoration of their humanity.

This never made sense to me. I would trade "being able to book a dental appointment during normal hours" for "eternal life and supernatural prowess" one-billion percent of the time, thank you very much, and I suspect I'm not alone. Hell, the world is full of people with chronic medical conditions far more damning than literary vampirism, and their reactions are not nearly as universally depressing. Many of them go on to accomplish great things, enjoy the time they have, and fall in love.

vAMP is a story of two people who don't know how much time they have left, but who want to spend it together. I hope you enjoy reading it as much as I enjoyed writing it.

Taylor Calder

by Taylor Calder
For my Doki

Six months into her infection Six months into her infection and Victoria still hates the smell of blood.

It's just after eight in the morning in France, and her client is telling her the exact size that items should be on the storefront page. Enough to fit columns of three in a standard browser window. Does she get that? Columns of three.

"Oui," she says, "oui." She lets them do most of the talking as a rule so they won't pick up on her accent, but right now she can barely speak at all. She is in the bathroom burning down to ash, or so it feels. She's afraid she's going to drop the phone. Or crush it.

Keep it together Victoria, she tells herself. You really need the money.

She tears the cap off the blood bag with her teeth. There it is, that metallic smell. It drips down her fingers. Revolting.

She tilts her head back and begins to drink. The virus's grip on her loosens as she does. Muscles relaxing, mind clearing, vAMP downregulating.

Relief.

Someone asks if she is perhaps having a morning glass of wine, to a chorus of mild French laughter.

Victoria returns it. Her teeth stained red. She tells them she missed her morning espresso and is doubling her dose to catch up. Not that it's espresso hour for her, either; it's just after two in the morning here in her Cabbagetown walk-up. They laugh again, but she curses at herself. She knows nothing of the coffee culture in France. They might not even drink espresso.

The white-hot edge of paranoia presses against her neck. Any inconsistency could lead to her getting reported, and getting reported would lead to a lifetime of experimentation at best, and at worst…

Images from the Hive chat come to her. Bodies mutilated, burnt to structural distortion, mouths open in permanent screams. Above the corpses, a sign reminds the staff that any suspicious activity among family or colleagues must be reported. The bottom corner features an image of a syringe over what could be either a maple leaf or a stylized flame – the logo for SOQA, the Southern Ontario Quarantine Authority. In one of them you could even see Commandant Todde, the province's interim leader and most valiant anti-vAMP crusader, giving the thumbs up to a pile of freshly-burned corpses.

Victoria sucks the blood from her fingers as quietly as she can while six thousand kilometers away, the committee discusses their choice of font. They have always liked Helvetica, they say.

Of course, she tells them in French. Licks crusting blood from the corners of her lips. Of course.

The call ends and her knees buckle inward. She hits the sink on the way down, and her shower, but it doesn't hurt the way it's supposed to. The way it used to.

They're getting more frequent, she thinks. The attacks. Until a week ago she'd been able to preempt them; one unit of packed red blood cells every twenty-eight hours and she'd be relatively symptom free. A little bit of the rage other vAMPs sometimes talked about online, but she told herself that was just a byproduct of her isolation. She would even watch part of a sunrise sometimes, without the full-body shutdown others had. She had stopped that, though. The idea of sitting up with a cup of tea, watching the sky pass through all the colors of blood, only to find that it was her last, was enough to put her off the idea forever.

She wonders how much time she has left, before she reaches Stage IV. Enough time to live, to travel, to paint? She's never even been to France.

Work mode, she thinks. You need to work. You can brood later.

Sitting in front of her MacBook, uncompleted projects staring back at her, Victoria puts her glasses on and her auburn hair up in a pony-tail, what she considers 'work mode'. That means no distractions, no pouting, no Sophia, no Hive. Although she allows herself one last chance to check for a text.

Zero messages.

That's fine, she tells herself. Perfectly fine. It's only been two days. A perfectly reasonable amount of time to pass without your girlfriend talking to you, especially since they had fought the last time they spoke. Not that it took much to push Sophia over the edge lately. She blamed it on medical school, long shifts, burnout. And yet she had time to spend with another clerk named Mandy. "Just hanging out," she had said. Victoria, who suffered a permanent kink in her neck from gazing at her feet in public, didn't understand how Sophia could make so close a friend so easily, without any other intent. But then again things seemed to come easily for Sophia. She had accepted her condition as a vAMP with greater ease than Victoria has ever known among the newly sired.

"It sucks," she had said. "It's awful. But this is my life now, and all I can do is make the most of it."

The most of it.

The viscera of several half-assembled websites lay before her. Graphics and code, annotated notes, a series of potential styles she had sketched up for a client in Nice. The client had hated them, had insisted Victoria redo them within a thirty-six hour timeframe. When she informed them, politely but firmly, that that was simply not a realistic request, although she would be more than happy to resubmit the designs in perhaps a week's time, they had yelled at her. Called her work sloppy, her professionalism lacking.

You are sloppy, she thinks. You are unprofessional. But it's not your fault you have to work these stupid hours. You didn't choose to get infected like some vAMP chaser. And it wouldn't be such a big deal if Sophia would just answer her texts. The SOQA could have busted her, she could be one of those charred bodies, so would it be so unduly arduous for her to call to call to call to...

Raising her fingers from the keyboard. vAMP, she thinks. That's not you, that's the vAMP. Don't let it take you, don't let it make you forget who you are. Not yet.

She takes her ponytail down and makes a cup of tea. Work mode can wait.

Calmed by the aura of her steeped Earl Grey, Victoria loads her encryption network and navigates herself to the Hive. This week's password is sanguine2.

<l'etranger> anyone else feeling down tonight?
<bloodspike> you mean EVERY NIGHT???
<bloodspike> yes :P
<l'etranger> hah
<l'etranger> i guess i meant more than normal
<miko> me
<miko> i saw my mom the other day across the street
<miko> i wanted 2 run up and hug her soooooo bad
<miko> but i had 2 keep walking... :(
Victoria types her reply.
<ladylasouris> That's awful miko
<ladylasouris> I know you miss her terribly
<bloodspike> hey lady
<miko> yeah i do
<miko> especially when im here
Miko, Victoria knows, is fourteen. Like most people with vAMP her age she's been forced into squalid living conditions. She shares a trailer somewhere in the Midwest with six other people, five of them much older men. All of them are infected. Victoria has been very careful not to ask for additional details.

<l'etranger> the cops did another sweep out here
<l'etranger> lost a couple friends
<l'etranger> shit's awful
#SireMe has entered #thehive

<SireMe> Hello

<SireMe> I'm looking for an Old Blood in the Washington State area to initiate me into your Beautiful Kind

<SireMe> Please I NEED it

#SireMe has left #thehive (Reason: lolbanned)

<bloodspike> fukin vamp chasers.........

<bloodspike> this is a gift for the chosen buddy not for losers LOL

A lo-fi fragment of Charles Aznavour plays over the grunt of a motor, the sound of plastic thumping against her MacBook's frame.

She has a text. From Sophia.

<ladylasouris> Um

<ladylasouris> I don't mean to cause a fuss but

<ladylasouris> I think I need some help

She reads the texts from Sophia's number again.

> I need you to text me the name of our blood supplier again

> Sorry I lost it lol

There's three things wrong with it. Sophia never uses capital letters, Sophia never says lol, and Sophia knows exactly who their supplier is: Sophia herself. The phone's casing cracks under her grip, but she can't control it. It's the vAMP's rage, not hers. Viral products hijacking her nervous system, making her erratic. She hates it. She hates hates HATES…

Blood, she thinks. I need blood.

A hinge comes loose when she opens the fridge door. Fumbling the bag, she finally tears into it, biting into the side like a wolf killing some small prey. She drinks the bag without breathing. When it's dry she runs her tongue over her lips.

Something has happened to Sophia.

Surviving as a vAMP, Victoria's first mentor had taught her, requires a certain amount of paranoia. With roving packs of slayers out to hunt you, government shadow troops hired specifically to track you, and a huge public information campaign architected to paint you as a ticking time bomb, it's best to assume that the worst has happened and will continue to happen. Her mentor had been a woman named Toni who had once worked as a school librarian. They lived together for a month following Victoria's sireing, until she came home one day to find the door to their apartment forced open. Victoria left and never went back. She never did find out what happened to Toni.

And now Sophia has vanished. She would never have sent that text. And if she hadn't sent it, then someone else had.

<miko> OMG

<miko> I'M SO SORRY :(

<miko> she seemed sooo nice

<ladylasouris> Miko we don't know what's happened to her yet

<ladylasouris> So let's be positive, okay?

<ladylasouris> She could be fine

<shard_of_porcelain> hav u been to her plac?

<ladylasouris> No I just received the text now

<l'etranger> ladylasouris, i'm sorry to say this but….

<l'etranger> well, let's occum's razor this, shall we?

<l'etranger> normally when one of us goes missing or stops responding it's because we've been caught

<l'etranger> either by the authorities or some rogue hunter

<ancestralcoven> Is there some place she was supposed to be tonight?

<ladylasouris> She said she had a shift in the emergency department

<ladylasouris> I think I'm going to be sick

Victoria met Sophia two months ago in the dangerous minutes before dawn. She was stumbling down the middle of the road in dirty scrubs, carrying a neon-pink backpack, clinging to the straps like that would stop her from falling. The newly infected are easy to spot once you've lived the process yourself. By the time you realize you're affected it's too late, your bodily systems are already losing the fight against a hostile takeover. Victoria dropped her groceries and ran to her. Sophia was unresponsive. "Oh dear," she had said out loud. "Okay, um, okay."

She carried Sophia on her back all the way to her third-floor walk_up, chased by the rising Sun.

With the blackout curtains drawn, she watched this enigmatic tanned woman snore in her bed. Sophia's legs were strong and smooth and she slept with her mouth slightly open. When she didn't wake after five hours, Victoria tilted the girl's head up and attempted to feed her.

Sophia awoke in an unfamiliar bed, to the image of a mousey red-head pouring human blood products down her throat while trying desperately not to blush.

She kicked Victoria off the mattress. And then, after cleaning up the mess that she had made, Victoria gave Sophia the talk.

There's still a faint stain, near the foot of her twin mattress. Sophia makes fun of it whenever she comes over, but never for long, and she always liked how close Sophia held her at night. What could she do? The text was a trap, surely. Sophia's family was across the country. The only other student she knew was Mandy, and Victoria had zero interest in speaking to her. So what else was there to do, other than check in on Sophia herself?

<ladylasouris> I'm going to her place

<ladylasouris> a +

<l'etranger> wait hear me out

She logs off, checks the time on her cracked screen. Almost two-thirty. She has three hours left until sunrise.

Grabbing her bag, she runs down the stairs into what's left of the night.

"The school gets it," Sophia had told her one night. "They know that SOQA is bullshit. There's other clerks that have gotten it, and they have a safe supply system in place."

"Is that how you get our blood?"

She didn't answer. At the time Victoria had assumed she had asked something foolish, but now she wondered. "Don't worry," Sophia had said, pulling Victoria closer. She could feel the thin layer of sweat on her skin. It was always odd to see their naked skin juxtaposed. Sophia's mother was the color of tea with milk in it. Victoria was just milk, even before the vAMP photosensitivity.

"I'll try, but…"

Sophia snored. Victoria smiled and kissed her forehead. "Dors bien," she said.

The city uses every opportunity to remind Victoria how scared it is of her.

The streetcar is lined with ads for SOQA. A silhouette of a spook in riot gear, and the message that lethal force is authorized for infected individuals not compliant with quarantine regulations. A stock image of a smiling nurse, her teeth artificially white, encouraging individuals to please report any friends or family with symptoms of vAMP. A young child playing in a pile of leaves, a fanged specter with glowing red eyes lurking in the background, a single line of text – Will You Let Her Have a Future? An awful design, the proportions off and the emphasis unclear.

She sits at the back, as far as possible from the only other passenger in the car. A woman in a business suit, tired. Victoria tries her best to look bored and not terrified. She's forgotten how much paler she is than normal people, how much more vibrant they seem. All that blood just under their skin. The woman taps her nails on her phone. She laughs.

Victoria tries not to look at the ads. They're a constant reminder of how this will end. Even if she avoids incineration, the average life expectancy of someone with vAMP is less than three years. Paris, she thinks. You need to make it to Paris once before you, well…

Whispers. The woman in heels is speaking to the conductor, discreetly pointing at Victoria, or so she thinks.

Oh God. She knows.

Victoria palms the railing to get off at the next stop. The streetcar skips it, picking up speed. The woman is still, trying to resist the urge to look back at Victoria. But it's obvious. It's so obvious obvious OBVIOUS…

No. Don't let it do that to you. Don't let the panic drive you into a frenzy, turn you into the animal they think you are.

Out, she thinks. Seizing the reins of control from the vAMP. I need out now. She palms the stop button. "Excuse me, but you missed my stop."

The streetcar continues on, as though she's a ghost.

He called them. SOQA. They're coming for her. The black tactical vans, troops in gas masks with UV batons. The woman in heels is breathing quickly, and if she's breathing quickly then she's scared, and if she's scared her heart is beating fast too.

That swift pulse of blood. Kick *kick*. Kick *kick*.

"Pardon me," she shouts. "But I'm going to need to exit the streetcar. Could you please open the doors for me?"

Silence. The street car is slowing. SOQA must be waiting. You idiot, she thinks. If they think there's a vAMP on board they'll torch the entire car with you and Miss Heels still inside.

"I'm sorry," Victoria says. "But for my sake as much as yours, I am going to have to insist on exiting the vehicle."

Victoria kicks the rear door. And again. On the third it falls away and she is out, in the middle of traffic. A Honda honks and brakes too late, its front nacelle crumbling on her thigh, sending Victoria to the ground. She hears a door open. Once they realize she's not dead they swear at her.

Victoria stands slowly, the headlights impaling her. "Jesus," he says, reaching for his phone. "She's a…"

Flashbacks to her school days, to the snickers of her fellow students when she stuttered through presentations. To the impossible weight of the spotlight. "Sorry," she says. "I…I'm sorry about your car."

She limps away, coat trailing behind her. For a moment she feels her lip quiver, but there's no time for that now. You just need a drink to calm you down and it'll be fine. Fine. Everything will be okay.

A semi blares its horn and swerves to cut her off, but she scrambles over the cab. The driver freezes as she scales the windshield. It tries to reverse but it's too slow. Victoria leaps over a chain-link fence and scurries into an alley to the growing sound of sirens.

Feet dangling from a fire escape, Victoria drinks from a travel container she had once used for her morning commute tea. The only sirens are the normal ambient noise of the city, and the only heartbeat is her own. But that's not what's on her mind. What's on her mind is that she, a woman who has never actually seen the inside of a gym except to pee, minutes ago made an eight-foot vertical leap over an eighteen wheeler.

The vAMP is getting worse, weaving itself tighter into the fibers of her muscles. Sophia once told her that increases in physical capability were the hallmark of Stage II, and that Stage II was when the disease pumped into overdrive. On the wards she had seen people die within months.

So you better find Sophia soon, she thinks, using all her available mental faculties to push thoughts of her prognosis away. That's all that matters tonight.

Wanting to see how far she can push herself, Victoria steps off the side of the fire escape, the air cutting across her face as she falls eight stories to the ground.

vAMP fills an ecological role that's obvious even to Victoria. As Sophia had once explained, most viruses have effects on the body ranging from negligible to life-threatening, stripping their host of resources while hijacking its cellular machinery to propagate itself. But vAMP does something else, it makes you stronger, faster, a fortress for the virus. It changes the structure of your muscle fibers, invades your immune system, even adds its own signaling pathway, which is where the name came from.

There's an intracellular signaling molecule in the body called cAMP. The 'c' stands for cyclic, a description of its chemical shape. The variant created by the virus has a configuration that changes under different conditions. The name they gave it was variable-AMP.

vAMP.

In front of Victoria is a set of glass doors, and beyond them is a second set of glass doors protected by a keycode, and beyond them is the lobby of Sophia's condo building. Inside that lobby is a desk where the nighttime concierge sits, eyes on his phone. If he sees Victoria trying to muster the energy to speak to him he doesn't seem to care, which is not an atypical response for her.

Hi! Sorry, I forgot my key, could you let me in?

No, that's stupid, he's going to ask your name and then what? Do you lie and say you're Sophia? What if he knows her?

Hi! I'm here to meet Sophia in twelve-seventeen. Could you buzz me in?

What if he knows she's not there? What if he saw SOQA come for her?

Hi! I'm sorry to bother you but Sophia from twelve-seventeen is in the hospital. Is it okay if I go grab some of her stuff? She gave me her key but not the front building code.

That could maybe work, or…

A young couple passes her and walk into the building. Victoria follows them, trying to act as normal as a pale woman with blood-tinged teeth can, but it seems to work. The woman's partner even holds the door open for her and motions her ahead, smiling. The concierge doesn't look up from his phone.

The three of them wait ten thousand years for the elevator to arrive. When the couple exits Victoria sits down in the middle of the elevator, head buried deep in her arms, as it rises all the way up to Sophia's floor.

She opens the door and she is home. A sacred place where no harm can come to her. She is in Sophia's apartment, with Sophia's geometrically perfected boxes of cereal and Sophia's open lacrosse bag and Sophia's waving porcelain cat.

She closes the door. It's cold. "Sophia?" She slips off her shoes and steps inside. "Are you home?"

It's cold. The balcony window is open. One pair of shoes are missing, the runners she wears to run errands. "Sophia?" No response. The bedroom is empty and the bed is made. The toilet is flushed. The bathroom sink is a hovel of skincare products. There's a prescription for a medication prednisolone, which Victoria has never heard of, and a half-full tube of toothpaste. There's no overturned furniture, no spilled blood to indicate a battle. Just an empty apartment and an open window.

She drops her bag. On the fridge is a sticky note – BUY TICKETS FOR SWITZERLAND. Switzerland? Neither she nor Sophia held a great affinity for clockwork or chocolate. Inside the fridge is half an apple and a bottle of a dreadful Austrian rosé that Sophia loves, in defiance of all good taste.

She tucks her feet under her on the couch, continuing to indulge the over-sweet wine. She calls Sophia again, hoping her phone is somewhere in the apartment, but the only tone she hears is her own. Where could she have gone? The hospital? She had persisted in doing night shifts in emerg, refusing to let SOQA stand in the way of her ultimate dream of becoming a cardiologist. But even if SOQA caught her they wouldn't have sent those texts from her phone. She wants to believe that Sophia was too smart to get cornered by slayers. Really, really wants to.

She finishes the wine. She needs to pee. Switzerland, she thinks. Why Switzerland? She knows little about it, other than that it shares a border with France.

A slab of memory falls on her in the bathroom. Victoria was sitting on this toilet when Sophia had first told Victoria about her theory of 'vAMP-time', approximately a million years ago. "France is a vAMP haven," Sophia had said while brushing her teeth. She scratched the back of her leg with her foot. "We should go there. Maybe they'll take refuge students. I heard that someone in the class did that with Ireland, got a direct transfer into the medical program somewhere. They were a national, but still."

Boarding a commercial flight was a fun fantasy, but a fantasy nonetheless. But that wasn't the part of it that seemed the most unrealistic to Victoria.

"You want to move to another continent with someone you've only dated for a month?"

"Someone who speaks the language." She spit toothpaste. "No pressure though."

"No, I'd like to, but it just seems rather fast. I'm afraid you would…"

"You're not accounting for vAMP time."

"Pardon me?"

"vAMP time is compressed. By a factor of four due to the imminent danger that we live in, what I call the carpe-diem factor. And then by a factor of five due to physiological differences." By that Sophia meant that they died sooner. "That means we've been dating a total of twenty vAMP months. So what I'm trying to say is that you really dropped the ball on my anniversary gift."

"They'll make fun of my accent."

"You'll be lucky if that's what they choose to make fun of." She spit again. "Whatever they choose, I'll be there to perform elective maxillofacial surgery when they do." She cracked her knuckles.

"What will they make fun of, exactly?"

"Mostly how strange you look. 'Look at her, her skin is so clear, untarnished by nicotine stains and ennui. And is that deodorant I smell?'"

Victoria pushed her glasses up her nose. "Such a barbarian. That's not at all what it's like there."

"Good thing I'll have you to show me around then. A starving artist like you, you'll fit right in."

There, on Sophia's toilet, Victoria finally allows herself a few tears. But only a few.

As she washes her hands, Victoria realizes that she hasn't checked in with the Hive since the incident in the streetcar. She opens the app.

<miko> np its horrrible

<miko> like ur infecting ppl when you bit them

<miko> remmber how shitty it was when U found out U wre vamped?

<miko> ur fuked if u think its ok to do that to other ppl

<bloodspike> hey i didnt ASK to have this hunger okay?

<bloodspike> besides its my fucking RIGHT to surfive

<bloodspike> **survive

<bloodspike> if people are going to try to KILL US because we're sick then FUCK EM

<bloodspike> kill em first

<ancestralcoven> That's quite barbaric

<bloodspike> self-preservation isnt barbaric you pussy

<vviz22> lol

<bloodspike> law of the JUNGLE

<bloodspike> besides it's my godgiven right

<bloodspike> is there anything more fuckin alpha than you being the one infected, but everyone ELSE being the victim? :P

#ladylasouris has entered #thehive

<ladylasouris> Bon soir everyone

<bloodspike> yo wazzzup??
<miko> OMG lady
<miko> did you find her????
<ladylasouris> No
<ladylasouris> I'm in her apartment right now drinking wine
<ladylasouris> Alone
<miko> :((
<vviz22> does she have a laptop?
<ladylasouris> Yes
<vviz22> get it

Sophia's MacBook is hot pink, one of her few traditionally feminine indulgences. Back in the living room Victoria opens it and finishes the wine. It glows, awake.

<ladylasouris> I don't know her password
<miko> guess!! maybe its ur name!!
<vvizz22> hmmmm
<vizz22> is she really tech savvy?
<ladylasouris> She once had to call me because her mouse was moving backwards
<ladylasouris> It turned out that she was holding it upside down
<vizz22> lol k so the drive probably isn't encrypted
<l'etranger> lady! what happened?
<l'etranger> is everything okay? do you need some help?
<ladylasouris> I can gain access to her files with the password?
<ancestralcoven> Yes
<ancestralcoven> Take the hard drive out
<ancestralcoven> Then connect it to another computer as a secondary drive
<ancestralcoven> You'll be able to read the files on it
<vvizz22> ^^^^
<vvizz22> hopefully you find something, we've lost enough vamps for stupid reasons
<vvizz22> good luck
<vvizz22> and i hope she doesn't get pissed at you for taking her laptop apart lol

Cross-legged on Sophia's bed, she connects the extracted hard drive to hers with significant coaching from <vvizz22>. Most of the files on it are just notes from school – clinical skills, physiology, all of it sorcery as far as she's concerned. But nothing like a journal, sticky notes, any clue to her daily routine.

<ladylasouris> Is there a more efficient way to search through this other than manually looking through each directory?

<vvizz22> here's a utility that will let you look at the file tree by size

<vvizz22> as well as most recently updated

<vvize22> might be helpful

It is. Deep within her drive is a thirty-gig directory named Research, with a flurry of recent activity. There's something odd in the folder, a .txt file updated multiple times.

1001588970 – vAMP POSITIVE

1001676378 – vAMP POSITIVE

1002117866 – vAMP POSITIVE

Seventeen entries, all the same. Identification numbers of a sort, but not any type that she recognizes. Underneath she had written a note – 17/17 what are the odds? A line of white light burns under Sophia's blackout curtains, making her skin itch.

Focus, please. The folder is full of academic articles related to vAMP, most of which she could never understand even with a dozen lifetimes. But there's one that catches her eye. JACKPOT.pdf. She opens it. A scan of a printout. The patient's name is John Todde. As in Commandant John Todde. There's identifying information of the processing laboratory, a health card number, and a single line in a desert of white space.

AMP type   VARIABLE

Commandant Todde has vAMP.

Victoria awakens to light in soft focus. Sophia's laptop. She reaches across the bed for her glasses only to find them on her face. Blinks, blinks again, still out of focus. Only when she takes them off to rub her eyes does she discover that her vision without her glasses is perfect. Twenty twenty.

In any other context this would be a miracle. Not now. It means her vAMP is progressing.

It's night again, the rest of the city deep in the dream state. In a few hours someone in Nice will be writing her a formal letter in French informing her that her contract is terminated. And here she is, scrolling through the Hive, re-reading their reaction to her bombshell about the Commandant.

<bloodspike> THAT'S FUCKED

<bloodspike> LIKE SERIOUSLY WHAT GIVES YOU THE FUCKING RIGHT TO POST HIS FUCKING PERSONAL MEDICAL INFO

<l'etranger> bloodspike crusader for patient rights lmao

<l'etranger> the guys an asshole

<ladylasouris> I'm more concerned about Sophia

<ladylasouris> What if something happened to her because of what she knew?

<ladylasouris> Something awful!

<l'etranger> hey hey itll be okay

<l'etranger> we're here for you

<miko> simp

<ancestralcoven> I am sure someone lurking here will post this information even if you do not

<ancestralcoven> It may be time to migrate to another hive…

<ladylasouris> I don't know where to post it if I wanted to

<ladylasouris> I feel like even if I screamed it from the rooftops no one would listen

<eruditetroglodyte> never liked rooftops, for screaming

<eruditetroglodyte> overrated

<eruditetroglodyte> much prefer crowded subways nowhere for anyone to escape to

She catches a glimpse of the Commandant in her mind's eye, his swept back bleached hair and unnatural teeth, and she wants to rip his throat out. The lives lost, the months she's spent hiding like a mouse, and he has vAMP too. She leaves cracks in the porcelain countertop from her grip.

That's when she hears it; someone is gently knocking at the door.

She goes still, thinking if maybe she pretends she isn't there she really will just disappear. She does not have any such luck. Stop it, she thinks. You're being silly. Slowly, she places her eye to the peephole.

No one is there.

More rapping and what might be a muffled "Hello."

It is her door, but not one connecting to the hallway. Out on Sophia's balcony is a woman tapping gently on the window, smiling. A smile she knows from social media stalking.

Mandy.

"You're an artist, right?" Mandy blows on her tea. "Sophia speaks highly of your talents."

"My graphic design?"

"No, she said you paint. Don't you paint?"

"I have." She sips her tea, avoids eye contact, accidentally makes eye contact to which Mandy smiles with her cheeks, avoids eye contact again. "How did you get on the balcony?"

"I flew."

Tea spills over Victoria's knuckles.

"Kidding. I jumped."

She cleans her hands. "Once upon a time that would have seemed equally preposterous."

Mandy laughs, crosses her legs the other way. She's dressed like she's on her way to present at a conference, pantsuit and bare arms. Toned, Victoria can't help but notice. Part of Sophia's medical school cohort. They had been working on something together, a research project, but Sophia didn't like to talk about it. She would either be short with her or go completely quiet when Victoria asked. She wasn't sure which she liked less.

"Do you know when she's going to be back?"

"She's doing a shift in the emergency department."

Mandy smiles, catching Victoria's lie in her teeth. The way it sits on Mandy's face is wrong, somehow, it's geometry uncanny. The face brushed by a new artist, one who can picture a visage in their head but struggles translating it to canvas. Mandy is not a very apt painter. "Is that what she told you?"

"Well, I mean she usually…I mean I'm sure she said something about…"

"Hey." She leans forward, two hands on Victoria's. Strong. Soft. "It's cool. I'm a…" She holds up her right hand, thumb and pinky adducted.

"Stage III." It comes out as a whisper, meant for her and not for Mandy. "Sorry, I…I don't think I've met a…"

"Oh, you almost certainly have. Don't believe the propaganda, we don't have fangs."

Whatever Mandy does have, Victoria's sure it's just as dangerous. "I'm surprised you're allowed to…I mean I'm surprised that you and Sophia are…I mean…"

"We've both been expelled for six months."

"Ah," Victoria says, less a revelation than an admission. She had her suspicions, but always talked herself out of it. It seemed easier than letting her mind construct scenarios about where Sophia really was going, all that time.

Mandy tilts her head and pouts, another practiced gesture. "Hey," she says, sitting cross-legged next to Victoria. "This is a lot, I know. Like for real, I am sorry. Sorry all this is happening."

"Me too." A voice so small she's not sure if she said it or merely thought it.

Mandy caresses Victoria's hands. "Blood. You're blood-starved, aren't you? Blood-starved vAMPs get fidgety. 'Akathisia minor', they call it."

"I've always been like this."

"A lucky guess, then. Unless there's something else you're looking for…?"

Mandy leans forward with her lips pursed, eyes closed a millimeter, moves slow like she's underwater. Victoria leans back just as slowly but without any of the grace, matching each degree, her phone held across her chest with two hands like a protective talisman.

"Excuse me," Victoria says. "I need to use the loo."

Sitting on the toilet seat lid with her pants on she opens the Hive.

<ladylasouris> Hello all

<ladylasouris> I have a situation I could use some help with
She explains.

<miko> umm thats sketch as hell

<l'etranger> sounds like shes into you fr

<vvizz22> she seems like a snake

Maybe, Victoria thinks. But snakes didn't end up snakes by accident, they evolved that way to survive in their own ecological niche. Maybe Mandy isn't any different. Maybe she herself isn't, either.

<ladylasouris> I have no idea what to do

<vvizz22> mind games not your forte?

<ladylasouris> To put it quite generously, no

<ladylasouris> Reading people was always Sophia's domain

<l'etranger> can you channel some of that? temporarily?

She pulls Sophia's hand mirror from the edge of the sink, a lipstick rolling off the edge as she does. This person you see, this anxious mess perched on a toilet lid, is this who you are? Sophia's photo negative, a woman whose skin burned in the Spring even before the vAMP dug in, who was starting to miss her glasses because at least they gave her something to hide behind. vAMP should have been a blessing for you, an excuse to retreat further inside yourself. It should have been hell for Sophia. Then why does she find it so much easier than you do?

<ladylasouris> Let's see

Victoria watches in the mirror as this woman straightens her posture, reigns in her fly-aways, searches along the edge of the sink for the fallen lipstick. Burgundy. It will match your hair, at least. The grease spread across her lips makes it feel like she's wearing another face. This person you see before you, borrowing a part of Sophia's face, what would this person do?

Mandy's on her phone when Victoria steps out. She doesn't look up until they're mere inches apart. "Oh wow, look at you. What's the occas…"

Wound up at the shoulder, Victoria cracks her palm across Mandy's cheek, phone tumbling out of her hands. "How dare you," she says. "You weren't invited here. You weren't invited to kiss me. You're intruding in Sophia's home and in my life."

The slap sends Mandy on a journey. Shock, then anger, and then finally to a profound sense of defeat. None of them seem practiced. "You hate me," Mandy says. "Whatever. I mean, it's…it's whatever." She breathes out through her nose, like a bull ready to charge. Back to rage. "Actually no, it's not 'whatever'. Do you know how much shit I'm dealing with right now? I'm in fucking Stage III. I have months left if I'm lucky, if you can even call it that, and I'm deep fucking shit with powerful fucking people. So I get that you're scared about Sophia being missing but…"

"I never told you that she's missing."

"*I'm* telling you that she's missing. *I'm* telling you that we pissed off the wrong, person and now he…"

"The Commandant. I saw the test results."

Mandy snorts. Wipes her eyes. "Those don't mean a fucking thing."

"I don't…" I don't see how that's possible, Victoria wants to say. But she must be missing something, something obvious, something that Sophia would have caught in an instant. "Here," she says, passing a box of tissues. She's starting to regret striking her, but not as much as she regrets regretting striking her. It would be nice to be able to retaliate against someone who had wrong her without feeling like she had done something even worse in doing so. C'est la vie, she supposes.

Victoria gazes out the wide windows of Sophia's condo. The moon is full. It's started to rain.

Just knowing that out there in the world are people who want to kill you, be they official government operatives or enthusiastic amateurs, is exhausting. Every stranger's glance, every pass by an open window, sends a jolt through your brain telling you that you could die here. It's the tax you have to pay for being prey instead of a predator.

For Mandy it was much more dire – she had been hunted down by a SOQA detective. Promised clemency if she helped locate another vAMP they were looking for, a classmate of hers who had somehow acquired some sensitive information about several people, including a high ranking member of government.

"How did she even…I mean, how did she get that information?"

"It was in the EMR, plain as day." Mandy puffs from what looks like a small USB stick. "She was blackmailing some hospital exec for access to blood. A good setup. But then, good things never last." She smiles. Her eyeshadow struggles to hide how tired she really is.

<miko> so she was in danger the whole time an never told u????

<miko> omg tru luv

<l'etranger> yeah TRU LUV is putting someone you care about in danger without them knowing

<l'etranger> straight outta hallmark

"Who do you keep texting?"

"The Hive."

Mandy opens her eyes and juts her head forward, her way of letting Victoria know that her explanation was inadequate.

"It's a chat room for other vAMPs."

"So you're just telling all of this to the world, huh? Does that seem like a particularly wise course of action to you?"

"They're my friends," she says, surprised at her own vulnerability. "They're all I have, them and Sophia." She clenches her fist. "Do you know where she is?"

Mandy exhales, the vapor coiling in the air. "No," she says. "I was hoping you did. Having her to trade to SOQA is my only out of this."

"Then get your coat."

"Are you stupid? SOQA must be watching this place."

"All the more reason for us to go. Look, if what you're telling me is true we're living on borrowed time, right? If we stay here and mope both of us are dead and neither of us gets what we want. If we find Sophia…"

"What? You hand her over and walk into custody?"

"No. You fight me for her. If you win you hand us in. If I win…" She realizes she doesn't know what would come next. France, via the Swiss border? Mandy's response is another cloud of vapor. She dons her coat. "Any idea where she would go?"

"No," Victoria says, typing. "But, I think I know how she left.

<ladylasouris> guys im about to do something

<ladylasouris> i plan on coming back but just in case hold on to this okay?

<ladylasouris> attached: jack-pot.pdf

<ladylasouris> a+

"See you down there," Victoria says, and alights from the balcony.

As she watches the street lights pass through the passenger window, Victoria can't remember the last time she rode in a car. When she closes her eyes she's just a girl out for a drive in the city, pop hits on the radio, songs she doesn't remember but that sound vaguely familiar, like they belong to another life she almost lived. "Donaldson, this admin person, are they a doctor?"

"You mean a physician? No, they're not."

"Yet they had all that blood at their fingertips, to use to protect themselves."

"And what, it should have been yours?"

"No, it should have gone to the people who needed it. Actually, I'm surprised they didn't take it for themselves. They're a vAMP, too, right? That's how Sophia got to them?"

"They're vAMP positive."

"Is there a difference?"

"I have a headache."

The hair runs up Victoria's neck. She's been here before, asking a question she has a right to the answer to and getting redirected, obstructed, obfuscated, made to believe it was wrong of her to ask. Being vAMP positive makes you a vAMP, doesn't it? Doesn't it?

<ladylasouris> Can you look into something for me?

<ladylasouris> Is it possible to be an asymptomatic carrier of vAMP?

<l'etranger> on it lady!

<l'etranger> are you safe?

<ladylasouris> For now, thank you

Street lights passing by.

A phone rings in the darkness. It glows with an image of Victoria's eyeless woman and the ringtone digs a pit in Victoria's stomach. When it goes unanswered it rings again and again, the same sixteen bars over and over again.

A door opens and a stocky shadow enters the room, rubbing his arms. "Jesus Christ," he mutters.

Mandy flicks on a lamp. "Good guess, but no."

Victoria closes the door to the study and leans against it. Mr. Donaldson is wearing slippers and hockey-themed pajama pants, and an expression slowly transitioning to confusion to surprise then anger and then...

Beam. It burns purple. Ultraviolet. The beam cleaves Victoria and she nearly vomits. Vision unfocused. When she comes to the light is on the ground, and Donald's arm is bent at an unnatural angle.

And the world goes red. She has him in her hand, a foot off the ground, his neck so close she can hear the blood flowing inside of it. He took Sophia. He has her phone. You deserve it. You deserve it more than he does. All that blood. All that blood.

She lets him fall to the ground. No. There's something else she needs more. "Where is she?"

"Listen, I've got ten thousand dollars in my safe, it's yours if…"

Victoria punts him. He wheezes.

"Please, they…"

Punts him again and again. He coughs up blood.

"Please, I just…the Commandant didn't want any leaks…"

"Didn't want anyone to know he's a vAMP?"

"He's a…what? He did it?"

"Did what? Did…"

Mandy pushes her gently aside. "Just tell us where Sophia…"

"No," Victoria says. "Don't 'just' tell us where Sophia is. Finish your sentence."

Donaldson looks to Mandy. "Does she know?"

She kicks his desk to the broken window. "Know what!?"

Mandy exhales. "The assays, they…"

"The assays for vAMP we ordered, the new one, they haven't…they haven't found a negative yet."

"Found a negative yet in whom?"

"The tests can detect any amount of vAMP, no matter how minute. Sophia went crazy. She didn't just steal medical records, she ordered tests under false credentials. On everyone important she could find admitted. The Commandant was in for treatment…when he found out he was furious."

"To be a vAMP?"

"To not! He was diagnosed with fucking leukemia, three months ago! You know who can't get leukemia? vAMPs. You know who can lift cars over their head? vAMPs! And there it was in his system and he hadn't been chosen. People like you get that gift, breaking my fucking windows and making my daughter cry, but someone like him? Someone trying to keep people safe?"

"Am I not a person? Is Sophia?"

He licks his lips, snorts. He doesn't have an answer for that.

She kneels down. "Mr. Donaldson, I'm sorry we broke into your home and I'm sorry we scared your daughter and I'm sorry that Sophia blackmailed you. In fact the only reason I've lived as long as I have is because of the blood you provided her. So I should thank you, really, I owe you my…well, whatever this is. But I love Sophia, the way any person loves anyone else, and I need to find her. So I need you to tell me where she is. And if you don't, I'm going to drink every drop of blood in your body." Not that there seems to be much left, the way the color drains from his face.

"I don't know," he says. "I tried to grab her outside her condo. Her phone slipped out her pocket as she stole my fucking car."

Victoria pushes his chin up, forcing him into eye contact. "And a successful man like you, I assume your vehicle is GPS enabled?"

Donaldson's adrenaline seems to be wearing off as they leave, two phones richer. "Please don't tell anyone about what I did, okay? Okay?"

"You're not bargaining from a particularly strong position," she says. But she knows that she won't.

"And don't tell anyone about the Commandant!"

"Hm? Oh, I did that two hours ago. Bon soir."

Mandy's hands shake on the drive back. She almost swipes an SUV trying to merge, and pounds the center console so hard she breaks the radio. It's the vAMP, and Victoria can't be far behind her. They might not even make it to dawn, and even if they do, what next? She slides Sophia's phone out of her pocket and unlocks it with her own birthday.

A notification. An unread message from the Hive. From bloodspike.

<bloodspike> U GET UR MEDICINE?

<bloodspike> U THERE??

<sophia2> yes i did

<sophia2> edrop me the tickets

<bloodspike> NOT UNTIL I TURN

<sophia2> im not waiting around for your transfusion to finish

<sophia2> 2 units for 2 tickets thats the deal

<sophia2> if you don't like it i'll go down the list to someone else

<bloodspike> HELLO?

The last message is from the day Sophia went missing. Victoria tries to remove her glasses but forgets she's not wearing them. There was medicine in Sophia's room. "What's prednisolone for?"

"What do you mean what is it for, it's used for fifty fucking things."

"Sorry I mean what does it…never mind." She switches to her own phone and Googles it instead. It's a corticosteroid with anti-inflammatory properties. It weakens the immune system. That makes no sense, she thinks. Why would she stop the only thing holding her vAMP in check?

<ladylasouis> @bloodspike are you here?

<vviz22> scroll up.

She does, going back two hours.

<bloodspike> fuck lady and fuck all u 2

<bloodspike> like its 1 thing 2 talk shit online but leaking sum1s personal medical shit is a SCUM FUCKING MOVE

<vvizz22> nope

<vvizz22>

<miko> FUCK U BLOODSPIKE

<miko> like seriously everyone here hates u lol

<l'etranger> ^^^

<bloodspike> u no its fucking pathetic that the gift of vamp is wasted on u LOSERS

<bloodspike> waste of my fucking time

<ancestralcoven> I assure you that the feeling is mutual

<ancestralcoven> Bon voyage

#bloodspike was BANNED from THEHIVE

<shard_of_porcelain> lol finally

Was <bloodspike> a chaser this whole time, trying to get Sophia to turn him? The car is starting to make her sick.

<ladylasouris> can you look up something for me?

<ladylasouris> has a drug called prednisolone or other drugs like that ever been studied for vAMP?

<ladylasouris> not for treating it for but initiating it

<l'etranger> wut

<miko> O_O
<miko> Y WOULD NE1 DO THAT??":??
<ancestralcoven> I'll take a look Lady

The screen on Donaldson's phone is cracked, the blue routed line not following any continuity. "Do you want me to look up directions?"

"Don't bother. I've been where we're going."

Through the windshield is an image of a large weeping angel, entreating donations. St. Michael's Hospital.

Donaldson's car is parked on the parkade rooftop, open to the moon. There's a half-finished iced coffee and a mess of blankets. It's dry underneath the car. She parked before the rain. The hybrid's chrome door door opens for her without resistance. "Oh. It was unlocked."

"No it wasn't."

The door handle clatters on the ground. "Ah." She settles in. Sophia was here, she can smell her, but not recently. She steps out, tries to close the door but it wobbles with a two inch gap. "So, where do we go from…"

Pillar of light.

It pierces the night air, searing them. It burns from the outside and in. Mandy vomits. Victoria's body buckles from the bottom up, as though melting over an open flame.

An ultraviolet spotlight from a circling helicopter, the beam shutting down all of the cellular processes that had come to rely on vAMP. Is this it? she thinks. This is all that's left of you with the vAMP stripped away. Her eyes are heavy. Mandy is screaming, but she can't find her breath.

Boots in unison, heavy steps. Men shouting. Assholes. A sound like leather being broken in. She turns to Mandy with great effort. She's shivering. Shouting. Pair of something.

Eyes wide, remembering something Sophia had told her. Paradoxical immune-mediated acceleration. In later stages of vAMP the immune system became dependent on it. Without a functioning immune system there's nothing to fight against vAMP. And with nothing to fight against vAMP…

It's not leather. It's the flesh growing under Mandy's skin. It's her skin struggling to manage the growing hypertrophy. And yes, there they are, fangs. But the hardest part to look at is her eyes, solid red but terrified. Confused. Stage IV eyes. Eyes that no longer understand what has happened to them, but are scared, all the same.

Mandy ascends through the air. For a moment it seems like gravity will never catch her, like she's truly flying, but she begins to slow near the apex. Not before she clenches the helicopter's landing gear. It maneuvers to shake her, freeing Victoria from the beam.

It returns as quickly as it had gone, her strength. Which is all well and good, except she's still surrounded by SOQA officers. With their bulky armor and muscular physiques they remind Victoria of kevlar eggs. It would be amusing if she wasn't staring down several automatic weapons. But for all their training, they are moving awfully slowly.

Or perhaps not. She can see the individual rotations of the helicopter's blades. It wobbles slowly to the ground, like it's sinking in gelatin. No, it's not moving slowly, she's moving incredibly quickly. Has this been what it's like for her this whole time? Has it been so long since she's been normal that she forgot, like that awful metaphor of the boiled frog?

A crack of gunfire. A stinging in her left shoulder. That's certainly one way to get her head back in the game. A second goes wide as she ducks, watching the weapon's bolt rock leisurely back in anticipation of a third.

Up until now a central thesis of Victoria's life has been that she was intrinsically incapable of affecting the world in any meaningful way. That she was an intangible spirit that only mattered when she was designing websites. One can imagine her surprise, then, when she rams her fist into the SOQA cop's big fat fucking face, shattering his helmet and God knows what else.

Oh, his gun. Victoria has no great interest in shooting anyone, but she points it in the air and pulls the trigger. It fires at the speed of Sophia's sleeping heartbeat, maybe slightly slower, and every few rounds the eggs take another step back, giving her much-needed space. One ascends the stairs and she kicks him back down, bowling down two others. Seems she won't be making a conventional escape.

She pushes off the parking lot railing, toward a billboard soliciting hospital donations. Dreadful font, she can't help but think. Something punches her in the back, perhaps a bird or a particularly large raindrop. The copter makes its landing too, in the middle of an intersection. Leaping across the rooftops, night air in her lungs, she can't help but think the whole exercise was, among other things, a spectacular waste of tax dollars.

Victoria wakes from her dream of adrenaline to find herself bleeding from a gunshot in an unfamiliar rooftop, smoke rising up from the distance. Mandy is dead and so is whoever else was in that helicopter, not to mention the officers she assaulted. The city will be hunting her now, and she's in no condition to run, let alone to fight.

She sees Mandy's eyes whenever she closes her own. What's worse, becoming a monster, or not living long enough to have the privilege? The city's response is a crescendo of sirens, its way of telling her that soon she'll have her answer.

<eruditetroglodyte > that copter was HER? holy shitballs

<eruditetroglodyte > ya girls on a rampage

<revolutionarygirlbootyna> i can legit see the smoke from my window

<miko> O_O !!

<eruditetroglodyte > RAMPAGE

<l'etranger> lol google the intersection where the copter went down you cant make this up

<l'etranger> #queenshitonqueenstreet

<revolutionarygirlbootyna> brb just heard a thump on my roof???

<miko> O_o ??

<ancestralcoven> UPDATE – THE CITY OF TORONTO IS DECLARING A STATE OF EMERGENCY

<ancestralcoven> Everyone please stay at home and stay safe

#ladylasouris has joined the hive

<miko> LADY!

<l'etranger> !!!!

<ladylasouris> bonsoir all hah

<ladylasouris> welb may maybe not for me

<miko> LADY ARE U OK???

<ladylasouris> bbleeding

<ladylasouis> quite heavily im affraid

<ladylasouris> c'est la vie i suppose

<ladylasouris> ii just didnt want to be all by myself when it happened

<ladylasouris> ssounds sillly to say it

<l'etranger> oh god no

<miko> WHERE ARE YOU??

<ladylasouris> under a night skyy

<ladylasouris> there are worse places t to go i su

<ladylasouris> suppos

<ladylasouris> e

Her phone slips. It hurts too much to roll over to it, and it's cold where her blood meets the night.

"Is that my lipstick?"

Eyes wide. She's lounging on the tared roof like a cabaret singer on a piano.

"I w – was having a…moment…"

"Such an artist. So melodramatic." The stars are out of focus but Sophia has borrowed their glow. "Hey, stick with me, okay? It's going to be okay."

"Such an awful…doctor…"

She's rising off of the tar. She doesn't want to leave Sophia behind but for all she knows the real Sophia is gone, just a plume of smoke like the crashed helicopter. For all she knows she's going to the same place, and their smoke will rise up together. It could be nice. It could be…

Blackness.

Victoria walks up the gallery's circular staircase and her Guest follows. TheHer the eyeless woman from her unfinished portrait. She's never seen her move but every time she glances back the woman is two steps behind her, limbs still, hands folded. "It's just at the top of the stairs," she says. Just is doing a lot of heavy lifting. She can't recall how long they've been walking.

Something drips through the eye of the staircase. "Oh no." The piece she submitted to this exhibition is a mixed media work – water would destroy it. "Oh no. Um. I need to…excuse me."

Taking the steps one by one as fast she she can, her Guest always behind but ever still. The liquid falls in thick ropes. Viscous.

It smells of iron. She can't see where she is going and can't see where she came from. She looks over the railing. She can't see the floor, can't recall if she ever could.

Ever up and up until at last Guest moved to point, painted finger aimed at the ceiling.

There it is, her work. A man's body pressed to the ceiling, bleached hair and uncanny veneers. A tapered piece of iron a foot wide juts from his abdomen.

Commandant Todde, impaled by a bloody spike.

She awakes in the hold of a monster. One arm in its grip and another embedded with its claws, it has a tendril down her throat, trying to devour her from the inside out. She can't scream. The tube comes loose when she pulls, hisses cool air at her. The beast's grip is a blood pressure cuff secured by velcro, its nails an IV. Hospital. She's in the hospital. Her eyes struggle to converge. "Hey!" she says. Someone turns to her, masked face in teal. "Help." She coughs. "Please help."

Eyes focus. Fortunately the figure appears to be a doctor. Unfortunately, there's a handgun shaking in their hands, pointed to Sophia. Behind the plastic face shield are eyes tinted red. They've been crying.

Some long, slow cognitive process comes to an end. <Bloodspike> is Commandant Todde. Todde is vAMP positive but not a true vAMP, and sick with envy for it. Under the guise of a chaser he came to Sophia with an offer – two tickets out of Toronto in exchange for a blood potent enough to turn him. Maybe she had caught on to who he was, or maybe she really did just hit the jackpot with his test results, but either way she made herself a nuisance. And so she had to be dealt with.

"Oh," says a voice obscured by a surgical mask. "You weren't supposed to wake up." They seem to be quite sad about it.

"Sorry," Victoria says reflexively.

A bellow through the halls. Like a bear about to charge, and yet also somehow like someone lamenting something awful that has happened to them.

Victoria jolts up. The doctor lowers the gun but their hand keeps shaking all the same. Looks at Victoria with a plea in her eyes. "I can't," she says, shaking. "I can't let him do to me what he did to…" She balls her hands into fists. Victoria watches the trigger nervously. "Please." Calm now. "Please, I heard what you did on the roof. You can have it, every drop. But don't let him do it to anyone else."

"Who?"

Another bellowing sob and somehow she knows. Todde.

"The antibody transfer worked too…he's not even remotely…God, the way he just pulled them apart at the neck. God, he's…" She exhales. "Don't let him have any of mine. Not a drop. I can't…I don't want to be a part of him."

"All of your what?"

As if to show her she points the gun at her temple and pulls the trigger.

There's screaming, from the halls. Molars crunching bone. A man softly crying. But for now there's something even more important. Something Victoria has needed for a long, long time.

With the body still convulsing, Victoria puts her mouth to the entrance wound and drinks deep.

She follows littered corpses and the sound of chewing. The entire hospital is a tasting menu, bodies served on marble flooring, barely tasted and, in some cases, spit back out. She pauses in front of the doors to the hospital chapel. Something is rotting inside.

Here. He's here.

When she was a little girl, Victoria was forced to visit a relative in hospice with an advanced cancer of the left breast. A blossom of pure rot, the smell was imaginable. The smell in the chapel is even worse. There, on the altar, sits what was once Commandant Todde, now eight hundred pounds of fungating tumor. He picks a wriggling woman and bites her external carotid, over the sound of her screams. The only recognizable part of him are his bleached hair and his cracked veneers. Goya, she thinks, *Saturn Devouring his Son.*

He tosses what's left behind him and grunts, licks what were once his fingers, and reaches for the next wriggling body in the pile. Sophia is there. Second from the top. She moves slowly, as though escaping from anesthesia.

There is a scream, that Victoria gradually realizes is her own. Her punches get lost on his abdomen. His backhand sends her through two layers of pews. Galloping toward her, spouting purulence. She flips over him, fails to stick the landing, slipping on viscera.

"You.ruiner.fault.all your."

She cracks what's left off his veneers. "Ta gueul!"

A statue of the virgin mother sails past her cheek, shattering stained glass. A pillar careens through, white hot. Daylight. Todde retreats from the light, squealing.

Cancer. That's what you are, that's what you've always been. First in spirit and now in flesh. You've become the monster in your own propaganda poster, the creature lurking just outside your vision, salivating over the blood of the innocent.

She dives into his belly. It's like kneading spoiled dough. He cuts himself on the glass as she pushes him through it into the street, and with every last pound of strength she lifts him above her head, knees buckling. The world's most putrid parasol.

Todde screams, as the sun blisters his skin. Whimpers, as his organs begin to fail. His weight pushes her an inch into the pavement. He pleas for mercy. He vomits up three fingers. She imagines herself and Sophia sharing a cup of tea, watching the morning sky pass through all the colors of blood. You were so afraid of what your last taste of daylight would be that you put it off over and over again, and here it is. Here you are.

She laughs. He doesn't like it. Malignant fists pummel her back, striking her gunshot wound. She winces. She almost lets go. She wants to let go so, so badly.

And then, suddenly, the burden is lighter. Beside her, ass to the wind in a blue hospital gown, is Sophia. "On three we toss this shit stain as high up as we can? Okay? Ready?" Victoria nods, shaking. "Okay. Three!"

She limps back to the chapel in the eclipse that Todde creates. The parabola of his flight takes him five stories up. Through a fractured portrait of the Virgin Mary they watch him crater in an overturned truck. He bursts, parts of him leaking down the sewer. Back where he belongs.

Aircraft fly overhead in formation. A column of vehicles in forest green approach. She doesn't know what's coming next. But for now she's happy to rest her tired body on Sophia's shoulder and sleep. Right back where she belongs, at long last.

<ladylasouris> The treatment centre in Genova was unpleasant, to put it mildly

<ladylasouris> Three months of immunotherapy

<ladylasouris> Chemo

<ladylasouris> Steroids, I never ate so much chocolate

<l'etranger> lol

<ladylasouris> Not to mention three surgery for my ACL

<ladylasouris> But we're doing well

<miko> yay!

<ladylasouris> Paris is different than I expected but in a good way

<l'etranger> really happy to hear that

<ancestralcoven> It's almost daybreak there, no?

<ancestralcoven> Cutting it close?

<ladylasouris> Actually we're trying a little experiment

The cafes in Paris are different than she expected, busy. Not out of frustration but determination. They have lives to live, and if you know what you want out of life, why would you wait? Victoria once had an answer to that question, but she can no longer recall what it is.

"Five minutes to sunrise," Sophia says.

"Are you nervous."

"No. I just want my cappuccino. You?"

"I would also like you to get your cappuccino, yes."

"If you start to feel sick you go back into the hotel immediately. Deal?"

"Deal," Victoria says. "And if we don't, we stay until the sun fully rises. Deal?"

"Full remission of photosensitivity after treatment takes time, even after the protocol. You could get hurt."

Someone with a brown paper bag bumps the back of her chair and does not apologize. But there's no need to. They just have a life to live. "Then I'm lucky to have a skilled clinician at my side."

"Four minutes," Sophia says. "Here we go."

They look up at the sky together, in anticipation of the dawn.

Taylor Calder is a writer and physician in Toronto. He's yet to encounter any real vampires in either his personal or professional lives, but he's keeping an eye out.

The story is a modern take on the Chinese folktale "Legend of the White Snake," with the setting moved to contemporary Taipei. Having lived in Taiwan for over sixteen years and having read various Chinese fables and myths over this period, I wanted to incorporate both these and my own experiences of cross-cultural romance, Taiwanese school and family life, and other aspects of local culture into a story. While I often write fantasy set in secondary worlds, I'll never tire of trying to capture different facets of Taiwan in fiction. The island often appears in the news due to its hazy political status, which sadly means its vibrancy, beauty, and uniqueness are often considered secondary.

Pat Woods

WHITE SNAKE, JADE TERRAPIN

by Pat Woods

To *Ilha Formosai* and all its stories

The first raindrops began to fall from the night sky as Xu was waiting for the street vendor to fill up the third bowl of red bean soup with *tangyuan*. Xu willed the old man to hurry up, though he kept his mouth shut out of respect. Old Lu was past seventy and didn't move quickly. Still, his tangyuan were renowned for their quality, and no one ever minded waiting. Xu had been there nearly fifteen minutes, and there was a long line of people behind him, unfurling umbrellas and putting up hoods.

Old Lu finally handed over a plastic bag containing four small cardboard bowls of the sweet dessert soup. Xu paid him and set off home, snapping his own umbrella over his head. The rain was growing heavier, but no one left the queue. Neither rain nor cold stopped Taiwanese from heading out for food; even summer typhoons barely slowed them down. Tonight of all nights, Old Lu would be doing business until he was sold out. It was *Dongzhi*, the Winter Solstice Festival, when families got together to eat tangyuan, the sweet glutinous rice-flour balls that symbolised union.

Xu's mother had demanded he pick up a bowl each for the family on his way home from his after-hours cram school. She wouldn't have tangyuan from anyone else, she'd declared, and Xu didn't argue, even though swinging by the vendor's cart added twenty minutes to his journey home, never mind the queuing time. He didn't mind; there'd been too many arguments at home lately. Xu didn't want to start another.

The traffic lights on Heping West Road changed just before Xu could cross. Rather than wait, he took the overpass, avoiding the puddles forming on the pale brick switchback stairs. A broken wall of the overpass was cordoned off by white plastic tape that writhed in the wind. He hurried across to the other side.

Just one more block till the MRT. Taipei's subway system was crowded, but warm and dry. With any luck he'd get a seat for at least part of the journey back to Banqiao, the southwestern district where he lived.

He was coming down the stairs when he saw two girls coming out of a bubble tea shop. It was hard *not* to notice them. They were both foreigners, and even more unusually, they looked around seventeen—the same age as him.

The taller girl had long blonde hair that snagged Xu's attention at once, even though it was tied in a long tail that wound sinuously over one shoulder. Her face was pale, though her cheeks were starting to flush now she was out in the cold. Xu thought she looked pretty—a different, foreign sort of pretty from the girls in his classes, with a longer nose and larger eyes, but pretty nonetheless. At her side was a shorter girl in a blue-green wool hat, perhaps a year younger than her companion. She had smaller, neater features, but with enough similarities that Xu guessed they were sisters. She was tugging on the older girl's arm and saying something. The older girl seemed reluctant.

Xu realised they didn't have umbrellas. *Of course not. They're foreigners.* Locals knew it could rain at any time in Taipei, and usually carried a small umbrella with them. These girls were probably tourists, here with their parents.

This put Xu in a bind. He wanted to help out and offer these girls the shelter of his own umbrella. On the other hand, that would mean speaking to them in English—and his English *sucked*.

Another hissing gust of wind came in, showering the streets. That decided it. Xu stepped forward.

"Hi," he said, before forgetting every English word he'd ever known.

They looked at him, expecting more. The smaller one had dark, lively eyes that drank in the world around her, though they narrowed with suspicion as they assessed Xu. The taller one had blue eyes. Very blue. They met Xu's own, and his breath caught in his chest.

"I have…umbrella," he said, hating his poor English, hating how stupid he must sound. *Do better!*

"An umbrella," he corrected himself. "Do you going to the MRT?"

The English wasn't right, but Xu couldn't remember what he should have said. Still, it got the message across. The tall girl beamed.

"*Xie xie ni*," she said, meaning 'thank you.'

Xu blinked. "You speak Chinese?" he said in Mandarin.

"Not very well," she replied, getting her tones so wrong that he barely understood. It was strange hearing a foreigner speak Chinese. "My little sister is speak me better."

Her sister was tugging at her jacket, making no attempt at subtlety. She said something too quickly for Xu to understand, though he guessed she wanted to get her older sibling away from this stranger. The older girl stayed put.

Xu grinned apologetically, drawing confidence from their shared ineptitude with a second language. "Your Chinese very good," he praised her in English.

"It's not," she demurred.

"It's really not," said her sister in Chinese. She was much more proficient. "Come on, let's go to the MRT. It's raining!"

Xu nodded, proffering his umbrella once more. The taller girl reached for it, but her sister's hand snaked out to stop her. There followed an exchange in English too rapid for Xu to follow, save the final sentence, as the older sister said, "It's OK." The younger one didn't look pleased, but Xu gave the girls his umbrella to share while he pulled up his hood. His jacket would get wet, but he didn't care.

He and the older sister talked as they walked, speaking in English, which seemed the easiest option. "My name is Xu," he said, using his surname, as all his friends did when they addressed him. Only his teachers called him Yong-xian, while to his family he was *Ge-ge*, "older brother."

"I'm Suzanne," said the tall girl. Her sister said nothing until prompted by an elbow.

"I'm Tilda." She was looking out at the night as she spoke.

"Nice to meet you," said Xu. His English was improving as his sense of accomplishment swelled. *I'm talking with foreigner girls! Pretty ones!* "Where are you from?"

"California, in the States," Suzanne said.

"Do you on… *Are* you on vacation?"

"No, we're students here. We start at Taipei American School next semester." Xu knew the school by reputation—an expensive academy for foreigners and local rich kids.

"Do you like Taiwan?"

"I don't like the rain!" Tilda said. Her eyes flashed as she glared around at the weather. "I prefer hot, dry places."

"I like it here," Suzanne said. "People are always so kind and friendly." She gave Xu a shy smile that made him feel six feet tall.

They made quick time to Longshan Temple MRT station. "I going to Banqiao," Xu said, pointing at an MRT map on a wall.

"We have to change at Taipei Main Station and go to Zhishan," said Tilda without looking, as though she already had the whole map memorised. She walked off without waiting for them.

"Thank you for lending us your umbrella," Suzanne said to Xu as they headed down the escalator to the platforms.

"It's OK," said Xu. Then he had a reckless idea. "Do you have LINE?" he asked. Everyone in Taiwan used the instant messaging app, which made extensive use of cartoon images and animations called stickers to communicate everything from hunger to rapturous affection. He didn't know whether foreigners used it. "Maybe we can study together. I can help you learn Chinese, you can help me learn English."

The sisters glanced at each other, and for an agonising moment Xu thought he'd pushed his luck too far. Then Suzanne said, "Sure! That would be really helpful!"

They took out their smartphones and added each other on LINE. Suzanne's profile picture was simple—she was in a white dress, smiling in the sunshine next to a lake. After some reluctance and a glance from her sister, Tilda added Xu as well. Her picture showed her in a closeup pout. Then their trains came, and they went in opposite directions, waving.

He hadn't reached Banqiao before the first LINE message came. It was a 'Thanks' sticker in the form of a clapping girl, then another one of three animals studying together. Xu replied with an anime character giving a giant thumbs-up, and his heart sang all the way home.

His joyful mood evaporated as soon as he walked through the door. Though they fell silent at once, it was obvious his parents had been arguing. Mama immediately put on a big smile and praised him for bringing home the tangyuan, while Baba opted for a stony yet expressive silence. Xu's sister Mei-Mei was summoned from her homework, and everyone tucked in. It was a nice moment, but the trouble began even before they'd finished.

"Save a few tangyuan," Mama said. "We need to stick them on the door."

"There's no need for that," Baba grumbled. "No one follows that old superstition these days."

"That's not so," Mama declared. "Lots of people do. It keeps bad luck away."

"Says who?"

"My friends Ms. Hung and Ms. Zhuang, and—"

"And Master Hai?"

"Well, yes, I think he said it works. I can't remember." Mama brushed off the question as unimportant, but Xu knew it went right to the heart of things.

Master Hai was…well, Xu wasn't sure exactly. He knew Traditional Chinese Medicine, a wealth of religious practices, and all sorts of ways to bring prosperity, good fortune, and spiritual wellbeing. Xu had seen his adverts on TV. Master Hai was an older man, but still handsome. He reminded Xu of Andy Lau, the Cantonese actor-cum-singer who sold out stadiums anywhere in eastern Asia in less than an hour. Master Hai was beloved by housewives and other middle-aged women; several of Xu's friends' mothers were his clients. As was Xu's mama, and thus the contention, for he'd talked her into adopting a range of new behaviours, and—Xu had overheard his father complaining—into donating money to his practice.

"Hai's a fraud," Baba said.

"Master Hai is a very intelligent man," Mama snapped back. Father's face darkened. "You kids should finish your homework," Mama said, and both Xu and Mei-Mei gratefully scuttled for the havens of their respective bedrooms. A closed door shut out most of the ensuing quarrel.

Xu had some homework, but first he took out his phone. There it was: a new message from Suzanne. His good mood returned.

—How was the soup?

—Very good! It was very (he tried to remember the word) *taste!*

—We say "tasty." Suzanne added a sticker of a contented-looking pig.

—Hahaha! Laughing sticker. *Thank you!* Thumbs-up sticker.

—When can we meet for our first language class?

Xu blinked. *She* was asked *him*? He hadn't expected her to broach the subject.

—Is Saturday OK?

—Saturday is great, but only after 2 pm.

—OKOK! A different thumbs-up sticker.

—I will be near Guting MRT. There is a Dante Coffee shop there. Meet inside?

—OK! Yet another thumbs-up sticker. Was he sending too many of those?

—Great!!! See you then. Good night!!! She sent a thumbs-up of her own.

Xu was ecstatic. He was meeting Suzanne again so soon! She must really want to…

Want to what?

Improve her Chinese? Make a friend? Or… (Xu hardly dared hope) …spend time with him?

Xu wasn't like his classmate Da-wei, a tall, handsome boy all the girls at school made eyes at, but he wasn't someone the girls made fun of or avoided. His spots weren't too bad, and he had a cool haircut. He'd kissed a girl called Jia-wen a few times, but her parents hadn't let her have a boyfriend, so they didn't hang out anymore. Maybe…

He shook his head. Foreigner girls didn't like Taiwanese guys, his older cousin had told him once. Lots of foreigners dated Taiwanese girls, but it didn't work the other way round. Suzanne just wanted to learn Chinese, and maybe make a friend, but once she started at her new school, she'd forget all about him. He almost didn't want to meet her on Saturday, but then he looked at her LINE picture again and decided it was worth it.

He dreamed that night of eating tangyuan with Suzanne and woke up looking forward to the day for the first time in a long time.

Their first language exchange consisted of thirty painfully awkward minutes followed by gradual relaxation.

"I don't really know how to teach," Suzanne said at the outset. "Can we just try to talk?"

"OK!" Xu was happy to do whatever she said. However, casual conversation proved difficult. They had too few words in common to do much more than list their family members and favourite foods. Their textbooks proved their saviour. They took turns following the lessons, helping each other with pronunciation and unfamiliar words. Within that structure, they improvised brief digressions revealing new words, which they wrote down in their notebooks. They ran through the BoPoMoFo Mandarin phonetic symbols until Suzanne could recite them without looking.

Deep into the second hour of what they'd scheduled as an hour-long class, they began to tire—not of each other, but of the mental effort of language learning.

"Can we meet again on Tuesday evening?" Suzanne asked.

It was the one weeknight when Xu didn't have cram school, but he agreed without reservation. Suzanne touched his arm when she thanked him and headed for the MRT. Xu didn't feel like standing around on public transportation. He wanted to run. He wanted to bound like a dog with a stick in its mouth. He walked all the way to Ximending, Taipei's number-one hangout for high schoolers, a neighbourhood full of stores and eateries, where he'd arranged to meet his classmates that evening.

"Why are you so happy?" Che-tien asked him. Xu smiled but said, "Nothing," and kept his secret. He'd share it sooner or later, but right now, this was his special thing. He wanted to keep it that way as long as possible.

Time passed, but Xu always found excuses to keep his sessions with Suzanne a secret. By degrees, his English came more easily. Words he'd learned years ago emerged from the depths of his memory and flowed into sentences, and then back-and-forth conversation. Suzanne's Chinese trickled, ebbed away, and then returned in a flood.

They didn't restrict their time together to coffee shops. When the weather and their schedules allowed, they went out together, to parks and night markets and other places of interest. They went to see a film and held hands in the darkness of the cinema. It was the most romantic moment of his life, though it was soon relegated to second place, as after Xu had walked her to the MRT, Suzanne asked,

"Are you going to kiss me goodnight?"

After a moment's exquisite hesitation, he did so, slowly brushing her lips with his own. She tilted her head up and they pressed together more tightly, just for a few seconds, and then parted.

They looked at each other. Then, as if some unseen spark had ignited them both, they were in each other's arms, their mouths opening, kissing passionately.

After that, it seemed to Xu that there weren't enough nights in the week.

His earlier fears proved unfounded; even after Suzanne began her new school, they continued to see each other. Sometimes it was for language exchange; more often it was a date.

"We are dating, right?" Suzanne asked him at one point.

"Absolutely!" Xu replied, and only realised later he'd done so in English.

His English grades went through the roof, and somehow dragged his other grades with them. Xu's teachers praised him, and his classmates begged for help. His academic improvement helped brighten things at home and gave his parents something to do other than bicker over Mama's continuing visits to Master Hai and the money she gave him. Xu didn't spend much time at home these days, so he missed the worst of it.

He tried to keep the relationship a secret, but his friends eventually found out by sneaking a look at his phone and seeing pictures of the two of them together.

"We have to meet her," Da-wei declared, after they'd all finished praising him.

"And her sister," Che-tien added, for Tilda had been in one of the pictures and the boys liked what they saw.

"I'll ask," Xu said. He and Tilda were on speaking terms, but he got the feeling that she was only friendly for her sister's sake and was waiting for him to mess up somehow. "Don't make it all about us," he added, knowing how much Suzanne disliked being the centre of attention. "Let's all meet as a group." He looked at Da-Wei. "Invite Su-ling and her friends, like we're all just hanging out together."

"We can see the Dragon Boat races," Chien-ming suggested.

The Dragon Boat Festival was only a few weeks away. The races in Taipei were always held along a stretch of the Keelung River at Dajia Riverside Park, where there'd be food, drink, music, and other entertainments. Xu and his friends seldom bothered to watch the races these days, but in this case Chien-ming had hit on a winner.

"Good idea," Xu said. "Suzanne mentioned she wanted to watch them."

"Let's organize it then," said Da-wei. "It'll be magical!"

Suzanne was also positive about the plan, and promised she'd bring Tilda. "I keep telling her she should get a boyfriend, too."

Xu always got a warm feeling when she called him her boyfriend. "Great! Everyone can focus on her instead of staring at us."

As the day approached, more plans were made. High on the priority list was figuring out who could procure a supply of alcohol to be mixed with something innocuous in a plastic bottle.

On the day of the festival, Xu was looking around his house, but without much hope. Then his eyes alighted on a decorated ceramic jar in the kitchen. He recognised it as the subject of his parents' latest argument—it contained a special wine Mama had bought from Master Hai, who claimed it was good for scaring away evil spirits. Baba had ordered Mama to take it back, and she'd eventually agreed to do so—only, by the looks of things, she'd hidden it in the kitchen amongst the cooking wines and sauces, where Baba never ventured.

Perfect. If Xu took it, Baba would never know about Mama's disobedience, while Mama couldn't punish Xu for taking it without revealing the truth.

He examined the label as he decanted the jar into a few empty bottles and mixed it with sweet oolong tea. *Xionghuangjiu*, realgar wine. It was traditional to drink the stuff during the Dragon Boat Festival, though he'd never tried it. It contained Chinese Traditional Medicine, but the oolong tea should mask its flavour. Xu mixed three bottles and headed out.

The day was scorching. A typhoon was supposed to be on its way, but not for some days. Xu and his friends positioned themselves at the back of a makeshift pavilion in Dajia Riverside Park, one of several erected for the convenience of spectators and the Dragon Boat teams when they were between races. Grinning and jostling, the boys shared some alcohol, starting with Da-wei's rice wine-orange juice cocktail. Suzanne messaged him to say she and Tilda would soon arrive. Xu met them and brought them to where his friends were, beaming with pride at getting to introduce his girlfriend to the group.

Since the girls were foreigners, Xu's friends were a little intimidated, and the language barrier stopped them from being too intrusive or boisterous. Soon, however, Tilda started showing off her Chinese and everyone started to relax. That wasn't all Tilda was showing off; she was in a very short skirt and a strapless green top that revealed plenty of skin. Xu's classmates couldn't stop staring at her, but Xu only had eyes for Suzanne. Despite their being in public, she let him kiss her on the cheek, and then—to cheers—on the lips.

"You've been drinking!" she mock-scolded him. "I can taste it!"

"They all have," Tilda added. "Look at how red all their faces are! You'd better have enough for us."

Da-wei passed Tilda the rice wine-orange bottle, which she emptied while the boys looked on in awe.

"You could have given me some," Suzanne complained.

"I have more," Xu said, reaching for his bag and pulling out a bottle. "I don't know if it's any good."

"Let me try." Suzanne opened it, sniffed, and wrinkled her nose. "What's in it?"

"Chinese medicine wine, with oolong tea."

"I guess I'll try it." Suzanne took a mouthful.

Immediately she went as pale as death.

"Is it bad?" Xu was horrified. "Spit it out!"

But Suzanne had swallowed, and something strange was happening.

She convulsed, almost choking on the drink. Her body writhed from side to side as if something inside her was pulling this way and that, trying to get out.

As her body twisted, it became thinner and longer, like she was a lump of dough being rolled into a fat, white *wulong* noodle. Her clothes blended into skin, her arms into her torso, and her legs fused together. Suzanne's neck stretched, her head narrowed, and her mouth split open, the skin opening as if on a seam that ran all the way back to her ears—which had disappeared.

In second, Suzanne was gone, and in her place was a long white snake, coils piling upon one another as gravity pulled them down.

Xu stared at it, unable to move. The snake looked at him, and its eyes were Suzanne's.

Xu retched and vomited, bringing up rice wine and orange juice that burned his throat.

No one else seemed to have noticed the horrifying transformation. They only saw the snake, and when they did, they began to scream and scramble away out of the pavilion. Panic spread, sparing only Xu, who was rooted to the spot, unable to take his eyes off the serpent.

Then Tilda appeared, her eyes flashing fire. She swept up the snake as if it'd been no more than a piece of string and glared at Xu.

"Don't try to contact usss," she hissed, and it seemed to Xu her teeth were sharper and that her tongue forked as she spat out the final syllable.

Then she was gone, and Xu was on his knees, dry-heaving, tears stinging his eyes.

No one seemed to know what had happened. They'd been looking the other way, or their memories were confused by alcohol, but as far as everyone except Xu was concerned, a snake had come out of nowhere and everyone had bolted. Xu's classmates asked after Suzanne as if she'd simply vanished in the panic with Tilda.

Xu knew what he'd seen. He couldn't explain it, couldn't understand it, but he knew. Suzanne, the girl he loved, had turned into a snake. Why? How?

He wanted to understand. He wanted to see Suzanne again, to hear an explanation that would convince him he'd gone momentarily insane and that everything would be all right. He wanted to tell her he was sorry—sorry for the drink, sorry for making it all happen, sorry for throwing up instead of trying to help her. But he could do none of these things. All he could do was cry, go home alone, and crawl into his bed with the door locked.

He tried to contact them, but neither Suzanne nor Tilda read the messages he sent, and his calls went unanswered. Xu put his phone down and closed his eyes.

He didn't get up again that day, or the next. When he closed his eyes, he saw Suzanne—her face, and then her transformation. All he could do was think about what he could have—should have—done. It was too late. He'd lost her now, lost her forever.

"You look terrible!" Mama exclaimed when he at last answered his bedroom door.

"You're going to the hospital," said Baba.

Arguing was pointless. Everything was pointless. They spent an hour in a waiting room full of masked, coughing old people before the doctor examined him.

"I can find nothing wrong with him," the doctor said. "He just needs rest. Come back in a few days if he doesn't improve."

He didn't. The weekend passed and he skipped school on Monday. Mostly he slept, or lay on his side, eyes open, staring at nothing. Food didn't help. His friends messaged him, and at first, he grabbed his phone, hoping it was Suzanne. It never was. Soon he just ignored it.

Tuesday came and with it another inconclusive hospital visit. Blood was taken. The results showed no physical signs of illness. That night, Mama proposed they call Master Hai.

"His problem isn't medical, so it must be spiritual," she told Baba. "Maybe an evil spirit has hurt him."

"Don't be preposterous!" Baba fumed. "And don't call that crackpot!"

But as soon as he left for work on Wednesday, call him she did.

Master Hai looked even more like Andy Lau in person than he did on TV. He was smooth and suave, dressed in an orange *changshan* shirt and wide pants, jade Buddhist beads on his arms and a necklace with a terrapin as its centrepiece. The shell was made of deep green jade, while its silver claws seemed to climb up Master Hai's shirt. Its tiny jet-bead eyes peered at Xu as the man stood beside Xu's bed. Every move he made was slow and deliberate, and as he listened while Mama detailed Xu's symptoms, he was as still as a statue.

"I must examine the boy myself," he said, his voice soft but authoritative. "Alone." Mama looked back as she left the room and kept on peering in until Master Hai shut the door.

"Now, my lad," he said. "What's the matter with you?"

Xu didn't reply. Master Hai muttered some words in a language Xu didn't understand as he clicked his beads and stroked the jade terrapin's smooth shell.

"Oh ho," he said, and his voice thrummed with knowledge—and something else, something entirely more sinister. "I know *exactly* what's wrong with you!"

He called Mama in and gave an exaggerated sigh. "It doesn't look good," he said, all woe and regret. "He's been afflicted by an evil spirit."

"Oh, Master Hai, no! Can anything be done?"

"Only one thing will suffice. I must take him to a place I know—Jinshan Temple. It is protected against ghosts and demons. Only there can I drive out the evil spirit and save your son." He paused. "I require many rare supplies for the ritual," he added. "Such things are…not inexpensive."

"I can get you all the money you need!"

So Xu was lifted up by Master Hai and carried downstairs as though he was made of bamboo. They travelled by Uber, which Mama paid for, to an out-of-the-way spot on the Xindian River between Taipei City and New Taipei. The temple had the usual swallow-tail roofs, vermillion pillars, and faded dragon carvings leaping from the eaves. Xu caught a glimpse of a tall pagoda with the name *Liefeng* emblazoned above it in golden characters as they went in.

It was draughty inside the temple. Xu shivered. The smells of old incense and paper money ash hung in the air. Master Hai took him past the shrine, where statues of various gods frowned down as if they disapproved of Xu. *Probably because I fell in love with a snake.*

He hadn't known, but now that he did, Xu didn't care. Suzanne had been the best thing that'd ever happened to him. So what if she was a snake in human form? Wasn't everyone these days saying you had to accept people and not discriminate against them for being who they were?

Master Hai lowered Xu onto a mattress on the floor and covered him with a blanket, and then busied himself setting up some kind of altar. Xu watched without interest as he arranged incense sticks in pots and set them burning, filling the room with a sweet, cloying smell.

"I must gather a few things," Hai said. "You take a rest, now."

As he spoke, he touched his jade terrapin necklace. Xu was immediately overcome by a drowsiness quite different to his weary apathy. He slept.

He awoke groggy and confused, unsure of where or even who he was. Someone was shaking him and speaking urgently, trying to get him to do something.

"Wake up, Xu! We have to go!"

He knew the voice, but even more familiar was her smell— her hair, her clothes, her breath.

Suzanne.

Xu wanted to leap to his feet and embrace her, to tell her that he was sorry, but his limbs felt like they were made of stone. He could barely see; his eyes were veiled by grey vapour.

"Wha…?" was all he could say.

"Come on!" Suzanne was pulling him to his feet, but he weighed a tonne and she couldn't support him. They both fell on the mattress. Xu smiled dreamily up into her face.

"I thought I'd lost you," he said.

"We don't have time for this!" Through the haze, Xu realised she was afraid. "We have to go before he gets back!"

"It's too late for that, my dear."

It was Master Hai's voice, but Xu couldn't turn his head to look. Suzanne shrank back, coiling in on herself. Slow footsteps approached.

"Did you think you could come here without my knowing it?" He sounded like a man who had it all worked out. "You should be at school. Where's your sister?" When Suzanne didn't answer, he said, "Doing as she's told, which actually surprises me. I thought I'd have far more trouble with her."

"You leave her out of it!" Suzanne hissed.

"I will." Master Hai's voice grew hard and cold. "*She's* obeying my instructions. You're not. What were you trying to do, save this boy?" He laughed a cruel laugh. "It's *your* fault he's like this! You charmed him, cast your spell on him, and now he's addicted to you. I'll cure him—when we've made a fat profit from his family."

"It's not fair!" Suzanne wailed. "He was nice to me! He doesn't deserve this!"

"Listen to yourself." Master Hai was standing over Xu now. "How can you talk about what's fair, or who deserves what? You know what the humans have done to us. They call us *yaoguai* and make monsters of us. They've hunted us almost to extinction to make their traditional medicine! There are so few of us left that no one even believes we exist anymore!"

His voice grew soft. "Don't we deserve to live? After what they've done to us, don't we have the right to use what little magic we have left to make our way in the world? Who cares if we leave a few gullible fools penniless? That's what *they* deserve."

"Not Xu! He's innocent of all that, he's… I love him!"

Xu's heart swelled. The strength her words gave him almost permitted him to move, but only almost. Whatever Master Hai had done had left him paralysed.

"Love a human?" Hai sneered. "Foolish serpent. How can a heart as cold as yours feel love?" He shook his head. "Suppose you do, then. What would you have of me?"

"Let him go," Suzanne said. "Cure him and let him go back to his family—without payment. They don't have much. Taking it would ruin them."

"And what do I get in return?"

Suzanne was silent, then said, "Name your price."

No! Xu wanted to shout. *Don't throw your life away for mine! I don't deserve you!* But his jaws were clamped shut.

"Give me your magic," Master Hai said. "Give me all your power. You're useless to me now. I won't ever be able to trust you to follow orders again. Give me your magic so I can put it to better use."

Don't! Xu wailed inside his head.

"Very well," said Suzanne. "But release him first. I will keep my word."

"As you wish."

Xu's drowsiness lifted and his limbs were freed. He sprang to his feet.

"Don't do this for me, Suzanne," he begged her. "I don't care that you're a snake!"

"It'll be all right, Xu," she told him. "Just take care of yourself, OK?"

"How can I? I love you, Suzanne."

"I love you too."

Xu put his arms around her. She kissed him and their tears mingled.

"Enough of that," Master Hai snapped. Holding the necklace, he began chanting in the same strange language as before. Suzanne jerked away from Xu and began to change. Xu's stomach churned, but he didn't look away. As Suzanne became a snake, a pale light was sucked out of her body. It leapt across the space between her and Master Hai and coalesced around his jade terrapin. Then it faded, leaving Hai looking younger and stronger.

At Xu's feet lay the white snake. He bent down and stroked her. Her scales were surprisingly warm. She barely moved; the loss of her magic had made her torpid. "I'll do something," he whispered. "I'll find a way to fix this."

Somehow Master Hai heard him. "You most certainly won't," he sneered.

Xu span around and launched himself at the magician, but Hai gestured, and Xu was suddenly on his back on the mattress, his head spinning.

"I'll keep my word as well," Master Hai said. He took out the money Xu's mama had given him and tossed it onto the mattress. "Take your money and go. Don't come back." Dismissing Xu, he picked up Suzanne and placed her on his altar. "I know just the place to keep you." He snapped his fingers and a glass case materialised around Suzanne. She looked horrifyingly like the poor reptiles on display in Huaxi Street Night Market—'Snake Alley,' as it was known, where serpents were once killed in theatrical performances before their meat and venom was served to eager customers. Bile rose in Xu's throat, but his anger forced it down.

"I'll tell everyone what happened!" he raged at Master Hai's back. "I'll tell them what you are, what you do!"

Hai turned and laughed in his face. "No one will believe you! With my own magic and your girlfriend's power, I can charm and control anyone. Do whatever you like." He gestured again.

Xu found himself outside Jinshan Temple. He tried to charge back in, but an invisible barrier blocked him. Xu swore and shouted, but it was useless. He could do nothing. Tears of loss and frustration welled up again, and he sat by the side of the road and wept for several minutes.

He wanted to go home, to shut out the world and pretend it had all been a horrible dream. Xu took out his phone to call Mama.

There was a LINE message from Suzanne.

Xu almost dropped the phone in his haste to unlock it and read the message. She'd sent it fifteen minutes ago, before she'd entered the temple.

—*Find my sister*, it said.

Xu messaged Tilda and she agreed to meet him at the same bubble tea shop where he'd first encountered them. As he explained what had happened, her hands clenched into fists and her face seemed to narrow. Her nostrils flared like the hood of a cobra.

"He took away my sister," she said, and her voice chilled Xu to the bone. "He took away her power—what makes her *her*. I can't believe he would do that to one of his own people."

Xu opened his mouth to speak but Tilda silenced him with a glare that had the force of a slap.

"Yes, I'm a shapeshifter, and a snake," she said, and her mouth opened to give Xu a quick glimpse of fangs. "Are you disgusted? Are you frightened?"

"I'm frightened," Xu admitted, "but not disgusted. Suzanne means everything to me, and you're her sister, so—"

"We're not true sisters," said Tilda. "We have different parents. But whatever she means to you is not one little piece of what she means to me." Xu didn't argue.

"She saved me when I was young," she said after a while, her voice softer. "It was in Hangzhou, over in China. A beggar—a human—had caught me and wanted to dig out my organs and sell them." Her eyes grew fierce again. "That's what you humans do to us," she hissed. "That's what you do to *anyone* who's different. You tell stories that make us out to be monsters, and then attack us every chance you get!"

Xu opened his mouth to protest, but Tilda fixed him with a glare. He shut it again. Tilda clenched her fists and took several controlled breaths before continuing her story.

"Suzanne bought me from the beggar before he could cut me up. She taught me how to use magic to stay safe and make sure you humans couldn't recognise us. I owe her more than I could ever repay."

"What about Master Hai?"

Her eyes blazed. "That traitor! He's a terrapin, like that necklace he carries around and uses to channel his magic. He's much older than us. We don't really know where he came from. He just found us one day and said we should work together. He knew how we could make money and actually have something like normal lives."

"By tricking people and stealing from them?"

She reared up in her chair. "How dare you judge us?! Do you know what it's like to live on the run, always looking over your shoulder, just waiting for someone to find out what we are and start the hunt? We may be part animal, but we're also part human, and we have the right to live in freedom, to enjoy ourselves and never have to worry that sooner or later, someone will try to kill us."

"It's terrible, what's been done to you," said Xu. "But that doesn't change the fact we have to save Suzanne. Will you help me or not?"

Tilda looked at him scornfully. "Of course I will, you idiot," she said. "I told you: *He took away my sister.*" She seemed ready to tear Master Hai apart with her teeth. "I'll make him pay."

"How?" Xu asked, awed by her anger. "I couldn't even get into the temple."

"I can get us in," Tilda said, "but that's the least of our problems. I can't beat Hai while he has my sister's power. If we can free her and somehow get her magic back, the two of us can overcome him."

"So, the problem is his magic," Xu said. "And it's all bound up in that necklace he wears?"

"That's right. If we can get it away from him, we can restore Suzanne and together we can deal with that treacherous shellback."

Her words rang like a gong in Xu's ears and his mind took fire. "Meet me at Nanshijiao Station," he said, naming the MRT stop closest to Jinshan Temple.

"Where are you going?"

"Home. I have to fetch something."

On the way to the temple, Xu explained his plan.

"You'll have to be quick," she told him. "I won't be able to keep him distracted for long."

At the temple entrance, Xu again felt the invisible wall. Tilda closed her eyes and spoke in the same unknown tongue Hai had used and the barrier was gone.

"Let's go!" Tilda hissed. Her eyes were glowing emerald and beads of sweat stood out on her brow as though she'd just lifted an immense weight. "He'll know we're here!"

They raced into the temple compound and past the god statues in the main hall. Was it Xu's imagination, or were their eyes following him? He felt buoyed, as if the gods were silent spectators somehow willing him on.

They burst into the room where Xu had been held before—and there was Master Hai, waiting for them with the jade terrapin in his hand.

"I told you not to come back," he snapped at Xu. Then he saw Tilda. "And as for you, I knew you'd be trouble."

"Let my sister go!" Tilda flared.

"She's better off where she is." Hai waved a hand at his altar, where Suzanne was still trapped in her glass prison. She looked smaller and weaker than when Xu had last seen her.

"If you've hurt her—" he began.

"She's safe—a good deal safer than if she was outside in the world with your kind," Hai said.

"Let her go!" Tilda shouted again.

"I think not." Hai grinned wickedly. "In fact, I think I'll take your power too and put you in there with her. You're no more use to me."

He muttered under his breath and Tilda flinched as if she'd been struck. She began to glow with a blue-green light. Hai moved his hands as if he was pulling something towards him, and Tilda's glow moved through the air.

"I'll kill you!" she raged, transforming herself in the blink of an eye. Her snake form was teal, and she was sleeker yet somehow fiercer than her sister. Hai hadn't been expecting her to change, and his spell was broken. Tilda darted off to one side. Hai grimaced and went after her.

But this put his back to Xu. Evidently he felt Xu was no threat. Xu didn't hesitate. He shrugged off the backpack he'd grabbed from home—the same one he'd brought to the Dragon Boat races. Inside were the two remaining bottles of realgar wine.

"Let's see how you like it!" he yelled, and twisting off the cap, he doused Hai with the contents of the first bottle.

Hai howled and swung around to face Xu, his mouth open and his hands reaching for him like claws. Steam rose off his body as though he was a pot of boiling water. But Xu had the second bottle ready and sloshed the wine right in Hai's face. He sputtered and gagged, swallowing a mouthful.

Then he jerked as Suzanne had done and began to shrink while his back swelled like a balloon being inflated. His long fingers thickened and merged. Xu leapt forward and snatched the jade necklace out of his hand just before it turned into a mud-brown claw. Hai's body collapsed in on itself, his limbs folding into his body and his head lowering into his chest as his shoulders hardening into a pitted, dirty green shell that covered him. In moments, a large terrapin was glaring balefully at Xu with jet-bead eyes.

Tilda appeared in her human form. "Quickly!" she shouted. "He won't stay like that for long!"

Xu ran over to the altar. There seemed no way to open the glass case and free Suzanne. In desperation he grabbed a heavy incense bowl and smashed the side farthest away from her. It broke, and Xu cried out in pain as a shard sliced his hand. Blood welled at the cut.

Ignoring it he put his hand in to lift Suzanne out. She coiled around his arm and up to his shoulder so he could remove her safely from the case. As she did so, she raised her head and looked at him.

"Give her the necklace!" Tilda cried.

Xu looped the jade terrapin around Suzanne's neck, and then set her down. First the necklace, then Suzanne herself started glowing with the same pale light Xu had seen before. Her reverse transformation was just as quick, and in a matter of seconds Suzanne was standing before him.

He wanted to hug her, but the look of absolute fury in her eyes stopped him dead. Her ire was directed at the terrapin, which was crawling away as fast as it could as Suzanne began to chant a spell of her own.

"I know what she's doing!" Tilda shouted to Xu. "Find something tall to stand on!" She blurred back into her snake form and wrapped herself around one of the temple's decorated pillars, ascending rapidly. Xu climbed onto the altar, hoping it'd be high enough for whatever was about to happen.

There was the sound of rushing water and suddenly the floor was awash. It was like the work of a typhoon condensed into seconds as the river behind Jinshan Temple burst its banks and swamped the temple grounds. Before Xu could blink it was lapping at his ankles.

In the midst of the torrent stood Suzanne, her eyes blazing white anger as she wielded her magic. The waters did not touch her. Xu feared she'd gone too far, that the river would sweep them all away, but as quickly as the water had come, it receded like the outgoing tide, retreating across the temple floor.

They had cleansed it, washing away the broken glass of Suzanne's prison and all Hai's accoutrements. Of Hai himself there was no sign.

Xu climbed off the altar and ran to Suzanne.

"Are you all right?" he asked, but those were the last coherent words he managed. The rest was hugging and kissing and each telling the other how worried they'd been.

"I'm sorry for how I reacted after you changed," Xu said.

"No! I don't blame you at all! I just wish I'd had the courage to tell you everything before. Can you ever forgive me?"

In answer, Xu kissed her again.

"When you've quite finished," said Tilda, "what are we going to do with that?" She pointed to Hai's jade necklace, which Suzanne still wore around her neck. Its green lustre had faded, and its silver sheen was tarnished. The dull jet eyes no longer sparkled.

They all looked at it. "What happened to him?" Xu asked.

"The river will take him far from here," said Suzanne, "but that's all. He's a terrapin, so he's used to the water."

"You let him off lightly, after everything he did," said Tilda. "But we can still teach him a lesson he'll never forget, now we've got most of his power." She reached for the necklace, but Suzanne stepped back.

"No," she said firmly. "He turned on his own kind. If we use his magic to hurt him, we'll be no better than he is."

"He'll come back for the necklace," Tilda warned her.

"Then destroy it," said Xu. "Smash it up. Then he won't have any reason to bother us again."

"Or enough power to threaten us," added Suzanne. "Yes, I agree. That's the best thing to do."

Tilda looked doubtful, but eventually nodded. Xu went out to the riverbank and picked up the biggest, heaviest stone he could find.

"I hope this gives you a headache, wherever you are," he muttered, and then smashed the necklace into fragments with a single blow. Jagged jade shards scattered across the temple floor. A faint orange radiance gathered about the pieces before drifting off towards the river like a patch of mist.

"What now?" he asked the sisters.

They exchanged a look. Xu was struck by a sudden fear that now he knew their secret, they'd leave Taipei—and him. He held his breath.

"I've got cram school this evening," Tilda said slowly.

Suzanne smiled. "Me too." She looked at Xu. "And I dread to think of how much homework we'll have waiting for us after missing a few days of school."

Xu sagged with relief, then remembered his mum. "I really need to get home," he said. "My family must be worried sick."

"Back to Nanshijiao MRT Station then," Tilda concluded.

They walked back together, but Tilda soon quickened her pace to give them some privacy.

"So…it's back to normal life," Xu said, not without some hesitation.

"That's what I want," Suzanne replied. "It's the only thing I've ever wanted." Then she reached out and took his hand. "Until now."

Hand in hand, they walked on in silence. They separated when their ways home took different MRT lines, but despite everything that'd happened, it felt like they were just saying goodbye at the end of another day, with the expectation that they'd be seeing each other again before long.

As Xu rode the subway home, his phone buzzed with LINE stickers. Suzanne's first was a rabbit declaring its love with hearts for eyes.

—*I love you too*, Xu messaged back, then added a sticker of an animated snake.

Suzanne replied with an exaggerated expression of shock, then one of a face crying with laughter.

—*I'll get you for that*, she sent.

Xu grinned.

—*You already got me*.

Pat Woods is a writer from Nottingham, UK, who moved to Taiwan in 2008 for an adventure that turned into a lifetime commitment. His stories have been published by Inklings Press, Spring Song Press, and elsewhere. He was nominated for the 2016 Pushcart Prize for his Sherlock Holmes pastiche "The Adventure of the Etheric Projection."

Why Mirror World?

We publish escapism fiction for all ages. Our novels are imaginative and character-driven and our goal is to give our readers a glimpse into other worlds, times, and versions of reality that parallel our own, giving them an experience they can't get anywhere else!

We offer free delivery within Windsor-Essex in Canada, an all-you-can-read membership program, blind-dates with books, and you can order our novels from our online store, or from your favorite major book retailer.

We appreciate every like, tweet, facebook post, and review and we love to hear from you. Please consider leaving us your comments online or sending your thoughts or questions to info@mirrorworldpublishing.com

Thank you.

9 781998 360086